Our Dear
Miss H.
is on
the Case

ALSO BY VIOLET MARSH

Lady Charlotte Always Gets Her Man

Our Dear Miss H. is on the Case

VIOLET MARSH

FOREVER

New York   Boston

Forever
Hachette Book Group
1290 Avenue of the Americas, New York, NY 10104
read-forever.com
@readforeverpub

First Edition: March 2025

Forever is an imprint of Grand Central Publishing. The Forever name and logo are registered trademarks of Hachette Book Group, Inc.

The publisher is not responsible for websites (or their content) that are not owned by the publisher.

The Hachette Speakers Bureau provides a wide range of authors for speaking events. To find out more, go to hachettespeakersbureau.com or email HachetteSpeakers@hbgusa.com.

Forever books may be purchased in bulk for business, educational, or promotional use. For information, please contact your local bookseller or the Hachette Book Group Special Markets Department at special.markets@hbgusa.com

Print book interior design by Taylor Navis

Library of Congress Cataloging-in-Publication Data
Names: Marsh, Violet, author.
Title: Our dear Miss H. is on the case / Violet Marsh.
Description: First edition. | New York : Forever, 2025. |
Identifiers: LCCN 2024043223 | ISBN 9781538739631 (trade paperback) |
ISBN 9781538739655 (ebook)
Subjects: LCGFT: Detective and mystery fiction. | Romance fiction. | Novels.
Classification: LCC PS3613.A76993 O97 2025 |
DDC 813/.6—dc23/eng/20230920
LC record available at https://lccn.loc.gov/2024043223

ISBNs: 9781538739631 (Trade paperback); 9781538739655 (Ebook)

Printed in the United States of America

LSC-C

Printing 1, 2024

To Uncle De and Gary, who took me to the Carnegie Museums of Pittsburgh and helped foster my love for history and objets d'art from the past.

Chapter One

E gad! Is that actual gold in this mud trap of yours?"
Miss Georgina Harrington instantly recognized the jovial voice of her most tolerable living relative, Percy Pendergrast. Glancing up, she could espy only her cousin's handsome face peering over the lip of the six-foot deep pit that she was currently kneeling inside. Knowing Percy, he was standing as far back from the overturned dirt as possible.

"I told you that my father was right about antiquities being hidden inside this mound!" Georgina shouted back. Her own words triggered a bittersweetness that lanced her euphoric bubble. After years of waiting and still more years of fruitlessly moving dirt, she'd finally accomplished her father's dream— their dream. Dear Papa should be sitting next to her, his narrow, scholarly hand sweeping away the debris to reveal these wonderful treasures. But he'd been gone, though, for a decade.

"You look like you're dusting," Percy observed with a shudder. "I still cannot fathom why you insist on descending into that dreadful hole and digging in the muck. What is the point, then, of hiring workers? People call me the family's spendthrift, but you simply toss away all your money into this giant abyss that you've half excavated yourself."

Tom and Jack, the local chaps whom Georgina had hired to help her shovel, exchanged a glance that she had no trouble deciphering. Clearly, they understood that nothing would keep their eccentric employer away from the mysterious heap of dirt.

She wished her own family could comprehend her passion so readily. At least Percy indulged Georgina, if only because of their mutually beneficial arrangement. In exchange for using his name for her antiquity appraisal business, Georgina paid him a small percentage of her commissions, and a slightly bigger one if he needed to appear in person or give a lecture.

Although Percy enjoyed the extra pin money, he had no appreciation for the actual historical pieces, except perhaps their beauty. He'd visited Herculaneum on his grand tour only because it was becoming a fashionable destination. But when Georgina had toured the site with her father and had watched the workers haul out marble statues and jewelry, she'd imagined herself in the middle of the seaside city during its heyday.

Percy would never comprehend the utter delight in communing with the past, so Georgina didn't try to explain. Instead, she moved aside in order for her cousin to see what she was so meticulously unearthing.

"Is—is that a gilded *face*?" Percy's shoulders and even torso were visible now as he leaned high above her.

"Helmet!" Georgina gazed adoringly at the perfectly formed nose poking through the dirt. Her heart squeezed with utter joy. "Judging from the cheek flap that I already pulled from the ground, I think it is iron covered with thinly hammered gold. I will need to study it more closely, but marvelous designs appear to be etched into the precious metal."

"A helmet, you say?" Another face—this one unfamiliar and undeniably handsome—appeared at the hole above Georgina. With his even features and straight nose, he looked like a statue of Caesar Augustus come to life. Even the sun seemed to recognize the newcomer's male beauty as it wreathed his head in a warm, brilliant glow. The auburn strands of his hair burned like fire.

Georgina had little use for pretty countenances, but her heart suddenly decided to beat in an odd, almost trilling fashion. She would have liked to attribute the irregularity to Percy bringing a stranger to her dig, but it wasn't concern causing her heart to trip.

Quickly, Georgina moved to shield her precious find from the interloper. Thieves—both lowborn and highborn—abounded everywhere. They could claim Georgina's discovery as their own or steal the grave goods to melt down.

As if understanding her precaution, Tom and Jack also strategically placed themselves to hide the partially unearthed treasures. Percy, as always, seemed blithely oblivious to their concerns or the need for secrecy.

"I see you brought a friend." Georgina didn't care that her tone sounded icy. She was icy right now.

Even Percy had no trouble understanding the undercurrent in her voice. "Oh, you needn't worry about Alexander. He's the loyal sort. Won't tell a soul. He's never gossiped to anyone about the scandalous scrapes that he's seen me get into."

"How reassuring," Georgina remarked drily, finding it odd that Percy used Alexander's first name rather than his last one or his title. Percy had never been the formal type, but he generally followed that social edict. Judging by the redhead's style of dress, he was clearly of noble birth, and if he was a good friend of Percy's, he was likely a roguish scoundrel as well.

"I promise I'm trustworthy," Alexander called, in a warm, genial baritone that had the surprising and exceedingly uncomfortable effect of resonating inside Georgina.

"Humph," Georgina replied. "A claim that both an honorable man and rapscallion would make."

Instead of being insulted, Alexander threw his head back and laughed. The deep, rich sound rumbled through Georgina, too.

"I am the former. I swear."

"Alexander is the loyal sort, and furthermore, he has no interest in English ancestry," Percy teased. "Now, if you were hosting secret curricle races, you might have a concern. He is the very devil when he has a set of reins in his hands."

"Percy is right that I have little regard for musty old heroes and even less care for the stuff they left behind. The present is much more engaging." Alexander grinned down and sent her a wink as if they were bosom friends. After living with her half brother for ages, Georgina didn't trust outward charmers. Their polished veneer often hid rough interiors. She also had little use for men who'd rather risk life and limb on a race to nowhere than spend any time learning the lessons of the past.

"I see," Georgina said as she gave him a polite but tight smile.

"I shall climb into the pit," Percy announced suddenly as if he were Julius Caesar declaring veni, vidi, vici—I came. I saw. I conquered.

Her cousin considered himself an athlete, but Georgina had trouble envisioning him scrambling down the rickety ladder leaning haphazardly against the wall of dirt. Although Tom and Jack—who had spent time as miners in the western counties— had shored up the sides of the trench with wood, it was a rather amateurish construction. Georgina was not missish about accepting a little peril if it meant touching history, and the men she'd hired had unfortunately endured more perilous jobs than this one. But Percy—Percy was pampered.

"I'll return to the carriage," Alexander announced. "Between the ladder, the descent, and the mud at the bottom, it seems a bit too much for me."

Some adventurer, Georgina thought—even as she acknowledged that her sardonic assessment was a rather uncharitable one. After all, she'd just been worried about Percy a few moments before. Something about Alexander disrupted her normal, practical bearing, which, in turn, irked her. Yet she felt oddly bereft to see his face disappear from the opening.

"Could you have found a ghastlier ladder?" Percy asked as he leaned down, his normally ruddy cheeks growing pale.

"Funds are limited," Georgina said crisply. Her father had bequeathed her a small monetary inheritance, along with the cottage and the parcel containing the barrows. It was enough to live on—barely—but her guardian, her half brother, did not permit Georgina free access to the largesse. To save on expenses, he'd even shut up her father's home and arranged for her to reside with him and his wife on their neighboring estate. Although the red-bricked manor house was much larger and more elegantly appointed than the five-bedroom abode, Georgina would have much preferred to live on her own property.

"Ergh!" A strangled sound erupted from Percy. He must have accidentally pushed the ladder away from the wall when he'd climbed onto it. The top swayed dangerously in the air with Percy clinging to the first few rungs. Miraculously, her cousin managed to keep the rickety structure upright as he attempted to wobble it back toward the sloped side of the pit.

Georgina scrambled to her feet. She, Tom, and Jack raced along the planks of wood that they'd laid down to protect the site. Georgina reached her cousin first. Years of wielding a shovel had gifted her with a strength exceedingly unusual among upper-class women. With one calculated shove, she managed to push the ladder and the increasingly panicked Percy against the safety of the dirt wall.

"What happened?" Georgina asked as she steadied the rails while Percy hastily climbed down.

"My shoe buckle caught on a rung," Percy explained as he pertly dusted off his light-blue silk breeches. Georgina glanced down at her cousin's footwear and had to hide a grin. Percy did nothing by half measure, especially when it came to fashion. The ornate silverwork inlaid with garnets and paste jewels stuck out almost an inch from the leather upper. No wonder the ostentatious piece had become entangled.

Georgina pressed her fingers into her temples and rubbed. "Why aren't you wearing your riding boots and a practical wool suit? You are in the countryside, not London."

"I brought my curricle since Alexander came down with me," Percy answered as he inspected the sleeve of his coat for any dirt or damage. "After he is happily ensconced at my family seat, I am planning to pop over to visit the lovely Lady Mowbray. She recently entered half mourning, and I thought a carriage jaunt might be just the activity to lift her spirits."

This time, Georgina could not stop her smirk. At twenty-six— just a year older than Georgina—Lady Mowbray was a young and exceedingly beautiful widow. Her parents had married her off at eighteen to an elderly earl, and according to Georgina's sister-in-law and her scandalmongering friends, the Dowager Mowbray was not so discreetly delighting in her newfound freedoms. A carriage trip was most definitely not the only riding Percy and Lady Mowbray had planned for today. It also explained why Percy had chosen shoe buckles dotted with garnet hearts.

"I wasn't expecting to muck about in the mud," her cousin continued as he gingerly stepped onto the board, his lips curled in distaste. Percy had inherited his ability to pout without looking ridiculous from his father's side of the family. Georgina, on the other hand, took after her papa and paternal uncles and aunts, including Percy's mother. With her dark-brown eyes and hair, extremely pale skin, and prominent cheekbones, Georgina always looked sober. Her sister-in-law, Anne, loudly bemoaned Georgina's grave appearance, claiming it was why Georgina had yet to make a suitable match. Since Georgina had never been given to vanity, the remarks didn't hurt...much. Besides, she hadn't desired any of the roués that Anne and Georgina's brother had not-so-slyly cast in her direction. Georgina dreamed of meeting a bookish man who wouldn't mind if his wife spent her time digging through the dirt or scribbling in her journal—which she realized was about as likely as her capturing a Pegasus. But she would be equally satisfied to remain unmarried as long as she gained control over her inheritance.

"No one forced you to descend into my pit," Georgina pointed out. Like Percy, she picked her way back to where she'd been diligently working. Her reason for moving cautiously wasn't to protect her old, mud-soaked frock, though. Rather, she didn't want to inadvertently hurt any antique material. For days, she'd been unearthing brittle pieces of iron that were evenly placed in what appeared to be a specific pattern. The sandy dirt around them was a curious color that did not match the rest of the soil. She didn't understand what they were, and she didn't want a single one disturbed until she had the chance to record its location. Although the rusty pieces didn't shine like the gold-encrusted helmet, she still felt drawn to them. Ancient hands had created them for some purpose. Every time Georgina ran her finger along the corroded metal, she couldn't help but wonder if the long-dead smithy had done the same.

"I am like a crow. I am attracted to shiny things," Percy admitted good-naturedly. Her cousin's wry humor and self-assessing honesty were one of the reasons Georgina was fond of him, despite the fact she generally did not tolerate feckless bon vivants.

"Talk of the devil, and he doth appear in the mud," Percy quipped as he suddenly slacked his already slow pace. "What is that glinting over there?"

As Percy bent to reach for a shard glittering in a beam of sunlight, Georgina grabbed his upper arm. "Please refrain from touching anything. I want to record where I found each object."

"Swounds, why would you do that? It sounds like a dreadful bore." Percy, however, did listen as he rose to his feet.

"It's the method that Karl Jakob Weber recommends. He is using it while excavating the Roman villa with all the papyri," Georgina said excitedly. She couldn't wait to write to the Swiss military engineer about her finds today.

"Who? What?" Percy asked as he leaned over again, this time to wipe away dirt that had landed on one of the garnet hearts decorating his shoe buckle.

"Karl Jakob Weber!" Georgina shouted.

"Repeating his name does not help." Percy pulled out a silk handkerchief and began to polish the semiprecious stone.

"He is assisting with the recovery of antiques in Herculaneum. I told you that I—or rather *you*—were corresponding with him. You need to remember these details. What if you encounter him?" A flare of familiar frustration burned in Georgina's chest. She wished—oh, how she wished—she could correspond with antiquitarians using her own name. But when she did, she received no response, and worse, her ideas were purloined without credit to her. But when she signed Percy's appellation, she garnered accolades and recognition... Well,

Percy received the boons. But if her work was to be stolen anyway, she'd rather choose who voiced her thoughts. And Percy, despite some of his hedonistic tendencies, was not really a bad sort.

"Balderdash!" Percy exclaimed confidently. "Do you think I'll bump into a German scholar at a London curricle race or boxing bout? I suppose he could possibly wander into my favorite coffeehouse, the Black Sheep, but there are so many of those establishments in London. If this Weber chap visited any of them, he'd likely head to Elysian Fields, since it's frequented by antiquarians."

Georgina rubbed her temples again, wishing her partner in deception possessed a bit more consideration of the game they played. "First, Mr. Weber is a Swiss mercenary in the Naples army, so there is a chance he might enjoy a bit of blood sport."

"I thought you didn't consort with those types." Percy grinned gleefully.

Georgina pretended to whack her cousin on the shoulder but only gave him a light bop. "I tolerate your presence, don't I?"

"Only because you lack other options," Percy happily pointed out. "And you do live with your brother, who makes me look like an utter dullard in comparison. He never met a cockfight he didn't like, and he is downright vicious with sword, fists, or pistol."

Georgina suppressed a shiver. Her half brother possessed a dark streak that Georgina had never trusted. She wished her father had noticed the black spot on Algernon's heart before he'd appointed the scapegrace as her guardian. But as much as Papa understood Greek and Latin texts, he'd always had trouble deciphering people.

"Will you let me touch that helmet of yours?" Percy asked.

"Certainly not." Georgina increased her pace. Percy may mean well, but his cavalier enthusiasm made him reckless and occasionally clumsy with objects he should treat with care. "It is very fragile."

"Wasn't it meant for war?" Percy asked. "How could I damage it?"

"It has been buried for untold years, and the iron has become brittle. Besides, it is highly ornamental. Perhaps it was only meant for ceremonies. Although if that were the case, why didn't they just make a crown or use a cheaper substance, like copper, for the base? The piece could have multiple purposes and functions. The gold leaf would have made the headwear exceedingly fearsome, especially with the sun glinting off it. The use of such a precious metal would be a clear display of wealth and power so maybe the helmet was used for battle after all."

"Georgina?" Percy broke into her musings.

"What?" Georgina blinked rapidly at her cousin, realizing that she'd nearly forgotten his presence.

"You're essaying aloud again."

Georgina heard twin snorts from Tom and Jack, who were standing shoulder to shoulder in the pit. She felt a sheepish grin stretch across her face. "I have a tendency to do that, don't I?"

Percy gave her head a friendly tap. "You do, but your fine mind does earn us plenty of accolades."

Earns you accolades, Georgina thought bitterly, but then she forced the sourness away.

"I'll let you look at the helmet," Georgina said. "But no touching."

Percy sighed laboriously. "I am not a child."

Georgina shot him a dry look. Percy was exactly like a rambunctious toddler, and he well knew it. "Put your hands in your pockets."

Percy pretended to pout, but he complied. With her cousin's grabby fingers properly contained, Georgina led him over to her most marvelous discovery. Even Percy reverently drew in his breath when they approached the half-uncovered helmet. Given the darkness of the barrow, Georgina had left her lantern near the piece of antiquity. The light caught not just the gold but the unique inlaid gems.

"Does—does it truly have rainbow-colored eyebrows and a mustache?" Percy asked. "That is not just an interesting but a bold choice."

The ancient craftsman had hammered out protruding, arching eyebrows at the bottom of the helmet's cap, right where the hinged face-plate had been attached. In the raised metal, the artist had inserted thin strips of an opaque rock comprised of pink, purple, blue, and black layers. Similar shards had been skillfully placed between the sculpted nose and the carefully crafted lips. The effect should have been garish, but the overall presentation was so fierce and finely wrought that the armor was simply stunning.

"I am not sure what the gemstone is," Georgina said, "but we've dug up a number of artifacts made from it, including a goblet and a remarkable brooch. It is a rather versatile material and must have been plentiful. They could have traded for it, but the sheer amount indicates a local source."

"Surely we would have heard of it," Percy said. "We both grew up in this area."

Georgina shrugged. "There are an untold number of nooks and crannies dotting the sea cliffs that could contain the mineral, and they are not precisely safe to explore."

Tom issued a smothered cough that turned into a choke. Jack whacked him on his back in a pretense of helping, but the glare

Jack sent the other young man was more telling. Smuggling abounded along Essex's coastline, and Georgina wasn't naïve enough to believe that Jack and Tom didn't play some lowly role in the local operations. But she purposely avoided thinking too hard about what had become a major source of income in the region after the decline of the wool industry. She was also careful not to dig anywhere near the shore on her property or to even visit the barrow at night. If Georgina sometimes spied mysterious lights from the window of her small bedroom on her brother's estate, she never made mention, even in her personal journals.

"When I was younger, I used to pretend I was a pirate smuggler and that a rock shelter on my father's property was my lair. It was grand fun," Percy said, seemingly unaware of the tension between the two workers. "Then I grew up and realized that being confined to a ship for months on end would be a terrible bore. Alas, travels around Cape Horn are not for me, nor are sojourns to the Caribbean. I must only visit the tropics in my imagination."

Not for the first time, Georgina wondered how she could be related to such a fanciful man. Shaking her head at Percy's whimsy, she bent to brush more soil away from her magnificent find.

Soon Percy was squatting beside her—the closest he'd probably been to a pile of dirt since his early boyhood days. He extended his hand toward the crest of the helmet, where a miniature, rainbow-gemmed dragon perched. Georgina slapped his fingers. He instantly withdrew and put them in his mouth to suck.

"I did not hit you that hard!" Georgina protested.

"You are terrifyingly strong for a woman," Percy pointed out as he made a show of shaking his palm. When he leaned over the helmet again, he kept his hands in his pockets. "It looks more like a crown than an item of war."

"I can imagine a warrior-king wearing it to his coronation," Georgina admitted.

Percy suddenly grabbed her arm, almost causing her to bash the precious object with the handle of her brush. "Percy, be careful."

"Georgina, what if it is *his*?" Percy's brown eyes were wide as he executed an excited bounce.

"Whose?" Georgina asked in confusion. Percy had little interest in history, and she had no earthly idea which dead English chieftain would make him this excited.

Percy rolled his eyes. "Who else would I be talking about?"

"I cannot even hazard a guess."

Percy gave her a shake. "Arthur! It must belong to him!"

"You mean King Arthur? The one of Round Table fame?" Georgina asked. Of course, Percy would make that assumption. She should have guessed. Her cousin had pored over his family's old copy of Thomas Malory's *Le Morte d'Arthur* until he'd irreparably damaged the aging spine.

"Obviously! What other Arthur bears mentioning? You said that you found a goblet! Do you think it is the Holy Grail?" Percy was almost vibrating now.

"Yes. The Holy Grail just happened to be under a mound of dirt in Essex," Georgina said drily.

Palpably insulted, Percy swept his arm out over the helmet. "Well, this just happened to be lying here in the mud."

"Percy, think for a moment. Even in many of the legends, the Grail was never recovered. And why would a drinking vessel used in ancient Jerusalem be carved from a colorfully banded rock that appears to be of English origin?"

"You have a way of plucking every thread of fun from a

situation," Percy remarked gloomily before he brightened. "But I still believe the helmet is his."

"If Arthur even existed—"

"What do you mean, *if*?" Percy crossed his arms. "Of course he was real."

"There are serious questions in the scholarly community about whether he was ever a living person," Georgina protested. "Bede never mentions him—"

"Because Bede was a dullard," Percy said huffily.

"Bede was a true historian, not a romantic novelist peddling trumped-up tales masquerading as—" Georgina began before Percy cut her off with a gasp.

"You take that back. Malory was a genius," Percy countered.

"He could weave a story, I'll grant him that much," Georgina said. "But even if Arthur actually walked on this earth rather than just in the imagination of his creators, why would he be buried in Essex?"

"Colchester isn't too far from here. Some say it was Camelot. The Romans called it Camulodunum, after all."

"The Arthur stories originated in Wales, so if he lived and died anywhere, it would be on the other side of Great Britain!" Georgina barely succeeded in stopping an eyeroll.

"When I present the helmet to the Antiquarians of England Society, I am going to say that it is Arthur's," Percy proclaimed, his lips tilting into a devilish smile.

"You wouldn't dare!" Georgina gasped. "We'd—you'd—become a laughingstock."

Percy's smug grin faltered. Although Georgina needed his name more than he required the fake reputation, "his" scholarly work gave him prestige in the family. Since he was the third son, his parents expected him to join the military or enter the clergy—neither of which aligned with Percy's natural temperament. But once Georgina had begun publishing articles as Percy, his father, mother, and older brothers had stopped pressing him to assume a respectable profession.

"Truly?" Percy asked.

Georgina nodded solemnly. "Yes."

"Well, I am at least going to tell my mates at the Black Sheep that it is Arthur's!" Percy declared.

Georgina rubbed her forehead, and she could feel the cool mud that her fingers left in their wake. She didn't care. "Please don't. And I wish, when you went to London, that you'd instead frequent Elysian Fields, where the classical scholars gather."

"Which is why Elysian Fields is so dreadfully dreary. Every patron is haranguing about someone long deceased. Plato this. Socrates that. Nero was mad. Caligula was evil. Hadrian and his wall. Caesar and his conquering. Cleopatra and Marc Antony made the beast with two backs. No one cares. They're all dead."

"At least they existed," Georgina said cheekily.

Percy gripped his heart. "Stop maligning my Arthur!"

"Then stop threatening to denigrate my helmet with a mere myth!"

"A connection to Arthur is an elevation, an honor!" Percy tossed his hands into the air with a grand flourish.

"Maybe at a place like the Black Sheep, but not Elysian Fields," Georgina scoffed.

"Actually, I think you'd rather like the Black Sheep," Percy said.

"A coffeehouse run by the daughters of pirates?" Georgina asked. "It sounds too adventurous for my blood. Besides, as a woman, I couldn't enter either the Black Sheep or Elysian Fields."

Percy glanced over at Tom and Jack, and then he leaned close to whisper in Georgina's ear. "The Black Sheep has opened a secret back room where women and men mingle. The furniture is sinfully comfortable. Sophia, one of the proprietresses, experiments with the coffee and makes it not just palatable but delectable. The patrons converse about all manners of topics. It is rumored that Lady Charlotte Lovett has taken part ownership and that she helped unmask Viscount Hawley as a murderous highwayman."

"Anne has mentioned the scandal, but I never pay attention to her gossipmongering."

"An heir to a dukedom is robbing carriages for his evil pleasure, and you're not interested?" Percy asked incredulously.

"Not really," Georgina admitted. "Although it has crossed my mind that I might have played a role—albeit a small one—in his capture."

Percy blinked. Twice. "Pardon? How could you possibly be involved? You have been rusticating in the country for years, and you don't associate with anyone in Society except your family."

Georgina shrugged as she returned to gently scraping dirt from the helmet. With the excitement of uncovering the antiquities, she had no time to think about solved mysteries. "I knew Lady Charlotte from my debutante days. She recently wrote asking if I could identify an ancient symbol carved into a cameo. I recognized it as belonging to the Chatti tribe of Scotland. It was shortly after I replied to her that Lord Hawley was arrested. I heard one of his victims was Lady Chattiglen, so perhaps the jewelry was hers and had been stolen by the viscount."

"Why haven't you told me this?" Percy demanded.

"It didn't seem of much import, and I have no way of knowing if the exchange of letters had anything to do with the unmasking of Lord Hawley." Georgina's careful removal of dirt revealed another glint of gold. Barely focusing on what she was saying, she leaned over to inspect the antique more closely. "Moreover, his arrest has little to do with my life or my work."

Percy shook his head with a fond expression. "You really are a countryside scholar."

"I have absolutely no desire to go to London."

Chapter Two

Two weeks later

Londontown was summoning her, and Georgina definitely did not want to heed the notorious siren's call. She had recently plotted out on paper the pattern of the iron scraps and stained sand from the barrow. The resulting image had taken on the form of a boat's hull. She'd even consulted with a local fisherman. Not only had he agreed that her sketch appeared to be part of a vessel, but he'd identified the iron as rivets for a ship.

But unforeseen circumstances were disrupting Georgina's efforts.

First, her brother and sister-in-law had suddenly and emphatically decided that Georgina must accompany them to London. She found their insistence exceedingly disconcerting. Anne had complained bitterly during Georgina's entire debut Season—the only time Georgina had ever traveled to the capital with them. Her introduction to Society had been lackluster at best, deplorable at worst. She had not inspired one gentleman caller, let alone an offer of marriage. After the three of them had returned to Essex, none of them ever made mention of Georgina returning to the city...until now.

"What, precisely, has changed?" Georgina asked aloud, her voice disrupting the quiet of her bedroom.

Ruffian Caesar, a small mutt of indiscriminate terrier origins, raised his curly head from his sun spot on the floor, where he was chewing on a turnip. He looked quizzical, but then again, the little dog always did. His one ear stood straight up while the other one remained permanently flopped over, the pointy tip missing. When Ruffian Caesar had been living on the streets in the nearby village, a neighborhood pack had attacked him. Georgina had chased the bigger dogs away and brought the bloodied pup home, much to the chagrin of Anne.

"You've noticed the increase in visitors this past week, haven't you, boy?" Georgina asked her faithful companion as she bent over to scratch his back, his wiry fur springy beneath her fingertips. "I know they've disturbed your sleep."

Given the terrier's small frame, he heaved out a surprisingly loud sigh, as if the influx of guests had personally affronted him. Georgina frowned. There'd been furtive knocks at the side door under her window during the nights. One dawn, a coach with an unfamiliar crest and covered in dust had arrived from the west, the direction of London. Another one with no markings had come from the northeast, its sleek black sides showing little dirt from travel. The family, however, had entertained no guests at supper. The visitors headed directly from the main entrance to Algernon's office, where they stayed sequestered for hours before departing.

Yet the bigger, more concerning reason for heading to London was Percy.

Georgina was sore afraid that her feckless cousin had disappeared along with her helmet.

She had not heard from him since he had departed for London

ten days prior. With their home relatively close to the city, the mail coach came regularly. There would be no reason for delivery delays.

Percy was known to disappear for weeks on end while frequenting gaming dens, boxing matches, horse races—any place where bets and liquor flowed freely. It had been one of the reasons his older brothers had pressured him to find a suitable calling.

"But Percy knows how important the helmet is! He can be thoughtless at times, Ruffian Caesar, but he isn't heartless. Surely he would at least send me a note?" Georgina asked as she rose to her feet.

The dog grunted as he returned to chewing on his favorite treat aside from a meaty bone. He gave his buttocks a wiggle while he munched on the turnip.

"I wish I could be as lackadaisical about it as you are." Georgina glanced at the pup. "You'd think Percy would have at least let me know how the presentation to the Antiquarians of England Society went. He was supposed to have given the talk four days ago. He better not have missed the lecture. Hopefully, he will visit me when I arrive in London and provide a full report then."

Georgina paced around her traveling trunk, stuffed with more books than clothes. They were due to leave in two days, and Anne had already inquired five times if Georgina had packed. Georgina never attracted this much notice from her sister-in-law. Something was definitely amiss.

"Ouch!" Georgina cried as she whacked her leg against her writing table. Her half brother had not seen fit to provide her with spacious quarters. Between the bed, her desk, and the trunk, she had little space to walk in circles. Still, she needed the exercise.

Ruffian Caesar raised his head again and emitted a rumble of displeasure at her squawk of pain. Georgina glared at her dog as she rubbed her abused shin. "I am so sorry to have disrupted your chewing, your excellency."

Just then the crunch of carriage wheels on the gravel outside Georgina's window filled the room. The terrier sprang to his furry feet. In one bound, he leapt onto the bed. His stubby tail shot straight into the air as he tipped back his head to yap.

"Shhhh! Quiet!" Georgina cried, scooping him into her arms. "You know that Algernon and Anne don't like when you bark. I barely convinced them to let me keep you. You must behave."

Ruffian Caesar twisted his head to deliver his best doggy glare, but he did settle. Georgina carried him over to the window as she tried to get a view of the equipage before it turned the corner for the main entrance. It was the same gold and white coach that had come earlier in the week. Georgina frowned as she studied its markings. She'd never put an effort into learning recent family crests, and for the first time, she regretted her lack of social knowledge. Still, she tried to instill it into her memory. This time, she'd sketch what she could recall and then leaf through the heraldry book in her brother's library.

As the carriage disappeared, Georgina pressed against the window as if somehow she would gain the ability to see around the side of the manor. It obviously did not work.

"I wish I could spy who the visitor is. Perhaps I should engage in some scouting. What do you think?" Georgina asked her furry companion. The dog sneezed and then stared longingly at a sun spot on the bed.

"I know. I know. I'd rather snuggle up and read Pliny the Younger. I've never been one for adventuring, but I'm afraid I don't have a choice. Something is afoot, and I need to find out what." Georgina bent and placed the terrier on the ground. He emitted a soft whine, but Georgina ignored his protest as she opened her door.

Looking both ways, she tiptoed into the hallway…and immediately stepped on a supremely squeaky section of the floor. Already tense, she jumped, which only triggered more horrendously loud screeches. Georgina looked around frantically, even though it was perfectly normal to exit her bedroom in the middle of the day. She saw no other human, but Ruffian Caesar's little head poked out of the crack in the door. He cocked his head to the side, making his mismatched ears even more noticeable.

With a rather disdainful snort, the dog emerged. Trotting on one of the many lavish rugs Anne had purchased, he padded noiselessly down the hall. He paused at the end to look over his shoulder. She swore he had a decidedly cocky gleam in his round, dark-brown eyes.

"Well, it is easy for you. You only weigh a stone, maybe even less."

Ruffian Caesar saucily wagged his tail and then scampered around the bend. Sighing, Georgina followed after her not-so-faithful hound.

"It is not my fault that I lack subterfuge," Georgina complained under her breath. "I am a straightforward person."

Her furry companion chose that very moment to snort again. Georgina glared at his sashaying behind. "I do believe you meant that on purpose."

Just then, Georgina stepped on another creaky board, this one somehow even louder than the first. It echoed down the hallway, but thankfully no one came to investigate.

Leaving the family's residential wing, Georgina entered the main section of the manor. She needed to literally and figuratively tread carefully now. Although she was allowed in this section of the house, her brother wouldn't want her spying on his guests. Up ahead, she could see the door to Algernon's office. It was closed, but if she placed her ear against it, maybe she could make out some words.

Once again checking to make sure no one was observing her, Georgina pressed against the panel. To her horror, it began to sway open. The smallest of yelps escaped her lips.

"What was that?" a cultured male voice asked.

"I am not sure," Algernon answered, and Georgina heard the scrape of a chair against wooden floorboards. "I'll go check."

Georgina clasped her hand over her mouth as she frantically scanned the hallway for a hiding place. Next to the door there was a heavy antique side table filled with the Meissen porcelain figurines that Anne loved to collect. It didn't offer much concealment, but it was better than nothing.

Georgina dove under it, whacking her leg in the exact same spot where she'd injured it earlier against her writing desk. Another high-pitched squeak emerged from her mouth. Ruffian Caesar, who still sat by the door to Algernon's office, swiveled his head in her direction. Despite the heft of the furniture, Georgina had jarred it hard enough that she could hear the figurines clattering above her head.

Even Georgina had to admit that she made an absolute rubbish spy.

Algernon flung open his door, and Georgina put her hands over her head and squeezed her eyes shut. Immediately, she realized her foolishness. Her stance would only serve to make her look more ridiculous when her half brother discovered her.

"It's you." Algernon's voice dripped with patent disdain.

Georgina opened one eye. Although Algernon had never been particularly fond of her, he generally didn't treat her with such open hostility. To her relief, she found her half brother staring not at her but at the dog. The good, good, *good* boy was still plopped in front of Algernon's office.

"Go! Shoo!" Algernon fluttered his fingers at Ruffian Caesar.

Ruffian Caesar just stared, happily panting. Algernon, who was not in possession of the calmest of temperaments, flushed a deep red. His regal, straight nose lifted in disgust.

"You have interrupted important business." Algernon glared at the pup as he threateningly drew back his foot. "Begone or I'll turn your hide into a rug."

Ruffian Caesar merely stretched out his compact body and yawned. Then, with a toss of his head, he rose and sauntered down the hall in thankfully the opposite direction of where Georgina hid in plain sight.

Algernon grunted. Yanking on the door, he turned back into his office. As he retreated, Georgina caught a glimpse of a white-haired man sitting in a chair. She could not tell, though, if his hair had actually turned that color or if he'd powdered it. She saw enough of his frock coat to ascertain that it was made of expensive patterned silk.

The door swung further closed before she could observe more, but it didn't shut completely. Although their voices remained muffled, she could hear snatches of conversation. She longed to move closer but now had no faith in her stealth.

"Veritable treasure..." It was her brother's voice. Georgina stiffened. Did he know about her discovery of the helmet and the other grave goods? Surely Percy wouldn't have told. Tom, Jack, and the other locals seemed loyal, and they knew the importance of secret-keeping. But they had families to support, and enough coin could knock their lips loose.

Georgina strained to hear more, but the discussion seemed to have shifted.

"...no need for..." the other man was saying. "...reputation is of the utmost..."

"Unbesmirched..." Algernon said. "Both her father and our mother's lines...William the Conqueror..."

Our mother? Were...were they talking about *her?* Georgina would have laid her hand over her heart if she wasn't afraid of knocking against the table supports. What could be the reason for her half brother to discuss her lineage? Was Algernon once again trying to arrange her betrothal? She had thought he'd given up ages ago. At twenty-five, she was no longer considered a young miss. Could it be that he was referring to her as a veritable treasure? Georgina knew for certain that Algernon regarded her as an annoying burden, but he would, of course, extol her virtues if he was trying to make a match.

"...the Marquess of Heathford...shoots, races carriages despite...misfortunate...let us arrange for the two to meet in London..."

Georgina grimaced. So that's why Algernon was so eager to bring her to the capital. She supposed she should be thankful that her brother was not again trying to tie her to an aging roué, but she would prefer a scholarly, older fellow. She did not want a man who still lived like a carefree child. She had enough of that while residing with her half sibling.

"...the terms?" Algernon asked. Although Georgina missed most of the sentence, she did not like his note of greed. A chill raced through her. The woman's family paid the dowry. What benefit could Algernon gain in marrying her off?

"...will transfer ownership...you...none the wiser..." the other peer said.

Ownership of what? Something the speaker possessed? But why would this unseen noble pay for Georgina to wed his son?

If the courtesy title was that of a marquess, then the gentleman must be high-ranking indeed. Why would he seek out a spinster? Was this son a truly diabolic profligate whom no other family would accept despite his lofty connections?

Georgina really should have paid more attention to Anne's gossipmongering. Then she wouldn't be so at a loss now.

"Good... with the terms of the trust left by my stepfather for my sister, it would be devilishly tricky otherwise..." Algernon's voice simmered with barely suppressed anger.

Georgina jerked to attention and nearly cracked her head on the underside of the table. Perhaps she had been right in the very beginning when she thought that Algernon might be referring to the grave goods when he'd mentioned treasure. The goldwork alone would garner a hefty price. Although scholars would put no credence in it being Arthur's, many of the collectors would believe the fantasy and happily part with a chunk of their wealth.

"No more of these.... unfortunate... violence traced... unacceptable." The visitor's words were even more garbled, but they caused an icy sensation to stalk through Georgina. What were the men discussing now? Had they switched the subject, or were the dire words about her?

Georgina rubbed her temples, her fingers moving at an almost frenetic pace. She was accustomed to drawing conclusions from disparate shards of information. But it was hard to piece together this conversation. What she did glean, though, sent horror cascading through her. Whatever plans that her half brother was forming, she seemed to be their linchpin.

Unease trickled down Georgina's spine, followed by the sensation of being watched. Slowly, Georgina turned her head. Unblinking emerald-green eyes greeted her. Georgina started, but thankfully she neither squeaked nor hit the table. Sweetheart, Anne's white cat, continued to regard Georgina with the curious aloofness that only felines could exude so flawlessly. Her gray-tipped tail twitched with deceptive laziness while she observed Georgina as she would a flea-bitten mouse.

The ominous sound of wood scraping against wood drifted from Algernon's office. The men were rising to their feet!

"I need to return to London posthaste," the visitor announced.

Georgina scrambled backward...and straight into the table support. Hot pain shot from her back through her body. She gave herself no time to absorb it as she continued her mad scuttle to freedom.

Porcelain clattered overhead. Something brightly colored caught the corner of her eye. Panicked, she turned to spy a harlequin figurine in mid-fall. Her gaze latched onto the exquisitely painted clown face with rosy cheeks and wide smile before the delicate bauble hit the floor. With the muffled thud, it landed beside Sweetheart on the rug. The cushioning of the carpet prevented the piece from shattering, but the delicate neck snapped. The grinning head bounced once, then twice, and then thrice, before it hit the wooden floor. Once on the smooth surface, it promptly rolled into a nearby drawing room.

Sweetheart mewled her displeasure at being nearly hit. Her green eyes glowed with accusation as she fixed them upon Georgina.

"What now!" Algernon's irritated voice floated from his office.

Smothering a gasp, Georgina crawled frantically toward the decapitated harlequin. Scooping it into her hand, she lurched halfway to her feet and flung herself in the direction of the drawing room, still some distance away.

Ruffian Caesar dashed back into the hallway. He ran straight for Sweetheart, who leapt onto the antique table. Algernon burst from his office, his eyes on the dog and then the cat. Thankfully, he did not notice Georgina.

"You mangy mutt!" Algernon cried out. "If you've caused Sweetheart to break one of Anne's figurines, you're back on the streets. I never should have allowed my sister to keep you, demmed nuisance."

Georgina half ran, half tumbled, and then dove into the parlor. Fortunately, Sweetheart's plaintive meows seemed to cover the sound. When Georgina was finally hidden from sight, she slumped against the wall, her hand pressed against her chest.

Algernon had a terrible temper, but he'd never struck Georgina. Though it wasn't just his wrath and spittle-laced lecture that Georgina wanted to avoid. She was deeply unsettled about the conversation she'd overheard. It wasn't due to her potential nuptials—she'd always handily avoided those types of entanglements. But there had been something…sinister. The half-heard words at the end of the discussion, a darkness simmering in the men's voices, a tension that had swirled from Algernon's office.

Two sets of footsteps passed in the hall. Even as Georgina heard them turn the corner and then fade away entirely, she still did not move from her position. She was definitely, most assuredly, not meant for stealth.

A cold nose touched her hand, and Georgina glanced down to find two brown eyes staring up at her. Smiling at Ruffian Caesar, she patted his wiry-haired head, leaving the strands standing up at all angles.

"I've really mucked things up, haven't I?" Georgina told him as she glanced down at the headless harlequin. "I best fix this before Algernon tells Anne about finding Sweetheart among her figurines. Algernon might not have noticed that this little fellow is missing, but Anne certainly will."

Ruffian Caesar just tilted his head, his pointy ear even more at attention than usual. Georgina sighed and rose to her feet. "Now just where did that clown head roll off to?"

"Miss Harrington."

At her softly spoken name, Georgina squealed and tossed up her hands. Even she had to admit that she sounded exactly like a pig stuck under a fence rail. Both figurine pieces flew into the air. In horror, Georgina watched as they started to crash back to the ground. She lurched forward and somehow managed to catch both the torso and the grinning head that she'd just retrieved from behind a settee.

Breathing heavily, she turned around to find Mary, one of the maids, staring open-mouthed. Mary quickly snapped her lips shut as she extended a letter in Georgina's direction.

"I'm sorry to startle you, miss, but a letter addressed to Lord Percy Pendergrast arrived in today's post. I know you were waiting for news, so I wanted to bring it to you straightaway." Mary, who was Tom's younger sister, knew all about Georgina's clandestine work as an antiquarian and Percy's role in the subterfuge.

"Thank you, Mary," Georgina said, glad that her voice sounded normal and not as frenetic as her rapidly beating heart. Who was trying to communicate with Percy? Another client? Or did the missive have something to do with his silence? "You were very kind to bring it to me immediately."

Mary beamed. "If you want, miss, I can fix the figurine and return it. I know exactly where Lady Craie likes them."

Georgina hesitated, even though she just wanted to hand over the harlequin and grab the missive. "If she catches you, inform her that I broke it. I don't want to get you in trouble."

"She won't notice me, miss," Mary said with confident cheek, "but it's kind of you to worry."

"Still, promise that you won't take the blame," Georgina insisted.

"I'll fess up to the truth," Mary promised.

"All right, then," Georgina said as she exchanged the broken figurine for the sealed letter.

As soon as Mary disappeared down the hall, Georgina tore through the wax seal and unfolded the note. When she scanned it, her heart clenched with brutal force. The Antiquarians of England Society was writing to Percy to ask why he had failed to attend their latest meeting, especially after he'd promised to bring a most marvelous find.

Georgina sank against the wall. Percy was truly missing. If she told his brothers, they would simply dismiss her worries and claim he was off carousing.

No one would look for him but Georgina. Though she was headed to London, she knew nothing of the city. She hadn't traveled there for half a decade, and even then she'd only attended Society events suitable for young debutantes. She wouldn't find Percy behind a potted fern in a ballroom. To search for him, she'd have to descend into a world she didn't understand and most definitely didn't have entrée to. How could she attend a horse race or a boxing match? She couldn't even enter a coffeehouse... or could she?

The Black Sheep has opened a secret back room where women and men mingle... It is rumored that Lady Charlotte Lovett has taken part ownership and that she helped unmask Viscount Hawley as a murderous highwayman.

Percy's words sprang into Georgina's mind, bringing with them a jot of hope. The Black Sheep was one of her cousin's favorite haunts. If the proprietresses and patrons didn't know Percy's location, perhaps they could tell her places to look.

Georgina straightened. When she went to London with Algernon and Anne, she wouldn't fall in line with their plans to wed her to this Marquess of Heathford. She would do everything in her power to avoid him and instead spend her time in the city tracking down Percy. Her first stop would be the Black Sheep and its secret room.

Chapter Three

"What do you mean there is no rice?" Alexander Lovett, the Marquess of Heathford, asked in absolute horror as he stared at his maternal cousin, Hannah Wick.

Not only did the proprietress of the Black Sheep not grasp the seriousness of the situation, but she appeared to be holding back laughter. Her eyes gleamed suspiciously in the light streaming from the narrow windows of the coffeehouse's front room.

"It must have gotten wet, and it molded. Believe me, you do not wish to toss it at the bride and groom. The bag is emitting a most malodorous stench," Hannah said, her voice a little too tight and controlled. Alexander definitely heard a twinge of mirth at the end.

"Then what will we throw when my sister and Matthew leave the wedding feast?" Alexander tapped his cane nervously against the wooden floorboards. If his right foot and leg weren't already throbbing and swollen from rushing around to arrange the surprise fête, he would have attempted pacing. After everything his twin and his best friend had endured to reach the altar, Alexander wanted the two people who he loved the most in the world to have the perfect celebration. Since they'd eloped, Alexander hadn't even been able to attend their ceremony.

"Don't worry. We have oats." Sophia Wick, Hannah's paternal

cousin and co-owner of the Black Sheep, patted Alexander's arm. Her accent had soft hints of her Caribbean upbringing and heritage.

"Oats!" Alexander shouted in dismay.

"It's what our ancestors originally used," Hannah told him sagely. "One cereal crop is as good as another at representing fertility."

"Must we use that particular word in the context of my sister?" Alexander asked.

"Well, what do you think hurling grains at newlyweds represents?" Hannah demanded, shoving her fists into her practical, linsey-woolsey skirt.

"Adherence to ancient tradition?" Alexander tried helplessly.

"Where do you want the cake?" Mr. Alun Powys, a theater owner, playwright, actor, and patron of the Black Sheep, asked in his lilting Welsh intonation. The black-haired man carefully stepped into the room. In his arms was the centerpiece of the feast—a three-tiered fruitcake covered in marzipan and icing made from expensive white sugar.

Alexander, who was given a pittance from his parents, had used most of this month's funds to procure the ingredients. He did earn some coin from the satirical articles he wrote under a fake name, but that income wasn't much, and he donated most of those funds to the causes he was trying to champion.

"Treat!" A hoarse, scratchy voice cried from the rafters.

Alexander's heart immediately and momentarily stopped beating. His whole body froze in horrified anticipation. Just as he'd expected, a lime-green blur dove straight toward the expensive confection. As Pan, the parrot, shot past Alexander, he spied a malicious, greedy glint in the bird's one eye.

"Noooooooooooooo!" Alexander launched himself forward despite the pain in his right leg that was hopelessly mangled from his parents' ceaseless efforts to "fix" his clubfoot. Years of horseback riding and curricle racing had gifted Alexander with the ability to react quickly, but that didn't mean he could make it to the precious pastry in time.

"Treat for Lovey!" Pan repeated gleefully, his gray talons outstretched toward the flawless white coating.

"Pan! Stop! Hannah and I spent hours making that!" Sophia called out desperately as Mr. Powys tried to carefully maneuver his body to protect the cake without sending it careening to the floor.

Another sharp, abrasive sound filled the air, this time an excited chitter of a capuchin monkey. Her black eyes bright against the pale fur of her face, Pan's "Lovey" bounced up and down on the shoulder of Lady Calliope, a poet and the daughter of a duke.

"Quiet, Banshee," Calliope ordered the primate in her genteel voice. Banshee, however, decided to live up to her name instead. Throwing back her brown-capped head, she emitted a string of very high-pitched and very loud calls.

Alexander managed to reach the cake just before Pan would have smashed into it. Thankfully, only feathers scratched his face instead of the bird's sharp claws. The parrot swooped over Alexander, Mr. Powys, and the cake with ominous intent.

"Pan, you are being a bad, bad, bad bird. Settle this instant!" Hannah's voice rose above the awful din, but it did little good.

"Circle the sweet!" Alexander called out, his cries bringing two more of their friends into the room. "Protect the pastry!"

"Is there a reason you're alliterating?" Hannah asked, even as she complied with the order.

"Just save the dessert!" Alexander shouted as everyone except Calliope quickly arranged themselves to stand shoulder to shoulder around the expensive delicacy. The noblewoman stayed in the far corner of the room as the excited capuchin climbed to the top of her head.

"Defend the dessert?" Mr. Powys suggested.

"Barricade the baked good?" Sophia offered.

"Not. Really. The. Time," Alexander said between clenched teeth as he traced Pan's trajectory through the air with his eyes.

Pan cackled—the effect rather bloodcurdling. Alexander winced as he watched the parrot sweep low above their heads.

"He should be on the stage," Mr. Powys observed drily. "I daresay, his evil laugh almost rivals mine."

"The parrot's is much better. You overdo yours." Calliope managed to utter the words with lofty dignity despite the fact that she was frantically waving her arms to grab the monkey.

Mr. Powys twisted his body to glare at the duke's daughter. Instantly, Pan's gray beak whipped toward the weakness in their human bulwark.

"Hold your positions!" Alexander barked out. "This is not the time for you two to engage in your feud! The enemy is Pan!"

"Don't you think you're being a touch dramatic?" Mr. Powys asked.

The militant look in Pan's single eye sharpened, and the bird gave a menacing flap of his wings. Talons extended, the parrot opened his beak so wide that his gray tongue was visible as he shrieked, "Attack!"

⁓ॐ⁓

Ten minutes later, all the humans sat slumped around one of the coffeehouse's long tables in the front room. Overhead, parrot and monkey cooed and chittered to each other as they shared the dried fruit that Sophia and Hannah had given them under duress. The cake miraculously sat untouched. Alexander wished he could say the same about the rest of them.

"Whyever did we let the monkey and the parrot attend?" Alexander asked to no one in particular as he rubbed the blood from the scrape on his cheek with his thumb.

"It was your idea," Hannah pointed out as she stared forlornly down at a small clump of her red hair, still in her hand after Pan had pulled it out.

"I know," Alexander moaned as he thunked his head down onto his crossed arms. "They were so instrumental in Lottie and Matthew's courtship that I thought it would be a grand idea to include them."

"You are ever the hopeless romantic." Sophia gave his arm a friendly pat. When he glanced at her hand, he noticed she had a thin scratch across her knuckles.

"My eye is burning," Mr. Powys announced, sounding concerned. Alexander lifted his chin to find the actor-playwright gingerly touching the inflamed skin above his right cheekbone. "It's puffing out already, isn't it? I am supposed to be performing as a prince tonight. I can't have a black eye."

"Perhaps you should play the villain, instead," Calliope teased him.

"How did I even acquire it?" Mr. Powys asked, ignoring Calliope's suggestion. "Everything happened so quickly. I think I even had feathers in my mouth at some juncture."

"My apologies, but it may have been my fault," Hannah confessed. "I was reaching for the wretched bird, and my elbow struck something. I believe I heard you grunt."

Mr. Powys waved the fingers of the hand not assessing the damage to his face. "Oh yes. I remember now. Remind me never to defend a wedding cake against a parrot again. It is a hideous business."

"Be glad you weren't holding the monkey." Calliope crossed her eyes as she stared ruefully at the golden tendrils in front of her face. Half of her fashionably tight curls had come loose, leaving some of her hair as tight as sheep's wool and some dangling in straight, limp bunches. "I was afraid I wouldn't have a single lock left on my head. I'll be glad when the bride returns, and Banshee can transfer her affections back to Lottie."

"When do you think Charlotte and Matthew will walk through the door?" asked Hannah with an uncharacteristic listlessness.

"Soon, I hope." Mr. George Belle, the proprietor of the city's best hackney carriage system, rubbed his cheek where Pan had rammed him. "I should have sent one of my drivers to collect the new spouses. Then Matthew and Charlotte would have arrived before the cake incident, and I would still be in ignorant bliss of what it feels like to have an angry parrot smash into my face. Or, perhaps, I should have just stayed in the back room when Alexander called for reinforcements and continued to peacefully count almonds with Mr. Stewart."

At the reminder of the treat that the Black Londoner had been preparing with Tavish Stewart, a Scottish-born printmaker and shipping merchant, Alexander straightened and tried to regain his initial energy. He turned toward the two men of business. "The almonds were not hurt in the scuffle, were they?"

"No. They're still safe in the back room." Tavish, a middle-aged man who was the groom's father figure, rubbed his shoulder where Pan had clawed him.

"And there are five—and only—five in each satchel?" Alexander double-checked.

"Yes. You were so concerned about it that we counted three times," Mr. Belle confirmed, only a tad testily.

"Why are you fanatical about the number of nuts? You do

realize that both Belle and Stewart maintain account books that involve much more complicated mathematics?" Mr. Powys asked as he continued to examine the bulge around his eye socket.

"He has been fervent about every aspect of the feast." Hannah rolled her eyes and then rubbed Alexander's arm to show that she meant no harm. "I suppose he is just being a good brother and friend."

"They have no immediate family to welcome them home but me," Alexander said softly. His parents were horrified that their daughter had chosen to marry a third son, who made an actual living as a physician rather than assume a more "proper" calling.

Matthew's father had never liked his youngest, and that sentiment only deepened after Matthew had unmasked his older brother as a murderous highwayman.

Sophia patted Alexander's other hand. Although she was not his cousin by blood, she had become one by choice. Initially, he'd patronized the Black Sheep to irk his mother and father, yet he'd grown fond of not just the establishment but of the proprietresses themselves. Now his beloved sister was one of the owners, and the three women had achieved brilliant success in opening the secret back room.

"We are all their kin now," Sophia said.

"Hear! Hear!" Tavish gave one of his kind smiles, his gray eyes sparkling. "We're a motley assortment of characters, but we somehow fit."

Alexander grinned jovially, but to his horror, he also felt the prick of tears at the back of his eyes. He'd learned at a very young age not to allow anyone to witness his true emotions except for his twin. Even then, he held so much back from Lottie, partly out of habit and partly out of not wanting to burden her with his pain. He'd done well in life maintaining a happy façade and had eventually made a host of friends despite being an outcast at his first boarding school. Yet he'd never experienced comradeship like he had the last few months at the Black Sheep when the people gathered today had banded together to save his sister from a terrible marriage to Viscount Hawley.

"What is the significance of the five bloody almonds?" Mr. Powys asked, providing exactly the distraction Alexander needed.

"It is originally an Italian tradition," Alexander explained, glad his voice sounded cheerful without a trace of deeper sentiment. "The nuts represent health, wealth, happiness, longevity, and..."

He trailed off as he belatedly realized what the last symbolized. Hannah smirked and exchanged a look with Sophia. The Wick cousins turned back to address the rest of the group and said simultaneously, "Fertility!"

Before Alexander could think of a response, the door of the Black Sheep scraped open. In the light spilling in from the outside stood his twin and her new husband. Matthew—who'd always been such a solemn sort—was grinning broadly, his brown eyes more alive than Alexander had ever seen them. And Lottie—Lottie was as radiant as every bride deserved to be. Alexander's heart grew warm with affection.

"Welcome home, Dr. and Mrs. Talbot!" everyone shouted.

Matthew stumbled back a step, obviously shocked by the unexpected welcome. Charlotte, though, laughed and tugged her husband forward. "Oh, this is wonderful! You even have a cake!"

"Which we defended with our lives!" Mr. Powys cried out. "We have the battle wounds to prove it."

"You're injured?" Concern immediately spread over Matthew's face as he donned what Alexander had deemed his physician countenance.

"We were mildly attacked by Pan. We have plied him and his lady love with dried fruit, and he is satisfied now." Alexander pointed toward the rafters with his eyes where parrot and capuchin were still happily munching, oblivious—or perhaps smugly indifferent—to the chaos they had recently unleashed.

"There's no mild about it," Mr. Powys muttered under his breath.

"Enough about the monkey and the bird. Sit! Sit! We want to hear all about your wedding." Alexander gestured to two empty spaces at the table.

As soon as the newlyweds sat, Charlotte regaled the group with the tale of her and Matthew's trip north to Gretna Green and back. Matthew interjected here and there, but mostly he seemed content to press against his new wife and not-so-covertly hold her hand under the table.

After the cake was served, the conversation turned to how the number of female patrons had been dramatically increasing at the Black Sheep. As soon as everyone had relayed the latest developments, Lottie pulled from her reticule a handful of dried wildflowers that Matthew had picked in Scotland for her wedding bouquet.

"Should I toss them or just hand one to everyone?" Charlotte asked.

"Toss," Hannah said. "It will be ever much more fun. You and Matthew can even pretend that you're escaping to your bedchamber."

"You can use the entrance to the back room for the ruse," Sophia suggested.

"Carry Charlotte!" Mr. Powys suggested.

"Carry! Carry!" Pan cried out.

Matthew swept a giggling Lottie into his arms. He, himself, laughed with such effortless joy that Alexander felt his own swell of emotion. He remembered their school days when Matthew, unwanted by his father and ruthlessly bullied by his older brothers, had never smiled. Even as an adult, there'd been a grimness about Matthew. But Charlotte had eased that festering pain. And Matthew had acknowledged Lottie's cleverness and given her the joy she'd been lacking under the stifling existence foisted upon her by her parents.

Charlotte hauled back and, with more strength than Alexander had anticipated, launched the flowers into the air. The delicate petals must have dried together, and they sailed in a clump right over everyone's head. The floral projectile attracted Pan and Banshee's attention. The capuchin screeched in a happy demand, extending one black paw. Pan immediately shot into the air to fetch his love's desire.

As Alexander followed the path of both bouquet and bird, he noticed that the door to the Black Sheep had begun to inch open. Charlotte must not have secured it when she and Matthew had entered. He hoped it was one of the coffeehouse's regular customers who would not be alarmed by the bizarre welcome party.

With a rather electrifying jolt, Alexander realized the newcomer dressed in a maid's attire wasn't a patron but the mud-stained scholar whom he'd met while visiting the childhood home of his friend Lord Percy Pendergrast. Despite the briefness of their meeting, memories of Miss Harrington had flickered into Alexander's mind at the oddest times over the last few weeks. She'd looked so excited, standing in the dark pit, a lantern near her skirts casting her in an almost otherworldly glow. But she hadn't acted like an ethereal sprite. Her tongue was too barbed for that, and even in her excitement, an innate sense of cool practicality radiated from her. She'd appeared more like a level-headed swashbuckler exploring a shiny new world than someone gently sweeping away dirt.

Alexander hadn't seen the helmet that Pendergrast and she had discussed. Miss Harrington had moved her body to shield it from his sight, and Alexander had respected her desire for secrecy. He'd met enough academics through his mother's salon and Matthew's collegiate connections to understand how competitive the various fields of study could become. Pendergrast really shouldn't have cavalierly brought Alexander to his cousin's dig site, but then the jovial rascal had a habit of being oblivious.

Besides, Alexander did not wish to learn anything more about English history—even if it involved gilded armor. He'd suffered enough "lessons" about his noble ancestry from his father. Alexander cared nought for the past—which he couldn't alter. Instead, his focus lay in a future that he could control or at least help improve. But even if Alexander possessed no interest in the goods of a half-forgotten time, he'd found Miss Harrington's unabashed fascination in them exceedingly intriguing. He didn't know exactly why, but he simply accepted that he did. Although he wasn't as unmindful as the blithe Pendergrast, he'd learned not to spend much time on introspection. He preferred instead to mock the foibles of society, especially when those shortcomings hurt the vulnerable.

Miss Harrington's gaze locked with his. He saw a flicker of recognition, then surprise, and finally something darker slip through her brown eyes. Before he could determine her exact emotion, Pan shrieked in triumph. His beak pierced the congealed bouquet. The lump of flowers burst apart, raining down upon the unsuspecting newcomer. Sprigs of the dainty yellow lady's bedstraw flowers, white oxeye daisies with their golden centers, and purplish bluebells landed on Pendergrast's cousin. Her snow-colored mob cap was festooned with so many bright colors that it looked like a satire of a jeweled crown. Several of the dried petals stuck to her cheeks, and one leaf dangled impishly from the tip of her nose.

His flower target destroyed, Pan decided to land on the visitor's head. Menacingly, he bent his body down over the woman's brow so that his one eye locked with her brown ones.

Pendergrast's cousin remained entirely unperturbed by either the floral or feathered assault. She simply raised a finger and jabbed it in Alexander's direction.

"You! There! Who have you told about the ancient gold-plated helmet? And what have you done with my cousin Percy?"

Although Alexander intellectually knew that Miss Harrington meant him, her vehement conviction was so strong that he couldn't help but look around. When his gaze returned to the lady, he found her regarding him gravely, despite the parrot perched on her floppy hat.

"I…uh…didn't tell anyone." Alexander spoke the truth. He hadn't, but her cousin certainly had, not that he was going to confess that. The woman, despite her solemnity, or perhaps because of it, looked intimidating—still intriguing in her serious intensity but also a wee bit frightening.

"Are you talking about King Arthur's gilded armor?" Hannah asked, sounding serious, but Alexander knew his cousin well enough to detect the impish undertone. Curious interest lit her grassy green eyes as she swiveled her head from Alexander to Miss Harrington to Alexander again. All his friends were doing the same.

"You *did* blab!" The woman advanced on Alexander, stabbing her still-pointed finger like a sword.

"No." Alexander helplessly waved the hand that was not gripping his cane. "I promise you; I did no such thing."

"Alexander didn't spill secrets." Sophia sprang to his defense as she shot Hannah a chiding look. "In fact, I overheard him telling Lord Percy that he should be more discreet about his discovery."

Miss Harrington paused, her brown eyes softening slightly as she studied Alexander. He was accustomed to women appreciatively scanning his face, then his broad shoulders and athletic chest, their gazes becoming much less enamored and often annoyingly pitying when they spied his cane and noticed his limp. But this lady wasn't admiring him, nor did her gaze stray from his countenance. She was judging him, and he wondered if she was trying to determine whether he'd revealed that she'd discovered the helmet instead of Percy.

Alexander gave a slight shake of his head. Pendergrast had told him years ago when deep in his cups that he wasn't actually a scholar, and it was his female cousin who possessed the real knowledge.

"You look vaguely familiar, but I am having trouble placing you," Calliope said with her typical directness. "Who are you?"

"Miss Georgina Harrington," Pendergrast's cousin answered crisply. "I am the sister of the Earl of Craie. You, Lady Charlotte, and I all debuted the same year. I was a wallflower, though."

Idiots, Alexander thought of the men who'd overlooked Miss Harrington. It didn't surprise him, though. She didn't possess the easy, warm demeanor that crowned most women as diamonds of the first water. Still, the unrelenting rogues should have detected her cleverness and solemn beauty. If he hadn't been away at university in Scotland, he would have paid her mind.

"Oh, I remember you now!" Calliope smiled sincerely. "You made the most unexpected quips. You were otherwise so quiet, yet the most devilish observations would escape your lips. You put me in silent stitches more than once."

"I recognized you straightaway," Charlotte added. "Thank you again for your letter regarding the Chatti symbol. It was instrumental in bringing down Lord Hawley."

"I do thank you for your kind words, but I am afraid I am not here to discuss the viscount or to reminisce," Miss Harrington replied politely but officiously. Alexander had no idea why her no-nonsense approach appealed to him. Perhaps because he'd never liked the fakeness of Society, even if sometimes he thought himself to be the greatest impostor of all.

Miss Harrington turned back to the Wick cousins, her expression resolute. "Who precisely did Percy talk to about the helmet?"

Sophia and Hannah exchanged a look. It was Sophia, the more diplomatic one, who spoke first. "Well, he was not particularly circumspect with his—"

"He told all and sundry," Hannah interrupted. When Sophia shot her an exasperated look, Hannah added, "What? It sounds like it is important for Miss Harrington to know the truth."

"He was flashing it around when I came for my cup of coffee about a week ago. We had an argument when I told him it couldn't be Arthur's since the man, if he existed, was Welsh. Everyone heard us," Mr. Powys agreed. "I don't think there was a patron in the back room who missed it."

Although Miss Harrington didn't exactly stagger, she seemed to crumple into herself. When she spoke, her clear voice had gone soft. "He—he brought the helmet here?"

Alexander instantly stepped forward, surprised by his almost physical need to assist this woman. When the ferrule of his cane thunked against the rough floorboards, Miss Harrington swung in his direction. Alexander paused as he realized that the fierce lady might not wish for his help.

"The piece was well protected in a velvet-lined box," Mr.

Powys added hastily, but Miss Harrington did not appear to hear.

Her eyes were locked on to Alexander's. "You are his friend, yes?"

He nodded. He wasn't as close to Pendergrast as he was to Matthew, but they were rather good mates. "I am."

"Did…" Miss Harrington paused and swallowed resolutely. "Did he talk about the helmet outside of the Black Sheep?"

Alexander really wanted to tell her that Pendergrast had been circumspect. Unfortunately, it wasn't at all in the rapscallion's nature. "I believe he mentioned having taken it to Elysian Fields. He wanted to stir up interest before his talk at the Antiquarians of England Society."

"Did you see my cousin after he brought the helmet to the Black Sheep?" Miss Harrington's face had turned a decidedly ghostly shade.

Alexander's own heartbeat began to skitter unsteadily. When Miss Harrington had first burst into the coffeeshop, she'd inquired about the whereabouts of Pendergrast. Although the rogue often disappeared for bouts of carousing, Alexander couldn't escape the whisper of unease that slipped through him.

"I have not," Alexander admitted.

"He hasn't stopped by here again, either, but that's not unusual," Sophia said quietly, obviously also sensing something was amiss. "He often won't pop in for weeks or sometimes even months if he's rusticating in the country."

"He's not at his ancestral estate," Miss Harrington said.

"He loves house parties," Alexander said, not adding *especially the risqué ones.* But he had a feeling Miss Harrington had a perfect understanding of her cousin's character. She did not strike him as either a sheltered miss or an unobservant one.

Miss Harrington whirled back toward him, her desperation

a palpable force. "Did he tell you that he was leaving for one? Where is it?"

Alexander hated dashing her hopes. "I do apologize. I was just speculating. He never mentioned a trip to the countryside, and I'm not aware of a particular party in our circle of acquaintances."

Miss Harrington's stiff shoulders slumped ever so slightly, but she quickly straightened them again. "I do not believe Percy left London...at least of his own accord."

Everyone exchanged a look. Hannah was the one who spoke first. "Well, that sounds ominous."

"Because it is." Unlike most people, Miss Harrington appeared unperturbed by Hannah's bluntness. "I know my cousin has a tendency to lose himself in drink and sport."

And women, but Alexander wasn't about to say that last part.

"But," Miss Harrington continued, "Percy missed his appearance at the Antiquarians of England Society meeting. He was supposed to talk about the helmet and its discovery on my behalf. As undependable as my cousin is, I do not believe he would betray me like this, especially without even sending me a missive."

Alexander shifted as his own trickle of concern turned into a flood. Pendergrast was an unpredictable sort, but he also possessed an unwavering streak of loyalty. Alexander had detected his friend's fondness for Miss Harrington whenever Pendergrast had spoken about his cousin. He wouldn't purposely hurt her. Even as dense as Pendergrast could be, he would have understood the importance of the presentation to the Antiquarians.

"I agree," Alexander said softly, just as Hannah exclaimed, "Wait! You're the one who actually unearthed King Arthur's armor?"

Miss Harrington's face twisted in exasperation. "It is not

Arthur's. It probably did belong to a king or, at least, a very important chieftain. But it definitely was not the property of someone who likely did not exist, and even if he did, Arthur would have lived in Wales, not by the Essex seaside."

"You are a real scholar," Mr. Powys said in his booming theater voice. He was half joking, but Alexander could see the flash of utter joy in Miss Harrington's eyes at the acknowledgment.

"Is it true, then?" Sophia asked. "Are you the one behind all of Lord Percy's works, or are you just the one who found the helmet?"

Alexander could see the hesitation in Miss Harrington's face and the desperation to rightfully claim credit for her own brilliance. But he also saw her fear of rejection. He recognized it because he lived it, never knowing when people would throw him to the side because of how he'd been born. For her, it was her gender. For him, it was his clubfoot.

"Did any of you actually believe that Pendergrast is capable of possessing a scholarly streak?" Alexander asked.

"He never wanted to discuss the discoveries at Herculaneum," Matthew said in that quiet but observant way of his.

"He also vehemently refused any invitation Mother or I made for him to speak at our salon," Charlotte added.

At each statement, Miss Harrington stood straighter and straighter. Her mouth even started to curve into a shocked smile.

"You can trust these people. Not only will they believe you, but they will guard your secrets," Alexander told Miss Harrington.

"You were aware of the truth all along? Even before you saw my dig?" she asked as she again studied him closely.

Alexander's body flushed warm under Miss Harrington's scrutiny, and prickles of awareness danced up and down his spine. He understood, though, that her assessment derived from intellectual and not sensual curiosity. Tamping down on his reaction, he nodded, hoping he looked at least a quarter as earnest as she did.

"Pendergrast confessed the truth to me years ago, but I would have realized it the moment I saw you in that pit." Alexander almost winced when he noticed that his voice had inadvertently deepened. Out of the corner of his eye, he saw Lottie shooting him with a curious look. But it was Miss Harrington's reaction that held him in thrall. Her cool brown eyes heated a fraction. His comment had clearly pleased her, and that pleased him.

"She was in a pit? Why was she in a pit?" Hannah asked.

"Obviously unearthing the helmet." Sophia shook her head in mock weariness. "You are forever opening your mouth without thinking."

At the Wick cousins' untimely observations, Miss Harrington visibly banked whatever glow had started to ignite. With a half smile, she regarded her small audience. "I suppose there is no hiding the truth now, especially since I may need your assistance. Yes, my cousin has been acting in my stead all these years. He is the visage; I am the intellect."

"You didn't just come here to look for your cousin. You want our help in finding him, don't you?" Alexander asked.

Miss Harrington nodded as another flicker of surprise drifted across her face. She clearly had not expected him to be so keen-witted. But then, given that he kept company with her cavalier cousin, he could forgive her for underestimating him. And he kept his identity as Willoughby Wright, columnist, carefully hidden, lest his prose mar his potential influence when he joined the House of Lords after inheriting the dukedom. He didn't precisely possess political aspirations, but he wished to champion certain reforms, and affably building relationships was more prudent than acquiring enemies.

"Yes, I am afraid I am in need of assistance," Miss Harrington admitted and then turned to Alexander's twin. "Lady Charlotte, I had heard that you unmasked Viscount Hawley and that you frequent the Black Sheep. I'd hoped you might give me some guidance on how to locate Percy. I have no one else to ask."

"I'll assist you." Alexander had no trouble making the promise. He too wanted to locate his friend, but even if the missing person had been an utter stranger, Alexander would have been eager to spend more time with Miss Harrington.

"Oh," Miss Harrington said, looking at him a bit uncertainly.

Alexander felt the sting of rejection, so he did what he always had. He smiled. Widely and broadly as if she hadn't inadvertently caused a twinge of hurt.

"We'll all help," Hannah vowed. "Finding a missing treasure and a nobleman sounds like a grand adventure."

"I wouldn't phrase it exactly in that manner," Miss Harrington said a little stiffly. After all, it was her relation who'd disappeared.

"What my cousin meant is that we all desire to help people unravel mysteries in their lives," Sophia broke in gently. "We will be happy to lend whatever aid that we can."

"But Alexander is in the best position," Lottie added as she moved to his side, quietly defending him, as she always did. Even though she did not even brush her shoulder against his, he felt his twin's support, and some of the old pain winked away.

"He is?" Miss Harrington still sounded dubious as she eyed him. Alexander noticed, though, that she didn't glance at his cane. Whatever reservations she held about him, they did not appear to be associated with his foot.

"He has access to all the spheres that your cousin inhabits," Sophia pointed out.

"Whereas I could only get you into drawing rooms," Calliope added.

"And I into the less savory venues," Mr. Powys continued.

"I'm the only one with access to both, and I also have connections to your cousin's inner circle, which no one else here can claim," Alexander said quietly, not wanting to scare Miss Harrington off if he seemed too eager to assist.

"And Alexander is eminently trustworthy," Lottie added, briefly resting her hand on his arm. "He knew your secret for years and never disclosed it, even before he met you. You can find no one more loyal."

Miss Harrington flicked her penetrating gaze over to him once more, and he saw her fear. Her own cousin had potentially abandoned her. Even if Pendergrast wasn't missing, he had definitely wronged her by carting the helmet all over London. She must think Alexander cut of the very same cavalier cloth.

"I won't betray either you or your secrets," Alexander vowed.

"Where..." Miss Harrington trailed off as if she still wasn't sure how she wished to proceed. Then she swallowed and seemed to arrive at a decision. "Where is the last place that you know my cousin went?"

"I met with him at the Black Sheep, but he said he was on his way to watch a fight at Championess Quick's Amphitheater," Alexander explained. "He frequents the establishment with some regularity, so it might be a good place to start. I can escort you there, but you must dress like a man. Championess Quick's may feature female boxers, but women can't openly attend the matches. Some, however, go in disguise."

Miss Harrington blinked. "There are women pugilists?"

Alexander nodded. "The prizefighters at Championess Quick's are true athletes. Some of them are handier with their fists and daggers than most men. Mary the Masher is the best I've seen with a cudgel."

Miss Harrington's eyes narrowed, and her accusation blazed back. "Do you like to watch women bloody themselves, Mr.... well, Alexander?"

"I enjoy champion matches where the participants are skilled and enjoy what they are doing," Alexander said evenly as he gripped his cane's bronze handle, which was cast in the shape of Hercules wrestling the Nemean lion. "I will agree that there are matches between women that are solely to evoke the prurient interest of male onlookers. Championess Quick's is no such establishment. The athletes do not fight bare-breasted, and she has instituted more rules than any other venue to promote sportsmanship. As someone whose strength and abilities are constantly underestimated, I like to support enterprises that allow outcasts to not just prove but celebrate their mettle. It is something I think you might understand."

Miss Harrington swallowed at his words, but she did not apologize. She did, however, give a curt nod. "I did not realize it was that type of place. I will accompany you there as soon as I can procure men's attire."

"Oh, no need to look for any," Hannah told her. "We have started to provide such clothing for our female clientele. One of the seamstresses at Powys's theater generally tailors them to fit, but she has provided us with a few ready-made pieces for our customers who need an outfit immediately,. We should be able to find something that suits you well enough."

"I am afraid that I have no coin to pay for them," Miss Harrington admitted.

Alexander sorely wished he could offer to cover the costs, but he had spent most of his allowance on Charlotte's white wedding cake.

"I can provide the money," Calliope said, and some of the tension fled from Alexander.

"Thank you." Miss Harrington bobbed her head in Calliope's direction. "I shall try to repay you—"

The duke's daughter waved away the offer. "I enjoy helping women defy Society's social dictates. Just make good use of the garment, even after your cousin and helmet are found."

Alexander thought he might have detected a glint of tears in Miss Harrington's eyes, but when she turned in his direction, they were once again clear and sharp.

"If it is acceptable to you, I would prefer to leave straightaway for Championess Quick's. I do not want to delay in finding my cousin." Miss Harrington's voice was back to its crisp tone.

"Understood. I want nothing more than to find Pendergrast too," Alexander said, hoping he seemed just as serious to her as she did to him. If she wasn't so desperate to find her cousin, he sensed that she never would have accepted his offer. Alexander wanted to prove his sincerity, but something told him it wouldn't be an easy feat—not with a woman as innately skeptical as the clever Miss Georgina Harrington of the Essex mud pit.

Chapter Four

What do you think of your clothing?" Lady Charlotte asked. "I've yet to go out dressed as a man, but I think I will try it soon."

Gathered with the other women in the Wick cousins' personal quarters, Georgina tugged on her thigh-length waistcoat as she glanced down at her breeches and stockings. "I feel lighter." Experimentally, she kicked out one leg and then the other. "Freer. It would be much easier to dig in this outfit than in skirts."

"I would avoid mud while wearing those," Hannah said. "They're silk."

"An outfit made of a more practical fabric," Georgina clarified as she took a few experimental steps. "My movement is definitely less encumbered without dragging around all those layers."

"Don't you feel gloriously unfettered?" Lady Calliope asked. "I used to borrow my brothers' clothing all the time as a girl. I absolutely love the garments that Miss Barrie makes."

Georgina nodded. "But how do I look? Are you certain I am not too curvy? We wrapped my chest with strips of linen, but is that enough? The bust is not the only area where a woman's form differs from a man's."

"That is the genius of Miss Barrie's designs," Lady Calliope said. "She has added strategic padding throughout to make the buttocks less noticeably curvy and the legs thicker."

Georgina had noticed lumps when she'd pulled on the breeches, but since she'd never worn male clothing before, she hadn't known it was unusual. Analyzing her thighs and calves for appearance rather than mobility, Georgina could see now that they looked more muscular. She tried to crane her neck over her shoulder to see her behind but to no avail.

"We really should invest in a mirror if we are to continue this additional service," Lady Charlotte said. "I have enough remaining inheritance from my great-aunt to purchase one."

Georgina found this much more interesting than the current shape of her bottom. "It is true, then? You are a co-owner of the Black Sheep?"

"Yes." Lady Charlotte nodded. "It is unconventional, but I've found I rather enjoy not fitting Society's expectations anymore."

Oh, how Georgina desired to control her own purse strings! Although she had not previously considered investing in an enterprise, the idea held appeal if it could afford her more financial independence. She didn't give a fig for her reputation, but she definitely cared about earning more coin to fuel her digging.

For the second time in less than a fortnight, she also wished she'd paid more attention to the identities of the nobility. Although she vaguely recalled the glittering Lady Charlotte and Lady Calliope from her debutante days, she could not remember their ranks or their families. She also still did not know the identity of Alexander—the man who was about to shepherd her around London. She had discovered that he was Lady Charlotte's brother, but that only confirmed he was part of the upper echelons of Society.

Alexander's association with Percy made her leery—as did his continued ability to wreak havoc on her senses. Discovering him in the Black Sheep had shocked her, and not just because she'd suspected him of revealing her secrets. Her skin felt tighter in his presence and a bit prickly—if prickly could be associated with the pleasant (if disconcerting) sensation. His all-too-frequent smiles unsettled her as did his eagerness to assist. Men typically ignored her—if they even noticed her at all. But Alexander's gaze had a way of lingering, and she did not know what to make of it. Clearly, her body didn't, either, with the way her heart occasionally tripped and her flesh continued to both heat and turn into goose-skin at the oddest moments.

Alexander's friends appeared to trust him implicitly. But although they had faith in the fellow, Georgina didn't. If she wanted to search London for Percy, though, it seemed like she would need to stay by the grinning noble's side.

"Does Alex—" Georgina was just about to ask if Alexander possessed a title when a polite but firm knock sounded at the door to the Wicks' quarters.

"I am sorry to disturb you, but is Miss Harrington ready? The bout starts in less than two hours, and I want to arrive early so we can mingle. Spirits are always high before a fight, and the men are less in their cups. It's the best time to glean coherent information." Alexander's smooth voice flowed straight through the door and right into Georgina. Again. Why did her body resonate so readily with his baritone? Such a thing had never happened other than with him.

"We were finishing up," Lady Calliope called. "We just need to affix her wig. You can come in if you wish."

Alexander entered the room with a wide, friendly smile on his classically handsome face. To Georgina's surprise, she felt the corners of her mouth twitch upward in response.

His gaze instantly focused on her, and Georgina shifted. She didn't think that Alexander was paying the most attention to her simply because she wore men's clothing. After all, he held her in the same regard when she'd been dressed in the plain clothes of a maid.

"Do I pass muster?" she asked.

"Now that is a thorny question." Alexander winked. "I will say that Miss Barrie is an excellent seamstress with an eye for transforming the wearer. You are remarkable in whatever clothes you don, Miss Harrington."

Georgina blinked. She did not recall any man ever speaking to her in such a teasing tone, especially accompanied by a wink, of all things. Gentlemen of Alexander's caliber had sneered at her during her come-out. They did not send her twinkling, flirtatious looks.

"If your tongue got any sweeter, cousin, it would literally drip honey," Hannah said, rolling her eyes as she approached with a wig.

Cousin. Alexander and Lady Charlotte's origins just became more interesting. According to Percy, Hannah and Sophia were the daughters of pirates. How did a noble family become linked with theirs?

But now was not the time to ask. Instead, Georgina eyed the powdered clump slowly descending upon her pinned-up coiffure. "I suppose the headgear can't be helped."

"Unfortunately, no," Sophia said. "Not unless we cut your hair. It is much too long to just wear in a simple queue."

Algernon and Anne would have her head if Georgina messed with her tresses. They had become obsessed with her appearance ever since they'd arrived in London. Georgina no longer possessed any doubts that her brother was trying to marry her off. If shaving her head would result in the termination of the secret betrothal, Georgina would gladly do it. But she had a feeling that something even more drastic would need to be done to prevent this union. Hacking off inches of her hair would only earn her endless lectures. The wig was decidedly less odious.

"This is actually one from my perruquier, whom I use for all my masquerade events. It has space built in to accommodate a lady's tresses," Lady Calliope explained.

Georgina would have turned to stare at the blond-haired woman, but Hannah was diligently working to secure the hairpiece. "You have a special wig maker for masques?"

"My half brother is the Duke of Blackglen," Lady Calliope explained. "He holds one almost weekly, especially during the Season."

Georgina felt her eyes widen. Even she, who knew little of Society, had heard about the notorious Blackglen. Algernon was forever moaning that he did not receive enough invites to the man's exclusive events. Anne had once let it slip that the duke considered Algernon a boorish sycophant. Although Georgina had little use for hedonists, she'd developed a fondness for the notorious rogue after learning that interesting tidbit.

"There." Hannah stepped back, examining her handiwork. "How does that feel?"

Tentatively, Georgina moved her head and then shook it more vigorously. "A bit heavy, but I don't think it will give me trouble."

"Are you ready for us to take our leave?" Alexander asked. "We really must be on our way."

"Yes," Georgina said, although instinct told her to run in the opposite direction. Alexander did not offer her his arm as a gentleman would, but she was, after all, posing as a fellow. Stiffening her shoulders, she tried to emulate a manly stride as she followed Alexander from the Wick cousins' quarters and down the stairs.

All went well until they reached his equipage in a nearby

mews. Georgina started at the sight of the curricle. She had ridden in Percy's... once. He'd delighted in driving it so fast that her stomach had lurched for nearly an hour after. But as bad as the nausea had been, her fear that they'd crash and break their necks had been worse.

"Are we going in that?" Georgina asked before she remembered to keep the horror from her voice.

"Yes. Championess Quick's Amphitheater is too far to walk if we want to arrive before the first bout," Alexander said. "Don't fash yourself. I'm good at the leathers. I know it doesn't have any covering, but no one should recognize you in your disguise."

Georgina wasn't worried about anyone noticing her. Even if she'd been dressed as a lady, she doubted anyone could identify her. She hadn't been to the city for so long, and even during her last visit, no one really knew who she was.

"Won't your curricle attract too much attention? We're investigating Percy's disappearance, after all. Is there time to take a hackney or perhaps stop by your residence for a more sedate vehicle?"

"People will notice if I don't show up in my normal transport," Alexander pointed out with what she was learning was his usual broad grin. "The whole point is being flashy. Besides, I don't have access to any other equipage."

Georgina blinked. Just how impractical was this man that he only owned an extremely lightweight carriage meant for racing about at speeds destined for disaster?

"It is sporting and manly. What use would I have of another conveyance?" Alexander spoke the words blithely with that wide, carefree smile still plastered on his face. Yet Georgina sensed something amiss. Perhaps it was because she had spent so much time in the company of Percy, who sincerely and regularly babbled such nonsense. Or maybe there was another reason for Georgina to detect a contradictory emotion beneath Alexander's layers and layers of cheer. Even though his countenance and voice gave nothing away, she felt a whisper of sarcasm and even bitterness.

"I would offer to hand you up." Alexander's chipper statement broke through Georgina's reverie. "But I am afraid it might attract attention given your attire. For the ruse to work, I cannot play the part of a gentleman."

"Oh, of course. Right." Georgina went to lift her skirts to place her foot on the step and realized she no longer had to contend with the burden of endless petticoats. With a rather sprightly bound, she launched herself into the speedy little carriage. A laugh of delight escaped her lips before she could stop it.

Although Alexander's expression hadn't changed, Georgina swore his grin was now genuine as he walked over to the other side of the curricle. He climbed into the seat smoothly and quickly, but he didn't move with the alacrity she had. She noticed he used his arm muscles to hoist himself aboard, never placing too much weight on his right side.

Given his gait, the cane wasn't just an affectation. Georgina wondered if his foot was the reason that he'd declined to climb into the pit with Percy that day. After all, her other assumptions about him kept being proven inaccurate.

"If our search for Pendergrast results in more outings, I could teach you," Alexander said as he expertly guided the matched bays onto the busy London thoroughfare.

"Pardon?" Georgina asked, confused by his words. "Instruct me how?"

"On driving my curricle," Alexander said, nodding his chin toward the reins. "It's not that much different from any other gig."

"I've only driven pony carts. My half brother's home is walkable to the local village and to my own property," Georgina admitted. Neither Algernon nor Anne wanted her using their precious conveyances.

"I can still show you how to manage the team," Alexander suggested, his expression bright and cheery while he maneuvered the horses through the snarl of traffic.

"Why?" Georgina asked, truly curious as to what had prompted the offer. The men who she knew hated when women took the leathers in their presence. Even Percy, with his random bursts of generosity, would never consider letting her drive. "Do you see it as a way to pass the time if we are stuck traveling?"

"No." Alexander shook his head. The sunlight caught in the strands of his auburn hair, giving him a halo of fire. He looked like Adonis, ready to challenge the gods with his mortal male beauty.

"Then your reason is?" Georgina pressed, trying to ignore the odd flutters in her heart. At five-and-twenty, she was too old and on-the-shelf for such girlish silliness.

Alexander slanted a look at her before turning his focus back to the heavily laden wagon in front of them. "I thought that if you were well-versed in the mechanics of driving a curricle, you would feel less trepidatious about riding in one."

"I am not apprehensive," Georgina quickly lied, a bit startled at how easily he'd correctly judged her.

"My mistake," Alexander said good-naturedly, without a hint of irony.

Georgina tilted her head to study him. She'd never actually met a true gentleman. All the so-called noblemen never lived up to the ideals they foisted on others. Could Alexander actually be one?

She had her doubts, but suddenly she heard herself confess, "Maybe I am a bit nervous. Percy drives like the devil."

Alexander laughed heartily. "That he does, but I promise I only do so during a race, and I wouldn't with a passenger who didn't wish to speed."

"Thank you," Georgina said, surprised to find that her muscles actually did uncoil a fraction. Instead of sitting ramrod straight, she allowed her shoulders to rest against the squabs. Despite the fact that Alexander was weaving the vehicle through the openings between the coaches, gigs, chaises, and simple farm wagons, he did drive more smoothly than Percy.

Alexander was silent for a moment. When he did speak, he started out cautiously as if debating his words. "There is another reason I offered to instruct you."

"Oh?" Georgina didn't know why, but her heart decided to beat at an almost painful rate.

"You seem like a person who has an unquenchable desire to understand precisely how things work. You also prefer to be in control."

Georgina almost gasped at his perfect assessment. "Did Percy tell you that?"

Alexander chuckled, the sound rumbling through Georgina's stomach...and then some place decidedly lower. A place that she did not know could rumble.

"Do you really believe Pendergrast is that preceptive?" Alexander asked amusedly without any malice toward her cousin.

"No." The word came out almost in a whisper, and Georgina didn't know if she was answering Alexander's question or giving a command to her own body. No matter what she was negating, she was decidedly uncomfortable with Alexander's ability to see the true her—even if his words flattered something deep inside her. It was a part that had yearned for years to be noticed.

But why by a man like Alexander, with his ever-present grin, his too-fast curricle, and his Adonis-surpassing looks?

Georgina needed to alter the path of this conversation. Immediately.

"Do you have a title that I should be using?" Georgina asked. Yes. That was a perfect inquiry. Make him feel exposed.

"Just Alexander is fine," he responded lightly without answering her question at all.

"But what should I call you when I am around others?" Georgina asked. "Isn't Alexander too informal?"

"My friends know I prefer my Christian name," Alexander said easily. "Besides, an antiquarian such as yourself should enjoy it. Alexander the Great and all. Although no need to include the 'Great.' Wouldn't want me getting a reputation for vanity."

Georgina had the distinct sense that Alexander was deflecting with a joke. Why did he eschew his title and last name? For so many men of his class, it became their entire identity.

"But we really should be discussing your choice of appellation when you're dressed as a man," Alexander said. Although he made an excellent point, Georgina suspected he was continuing to purposely divert the discussion.

"I suppose George Harrington will work. I don't think anyone will associate it with the real me. I'm not known in London. We can even say I'm Percy's cousin. He has a bevy of them, including many males."

"A pleasure to meet you, Mr. George Harrington. I'd extend my hand for a shake, but I think you'd feel more at ease if I kept both of them on the reins."

"Thank you," Georgina said, surprised again by Alexander's honest consideration. Could the man actually be as pleasant as he seemed? Or had he, like Algernon, just acquired the proper manners to dupe people into believing him to be a good, upstanding fellow? For the sake of her mission to find Percy, she hoped it was the former. But if she found Alexander to indeed be trustworthy, would it make it harder for her to battle these odd sensations?

⚬⚭⚬

"Don't look in that direction," Alexander warned Georgina as they walked through the crowds gathered near Championess Quick's Amphitheater.

They were in the outskirts of London in a rougher section than Georgina had ever visited. Men in their cups stumbled down the street. Two had almost knocked her over. She noticed that Alexander angled his body and his cane to create almost a bubble around her. It felt odd to have someone watch over her. No one had since her father's passing.

"Why?" Georgina asked as she averted her gaze.

"Cockfight," Alexander said, his disgust palpable. "It is a despicable pastime."

"For a lady to observe?" Georgina asked, curious if he was simply watching out for her virtue or if he actually shared her opinion on the practice.

"It's not pleasant for anyone with an ounce of compassion to witness," Alexander said vehemently, his mien serious for once.

"I thought you enjoyed blood sport?" Georgina turned the statement into a question.

Alexander's face twisted. "There is no sport in two helpless creatures being forced to fight to the death. It is worse when one is noticeably weaker. I like bouts between two evenly matched human champions who want to exhibit their abilities. There's a thrill in watching talented people display their strength, is there not?"

By the time Alexander finished speaking, his expression had returned to its normal sunniness, as if the storm clouds had never existed. But his cheer did not make his question any less pointed.

"I have never thought about it in that manner," Georgina admitted.

Alexander suddenly paused in front of a large building. Pulling back one of the double doors, he said, "Now that we've arrived at Championess Quick's, you'll have the opportunity to witness the best of the best."

"Here! Here!" A throaty female voice floated out to greet them. "I do like hearing my establishment praised."

"Championess Quick." Alexander inclined his head to the tall woman in her fifties.

Like a hostess welcoming her guests to a grand ball, the boxer stood just inside the entrance. Her brown and silver hair was covered by neither powder nor cap. Instead, the tresses had been braided and woven into a crown. Something about the hairstyle made Georgina think of the olive leaves worn by the winners of the ancient Greek Olympics according to Pausanias. The woman was certainly built like a legendary Amazon. Her simple linen jacket must have been specifically tailored to cling to her broad shoulders and her defined arm muscles. Her skirts were unconventionally short and fell only to just below her knees. Her pristine white Holland drawers and stockings seemed designed to highlight the strength of her legs rather than obscure her powerful form. She had a longer face than strictly fashionable, but it only bestowed a harsh but handsome beauty upon her.

"Alexander." Championess Quick regally tilted her chin to acknowledge him. The woman's eyes slid over Georgina once, then twice, and finally much more slowly. A devilish glint appeared in her blue-green eyes. "I see you've brought a friend..."

Championess Quick paused, and Georgina froze, certain the prizefighter would reveal her secret. Another beat passed, and Georgina glanced in panic toward Alexander. He appeared utterly relaxed.

"What is his name?" Championess Quick finally finished, putting the slightest emphasis on "his."

Georgina heaved out the breath that she'd been holding. It was obvious that the boxer *had* guessed Georgina's gender, but it was equally clear that she would not reveal it.

"Mr. George Harrington," Alexander supplied. "Mr. Harrington, this is Championess Quick."

"Pleased to meet you, Mr. Harrington." A secret half smile touched the boxer's lips as she said the last two words.

"Likewise," Georgina responded in her deepest voice. She might have tried a little too hard as the single word ended in a rather dramatic coughing fit.

Championess Quick whacked Georgina on the back. At the strong but fortunately not painful blow, Georgina almost tipped over onto her face. As she stumbled, Championess Quick bent over to whisper in her ear.

"Not so low, dearie. You'll give yourself away in a trifle. Just slightly deepen the natural timbre of your voice."

Advice given, Championess Quick started to turn away, but Alexander stopped her with a question. "Championess Quick, have you seen Lord Percy Pendergrast lately?"

The prizefighter paused and pursed her lips in consideration. "I do believe he was last here over a week ago when Kate Ball fought Mary Henderson. He was one of the few who bet on Kate. It was a tremendous shock when she won. I don't believe I've seen him since, but I may simply not remember."

Alexander laughed good-naturedly. "You recall everything about your regulars. If you said he didn't show, then he wasn't present. Do you remember anything in particular about Pendergrast on the day of the Ball-Henderson match? Was he his normal self?"

Championess Quick again thought before answering. "He was in high spirits, even for him, but he did win a lot of coin. Perhaps he was a little deeper in his cups than usual. He normally likes to be more sober during the matches, but nothing too unusual."

"Did he mention any of his plans?" Georgina asked, forgetting to roughen her voice.

Championess Quick motioned with her hand for Georgina to deepen her tone as she asked, "How do you know Lord Percy?"

"He's my cousin." Georgina finally managed to properly modulate her fake speech. She was a bit hoarse but passable.

"Mr. Harrington is telling the truth," Alexander said. "Pendergrast introduced us himself. The two of them are very close, and Mr. Harrington is worried. We haven't heard from Pendergrast in over a week, and he missed an important obligation."

"Lord Percy mentioned something about heading to Elysian Fields, but I am afraid that is all I know. You may ask my staff if you desire. Later this evening, I will inquire if they know more than me. If they do, I will send you a missive."

"Thank you," Alexander said. Championess Quick gave a quick nod of acknowledgment before she turned to greet her other customers.

"Incredible, isn't she?" Alexander asked. "You should see her in the ring. She's excellent both at bareknuckle fighting and with short swords. But her true genius is promoting. She started out with nothing but earned enough to build this amphitheater. She created an entire empire all the while singlehandedly raising her daughter—who, by the by, is unbeatable with the quarter-staff, even against male opponents."

Georgina glanced over at Alexander. He did not speak about women as many men did, especially about females engaged in a profession some would consider close to prostitution. He mentioned nothing about Championess Quick or her daughter's physical attributes but only characteristics more often ascribed to men.

"You truly do admire and respect her," Georgina observed.

"Just watch her navigate through the throng."

Georgina glanced around the packed but cavernous building with its high ceiling and large windows to let in light. In the center was a wooden platform with a pit surrounding it. Lower-class fellows crowded shoulder to shoulder in the depression as they jostled for better positions. Championess Quick had moved to the tiered seating that was filled with gentlemen in fine silks and expensive wool suits. As Georgina studied the faces of the people in both sections, she realized that a few possessed rather feminine features. Alexander was right. She wasn't the only woman in disguise.

Championess Quick was leaning over a group of seated noblemen. A young chap moved his right arm as if pretending to strike an invisible foe. Championess Quick gently shook her head. Standing up, she demonstrated what Georgina assumed was the proper way to land the blow. The fellow watched her closely, mimicking her actions.

"Do gentlemen accept advice from Championess Quick?" Georgina asked in shock.

Alexander chuckled, and Georgina sorely wished he'd stop making the deep, intoxicating sound. She was tired of battling its effects.

"No one admits to it openly, but they take lessons from her. I hear there's a waiting list. Championess Quick is selective, too. I'm fortunate she agreed to teach me. She showed me how I can use my cane to defend myself and a few ways to balance with my bad leg. The best strategy for me is to get my opponent on the ground," Alexander told Georgina.

Unbidden, an image of a shirtless Alexander popped into Georgina's mind. If she thought his laugh had an odd impact on her nerves, the image did much more damage. A sense of something she could only categorize as need rushed through her. Desperate not to deal with any unwanted yearnings, Georgina blurted out the first sentence that came to mind.

"I thought you said no one confesses that she taught them."

Alexander winked once more. "I believe I can trust you. Besides, I thought you'd be interested in my endorsement of Championess Quick's lessons."

"Whyever would you think that?" Georgina asked, with perhaps more tartness than necessary. But a horrified part of her wondered if Alexander suspected that he'd been boxing half naked across her imagination.

Alexander leaned close, and an annoying flush of warmth rushed over Georgina's face and neck. She was so unsettled that she almost missed his comment.

"She teaches women as well."

Was Alexander envisioning her boxing bare-chested? Georgina's entire body burst into flames of embarrassment.

"I'm not really an adventurer," Georgina blurted out in a panic.

Alexander shrugged with a nonchalance that Georgina certainly didn't feel. "Knowledge of how to fight might prove useful during our search for Pendergrast."

"Do you expect me to beat the answers out of people? Even if I did take instructions from Championess Quick, I am not exactly what one would classify as intimidating."

To Georgina's surprise, Alexander did not laugh. In fact, his mouth flattened into a rather sober expression. "I meant in defense. If your cousin was truly abducted, we could be facing danger ourselves."

The unease that Georgina had felt since overhearing Algernon's clandestine conversation burgeoned inside her. She had no idea if the discussion was related to Percy's disappearance, but she couldn't escape the sensation that peril was barreling toward her.

"I don't possess the pin money to afford lessons," Georgina admitted. "I have an inheritance from my father, but my half brother controls it."

"If you'd like, I can show you a few maneuvers," Alexander volunteered, his customary affable grin back.

Georgina did not understand his continued kindness. He had already offered to show her how to drive a curricle. Did he pity her? Was there perhaps an ulterior motive to his generosity? Maybe he was behind Percy's disappearance after all, and he meant to disarm her with his charm.

Georgina was just about to question his benevolence when Alexander lightly bumped her arm and began to guide her through the crowd. As they walked swiftly, he bent his head near hers so no one could overhear. She wondered why he even bothered. The din inside the echoey building was overwhelming, making it hard to hear a person even when standing directly across from them.

"Do you see that scholarly-looking fellow seated in the far corner and scribbling away?" Alexander asked. "He's the Earl of Clifville and an antiquarian whom I've seen at the Elysian Fields coffeehouse when Pendergrast dragged me there. If I am remembering rightly, his ancestral seat is in Essex."

A spidery sensation whispered down Georgina's spine, and she repressed the urge to shiver. Frantically, she searched her mind to recall if she'd heard his name before. "Do you think he caused my cousin's disappearance? Does he have a particular interest in English history?"

"I am not very familiar with his work," Alexander admitted, "but he seems like a nice enough fellow, if a bit of a dullard. I honestly cannot imagine him bestirring himself from his books long enough to plot a kidnapping. But he might have some useful information. Despite his retiring nature, I heard he's a favorite of King George, and he might have access to gossip that I never would."

As they approached the tall, slender man who appeared to be in his thirtieth year, Georgina realized that the earl fit her ideal almost perfectly. He possessed the rawboned build of an academic who spent most of his days at his desk, forgetting even to eat as research consumed him. Even now, despite the cacophony of sounds, Clifville diligently wrote on scraps of paper, a book laid across his knees as a desk. Beside him on a nearby windowsill perched an open ink bottle. Although Georgina had never attended a fight before, she assumed the sight was an unusual one.

"Lord Clifville," Alexander shouted, but the earl did not appear to hear. He just kept scratching his quill over the parchment. Alexander had to call him three more times before Clifville finally raised his head. Blinking slowly, just like

Georgina would have done after being pulled from her writing, he waited several beats before he focused on Alexander's face.

Georgina's unease fled. Alexander was correct. Clifville didn't seem the kidnapping sort—not that she knew what a kidnapping sort would be like.

Georgina took the time to study the peer. He had slight hollows under his cheekbones, and his Adam's apple stood out. He was pale without the use of face powder. His brown hair was tied back into a queue with a simple black ribbon that matched the plain practicality of his unadorned wool suit. He seemed dressed for a stroll in the country rather than for a London boxing match. Although not classically handsome, his face possessed an austere appeal. He exuded a quiet solidness that should have intrigued Georgina.

Yet despite being confronted with her very fantasy, she felt decidedly...unmoved. Her heart did not flutter, let alone jump. There wasn't even the occasional odd beat. No unusual sensations rumbled through her. Nothing was rumbling at all. Her breath didn't seem caught in her throat or even shortened. She felt absolutely normal...unlike when a certain redhead sent a ridiculously cheery smile her way.

"I'm Alexander, Lord Percy Pendergrast's friend," Alexander explained as the earl still stared at him owlishly.

The scholar shook himself as if waking up from a long nap. "Oh yes. Alexander. I remember you now."

"This is Mr. George Harrington, Lord Percy's cousin," Alexander said by way of introduction to Georgina. "He studies the classics, too. Pendergrast seems to have gone carousing again, and Mr. Harrington was trying to locate him. Have you seen him lately?"

Clifville's eyes suddenly brightened as he turned to Georgina. Yet even as the man's excited gaze met hers, she still felt...well, the exact same as she always did. No excited stir-rings. Not even a feeble one.

"Lord Percy did stop by Elysian Fields a few times recently. He brought with him a most marvelous helmet. Very ancient, but it did not appear Roman. He claimed it belonged to Arthur, but it is not likely to have been possessed by a mythical legend. I was looking forward to his presentation at the Antiquarians of England Society, but he did not show. A grave pity."

The earl seemed to speak the same language as Georgina's very soul, but still...quietude. Not a flare. Not a flame. Not even a small spark. She only felt frustration at her cousin's cavalier handling of her helmet.

"Did anyone show particular interest in the piece?" Georgina asked, remembering at the last moment to lower her timbre.

"Well, of course, everyone gathered around," Clifville said. "We were all exceedingly impressed. Lord Percy never ceases to amaze me. When speaking with him, he does not appear that interested in the ancient world, yet his articles are superbly knowledgeable. I would not have thought him of the tempera-ment to systematically search for antiquities, yet it appears that he is very deliberate in his digging."

Pride whipped through Georgina, but no other emotions sparked.

"Did anyone seem abnormally intrigued with the helmet—an obsession beyond professional curiosity?" Alexander pressed.

Clifville rubbed his chin with his narrow fingers. "Well, there was that rather boisterous newcomer: Lord Henry Talbot."

Georgina started at the name that she'd almost forgotten. He'd been one of the callow youths who'd viciously mocked her during her come-out. Algernon had originally been keen on her marrying the second son of a duke, but Lord Henry had scoffed at wedding a wallflower.

To Georgina's surprise, Alexander also visibly stiffened. He seemed to pale under his bronzed skin. For a moment, a haunted light flickered in his hazel eyes. But suddenly it was gone, and he was back to smiling. "Good lord. What is a devil like Henry Talbot doing at Elysian Fields? It is much too tame for him."

"He made mention of his father wanting him to improve his reputation after his older brother, Lord Hawley, was arrested for something dreadful—highway robbery, I believe." Clifville lifted his narrow shoulders into a shrug. "It is a grand scandal, but I don't know the details. I rarely pay attention to gossip. But Lord Henry was completely enamored by the idea of the helmet belonging to King Arthur. He offered to buy it, but Lord Percy declined—very vehemently, if I recall. Seems he isn't interested in selling."

"Is there anything else you remember? Did he talk about any places where he planned on going?" Georgina asked, her heart squeezing as she thought of the danger that her cousin could be in. Dear Percy might have foolishly displayed her helmet all around town, but at least he'd refused to part with it.

"Not that I recall." Clifville settled back into his seat. "As I said, he mentioned the Antiquarians, but that was all. If you don't mind, though, the bout is about to begin, and I am here to observe it for historical purposes."

"Pardon?" Georgina asked as her estimation of the man began to drop. Did he truly think he could twist his attendance at a boxing match into research about antiquity?

"I am writing a paper on the veracity of the Amazons and thought it prudent to watch modern female fighters," Clifville explained. "Many men claim it is impossible for women to have performed the feats of warcraft ascribed to legendary warriors by Greek historians, but I have heard that some of the female competitors here are better than males in their particular disciplines."

Georgina had evidently misjudged Lord Clifville's intellectual bent. He did have a legitimate academic reason for his presence at the amphitheater.

"Lizzie Quick, Championess Quick's daughter, is one of them," Alexander said. "She is to fight Jane Hawkins first with the quarterstaff. If the bout is a fast one—and it normally is with Lizzie—then the second fight will be a bare-knuckled one between Agnus Cooper and Joan Foy."

"You seem knowledgeable," Clifville said. "Would you two care to join me?"

Alexander turned a questioning look in Georgina's direction. She debated for a moment. If the competition was about to begin, they could no longer move freely about the building to question the attendees and staff about Percy. But should Georgina stay at the match when no more investigating could be done? She abhorred blood sport, but part of her wanted to see the women engage in fisticuffs, especially after meeting the peerless Championess Quick.

A sudden cheer rang out. Georgina swung around to see two women take to the floor. They both wore ensembles similar to Championess Quick's—shortened skirts, tailored jackets, Holland drawers, and white stockings. In their hands, they held thick wooden sticks. It was easy to identify Championess Quick's daughter. She possessed the same regal bearing as her mother, her chestnut-brown hair also woven into a crown.

At the first crack of the women's quarterstaffs, Georgina plunked herself down beside Lord Clifville. By the second, she was leaning halfway over her knees for a better view. After the third, she started peppering Alexander with questions.

It was glorious watching the women whirl, duck, and charge. The wood whistled through the air, almost creating its own wild song. There was fierce beauty in the fighters' footwork and their magnificent strikes. Excitement and perhaps even a sense of pride thundered through Georgina. Lizzie and Jane's prowess made Georgina wonder about her own hidden depths. What would happen if she did take Alexander up on his offer to teach her how to fight?

Chapter Five

"Why were Agnus Cooper and Joan Foy holding a half crown in each hand?" Miss Harrington asked Alexander as they left the amphitheater. "Was it to give their blows more heft? Does it make it more painful? I thought you said that Championess Quick's rules improve safety, but don't the coins make things more dangerous?"

Alexander grinned at Miss Harrington's unbridled enthusiasm. She'd stopped trying to hide her enjoyment of the fight after Lizzie Quick and Jane Hawkins had exchanged six strikes with their quarterstaffs. Poor Lord Clifville had barely been able to ask a single question. Georgina had just fired away her inquiries with nary a pause.

Not that Alexander minded. He rather liked her endless queries.

"The pieces of sterling are to prevent the competitors from gouging each other's eyes or from scratching, which Championess Quick strictly forbids," Alexander explained. "That's why she requires them to carry the money."

"That happens?" Miss Harrington asked, looking horrified.

Alexander nodded grimly. "I've seen it myself. It's terrible. Jack Broughton introduced rules a decade or more ago to help prevent deaths in the ring. But it is still chaotic. Like I said earlier, Championess Quick has developed her own set of laws. She believes in less blood and more talent."

"The more I learn about her, the more remarkable she becomes," Miss Harrington said.

"She also runs a charitable boxing academy for youths from the street. It is to protect them from unscrupulous promoters and to provide them with a way to make a living." Alexander had donated funds as Willoughby Wright after he'd penned a piece about the prurient cruelty of unregulated bouts between poverty-stricken competitors. Even Championess Quick had no idea that he was the one who'd sent her the money. Nor did she realize he'd penned the short story about a rich man pompously attiring himself for watching a fight by determining which colors would go best with blood splatters.

Uproarious laughter drew Alexander's attention away from his conversation with Miss Harrington. Instantly, he wished that he hadn't glanced in that direction. A throng was gathered in the yard of a nearby tavern for a cockfight. The crowd likely had been so big that the owners of the birds had moved the event outdoors. Such entertainment must be a semi-regular occurrence—not enough for a proper sunken cockpit with tiered seating, but enough for a crude stage rimmed with a low, mostly see-through wicker fence.

Alexander and Georgina were still some distance away, but he could make out the fowls. The size difference between the two sickened him. A huge meaty rooster with dark coloring and spurs on his feet strutted in his cage while a small, fluffy white one cowered in his. Alexander had never seen a chicken like it. Its profusion of feathers looked almost like a mammal's pelt. Massive tufts grew from its crown and legs, making the bird appear like it was wearing a fur hat and boots. The extreme plumage would encumber the already undersized rooster, giving its opponent something to grab and tear.

Rage and disgust filled Alexander as he realized that this round was merely for the depraved humor of watching the stronger animal torment the weaker. A familiar sense of helplessness washed over Alexander as memories of old jeers mixed with the current taunts.

The faces of Viscount Hawley and his younger brother, Lord Henry, lurched into Alexander's mind. He saw their sneers as they and his mates pushed him into the manure heap outside the boarding school's stables. Phantom throbs pulsed in Alexander's arms, chest, and legs. In his vision, he saw his own cane lifted against him as the boys laughed. He heard his only friend Matthew cry out for his older siblings to stop, but the other students held him back.

"Alexander?" Miss Harrington's voice broke through Alexander's pain. "Alexander?"

Dimly, he turned in her direction. She stared at him with worried brown eyes.

"Are you all right? You're so pale, and you're rubbing your leg. Did you twist it?" Miss Harrington spoke with concern and not pity—a difference that Alexander knew too well.

"I am fine. I'm just revolted by man's degenerate nature. That white bird can't defend itself. They're sending it to slaughter for their own enjoyment." The words flew out of Alexander's mouth before he remembered that he was speaking to a sheltered miss. It was clear from her questions during the prizefight that she knew little of modern violence, even if she had read and studied ancient wars.

"We should stop the fight," Miss Harrington declared.

Alexander turned fully in her direction. Was this the same

woman who had declined his offer to teach her how to defend herself and claimed that she was not an adventurer?

"How? I may hold a courtesy title, but those men won't listen to me," Alexander said. His earliest satire had been a very ribald one about men strutting around and striking each with their own erect cocks. It had been his juvenile attempt to criticize the link between masculinity and blood sport. The tale had sold fairly well, but he'd never found an organization to donate the funds to. Banning animal fights was one of the laws that Alexander wanted to champion when he became Duke of Falcondale.

Miss Harrington jerked her head toward the row of cages set up close to the stage. "If I free the other birds, their escape will ignite a proper commotion. In the confusion, we can grab the fluffy one and escape."

"I thought you were supposed to be a scholar, not a swash-buckler," Alexander said in disbelief.

"I cannot watch another creature harmed. You should have seen me when I fought off the neighborhood dog pack with my reticule to save Ruffian Caesar," Miss Harrington said, utterly and completely serious.

"Who is Ruffian Caesar?" Alexander asked in confusion.

"The terrier whom I rescued," Miss Harrington explained. "We better hurry. They are about to open those two roosters' cages, and I am afraid that little white one won't last long."

"But Miss Harrington, I can't run," Alexander pointed out.

"We'll meet by your curricle."

Before Alexander could stop her, Miss Harrington seam-lessly wormed her way through the onlookers. With her petite form, she could sneak through the spaces in the milling group. If Alexander tried to follow her, he'd only attract attention, which could land Miss Harrington in more than just a spot of trouble.

It struck him that her daring plan to rescue the chicken wasn't entirely out of character. After all, in the space of half a day, she'd already donned two costumes to track down her flighty cousin.

Alexander followed her with his eyes the best that he could. Here and there, he spied her for a moment before she disappeared again.

Although he had no idea how exactly to protect her, he couldn't just stand on the street and desperately hope her hastily planned mission did not go awry. Picking up his own pace, Alexander headed over to the man collecting coin from the spectators. After paying the fee, Alexander made his way to the part of the stage closest to the coops.

From his new spot, he watched Miss Harrington slink up to the caged creatures. Alexander's heart clenched, and he gripped the head of his cane so hard that the Nemean lion's teeth dug into his palm. Fortunately, the cockfight had begun, and everyone's attention was riveted to the stage.

Sweat dripped down his back, and his muscles tensed. Alexander continued checking the crowd and Miss Harrington's progress. Slowly, she lifted each of the wooden pegs holding the cage doors closed until they were almost out of their looped pinning but not completely. Both Alexander's curiosity and admiration grew. Miss Harrington clearly had a plan, and he hoped for both their sakes that it worked.

When she'd finished loosening all the fastenings, she disappeared behind the stack of twenty-four cages. With a resounding bang, the entire pile crashed to the ground. Miss Harrington must have also dived to the dirt because, even though Alexander looked, he could not spot her, not even the top of her white wig.

The doors to the coops bounced open. Angry roosters flew haphazardly into the throng and darted along the ground, hissing and flapping their wings. Men shouted as talons scraped their faces and shoulders. Some of the birds had already been fitted with metal spurs, and the spectators screamed as they ducked and even fell to the ground. The chickens stampeded over the prone humans, their beady eyes glowing with malicious glee. One perched on a gentleman's head and crowed as if seeing its first sunrise. Alexander couldn't have written a better scene.

The onlookers who hadn't fallen to their knees batted at the aerial poultry, driving the fowls straight onto the stage. The roosters rage-squawked as they awkwardly but determinedly fluttered straight at their handlers. The owners raised their hands to protect their faces as curses spewed from their lips. In the ring, the bigger rooster abandoned the furry white chicken. The hefty fowl opened its beak wide as a hideous screech escaped from its muscular chest. The startled fluff ran around in a tight circle, seemingly too overset to even make a sound.

Miss Harrington leaped onto the stage and scooped up the small rooster. In her haste, she tucked it under her arm backward. As she bounded away, the poor creature's body bounced this way and that, but its fleecy head remained perfectly straight in that peculiar balancing habit of chickens. If Alexander hadn't been so worried for Miss Harrington, he would have laughed.

One of the match organizers lunged in her direction, and his thick fingers nearly caught the back of Miss Harrington's coat. Frantic to protect her, Alexander did the only thing that he could think of. He smashed his walking stick through the wicker fencing around the stage and transformed into a gentleman in high dudgeon.

"What is the meaning of this travesty?" Alexander shouted loud enough that the owners of the birds could hear him over the cacophony. A few of the men closest to him quieted down, interested in the new spectacle.

"I paid good coin to watch a cockfight," Alexander continued to yell. "Instead, I—*I*—am attacked by a flock of poultry! Do you not know who I am?"

"I also want an accounting!" The gentleman who'd had a rooster crow on his head hopped up from the ground.

Alexander whacked his cane against the wooden boards again. The crack echoed through the tavern yard. The chaps gathered around the stage began bumping each other with their elbows. As the crowd quieted and their attention turned to Alexander, the organizers of the bout looked at each other in pure panic. Miss Harrington slipped away, the fluffball now secure against her bosom. The other roosters began to flap and dash to freedom, their thick necks bobbing from the effort.

"Recompense! I demand recompense!" Alexander hollered, punctuating each word with a strike of his walking stick.

The throng took up his cry. In unison, they shouted. "Recompense! We demand recompense! Recompense! We demand recompense!"

The man collecting the coins clutched the purse close to his belly as he ducked his head and began to dash away. A collective roar filled the air.

"Get him!" a rough voice called out.

"Attack them all!" another cried.

The throng surged forward, some to tackle the fellow with the proceeds, the others to bring down the two onstage. Alexander took the opportunity to stroll away unnoticed. Reaching the street, he hummed a jaunty tune as roosters darted around him. Passersby gasped as armed chickens filled the thoroughfare. Some of the fowls emitted joyous battle squawks before they raced down side alleys to their freedom.

As Alexander walked by a bakery, he paused. He had little coin left for the month, but Miss Harrington would probably want to feed the white puff. Changing to a whistle, Alexander strolled into the store and bought the cheapest bun. Stuffing it into his pocket, he headed to the curricle, where he found Miss Harrington perched on the seat, the chicken nestled in her lap. Although the pouf on top of its head obscured its eyes, its slumped neck revealed its frightened exhaustion. Miss Harrington, however, was the very picture of excitement.

Her cheeks glowed a soft, wonderful pink, and her brown eyes sparkled with fierce joy. Her bound chest still moved up and down from the exertion of the rescue. The wig had slipped a fraction, revealing her tightly pinned brown hair and giving her a rather jaunty appearance. She simply shone with life.

Alexander's heart felt like it did when he took a sharp bend during a carriage race and one of its wheels lifted dangerously. And just like then, he wasn't about to exercise caution.

At his approach, Miss Harrington turned. For once, she did not fix him with a half-skeptical look. Although she did not precisely smile, she looked happy and perhaps a touch relieved.

"You were brilliant!" Alexander told her as he hoisted himself into his curricle. "Your scheme worked perfectly. I do believe you liberated every single rooster and not just your fluffball. The streets were filled with fleeing fowl. They'll never collect the birds."

Miss Harrington beamed, and her wig dipped a bit further. And so did Alexander's heart. She looked utterly and completely fetching.

"I did not know that I possessed the ability to do something like that." Miss Harrington's expression turned introspective but no less enthusiastic. "I must have been inspired by the prizefighters at Championess Quick's. It was so exhilarating watching their bouts."

Miss Harrington had been the thrilling one. The way the coops had clattered to the ground had been truly marvelous. Alexander could still see her flying onto the stage and scooping up the befuddled rooster.

"Do you think we should leave now?" Miss Harrington asked. "Could they be chasing us?"

Alexander shook his head. "They are otherwise occupied. I turned the crowd against them. The spectators are determined to see blood flowing, having been deprived of the promised cockfight."

"Normally, I abhor violence, but I do believe those men deserve their comeuppance, tormenting helpless creatures like that for money." Miss Harrington sighed deeply as she gazed down at the chicken. The rooster remained frozen in shock, oblivious to the adoring gaze he was receiving.

Foolish fowl. Alexander would cherish such a look from Miss Harrington. He definitely wouldn't remain a motionless lump.

Suddenly, Miss Harrington raised her chin to look at him. Although her eyes were not as soft as they were when directed at the chicken, there was warmth in them. "You are cleverer than I suspected, Alexander. It was quick-witted of you to cause a scene to help me escape. Thank you for coming to my rescue. If you hadn't acted so quickly, that beefy man would have certainly caught me."

Alexander swallowed at her sincerity. There was a time in his life when he'd been starved for true compliments, and Miss Harrington's words touched that long-buried need. His heart thudded against his chest like a horse's hooves against cobblestone.

As Miss Harrington started to turn from him, her wig tilted

even more. Alexander reached up to right it. When his hand brushed against the side of her head, she froze, her face inches from his. If he dipped just a little closer, their mouths would touch. Alexander's gaze flicked to her pink lips. Her tongue darted out as she nervously wet them, leaving behind a bead of moisture. Alexander wanted to brush it away—with his thumb, his lips, or even his tongue—it didn't matter.

"Miss Harrington?" His voice sounded guttural to his own ears, and he hoped she understood the question he was asking.

"Yes?" She sounded uncharacteristically hesitant and maybe, just maybe, a little hopeful.

"Miss Harrington," he started again, "may I—"

"Baaaaaaaaaaaaaaaaaawwwwwwwwwwwaaaaaaaaawwwwww-wwwwwk!"

Both Alexander and Miss Harrington flew back at the chicken's panicked cry. Its faculties—although limited—had returned. Even with its downy head thrown back as it moaned its woes to all and sundry, only its gray beak was visible through its plethora of feathers.

"I suppose the chicken wants us to leave," Alexander joked, although he wasn't sure if he should throttle or thank the fowl. Kissing Miss Harrington would have not been the wisest decision for many reasons. But the foremost was that Alexander's personal code did not allow him to trifle with hearts. As much as Miss Harrington intrigued him, he had no intention of wedding someone whom his sire deemed appropriate. Although Alexander wasn't precisely sure of Miss Harrington's bloodlines, she was the legitimate cousin of a duke whose maternal lineage traced back to the Norman invasion. And Alexander's father wanted nothing more than flawless, unblemished prestige and respectability for his next heir—an heir with a perfect body and no clubfoot. Alexander had sworn as a boy—when fever, chills, and pain had racked his body when fighting infection from another botched surgery—that he would never give the duke the satisfaction of a faultless grandson. Yes, he'd marry and have children, but he'd either choose a wife with questionable roots or wait until after his father had left this earth.

But it was too fine a day to dwell on such darkness. Alexander reached into his pocket and pulled out the bun. "Here. Perhaps this will calm the bird. I bought it for him."

Miss Harrington regarded him thoughtfully. "That was kind of you."

Alexander shrugged. "The poor creature had a nasty shock."

As Miss Harrington ripped apart the bread, Alexander lifted the reins and clicked twice to the bays. When they reached the main thoroughfare, where the traffic inched along, he glanced over at the chicken on Miss Harrington's lap. Its white plume waved merrily in the air as it enthusiastically pecked at the crust.

"What are you going to name him?" Alexander asked.

"Crinitus Legatus," Miss Harrington said crisply.

Alexander barked out a laugh, feeling back to his normal self. "You're giving that ridiculous creature the title of a Roman general? Although I suppose I shouldn't be surprised, since you bestowed the honor of emperor upon your mutt from the streets."

"It is a perfect appellation. I did call the rooster General Fluffy," Miss Harrington pointed out.

"But since Crinitus Legatus is in Latin, it is absurdly dignified for a fowl, especially that one."

"Well, I like it."

"Fluffus Legatus?" Alexander suggested. "It has a more pleasing sound."

"I beg to differ. His name shall remain Crinitus Legatus."

"Fluffus Legatus."

"Crinitus Legatus."

"Fluff-us."

"Crin-it-us."

"You know I can keep this up the entire ride back to the Black Sheep," Alexander pointed out, feeling gloriously lighthearted.

Miss Harrington regarded him with solemnity tinged by amusement. "So can I."

Alexander threw his head back and laughed. Miss Harrington may have the power to disrupt his vow to never fall for a gentlewoman, but Alexander found her presence just too delightful to part with her just yet. Besides, he'd made a promise to help her find Pendergrast. He couldn't break that oath and abandon a friend in potential danger. Besides, what was the harm in indulging in a bit of diversion for a few days or even a week or two? As long as Alexander's and Miss Harrington's hearts didn't become truly entangled, no harm would come of a new friendship peppered with light flirtation.

⚜

Later that day, Alexander glanced over at Miss Harrington as he drove to her half brother's townhome in fashionable Mayfair. Once again, she had on the maid's outfit that she'd originally worn to the Black Sheep, but she carried the male clothes in a satchel. She looked sterner under the floppy mob cap than she had in the white wig. Alexander supposed it was the contrast between the oversized, almost comical, ruffles and her serious mien. But he found her equally charming, no matter what attire she donned.

"Now that we are settled on a name for the poultry—" Alexander began.

Miss Harrington shot him a rather waspish look. "It is not settled."

"Everyone agreed that Fluffus Legatus suited him the best—even Pan," Alexander pointed out cheerfully.

"I am not going to allow a parrot to dictate to me," Miss Harrington huffed. "Besides, Crinitus Legatus is *my* rooster."

Alexander decided not to counter that statement. He sensed that Miss Harrington wasn't happy about her decision not to bring the bird home with her. Her half brother and sister-in-law would apparently not accept a pet chicken. The Wick cousins had offered to house the fowl, but Pan had thrown a proper fit. In the end, Alexander had agreed to take in the fluffball, who was currently in a makeshift coop cobbled together from two baskets.

"Let me begin again," Alexander said. "Speaking of appellations, may I suggest we use Christian names? It is terribly forward of me to ask, but I can be roguish that way."

Miss Harrington shot him a grumpy expression, yet he sensed an undercurrent of amusement. "I already call you Alexander."

"I'm asking permission to call you Georgina—or George, as appropriate for the circumstances at hand. Of course, I'll still use Miss Harrington when social rules require." Alexander didn't know why, but as he spoke, a curious nervousness descended. He didn't want her to reject his offer, and it baffled him that he cared this much about her response.

To his relief, she gave a curt little nod. "I suppose I can allow that. We do share chicken custody, after all."

Alexander laughed heartily as he pulled his bays to a stop a little distance from her brother's address. Georgina had confided that she had sneaked away, and she didn't want to draw attention to her return. Alexander climbed down from his curricle and headed around the vehicle to hand Miss Harrington down now that she was in female attire again.

As soon as her bare hand met his gloved one, a jolt bolted through him. Her grip was stronger than he'd expected, but then again she'd spent her days shoveling and sweeping away dirt—not the life of a typical highborn lady. He liked the strength in her fingers and the confident way she dismounted from the carriage. Although he'd braced himself with his cane and good leg, she barely used him for support.

When her feet touched the ground, they should have released each other, but they didn't. Alexander kept his hold light, allowing Georgina to pull away. Yet she remained standing in front of him as a gentle summer breeze swept over them, carrying with it the scent of late-blooming roses.

"Why if it isn't Alexander the Galling!"

The familiar taunting voice broke the spell weaving around Alexander. He immediately dropped Georgina's hand and sprang away from her. Reaching deep inside for his jovial mask, he turned to face Lord Henry. As he saw the handsome man's smirking mug, Alexander reminded himself that he wasn't the scrawny, cowering boy that he'd been. He knew how to fight back, and he wouldn't let anyone or anything intimidate him.

"Talbot," Alexander said, refusing to revert to formality for such a blackguard.

"I don't know if I should be showing you gratitude or if I should thoroughly thrash you like I did when we were lads." Talbot stepped so close that the tips of his ridiculously buckled shoes almost touched Alexander's.

The move was meant to cow Alexander. As a boy, he would have tried to slink back. But as a man, he stood firm.

"You will find me not so easy to trounce anymore." Alexander kept his voice light and bright. He wished to hell that

Georgina wasn't learning about the humiliation of his past, but it couldn't be helped. He shoved the embarrassment away along with his old vestiges of fear.

Talbot's eyes narrowed as he started to lift his fist. Alexander just raised his eyebrow and tutted. "Engaging in fisticuffs in the broad daylight in Mayfair. My, my, you haven't changed a whit since school."

With what appeared to be a great effort, Talbot slowly extended each finger and then pressed his hand against his thigh. "Your role in bringing about the arrest of my elder brother has greatly changed my circumstances. On the one hand, it appears as if I will soon become the heir apparent and then the duke when Father shakes off his mortal coil. On the other, it will be because my brother's neck will have snapped at the gallows."

Out of the corner of his eye, Alexander saw Georgina lift her hand to her mouth. Her gaze bounced from Alexander to Talbot and back again.

"Your brother chose to kill people merely because it excited him. His hanging will hardly be my doing," Alexander said stiffly. "Now if you do pardon me, I must be—"

"You exposed him." Talbot shoved his face in Alexander's.

Alexander didn't flinch, but he did tighten his grip on his cane. If Talbot attacked, Alexander needed to be ready. As much as he'd boasted that Talbot wouldn't find him such an easy target as before, the bigger man was a skilled fighter who had the full use of both legs. If Alexander had a hope of besting him, he needed to immediately bring Talbot to the ground.

"Father is worried that the king will strip him of his titles because of Hawley's little mistakes—" Talbot whined.

"Murder is hardly a little mistake." Alexander probably shouldn't antagonize the brute, but he could not allow him to dismiss others' lives with such abhorrent casualness.

"Why should I suffer for Hawley's bloody sins?" Talbot snarled. "I thought when Father ordered me back from our shabby property in Essex that I could finally enjoy London again. But now I'm saddled with all these rules on how to appear proper and distinguished."

Alexander froze at the mention of Essex. He'd forgotten that the Duke of Lansberry had property there. Clifville had mentioned that Talbot had displayed a peculiar interest in Georgina's helmet when Pendergrast had brought it to Elysian Fields. Could Talbot be responsible for Percy's disappearance?

Surreptitiously, Alexander hazarded a glance at Georgina. While she didn't look particularly surprised at the reveal, she was eyeing Talbot with suspicion.

"Why were you in Essex?" Alexander tried to make his request sound as offhanded as possible since the bully would never respond to a demand.

"It was the property that Father assigned me to manage. It is depressingly small with a crumbly old house and not near the water. Father allowed me to set up my nursery there after I married Lucinda. She likes it, but heaven knows why. There is nothing to recommend the place other than its relative proximity to the capital. I left her and the children rusticating there when I moved back to London. It is much more peaceful living away from the brats."

Georgina made a sound of disgust, drawing Talbot's attention. Instinctually, Alexander moved to block her from view. Although Talbot normally barely registered the presence of servants, he'd never tolerate one showing disrespect. Alexander didn't want Georgina in the man's line of wrath. And if he recognized her, Georgina would face a scandal.

It was too late, though, for Alexander to shield her. Talbot's gaze had already locked onto her face.

Talbot advanced slowly on Georgina. "You look oddly familiar, and I don't generally consort with maids unless it is for one thing. Did I tup you once?"

This time, Alexander stepped fully between them. "That is enough. Stop harassing her. Your frustrations are with me."

"Oh, are you trying to play the role of a gentleman now, *Lord Heathford?*" Talbot used Alexander's courtesy title like a mocking insult, just as he had when they were lads. Alexander sensed that it had always irked Talbot that Alexander had possessed a status he would likely never obtain.

A strangled sound emerged from Georgina. Hearing the absolute horror in her gasp, Alexander turned toward her with panicked concern. Accusation burned in her brown eyes. She lifted a shaking finger in his direction, just as she had at the Black Sheep.

"You. *You!* You're Lord Heathford? *The Marquess of Heathford??*"

Stupefied by the venom in Georgina's voice, Alexander blinked. What did Georgina think he'd done now? Had Pendergrast told a Banbury tale about him using his title? Could Alexander have inadvertently made a mistake in the past that harmed Georgina?

Pain sliced through him at the last thought. If he had hurt her, he would have to find a way to quickly repair whatever damage he'd wrought. His heart couldn't withstand any more loathing looks from Miss Georgina Harrington.

Chapter Six

A re you the Marquess of Heathford?" Georgina repeated, unable to stop her voice from rising sharply at the end. Blades of betrayal pierced through her heart, burying themselves in her spine. Here, she had begun to trust the man, even *feel* things for him. She'd risked her reputation and worse to rescue a chicken because of how upset he'd looked watching poor Crinitus Legatus await his fate at the beak of a hulking rooster.

And now she had discovered that Alexander was the fiancé being foisted upon her. No wonder he had studiously kept his full name and rank a secret. He must have realized who she was to him and had hoped to covertly charm her.

What, though, could his reason be for wanting to marry her so desperately? She would not even entertain the idea that he could have fallen head over heels in love with her when he'd espied her digging in the pit. Had he wanted her helmet and her treasure that badly? Had he been the one to kidnap Percy? Was today an elaborate ruse to fool her into trusting him? What about his companions at the Black Sheep?

Georgina physically staggered backward under the pressure of the questions bearing down upon her. Alexander—or Lord Heathford, the heartless rogue—stretched his hand forward as if to lend her assistance. The callous actor even feigned a look of concern. Georgina shrank away from his fingers.

"Are. You. Lord. Heathford?" she demanded again, not caring that she sounded like a shrieking harpy.

"Yes," he breathed out, "but—"

Lord Henry's sneering voice interrupted whatever lie Alexander was about to spew. "He is, and I am beginning to think you're not a maid at all. You look deucedly familiar."

Of course she did, since they'd been practically betrothed by his father and her brother. Although to be fair, Georgina had utterly forgotten that Lord Henry was the brother of the now-infamous Lord Hawley. In the past, she'd only been vaguely conscious of him being the Duke of Lansberry's second son. What she had clearly remembered, though, was his smooth, mocking voice when she'd overheard him as he walked by her in a crowded ballroom.

Miss H reads so many books about old, grimy things that I swear she's becoming one herself. She's recently acquired a distinct layer of dust after being tucked away in cobwebbed corners all Season! What was my father thinking to suggest that I wed such a boring relic?

Lord Henry had spoken the words loudly to his friends, but Georgina knew he'd meant for her to hear. After all, he stared straight at her as he'd passed where she sat. His cronies had glanced at her when they'd strutted by, their contemptuous laughter ringing in her ears.

As both Lord Henry and Lord Heathford studied Georgina now, sweat dripped down her back. She would not crumble under the handsome men's scrutiny. She wasn't the same young miss who'd spent every night in London crying in her bedchamber at the cruel words spoken about her lackluster debut. She hadn't wanted to be a diamond of the first water anyway.

"It's time for you to leave us be, Talbot," Alexander said as he once again placed his body between her and Lord Henry. Earlier, she'd thought he was protecting her and had felt reluctant warmth toward him. Now she wondered if he simply saw Lord Henry as an obstacle for whatever dastardly interest Alexander had in her.

"Do you think you can force me to do anything?" Lord Henry's chiseled face twisted as he poked Alexander in the chest. "Do you need a beating to remind you of your station?"

A surge of protective anger rushed through Georgina just like before when Lord Henry had alluded to bullying Alexander. This time, though, she shoved it aside. She would spare no feelings for the man who had betrayed her.

"We're in the most fashionable section of London in the late afternoon." Alexander spoke with a lightness that had originally impressed Georgina and now just sickened her. Before, she'd thought it admirable that he'd maintained such poise in the face of an old tormentor. Now she just regarded it as more evidence of his nefarious acting skills. He should be treading the boards with his friend Mr. Powys.

"Are you hoping for someone to rescue you?" Lord Henry sneered. "One facer is all it will take to unman you."

"Do you think your father will be pleased to hear of his son's involvement in a violent scandal?" Alexander asked. "Will news of you attacking me reach the ears of the king? Any gossip about your family—no matter how seemingly trivial—has become the juiciest tidbits to share over and over and over. I am sure more than one person on this street has pulled their curtain back and is watching our exchange with very curious eyes."

"You think you've bested me, Alexander the Galling, but we

won't always meet in such a public place. I will find you again," Lord Henry snapped.

"I'll be ready." Alexander showed not a speck of animosity as he grinned widely.

Lord Henry clenched both of his rather substantial fists, but he did not take a swing at Alexander. Instead, he turned on his heel and stomped up the street. To Georgina's dismay, he marched up the steps of a nearby townhouse. How had she forgotten that the Duke of Lansberry had a residence so close to Algernon's? But then again, she never dwelled on those awful months in London.

Deciding to make her own escape, Georgina whirled toward the gate to her half brother's garden. The front steps were closer, but she couldn't stroll through the main entrance. Algernon and Anne would certainly cotton on to the fact that Georgina had slipped away for the day.

"Wait!" Alexander called, and Georgina could hear the tap of his cane as he followed her.

She ignored him and kept barreling forward. To her horror, she felt hot tears sting her eyes. She didn't let them fall, but it appalled her that she had to struggle to keep them in check. She would not let this man make her cry, not when she hadn't sobbed for years.

"Why did my title trigger this reaction?" Alexander called after her.

Georgina just moved faster. She did not owe him answers.

Reaching the wrought-iron gate, she struggled to unlatch the unfamiliar fastening. As she lifted the metal handle, Alexander appeared at her side. Concern marred his handsome features, and for once, he wasn't grinning like the famed cats of Cheshire.

"If I did anything to upset you, I apologize, Georgina," Alexander said. His use of her Christian name sent a new shard of betrayal stabbing through her. He'd made her start to trust him, and she would never forgive him for that.

"You no longer have permission to call me by my Christian name," Georgina informed him as crisply as she could while yanking open the gate.

His feigned look of hurt was so realistic that she almost faltered. But she didn't let his falsehoods sway her. Resolutely, she strolled into Algernon's garden. "Do not follow me."

"Miss! Miss!" The wan face of Mary, the maid who'd come up with them from Essex, appeared above a bush covered with brown, half-dead roses. She looked as wilted as the drooping flowers. Dark circles had formed under her eyes. Now instead of only looking haunted as she had since before leaving Essex, she wore a panicked expression.

"What is it, Mary?" Georgina asked, concerned by the young woman's almost palpable fright.

"My lord and lady noticed you were missing. They're putting up an awful fuss. You must come in straightaway." Mary glanced back to the house, her voice trembling a bit.

"Will you be all right?" Alexander asked, his voice no longer jubilant but concerned. The man was truly a marvel at manufacturing emotions.

Georgina turned to him, wishing him to perdition. "I will be if you leave now."

The words weren't precisely true. Although she would feel a mite better without the betraying blackguard hovering near, his presence might actually calm Algernon. After all, finding that they'd spent the day alone together would be the perfect excuse to force the marriage. But if Alexander could lie, so could Georgina.

"Are you certain?" Alexander followed Mary's gaze back to the brick façade of Algernon's home.

"Just go!" Georgina ground out, not needing to act to infuse her voice with desperation.

Alexander hesitated for only a moment longer. "If you need assistance, send a missive to me at the Black Sheep. I will come to you as quickly as I am able."

Georgina said nothing. She only stared at him coldly until he executed a curt nod. With seeming reluctance, he finally strode away. Georgina watched him, bitterness welling in her chest. She had been a fool to think, even warily, that she had discovered an ally in such a man. Her first judgment had been accurate. He was just another handsome devil like Algernon.

As soon as Alexander climbed into his curricle and drove off, Georgina gripped Mary's shoulders. "Do my brother and sister-in-law know that you helped me sneak away?"

Mary shook her head and held out a bundle. "Here are your clothes, miss. I can help you put them on."

Georgina had no lady's maid of her own. Anne found it an unnecessary expense, especially since Georgina never attended Society events and rarely even visited their neighbors in the countryside. Georgina did not mind fixing her own hair and preferred the simpler, practical clothes that she could don herself. It made her expeditions to her own property much easier.

Mary, who had dreams of becoming a proper lady's maid, had assisted Georgina in the past whenever she had to attend one of Anne's dinner parties. It was the reason Anne had decided to bring Mary with them from Essex. Georgina had always liked the previously cheery young woman, and she regretted turning to her this morning when she'd needed help to flee Algernon's townhouse. The poor dear clearly did not have the temperament for subterfuge.

Fortunately, the garden had a small stand of trees that Georgina could use to shield herself as she changed back into her dress. If she walked in wearing maid's clothes, Anne would instantly know that Mary had lent them to Georgina. Anne always paid attention to details as much as Algernon overlooked them.

When properly attired in a gown that had been one of Anne's castoffs, Georgina hurried after Mary to the blue drawing room. Inside, Algernon paced while Anne plunked out a rather angry tune on the spinet. Algernon stopped midstride when he caught sight of Georgina standing in the doorway. Ire washed over his otherwise angelic features, bestowing upon him the look of Lucifer after his fall. He had inherited their mother's beauty and his father's stalwart frame. Despite reaching his fortieth year, he had not a single strand of white in his brown hair, and his perfectly formed face remained unlined. He was a man of little worry, but often of great rage.

"Where were you?" Algernon demanded. "You did not have permission to leave my premises."

"I do apologize," Georgina said softly. "I must have fallen asleep in the garden while reading. It was such a pleasant summer day that I didn't awake until now."

"Balderdash!" Anne slammed down a random set of spinet keys, and a horrible jangle rent the air. At eight-and-twenty, she possessed a regal beauty. No matter what waspish words spewed from her mouth, she always moved with grace. Even now, despite the anger roiling from her, she rose from the instrument's bench with the elegance of a queen. "I personally helped the staff scour the flowerbeds. You weren't there. You weren't anywhere in the house."

"Whyever does it matter if I took some air?" Georgina lifted her chin. "No one in Society pays me any mind."

"You cannot go about London unaccompanied!" Algernon stomped over to the mantel and slammed his fist onto the elegantly carved wood. "How can you be so meek, yet so abominably willful at the same time? You shall be the death of me if I cannot marry you off."

Georgina resisted arching an eyebrow. Was her brother finally about to admit why he'd dragged her to London? "I am too long in the tooth for matrimony."

"Which is why your reputation must stay pristine!" Anne's sweet voice rose slightly at the end as she floated toward Georgina like a flower petal carried by the wind, although her words were those of a stinging wasp. "You have nothing but your lineage to recommend you. Your dowry is middling, and you spend all your time reading dusty old tomes. No one wishes to converse to his wife in dead languages."

"If I am such a burden, just allow me to live in my late father's house. There is no need to haul me to London in hopes of a match." Georgina tried to remain calm when she wanted to rage back at Anne. She loathed being reduced to her value on the marriage mart, but that's all Anne or Algernon ever saw.

"I have arranged a union for you." Algernon struck his hand against the fireplace again. "The Duke of Falcondale is miraculously impressed that you can trace multiple bloodlines back to the original Norman earls and to William the Conqueror himself. He has been looking for a match for his misbegotten son and heir apparent for almost as long as I've been trying to wed you off."

"What if I don't wish to marry this man?" Georgina asked.

"I. Do. Not. Care." Algernon bit out. "This is my decision, and unless you want to be reduced to a diet of bread and water for the rest of your miserable existence, you shall marry him. I will not have you pulling any schemes like you have in the past. You will act the presentable miss for once in your life."

Algernon advanced on her. His brown eyes glowed with an intense light that she'd never seen in them before. She was accustomed to his anger, but this was something deeper and dangerous. And it frightened her. Involuntarily, she took a step back.

"If he says he is superstitious, do not claim that you were possessed by the ghost of a Roman noblewoman when you visited Herculaneum." Algernon held up a blunt finger as he began to tick off the ways she had chased away suitors in the past. "When he asks you to sing a lighthearted melody, do not recite excerpts from Plato's *Dialogues* in Greek. In fact, do not discuss Plato in any language. After he shows you a precious antique that he spent a fortune to purchase, never tell him it is a fake. And definitely, under no circumstances, should you start categorizing all the piece's flaws!"

"It really would be best if you just kept your mouth firmly shut, dear." Anne fluttered near Georgina's elbow.

"Why is the Duke of Falcondale so eager for his son to marry me if I have so little to recommend me?" Georgina asked the question she'd been wondering. Alexander may walk with a limp, but he was a handsome man and heir apparent to a dukedom. Surely women more elegant and refined than Georgina would agree to marry him. Was Alexander hiding dark secrets?

"That is not for you to know," Algernon bellowed. "You are not to ask more questions. Go to your room and stay there until I summon you. I will not have you sabotaging this."

Before Georgina could protest further, Algernon rang for the servants. Two footmen appeared with such alacrity that

Georgina realized they'd been standing nearby, waiting for her half brother's signal. Her disappearance really had upended the entire household.

"Escort my sister to her room," Algernon ordered. "See that she is properly locked inside and bring the key and any copies directly to me."

"You're trapping me in my quarters?" Georgina asked aghast. "This isn't a fairy tale, and I'm not Persinette."

"No, you're definitely not a fair princess," Algernon snapped as he waved at the servants to take Georgina away, "so don't expect a prince to free you."

Georgina knew she had no knight in shining armor ready to do battle for her. Today's revelation about Alexander had only substantiated what her heart had always known. She was on her own, as she had been since her father's death. No one was riding to her rescue on a gallant stallion, but if she was imprisoned by Algernon, who would save Percy?

⚜

"Please desist in giving me that look, Ruffian Caesar," Georgina said as her faithful mutt cocked his head to the side while she knotted her bedsheets into a rope. "This escape plan always works in stories."

Ruffian Caesar snorted, tossing his head dramatically. His floppy ear flipped up and then back down again.

"Yes, I realize I am speaking of fictional tales, but I am sure it has worked. I have no other choice. I am on the second story, and there is no handy tree in the vicinity." Georgina yanked off another sheet and twisted it tightly before folding it in half to add to her chain.

Her terrier stretched his front paws, his mouth opening into a huge yawn. Clearly unimpressed with their conversation, he began to roll on the floor, his stomach pointed toward the ceiling. He paused mid-wiggle and sent her a mournful look, clearly disappointed by the lack of belly rubs. Sighing, Georgina put down her handiwork and squatted down next to the little rascal to deliver the demanded scritches.

"I know it could be dangerous," Georgina admitted quietly as her fingers ran through Ruffian Caesar's curls. "But then, what choice do I have? It has been two days already, and I need to find Percy."

Ruffian Caesar's rough tongue scraped against Georgina's knuckles. She realized that the little dog was probably just thanking her for the scratches, but she liked to think that the gesture was meant as encouragement. Georgina needed support, even the slobbery, canine kind.

Blinking back sudden, unexpected tears, she admitted her biggest fear. "But where do I go, Ruffian Caesar, if I do make it safely to the ground? I cannot return to the Black Sheep, as I do not know if I can trust them. They were all so kind. It is not as if they lured me there, but perhaps I stumbled into their nefarious plans to steal my treasure. Yet, if they kidnapped Percy, why didn't they simply abduct me when I bumbled through the door? It was obvious that I was there in secret, and that no one knew where I was. I made an easy target who didn't need to be further duped."

Georgina stopped talking and petting Ruffian Caesar. Instead, she raised her hands to her face and scrubbed. Hard. "Or am I only searching for plausible excuses because I liked them? Even Alexander had begun to seem tolerable."

More than tolerable. Unbidden, a memory of their time in the carriage flashed into Georgina's mind. Once again, Alexander was fixing her with that charming smile of his, a mischievously warm twinkle in his changeable hazel eyes.

Speaking of appellations, may I suggest we use Christian names? It is terribly forward of me to ask, but I can be roguish that way.

Even the recollection of Alexander's words caused Georgina's heart to soar and then plummet and soar again. His voice had swept over her with an intimacy that had felt akin to a caress. And she'd melted enough to agree to his request.

Foolish, foolish woman. She wasn't a young miss anymore and shouldn't fall for such claptrap.

But her fine intellect refused to cooperate. Instead, her imagination served up an even more disarming remembrance of Alexander fixing her wig. For a moment as she'd stared into his eyes—that curious, compelling mix of green and brown hues—she'd thought he'd lean forward a few more inches and kiss her. And she'd wanted him to. Her whole body had tingled with glorious anticipation, awakening sensations she'd never encountered before.

"But he was just manipulating me. Right, Ruffian Caesar?" Georgina asked, ashamed by the heat pricking her eyes once more.

At the sound of his name, the terrier glanced over his shoulder, his tongue lolling out. A sneeze caught him in just that moment, and his little chin jerked forward.

"Oh, what do you know!" Georgina cried in frustration as she angrily tied another sheet to her makeshift ladder.

The terrier bounced to his curly feet. After three luxuriant stretches, he padded over and bumped Georgina's knee in a clear demand for more attention. She was just about to give him another pet when she heard a key scrape against the lock on her door.

Frantically, Georgina started to gather her bedsheet-rope.

Ruffian Caesar bounded over to the door and plopped down on his haunches, ready to guard or to greet. Still collecting cloth, Georgina glanced nervously at the ornate handle. Judging by the angle of the sun outside her window, it wasn't time for a meal. Who could be barging in?

Anne stepped into the room, the picture of summer beauty in her sack-backed dress with its cheerful print of small red roses on a yellow background. Although already pale by nature, she'd caked on talc and tragacanth water to achieve porcelain perfection. As fashion dictated, she'd rouged her cheeks and painted her lips into a perfect moue. But instead of a pleasant, genteel expression to match her attire, outrage twisted her visage.

"What is the meaning of this?" Anne demanded, her eyes fixed on Georgina's makeshift ladder.

"I was bored and found that twisting the sheets calmed my nerves." It wasn't a very good excuse, but there really wasn't a lie to obscure what Georgina had been doing. "It is similar to how you pull the gold threads from your old ballgowns when you require a soothing activity in the evenings."

"I am not a fool," Anne said, her tone sweet on the surface but simmering with a poisonous undertone. "You were trying to escape."

"I—" Georgina wasn't sure how to defend herself, but Anne didn't give her another chance. The other woman marched into the room and tried to snatch the bedclothes from Georgina's hands. However, she was no match for Georgina, who yanked back. With her dainty slippers giving her little traction, Anne skidded across the floor. An excited Ruffian Caesar circled happily. Anne screeched and tried to stop her slide. Unfortunately, or—from Georgina's perspective—fortunately, Anne lost her balance. She tried pinwheeling her arms, but to no avail. She plunked down on the ground, her voluminous petticoats cushioning the fall but also forcing her stocking-clad legs into the air. For a moment, Anne floundered like a fish as her numerous undergarments formed a veritable sea around her.

"Help me!" Anne shrilled, her voice no longer honeyed. "Help me up this instant!"

Georgina ignored her sister-in-law as she plucked up her terrier. Arms full of bedsheet and squirming canine, she dashed toward the window. Her rope ladder wasn't long enough to reach the ground, but it would have to suffice.

"My lady!"

At the shocked exclamation, Georgina glanced over her shoulder to see two footmen burst into the room. Unlike with the staff in Essex, she didn't know their names. One of them extended his hand to Anne while the other glanced at Georgina, clearly unsure how to respond. Turning her attention away from the men, Georgina furiously worked to open the sash. Ruffian Caesar began to bark in her arms, his upright ear perked in excitement.

"Get her!" Anne demanded.

The closest footman grabbed Georgina about her belly, pulling her back across the room. Although he kept his grip relatively gentle and respectful, Georgina couldn't break free.

"I am sorry, miss," the young man whispered softly, but despite his words of regret, his arms remained an inescapable prison.

Batting away the other servant's hand, Anne scrambled to her feet. She no longer looked like genteel sunshine. The panniers under her skirts had slipped about her waist, leaving one hip notably higher than the other. Her nose glowed red from smeared rouge. Like a misplaced mouse's tail, her velvet beauty patch dangled from her upper cheek.

"Take her to a servant's room. One without *any* windows!" Anne didn't even try to straighten her attire as she shoved her hands onto her hips.

"Will you walk yourself, miss?" the footman holding Georgina asked hopefully, clearly not relishing carrying a struggling woman through the house.

Fighting down a frustrated battle cry, Georgina reluctantly nodded. She wasn't one of the fierce warrior women at Championess Quick's, and she had no hope of overpowering even one of the footmen. The young fellow was giving her a chance to retain a shred of her dignity.

"This way, Miss Harrington," the other servant said politely as if leading her to the parlor for tea.

Still clutching her dog to her chest, Georgina allowed the two youths to lead her through the luxurious main hallways to the narrow, austere servant passageways. Anne followed, stamping instead of gliding regally. Maids carrying buckets and linens squeaked in surprise as the two ladies of the house paraded through the lowly corridors. Finally, the four of them reached their destination.

"Do you wish for us to bring you anything from your room?" one of the footmen asked.

"She is to have nothing, not even one of her precious books or a scrap of paper!" Anne decreed as she lit a candle. "It is enough she has that mutt of hers! Now leave us!"

With final apologetic looks aimed at Georgina, the two hastily retreated. Anne firmly shut the door and whirled on Georgina.

"The Duke and Duchess of Falcondale will call upon us tomorrow, along with their son, Lord Heathford. I came to warn you that I expect you to look and act presentable at the meeting. If you continue to resist this match, you will discover a much worse fate than simply being removed to a small, windowless room in the servants' quarters." Anne jabbed her gloved finger in Georgina's direction, her other hand on her hip. The fact that the desperately elegant lady had assumed a position associated with fishwives revealed the utter depths of her ire. "I will not have you ruining all our plans. Not now."

"What plans?" Georgina inquired, proud she had enough pluck left inside her to ask such a bold question.

Anne stilled. She might have even paled, but Georgina couldn't tell beneath all the white and red paint. "Do not fash yourself with trying to comprehend what I meant. You only understand the language and objects of the long dead. Stop trying to interfere with the schemes of the living."

Georgina ignored Anne's harsh words, determined to press further. Her sister-in-law seemed to be teetering at the edge of her control, and she wanted to shove her over the precipice. "Why are you so invested in my union with the Marquess of Heathford?"

Anne ignored the question as she stamped over to the door. Yanking it open, she paused at the threshold. "Just know that Algernon and I will do anything to see that this wedding happens even if we must starve you into submission. Your only way out of this room now is through marriage to the marquess."

With that parting salvo, Anne stomped into the hallway, taking the only candle with her. Georgina sank down onto the small, straw tick mattress on the floor as her sister-in-law locked her inside. Darkness descended over the tiny but clean space. The only light was thin slivers drifting in from the gaps between the door and its frame.

Georgina felt a cold, wet nose poke her cheek, followed by two rough licks. She ran her hand down the curly fur on her dog's back.

"Oh, Ruffian Caesar, what am I going to do now? I can't even save myself. How am I going to rescue Percy?"

In the blackness, no answer came. Georgina leaned her head against the rough plastered wall and did her best not to succumb to sobs.

Chapter Seven

When Alexander flipped the page to one of Georgina's treatises, Fluffus Legatus shifted in his perch on Alexander's lap. The bird ruffled his white feathers before settling again.

"Oh, I do apologize," Alexander told the fowl with a wry humor that did not reach his heart.

It had been three days since he'd left Georgina in the garden of her half brother's house. He could not shake the feeling that he had made a grave mistake in departing. The little maid had been a fretful wreck. Although Georgina's inexplicable anger toward him masked most of her nervousness, he'd sensed that she'd been unsettled by the revelation that her family had noticed her absence.

But Georgina had clearly wanted him gone, and he would not force his presence upon any woman. He wished he knew what he'd done to make her react so violently toward his title. Perhaps he would never discover the truth, and he wouldn't pressure her to reveal it.

But that didn't mean that he wasn't worried about her. Calliope, at his behest, had even sent Georgina a missive two days ago, but there had been no answer.

Alexander was also concerned over Percy's presumed disappearance. None of the other patrons of the Black Sheep had offered more information about his whereabouts. Alexander had even called upon a few mutual friends, but no one seemed to know Percy's location.

"I do hope your lady-savior and her rascal of a cousin are safe," Alexander told the puffball on his lap.

Fluffus Legatus simply shoved his head under one luxuriant wing. He was not the most emotive of companions. However, he would serve as the perfect irritant to Alexander's parents, who'd commanded his presence at their townhouse.

Alexander had already been waiting over an hour in the green salon, but that wasn't unusual. Hence why he'd brought along the pamphlet that he'd purchased after escorting Georgina to her home.

Georgina's dissertation analyzing Pliny the Younger's description of the eruption at Mount Vesuvius was not likely to yield any answers into why she'd looked at Alexander with such betrayal. But he could not resist learning more about the lady, even though he did not generally like reading about history. Yet he found himself enjoying her crisp, precise observations. She wrote as she spoke, and he could hear her voice as she conjectured that not just Herculaneum lay under the volcanic rubble but the elite town of Pompeii as well.

"What is that?" Alexander's mother asked, disdainful horror causing ripples in her otherwise placid voice.

He glanced up to find her staring at the chicken in revulsion… at least with her eyes. His mother rarely allowed displeasure to touch any of her other features.

"This is Fluffus Legatus," Alexander said cheerfully. Carefully holding the rooster with one hand and gripping the arm of the chair with the other, Alexander rose to his feet. His mother's gaze flashed condescendingly between his supporting palm and the poultry.

"Why is that…that thing in my second-best salon?" Lady Falcondale demanded.

Because you don't invite me into the best drawing room. But Alexander never took the direct approach to needle his parents.

"Haven't you heard? A pet chicken has become the fashionable companion of London." Alexander accompanied his lie with a brilliant smile. "Feathered friends are cropping up in parlors all over the city. That is why I brought dear Fluffus Legatus. I do know how much you like to be in vogue."

The corner of Lady Falcondale's left nostril twitched ever so slightly. "I have not witnessed this."

Alexander nonchalantly shrugged one shoulder. "Well, they are more popular among the younger set. Why have a pet that only attracts fleas, when you can have one who eats them?"

The right side of his mother's nose began to tremble too. She clearly remained skeptical of Alexander, yet she also did not want to make a social blunder that would cast her as old-fashioned.

"Good lord, what is that atrocious creature?" Alexander's father bellowed as he strode into the room like a knight about to mount his battle steed.

"Father, meet Fluffus Legatus. Fluffus Legatus, this is the esteemed Duke of Falcondale." Alexander held out the chicken. Although it extended its head, causing its pouf to bob about wildly, it otherwise did not appear either pleased or displeased to meet a peer of the realm. Falcondale, on the other hand, turned a wonderful shade of puce. Alexander's father possessed a narrow, aristocratic face that normally looked suitably noble. It did not when red-violet, which is partially why Alexander made it his mission to turn his father's countenance into that glorious hue.

"Lady Falcondale," the duke growled—he would never be

so coarse as to call his wife by her first name. "Do something about your son!"

"Alexander, cease antagonizing your father. You know my nerves can't take it when you two are at odds." After speaking the last line, Lady Falcondale allowed her hand to flutter to her forehead for good measure. Then she sank with exceeding grace into an intricately carved chair upholstered in the finest green-and-white striped silk.

"I am only introducing His Grace to Fluffus Legatus. You two always insist that I act fashionably, and I am simply adhering to the latest in social graces." Alexander slowly moved the bird so that its head remained straight while its body gently swayed.

The duke turned a lovely aubergine. Since the day was exceedingly hot, especially for London, the peer even had a sheen like the fruit.

"Be serious for once." Falcondale glowered, but the effect was rather diminished by his purpleness.

Alexander kept grinning like a fool. Humor had been the only thing that had saved him—other than his twin sister. "I always endeavor to be good-natured, Father. Didn't you always demand that of me?"

Falcondale ignored Alexander's question and flicked his eyes over him. "Your attire is not acceptable. I told you in the missive to wear your best suit."

"This is the one that you had made for me at the start of the Season." Alexander spoke easily despite the stiffness in his heart. Falcondale preferred to control every aspect of how Alexander looked to the outside world, including ordering his attire and his curricle. It was an obsession stemming from the fact that no matter how many quacks his father had called upon, none of them had ever been able to improve Alexander's limp.

"Your waistcoat does not have enough ornamentation. You are meeting your intended today, and you need something to distract from your cane," Lady Falcondale said crisply.

Alexander started at the word "intended." Suddenly, the presence of both of his parents made sickening sense. Alexander wondered if this is how Charlotte felt a few months ago when his mother blithely let slip that she was being forced into a betrothal. That casual announcement had involved clothing, too.

"I have already told you both that I will not marry who you select." Alexander gripped Hercules and the Nemean lion and prepared to walk from the room.

"You shall wed!" Lord Falcondale bellowed. "If you do not, I shall cut you off!"

Alexander laughed at the absurdity. "What funds do you give me now? Will you stop providing me with clothing? You would be too embarrassed to see your son in the rags of a pauper. Matthew's friend, Mr. Tavish Stewart, will employ me as a clerk. Do you truly want your heir working for a merchant and a printmaker?"

Alexander had long considered finding employment, but becoming a tradesman would all but destroy his chances of making a difference in the snobbish House of Lords. He'd witnessed how the nobility had treated his best friend when Matthew had elected to work as a physician. If Alexander had any hope of forming alliances to pass the laws he wanted, he needed to maintain his status as the son of a nobleman, even if he found the restrictions ridiculous. He might have little in discretionary funds, but he lived a comfortable enough life that enabled him to form friendships that would help him become a better, more influential duke in the future.

He realized how privileged he was to make such decisions. Despite his clubfoot, Alexander could easily obtain a job with his status, education, and identity as a male member of the nobility. Unlike many who walked with a limp or who had a missing limb, he had connections and resources that helped shield him from the worst biases. He also did not have to face the restrictions thrust upon his sister, his cousin, and other women, nor did he have to constantly battle the prejudices that Sophia and Mr. Belle faced due to their African heritage.

"You owe me a well-formed heir!" Lord Falcondale shouted as he drew himself to his full height.

Alexander did the same. Even with his uneven legs, he had an inch on his sire. "I owe *you*? I spent the first decade and a half trying to do everything to please you. I suffered through hell for you to get your perfect heir."

"Then tupping a wellborn woman should be easy in comparison!"

"That is insulting to the lady in question," Alexander said. Rage filled him as he thought of how his father had treated Charlotte like a commodity. Swounds, the duke had almost married his daughter to a murderous fiend just so he could have more ducal grandchildren.

"Your Grace, your language," Alexander's mother said calmly as if she was simply ringing the servants to bring around seedcakes.

Lord Falcondale turned on his wife. "This! This is your fault. If you hadn't borne a son with a twisted, bent foot, none of this would be necessary."

Lady Falcondale froze, and her loathing gaze found Alexander. "I am not at fault. It is his leg."

"It is celestial punishment for your family's misdeeds! It wasn't enough that your sister brought dishonor to my good name by running off with that man and making me the brother-in-law to a stinking pirate. Oh no, the penalty for her misjudgment was suffered by my heir!"

The words would hurt more if Alexander had not heard them so many times before. Old pain did flicker, but mostly he felt weary. It would do no good to bring enlightened ideas about medicine and science into the conversation. He would always be the wicked son who'd shamed the Falcondale legacy.

The fact that he'd helped Charlotte elope with Matthew had only made Alexander sink lower in his parents' esteem. Now that they could not claim "honor" through Charlotte's union with an heir to a dukedom, they'd clearly become more desperate to marry him off. But he doubted that aristocrats wanted to wed their daughters to a man who'd unmasked a viscount as a murderer. Worse, Alexander had handed a noble over to mere dragoons—a fact not easily forgiven privately even if applauded publicly.

"I shall leave the two of you to sort out who is to blame for the circumstances of my birth." Alexander started to move toward the exit with Fluffus Legatus still tucked under one arm.

"Halt!" Lord Falcondale shouted. "We are due to meet the Earl of Craie and his sister in an hour's time."

Alexander froze. He stopped so suddenly that the docile Fluffus emitted an atypical *bock*. Hadn't Georgina mentioned that her half brother was Lord Craie? But the coincidence seemed too great. Still, he couldn't depart without learning more.

"What is the woman's name?" Alexander asked, not turning around but not leaving, either.

"Miss Georgina Harrington," Lord Falcondale said. "You wouldn't know her."

It *was* her. Alexander kept his back turned so his parents couldn't see the play of emotions over his face. He did not want them to know about Georgina's escapades, even if it would result in them not moving forward with the betrothal. Protecting her was first and foremost.

As his father blathered on about William the Conqueror, bloodlines, and biddability, Alexander tried to examine how he felt about the news. He was absolutely and entirely poleaxed. The very woman who sparked his interest was the miss that his parents wished for him to marry.

Yet he also felt thunderous relief. If he accompanied his parents, he could confirm her well-being. And if she needed assistance, hopefully she would figure out a way to surreptitiously send him a message…if she even trusted him enough to do so.

Could this blasted betrothal be the reason for her reaction to his name? Perhaps she thought he had been attempting to manipulate her emotions. He would probably feel the same if the circumstances were reversed. She'd already accused him of stealing her precious helmet. Perhaps she thought he'd marry her for it? As absurd as that sounded, he didn't think Georgina would consider it ridiculous. If a villain had indeed abducted Percy for the antiquity, it might not be too far-fetched for someone to enter into matrimony for it.

"Given your latest brush with scandal, your blasted foot, and your sister's dismal marriage, Miss Harrington is the best match I could make. Had I married you off earlier, the selection would have been better," his father concluded.

Alexander made sure his jovial mask was firmly in place as he turned to face his parents. "I'll at least meet her."

Falcondale grunted, and some of the puce left his face. "It is about time that you listened."

His mother, however, was not so easily tricked. Although her eyes did not narrow—for fear of wrinkles—she had a way of staring that felt just as skeptically penetrating. "Do you know this chit?"

Alexander delivered his smoothest smile. "As Father was talking, I realized that she is the cousin of my dear friend, Lord Percy Pendergrast. Since the meeting is prearranged, I do not want to be so rude as to fail to show and hurt his relation's feelings."

"Another third son," his mother sighed. "Why must you always consort with the lesser-born offspring?"

He didn't actually. Alexander had cultivated a diverse group of companions, but he wasn't about to explain to his parents that he preferred broad social circles. They didn't understand his views on society any more than they listened to his ideas for improvements to the estates. Alexander was simply a failure in their eyes, no matter how much he prepared himself to inherit the dukedom.

"We should be thankful that his connections are at least beneficial this time." Falcondale glowered at Alexander. "You will not ruin this match."

Alexander grinned with a lightness that he didn't feel. "Then we best be off, hadn't we?"

Falcondale emitted a sound somewhere between assent and annoyance while the duchess reluctantly rose. As they made their way to the family coach, Alexander deliberately looked straight ahead. He didn't want his parents detecting his eagerness to visit with Miss Georgina Harrington.

Then they might think they'd won.

But Alexander was only agreeing to this meeting to ensure that the lady and her cousin were safe—not because he wished to see those solemn brown eyes cast in his direction again. Certainly not because of how he'd felt when he'd straightened her wig. And definitely not because he wished to pursue a romantic relationship.

Because he'd never marry a woman whom his father had selected.

⁂

"I cannot believe that you brought that thing with you," Alexander's mother whispered as she warily eyed Fluffus Legatus. They, along with the Duke of Falcondale, were waiting in an exceedingly blue drawing room at Lord Craie's. The walls above the white wood paneling were painted the color of the sky just before dusk when hints of gray appeared. The chairs were upholstered in a hue just a bit brighter. Even the Persian rug and the ceramic knickknacks were studies of the shade. It was meant to appear elegant, but Alexander felt like he was trapped in a Delft vase.

"I could not meet my lady-love-to-be empty-handed," Alexander said merrily.

"You should be bringing flowers, not poultry." Falcondale frowned stormily in the chicken's direction.

Fluffus remained oblivious to the fact that it was once again the center of the conversation. He simply perched on Alexander's lap and twisted his head this way and that. Alexander had no idea how the excessively feathered creature could see anything with the giant pouf on his head.

"Are you sure these types of pets are actually popular?" The duchess glanced nervously in Fluffus's direction. "It is a barn-yard dweller, after all."

"Oh, ladies are getting their portraits painted with their chickens on their laps," Alexander lied gleefully. "You would look wonderful holding a red-combed rooster in one, Mother."

Once again she shuddered with her body while keeping her mien a motionless but pleasant mask. "No thank you. There are limits to what I will suffer for fashion."

But not on what you make your children endure for the sake of appearances. Alexander, however, did not voice those words aloud. He only maintained his carefree façade.

"You are writing Miss Georgina a poem." The duke looked down his nose at the vellum and inkpot that Alexander had requested from Lord Craie's butler. "Is it necessary to gift her with a fowl as well?"

"Very." After all, Alexander required Fluffus's, well, fluffiness to obscure the secret missive to Georgina asking if she required saving. He couldn't very well include a message like that in the utter romantic dribble he was penning. It was very likely either his parents or Georgina's relations would skim his overwrought stanzas. They wouldn't, however, think of checking the chicken for contraband.

Suddenly, Fluffus Legatus decided it was high time to start clucking. Alexander found it rather soothing, but his parents clearly did not. His mother's nostrils began their almost imperceptible dance as she angled her body away from Alexander and the bird. The duke deepened his ever-present scowl.

"Are you certain that it will not frighten or disgust Miss Harrington?" His mother dabbed her nose with a finely embroidered silk handkerchief.

"I have it on good authority from Pendergrast that his cousin is enamored with banties such as these." The half falsehood slipped easily off Alexander's tongue. He was pleased with himself that he'd discovered a way to deliver Georgina's pet to her. If her half brother was as keen on this marriage as Falcondale, then the man should agree to house Alexander's "gift."

Just then, footsteps sounded in the hall. As Alexander's parents rose slowly to their feet, he used the opportunity to hastily scribble a note. After hiding it in his sleeve, he grabbed his cane. When the ferrule hit the wood, his father glanced at the implement with unveiled disgust. Alexander just grinned.

Georgina's brother and sister entered first, mostly blocking Georgina from Alexander's view. He could only see a small portion of her silk skirts behind her sister-in-law's. Paying scant attention to the introduction, he tried to gaze around her relatives. Damn it. Was Georgina well?

When he finally espied her wan, colorless face, rage burst through him. Her eyes—her normally beautiful, sharp brown eyes—looked dull and frightfully resigned. There was a brittleness about Georgina that reminded him keenly of his twin's when she'd been almost forced into marrying a murderer.

Alexander wanted to step forward and whisk Georgina away. But he couldn't. As much as he believed the lady to be in peril, he wasn't absolutely certain. Judging by her reaction to learning his title, she clearly did not wish to wed him. But if he grabbed her hand and ran away with her, he would be sentencing them both to quick matrimony. If she wanted to be free of her half brother's residence, Alexander would need to be clever about planning her escape.

"Oh!" Lady Craie executed a little jump as she caught sight of Fluffus Legatus. She instantly tried to smooth her features, but she wasn't as good at hiding her thoughts behind pleasantness

as Alexander's mother was. "You brought your pet. How...
utterly...charming."

"It is a gift for Miss Harrington," Alexander told Lady Craie,
using every ounce of his carefully cultivated charm.

"How...how generous." Lady Craie's expertly painted
lips started to curl toward the floor. With visible effort, she
attempted to raise them. But no sooner had she lifted her mouth
into a pleasant smile than the sides popped down again.

"It is a very unorthodox present." Lord Craie didn't even
attempt to obscure his distaste as he sidled away from Alexander and Fluffus Legatus.

The Duchess of Falcondale grabbed the fleshy part of Alexander's upper arm and twisted. Clearly, she realized his deception about the popularity of fowl companions. Alexander kept
his grin firmly affixed to his face as he studied Georgina.

She was staring at Fluffus Legatus with a look of disbelief.
Slowly, she raised her eyes to Alexander's. He could easily detect
her internal debate. It was apparent that she did not know what
to make of him or whether to trust him. But he had no doubts
about her. Something was dreadfully wrong.

"It is very fortunate that I had my rooster with me when I
came to call on my parents," Alexander said, keeping his voice
bright as he tried to send Georgina secret reassurance with his
words. "I was not aware that I was to meet Miss Harrington
today. In fact, I was not privy to my parents' decision to begin
marriage negotiations on my behalf. But I am glad to bring
such a fashionable present."

His words earned him another vicious pinch from his
mother, but the short burst of discomfort was worth it. Some of
the dreadful hopelessness in Georgina's eyes cleared. Her chin
lifted further. He had not won her confidence, but he had at least
startled her from her stupor.

"Fashionable?" Lady Craie asked, her voice quavering between politeness and derision.

"Oh, yes. The Duke of Blackglen purchased a pet rooster, and now they are all the rage in his circle," Alexander gleefully lied. Blackglen was always up for a good lark, and he was the older half brother of Calliope. Alexander would have her write to her brother and explain the joke in case it ever reached his ears. Knowing Blackglen's sense of humor, he might even start hauling around a fowl himself. If Alexander's fib actually resulted in a chicken craze, it might be a strategic blessing. Once the nobility acquired affection for their pet poultry, it would be easier to pass laws protecting chickens against blatant cruelty.

"Blackglen has a cock?" Lord Craie asked with interest.

Alexander did his best not to snort at the earl's poor choice of words. Really, the man could have just said *rooster.*

Lord Craie turned to his wife in excitement. "Dear, why weren't you aware of this? If only I'd realized before we ran into him at Mr. Powys's theater. I could have had one with me. Perhaps he would have been more amenable to chat."

"If you do purchase a chicken, you must find one with dark feathers," Alexander said, not wanting Lord Craie to abscond with Fluffus. "Those are the most popular, as Blackglen's is the color of pitch. I had the devil of a time securing this one, since they are selling with such alacrity. I had to settle for snow white, which is the least desirable of colors, I am afraid."

A sliver of relief crept through Alexander as he saw a twinkle flash in Georgina's brown eyes at his blatant falsehoods. She still looked horribly piqued, but her indomitable spirit was reviving. It worried him that her half brother and his wife had been able to suppress it in the first place. What had they done to Georgina?

Alexander slipped the secret note from his jacket's sleeve and covertly buried it among Fluffus's numerous feathers. The bird emitted a single cluck but then appeared to accept its new fate as impromptu carrier pigeon. Alexander handed the bird over to Georgina. She immediately cradled the creature, affectionately running her hands over its body. Closely, he monitored her expression for any change. When her lips pursed together ever so slightly, he realized she'd discovered his missive.

"Oh, but I almost forgot the sonnet that I penned for you!" Alexander exclaimed, intent on providing a distraction so Georgina could read his message.

"You—you wrote me a poem?" Georgina blinked, clearly nonplussed.

"Since I didn't know what you looked like," Alexander lied, "some of the descriptions will not be accurate, but please accept my humble attempts nevertheless."

Alexander made a show of thumping over with his cane to the table where he'd been writing, knowing that everyone's eyes would be drawn to the sound and not watching Georgina. When he turned back in her direction with his horribly written stanzas in hand, he thought she gave him a nod. Did that mean that she'd read his note and was in trouble? Alexander's heart pinched, and he forced himself to remain calm.

"What is the name of the bird?" Georgina asked rather woodenly.

Alexander wondered if she was trying to send him a message. "Fluffus Legatus."

"I like it," she said. "It has a much better sound to it than if you had given the bird a fully Latin appellation. *Crinitus* is not suitable."

Alexander now had no doubt. Georgina was definitely

signaling that something was amiss. She would never other-wise concede to the name of Fluffus.

But as much as Alexander wanted to play Georgina's prince and release her from her locked tower, there was someone else—two someone elses, in fact—who were better positioned to free her. He just hoped that Georgina trusted him enough to know that he would see to her rescue even though he had to walk out the door without her today.

Chapter Eight

⸎

"Did I judge him wrongly again?" Georgina asked her growing menagerie a day later. Ruffian Caesar's warm body was pressed against her leg, just as he'd been throughout her entire ordeal. He was a loyal mutt, never leaving her side in the darkness.

Crinitus Legatus was much less faithful. Georgina could hear him scratching on the other end of the room in his fruitless search for food. Or, at least, Georgina hoped it was fruitless. Although she tolerated bugs when digging through the mud, she didn't want to share her living space with them in the dark.

Spidery sensations crawled up and down her arms as she imagined little legs running across her body. Biting her lips, she rubbed the sleeves of her gown.

"Do you think he'll come?" Georgina buried her fingers in Ruffian Caesar's wiry curls. "It was awfully clever of Alexander to use Crinitus Legatus to hide his message. His sonnet, though, was exceedingly awful. I suppose he wrote it as an excuse to ask for pen and paper."

Georgina's mouth quirked upward as she thought of the ridiculous words. Anne had insisted on reading the romantic rubbish out loud. Alexander had not shown a hint of embarrassment but had grinned good-naturedly the entire time. His parents—or rather, his father—had winced. His mother only allowed a pained expression to reach her eyes.

"I hope we together grow olden / as much as your tresses are golden." Georgina repeated the ridiculous line into the endless shadows of her prison, hoping levity would bring some lightness. To her surprise, she did feel a mite better. A soft laugh even escaped her lips. "That rascal very well knows that my hair is brown. I wonder if he was obscuring the fact that we'd met prior or if he was trying to assure me that he is not going to force me into marriage."

"Gah!" Georgina howled her frustration into the darkness. "I need to escape from here and find Percy!"

Ruffian Caesar shoved his cold nose into the palm of her hand and began to lovingly lick her fingertips. Crinitus Legatus, however, was startled by her shout. He emitted a frightened *bock*, and she could hear his wings rustling as he commenced panic-flapping. She had learned in the past night and day that this was an exceedingly common occurrence for the easily alarmed bird.

Suddenly, brightness seared Georgina's eyes. Lifting her arm to shield them, she heard Crinitus Legatus emit terror-cries to accompany his increased panic-flapping. The *cluck-cluck-baaawaccks* were quickly followed by a piercing scream—Anne's own terror-cry to be precise.

Georgina lowered her hand just in time to witness Crinitus Legatus flying straight into her sister-in-law. Anne pinwheeled backward, her hands waving frantically. Her shrieking abruptly stopped when a clump of Crinitus Legatus's tail feathers fluttered into her mouth.

Mary, who had been meekly standing behind Anne, sprang

into sudden action. She grabbed the bird with surprising dexterity and cradled the quivering white puff against a pile of silk draped over her arm.

For a moment, Anne stood in frozen disbelief. Down covered her head like a snowy wig. The feathers sticking up from her shoulders gave the appearance of wings, although her expression was far from angelic.

"How…" Anne began but then paused to spit out white fluff. "Do you." Spit. "Know." Spit. "Lady Calliope?" Spit. Spit.

"Lady Calliope?" Georgina repeated, still a little befuddled after the burst of light and Crinitus Legatus's impressive feathering of Anne.

"She is." Spit. "Downstairs." Spit. "Calling on." Spit. Spit. "You." "Oh, would someone." Spit. Spit. "Get this blasted." Spit. "Fuzz out of my." Spit. "Mouth."

Georgina thought rapidly. Had Alexander informed Lady Calliope about her plight? If so, it was a good plan. Anne would never turn away someone of her rank.

"Oh, yes. We met during my debut. We've corresponded ever since." The half lies tripped with surprising ease from Georgina's mouth. Perhaps she had gleaned the talent from watching Alexander yesterday when he'd fabricated an entire chicken fashion trend.

Anne paused in wiping her silk handkerchief over her tongue. "And you didn't tell Algernon or me about your connections? She is the sister of the Duke of Blackglen! Do you realize how hard your brother has tried to befriend His Grace?"

"You were never interested in my correspondence," Georgina said softly.

Anne started to put her arms akimbo and then stopped. "That is because I thought you were writing to boring antiquarians, not to the half sister and daughter of a duke! Oh, never mind! We don't have time to discuss your foolishness. Lady Calliope and Lady Charlotte are waiting."

"Lord Heathford's sister is here, too?" Georgina asked as more hope surged through her. It was sounding more and more as if the ladies were a petticoated rescue party.

"Yes." Anne's eyes narrowed suspiciously. "How did you know that Lord Heathford's sister was Lady Charlotte? You rarely pay attention to the aristocracy. Your social blunders gave me numerous headaches during your debut."

Georgina thought quickly, wishing her sister-in-law wasn't so observant when it came to matters of the peerage. "Well, Lord Heathford mentioned it yesterday, but his mother shushed him. I believe Lady Charlotte was recently involved in the Viscount Hawley scandal."

"Oh," Anne said, her shoulders relaxing. "I suppose he did. I debated about allowing Lady Charlotte to enter my home, as I am not certain how Society will judge her involvement in the unmasking of a murderer. But I could hardly deny Lady Calliope entrance, and Lady Charlotte is a relation of your intended."

"Are they requesting to see me?" Georgina asked, desperate to escape her makeshift cell.

"Unfortunately," Anne said, beckoning Mary forward, who was still clutching Crinitus Legatus against what Georgina now recognized as one of her own more elegant gowns. "Mary is here to dress you. I expect you downstairs in ten minutes. I will be present the entire time, so do not even think of engaging in any nonsense. Also, bring that wretched bird with you. They have hens."

⚭

"What do you think of the weather that we've been having?" Lady Charlotte asked Anne as she lifted her teacup from its bluebell-patterned saucer.

"It is so dreadfully hot," Anne moaned, plunking down her own drink. "The sun is beastly when you step outside. I have been staying indoors to avoid the worst of its effects."

Lady Charlotte made some sympathetic clucking sounds, which caused the hen in her lap to perk up its head. The one perched on Lady Calliope even *bocked*. Crinitus Legatus, being the haughty gentleman that he was, ignored the entire affair and did not even twitch his pouf.

Seeing the ridiculous birds snuggled in the ladies' silk gowns, Georgina was absolutely certain that Alexander had arranged for the women to come to her rescue. Only the irrepressible lord could have sent them with poultry in hand. Each time Georgina felt a hint of panic, she merely glanced at one of the beaky faces, and a warm reassurance washed over her.

"I personally enjoy taking a turn outside when it becomes stuffy, but I can understand wanting to avoid the worst of the midday rays," Lady Charlotte murmured in her soothing voice.

Anne formed a perfect pout of horror. "Oh, I could never step even a foot into the afternoon heat! I would simply melt."

"That is a shame." Lady Calliope dramatically clasped her hands over her bosom.

Anne glanced at her suspiciously. "Why would you say that?"

"I was about to suggest that we adjourn to your garden. When Lady Charlotte and I disembarked from the carriage, I noticed that you have such lovely plantings," Lady Calliope answered.

"Yes!" Lady Charlotte said. "And I spotted those charming benches under the shade trees!"

"Miss Harrington, what do you think about partaking in a little fresh air?" Lady Calliope asked. "If I recall from our debutante days, you delight in nature. Is my memory correct?"

"Perfectly," Georgina answered quickly before Anne had a chance to speak.

"That settles it. The three of us will sit outside." Lady Calliope rose to her feet. She turned to Anne and unceremoniously deposited a hen on her lap. "Please watch Precious for me. She is a dainty sort and cannot tolerate a scorching day. I am sure you will take good care of her."

"But—but—" Anne began to splutter. "I—I could join you."

"Please don't fash yourself," Lady Charlotte assured Anne in a kind voice as she, too, placed her fowl on Georgina's sister-in-law's lap. "We would not want you to suffer the sun."

"You look exceedingly fashionable with two birds!" Lady Calliope exclaimed, clasping her hands together as she loomed over Anne. Before the countess could hand one of the feathered creatures back, Lady Calliope spun away and headed toward the open doorway.

Lady Charlotte offered her arm companionably to Georgina. Tucking Crinitus Legatus into one elbow, Georgina stood and accepted Lady Charlotte's gesture. Although she trusted that Anne would not harm the pets of the two esteemed ladies, she was not certain that her sister-in-law wouldn't take out her frustrations on the poor rooster.

Quickly, Georgina led her two visitors through the house. When they reached the sanctity of the garden, Lady Charlotte and Lady Calliope turned toward her. No longer did their eyes shine with mirth as they studied her with palpable concern.

"My twin sent us," Lady Charlotte whispered as she drew Georgina behind a copse of trees.

"He was worried that you were being mistreated by your

brother," Lady Calliope answered. "If Alexander was wrong, we do apologize for any intrusion."

"He—he was not incorrect," Georgina said, suddenly embarrassed to admit that she'd been locked up in the dark for days. Although she knew others had suffered greater ordeals, there had been something deeply degrading about being kept in pitch blackness and released only for command performances.

To her relief, the women did not press for details. Lady Charlotte merely grabbed Georgina's free hand. "Would you like to stay with Lady Calliope's family? I would offer myself, but I am afraid that your brother and sister-in-law would not allow you to stay in the household of a mere physician."

"But they won't be able to deny the invitation of a daughter and sister to a duke," Lady Calliope said with a confident smile. "Alexander told me that your half brother is keen on impressing mine. He wouldn't want to risk getting in my bad graces. Everyone knows Blackglen dotes on me and my siblings. We're considered his only soft spot."

"Are your parents willing to host me? And they won't mind if I leave unchaperoned to look for Percy?" Georgina asked, surprised by Lady Calliope's generosity. Her father's household was one of the wealthiest in England—second only to the king, according to some whispers. Would they want to potentially invite scandal into their home? Georgina had no intention of giving up her search for her cousin, especially after the investigation had been delayed for days.

Lady Calliope merely waved her fingers. "Of course, to both. We have scads of room. My siblings and I are always inviting guests who come and go of their own accord. Mother jokes that she loses track of who are her children and who are their friends. You will be very welcome as will your adorable rooster."

"I have a dog too," Georgina said.

"We're absolutely mad about canines." Lady Calliope looped her arm around Georgina's shoulders. "And don't fret about your sister-in-law. Charlotte and I will handle her."

Georgina allowed herself a small smile as she recalled the women dumping the hens on a nearly tongue-tied Anne. Yes, they were very effective at taking advantage of Anne's need to impress higher-ranking members of society. Alexander had been wise to send them.

"There's no need to linger. Let's go inside and get this settled." Lady Charlotte gave Georgina's arm a kind, sisterly pat. "I promise we'll be quick. You'll soon be on your way and free to seek your cousin's whereabouts."

⚜

Lady Charlotte was true to her word. In less than a quarter of an hour, Georgina had been bundled into Lady Calliope's family coach along with a wide-eyed Mary, a befuddled Ruffian Caesar, and a clueless Crinitus Legatus. Within twenty minutes, the vehicle pulled up to a massive Mayfield mansion. A stream of servants immediately appeared as they efficiently dealt with Georgina's meager belongings. Mary disappeared with the staff and the two hens, leaving Georgina holding Ruffian Caesar in one arm and Crinitus Legatus in the other.

"Alexander wished for me to let you know that he's waiting for you in one of our drawing rooms," Lady Calliope whispered in Georgina's ear as they along with Lady Charlotte ascended the main steps. "He understands if you do not desire to meet him and wanted it to be abundantly clear that you have no obligations. But there are things he would like to explain, if you are willing, and he wants to give you an update on his inquiries into your cousin's disappearance. I'm afraid, though, that none of us have learned much of anything."

"I—I would like to see him, Lady Calliope," Georgina admitted, not just to her companions but to herself.

"Oh my, there is no need to be so formal, especially now that you will be my guest for the foreseeable future. Just call me Calliope."

"Please use my Christian name as well," Alexander's sister added. "May we address you as Georgina?"

Georgina had never had close female friends before, and after everything that had transpired, she was beginning to trust that these two were most assuredly not after her helmet. Tears pricked her eyes as she bobbed her head in assent. Welling up was apparently becoming a regular occurrence. Although she had never considered herself to be an emotional sort, the last few days had driven her feelings to the surface.

Before Georgina had a chance to collect herself, Calliope opened a pocket door to reveal a richly appointed drawing room. But Georgina barely noticed the bold, bird-covered wallpaper and intricately molded ceiling. Her focus was entirely on the man clamoring to his feet. Even with his uneven gait, Alexander moved swiftly toward her. Worry marred his usual handsome, devil-may-care mien.

Georgina's already rioting emotions billowed. Since her father's death, no one had rushed toward her with concern. They hadn't run their eyes frantically over her, checking for injuries. They certainly did not begin to reach for her and then stop uncertainly. Yet Alexander did all those things.

Through the years, Georgina had become inured to being disregarded, but she'd never had the opportunity to develop a defense to being fussed over. Alexander's honest reaction caused something to break loose inside her.

"Are you hurt in any manner?" Alexander asked, his voice a shade deeper than Georgina recalled it being.

"No," Georgina said truthfully. Her half brother and sister-in-law hadn't touched her body, and she didn't want to talk about herself right now. She needed to know what was happening in the search for her cousin. "But what have you learned about Percy? Calliope mentioned that you've been looking for him, and I deeply appreciate that."

Alexander studied her face. For a moment, Georgina thought he'd press her about the last four days. To her surprise, he instead promptly answered her question. "I've discovered very little. Our mutual friends know nothing about Percy's whereabouts. I did stop by Elysian Fields, but the patrons who were there hadn't been present when Percy brought in the helmet. I was planning to pop by the coffeehouse again today when the establishment is at its busiest."

"I want to go with you," Georgina said immediately. Now that she was liberated, she wasn't about to sit in a comfortable house and fret while Alexander searched.

A cautious smile spread across his face. "I was hoping you'd trust me enough to accompany me again."

An odd emotion jangled inside Georgina, and she realized that she'd begun to put her faith in Alexander once more. And that uneasy acknowledgment made her next words a tad more brusque than she'd intended. "Well, you did engineer my rescue in a way that ensured I wouldn't be forced to marry you. I no longer believe you were scheming to wed me."

Alexander's expression turned worried again. "What did happen after I left that day?"

"I..." Georgina faltered as she glanced nervously in Charlotte's and Calliope's direction. Both women were so strong. What would they think of Georgina's weakness?

"Would you like Calliope and me to leave?" Charlotte asked quietly.

"My servants do not even know Alexander is here. Even if they did, they would not utter a peep. My siblings and I are constantly causing trouble that never leaves this household," Calliope promised.

Georgina nodded her head. Logically, Alexander was a man she should be running from, but instinct told her that he might be the very one to run toward.

After Charlotte and Calliope departed, neither Georgina nor Alexander spoke. He waited patiently, his gaze still scanning her for any hidden wounds.

"Algernon and Anne really did not harm me, but they were not pleased that I was going about London unchaperoned," Georgina finally said. She paused and glanced toward the carpet as a shame she could not stop filled her. "They...they locked me in my bedchamber. When Anne discovered me creating a ladder from sheets, I was placed in a windowless room in the servants' quarters."

Alexander swore softly but vehemently. "Was it to force you to marry me?"

Georgina sucked in her breath and found her old courage. She lifted her chin and nodded. "Yes. They are both very keen for this match, but I do not know why."

Alexander stepped forward and lightly gripped her shoulder. "I knew nothing of our planned betrothal until yesterday. My parents wished to finagle me into meeting you. I have rejected all their other attempts at matchmaking. Please know I would never coerce any woman into marriage."

"As I said, it is obvious in how you planned my rescue," Georgina said, shakily. "I never would have cast myself in the role of a fair maiden needing saving, but apparently I did. Thank you for not abandoning me, especially after I constantly misjudged you."

Alexander dropped his hand. "If you were tying sheets together, you were hardly a damsel in distress. It's not your fault that our country's laws give guardianship of free-thinking adult women to their male relations. Algernon should not have this much power over you. A few months ago, Charlotte was in a similar predicament."

"But she saved herself," Georgina pointed out, yet Alexander's words soothed some of the rawness inside her. He was right. She had not been a placid victim. Given time, she would have tried to escape again. She would not have simply accepted her fate.

"My sister also had help from Matthew and everyone you met at the Black Sheep. And you will ultimately rescue yourself, too. You just needed assistance in leaving your bastard of a brother's abode. But I have faith that you'll figure out how to wriggle your way out of his control entirely."

Georgina knew physical strength would not help her wrest the reins of her life away from her brother. Only cleverness and a healthy dose of luck would manage that. But her mind kept returning to the moment when the footman's arms had closed around her and dragged her from the window. She'd been so helpless then—an utter pawn at Algernon's and Anne's mercy.

"Teach me to fight." The words flew from Georgina's mouth before she could stop them. But after she spoke, a satisfaction swept through her. Why should she swallow back the request? Didn't she have the right to defend herself? Perhaps fisticuffs did not fit with her original notion of being a scholar, but even her father had taken fencing lessons.

Alexander did not appear nonplussed by her demand. Instead, one of his wide grins spread across his face. "Do you wish to start straightaway while we're waiting to leave for Elysian Fields? If your cousin really has been abducted, it will be good for you to know how to defend yourself."

Once again Georgina viscerally felt that iron grip around her middle. "Let's begin now."

She wondered for a moment if Alexander sensed her panic, for his hazel eyes turned a softer golden-brown hue. He did not question her, though. Instead, his ever-present smile grew warmer.

"In that case, I'd say it is the perfect time to make use of the best feature of Estbrook House." Alexander winked.

Chapter Nine

Alexander thought Georgina looked every inch the scholar despite her clenched fists as she stood in the center of the Estbrook ballroom. Her sober expression almost verged on a grim one, her body rigid. She contrasted sharply with the whimsical setting. She was certainly not the ethereal Venus to the painted cupids playing their golden harps on the ceiling above her.

No, she did not suit the cavernous room with its expensive gilt mirrors and luxurious silk draperies. She was definitely more at home in her Essex mud pit. Yet she was not exactly out of place, either, because Georgina had a way of commanding the space around her, even if she did not realize it.

"What is my first lesson?" Georgina asked, her chin set at a stubborn angle, her feet spread apart...but not in an appropriate stance. Her weight was balanced unevenly, making it more likely for her to topple over.

Without thinking, Alexander walked over and lightly grabbed her hand. "First thing, do not tuck your thumb into your fist. It's liable to get broken like that."

"Truly?" Georgina asked in surprise. "It feels natural to hold it so."

"This is the way." Alexander began to automatically rearrange her hand. By the time he touched her second finger, something shifted inside him when his thumb rubbed against a callus. Smooth and rough, her skin was an intriguing mix of contrasts. His heart constricted and then, just as suddenly, expanded. Deeply affected, he glanced up…and straight into Georgina's solemn eyes.

Alexander swallowed hard and quickly returned his gaze to her fist. Moving much quicker now, he corrected her hold, trying his best not to notice her slender fingers between his bigger ones. Even when he stepped back, his breathing remained terribly uneven. He was not a green lad, but being in this close proximity to Georgina evidently turned him into one again.

"It feels awkward," Georgina remarked.

Her words so perfectly described the current sensations rioting through him that Alexander was almost afraid he'd spoken his feelings aloud. It took him a moment to ascertain that he hadn't.

Swounds. Perhaps he shouldn't have offered to teach Georgina. It had seemed a grand plan at the time. He'd expected to feel the pull of attraction, but not to this extent. He felt…flustered, which wasn't like him at all.

"You'll become accustomed to it with practice," Alexander said and then immediately wished he hadn't uttered the last word. Images of an entirely different type of practice sprang up in his all-too-fertile imagination. Mouth against mouth. Hands intertwined. Hearts pumping madly.

Firmly, he forced his mind away from such lustful thoughts. Georgina was here to learn. Now was not the time for fantasies.

Alexander cleared his throat and straightened his shoulders. "Before we begin anything, there is an important lesson that I need to impart."

"Yes?" Georgina asked, clearly oblivious to whatever feelings were pounding through him.

"You must always act with intent." As soon as the words left Alexander's lips, he realized he could be talking to himself instead of instructing Georgina about fighting. He'd purposely lived a frivolous life, but something told him that he could not take his relationship with this woman lightly.

"Pardon?"

"If you strike a man, you must make the blow count. If not, you could only further provoke him. You most likely will be smaller, slighter, and weaker. What you do possess is the element of surprise. You must not just catch him off-guard but place him at a disadvantage. To do that, you must be decisive."

A confident smile stretched over Georgina's wan countenance, and Alexander felt a corresponding lift in his own heart. He hadn't liked how suppressed her spirit had been since her brother and sister-in-law had imprisoned her. But Georgina was strong and practical. She wouldn't allow Lord and Lady Craie to subdue her for long.

"I am always decisive," Georgina said in her crisp, no-nonsense tone.

Alexander wanted to grin, but for once, he didn't. Now was one of the rare times when he needed to be serious. "Even if being determined means gouging out a man's eyes or striking him in the cock with your shin?"

Georgina's eyes widened. He'd shocked her, as he had meant to. The surprise did not last long. Her expression turned thoughtful and then resolute. "I suppose those would be the easiest ways to disarm someone. Vicious, but ultimately necessary if one's person is under attack."

"How is it that you manage to make fighting sound like a scholarly pursuit?" Alexander asked, truly charmed by how her mind worked.

Georgina shrugged. "Is it not? You forget that I cut my teeth on ancient Roman texts. My father read me Herodotus's *Histories* as a bedtime story. If you recall, the Scythians made cups out of their victims' skulls."

"I am afraid that the actual employment of violence is very visceral and not at all academic. You must practice until it becomes innate."

Georgina's lips quirked ever so slightly at the corners. "Are you offering your eyeballs as a sacrifice to my betterment?"

"Swounds, no." This time Alexander couldn't help his laughter. "I am rather attached to them. In fact, they are the feature that I'm most vain about."

"I can see why. They are a kaleidoscope of ever-changing color."

Heat immediately whooshed through Alexander, lighting him like a forge. Although he'd exchanged his share of flirtatious quips, he hadn't expected such a whimsical observation from Georgina.

Apparently, neither had she. Her pale face instantly pinkened, the flags of color softening her otherwise somber features. Yet even though he sensed her unease and embarrassment, she did not lower her gaze.

Yes, she was a decisive one.

He could have crafted a clever, lighthearted reply, allowing them both a reprieve from the tension swirling around them. But he couldn't bring himself to turn this moment into something frivolous.

He could also have lowered his voice and made some soft, teasing reply to deepen the pull of attraction. But a romantic entanglement would only complicate their desire to avoid their relations' matrimonial machinations.

So he did neither. He simply changed the subject. "The goal is to surprise and disable your attacker to give you a chance to run away. It is not so much a fight as it is an escape."

"Escape," Georgina repeated the word, and that haunted look returned to her brown eyes. "That word has new meaning now."

Alexander yearned to reach for her, to offer comfort, but he didn't know if she'd want it. The last thing he desired was for her to feel trapped again.

"Perhaps we should wait for more training," Alexander suggested. "We will need to be in close proximity when I demonstrate some techniques, and I do not want to distress you further."

"No," Georgina said resolutely. "Knowing I have some means to defend myself will far outweigh any discomfort that I may feel. You were right when you said that I prefer to be in control of a situation, and that includes my own fears."

The admiration Alexander had felt for Georgina since the beginning swelled even more. She was fierce and bold in unconventional ways.

"How do I properly kick a man in his cock? Do I just kick out like so?" Georgina swung her leg straight out and almost toppled over.

Alexander smiled at her enthusiastic determination. It was apparent that Georgina did not do anything by half measure.

"It is best to use your shin—halfway between the knee and ankle," Alexander instructed. "You can even kick from behind. Brace yourself beforehand, and don't madly toss your leg into the air. Be as deliberate about this as you are about uncovering your treasures."

"What if a man snares me around the middle?" Georgina asked, her voice grim.

"Is that what happened?" Alexander asked softly.

Georgina visibly set her jaw. "Yes. A footman grabbed me at Anne's command. He was not unduly rough, but it was uncomfortable."

"You can twist your body and elbow an attacker in the face," Alexander said. "Would you like me to demonstrate?"

"Yes," Georgina said. And to Alexander's shock, she strode over to him and wrapped her arms around his middle. His mind utterly and entirely blanked.

He had been trained by both Championess Quick and her daughter. He was accustomed to grappling with women and found nothing overtly sensual about it. But with Georgina…

It was different. Very, very different.

He felt like he did when flying over a hedge while racing his horse in the new style from Ireland. His heart had certainly left its place in his chest and seemed to be sailing up his throat. Even his breathing had changed as he exhaled in irregular puffs.

"If I were bigger and stronger than you, how would you free yourself?" Georgina asked, her voice so damnably even. Didn't their closeness affect her at all?

"Like this," Alexander said as he pushed past the sensations saturating his body. Using his cane for support as Championess Quick had taught him, he twisted in Georgina's slim arms. Lifting his own limb, he demonstrated how he would smash his forearm against her face, stopping just inches from her nose.

"You do not actually hit directly with the elbow then?" Georgina asked, her voice both clipped and thoughtful. She was clearly committing everything to memory in that logical way of hers.

"It is best to use whatever position you find comfortable as long as you are employing maximum force when ramming into the villain's face."

"I shall keep that in mind." Georgina gnawed on her lip as she clearly focused on how she would complete the action.

"If you pivot further," Alexander said as he demonstrated the next move, "you can kick your leg into his groin while he is staggering backward."

"Can I try?" Georgina asked eagerly, her arms dropping from his waist.

He immediately missed the slight pressure, yet he hesitated to gather her into his arms. It wasn't just his own reaction that concerned him. He wasn't sure if she was prepared—even in a feigned situation—to be gripped by a man.

"Are you truly ready?" Alexander asked.

Georgina nodded. "I believe so."

Alexander placed his cane on the floor. Slowly and carefully, he encircled Georgina, giving her a chance to pull away. But she stood there resolutely, her chin tilted skyward, her shoulders noticeably tight. For a moment, he could feel her smaller frame against his larger one. She was slender but not delicate.

Everything inside Alexander seemed to bolt at the same time and settle into a fast *clip-clop*. When he first heard Georgina's shortened breaths, he thought she was experiencing the same sensations as him. But when she whirled in his arms and just stood there with her head lowered, he realized something was amiss.

"What's wrong, Georgina?" Alexander gently laid his hands on her shoulders and leaned down to look into her face. Unfortunately, just as he bent, her head shot up. Her crown whacked soundly against his nose.

Familiar pain burst through Alexander as warm blood trickled down his face. Even if he'd had two good legs, he would have wobbled. Instead of bringing them both down, he released her and allowed himself to crash. Clearly startled from her previous panic, Georgina emitted a surprised sound somewhere between a squeak and a shout.

"Oh no!" She dropped down beside him, hovering anxiously near his head. "Did I hurt you? You're bleeding! Should I get you something? Would a warm compress help? A poultice of some type? This is not at all part of my knowledge."

Despite the unwelcome throbbing, Alexander felt a smile stretch across his face. "But it is within my expertise. Don't fash yourself. It is not my first bloody nose, and I daresay it won't be my last. You didn't break it at least. How's your head?"

Georgina leaned over him, her solemn brown eyes scrutinizing his face with scholarly intensity. No wonder the antiquities that she appraised gave up their secrets to her. Right now, he'd promise her anything.

"I am good, but are you certain that you are fine?" Georgina's hand brushed against his face.

Her fingertips caused a delicious friction, leaving a trail of delightfully sparkling sensations in their wake. His breath . . . his breath simply whooshed from him. Before Alexander could summon a sound, Georgina reached into her pocket with her other hand and produced a simply embroidered handkerchief. The linen swatch was as practical as she.

Yet when she began to wipe the blood from Alexander's chin, she did not do so with efficient, deft strokes. Oh no. That would have been too kind.

Instead, she drew the cloth slowly across his flesh. As she carefully dabbed at the blood, she chewed at her lower lip. Alexander knew then that she wasn't as unaffected by his presence as she'd seemed.

The air slammed back into his body and, with it, heady desire. He reached up and touched Georgina's cheek, her smooth skin warm against his palm. Her brown eyes widened, but she did not pull back. Perhaps she even leaned a little more firmly into his cupped fingers.

He longed to lift his head, to graze his lips against hers. Nay, not merely graze, but to press their mouths together. Would she kiss with the same intensity that she did everything else?

Swounds. He was supposed to be showing Georgina how to defend herself. This wasn't the time or place for seduction, not to mention the blood gushing from his nose.

He mustered up one of his teasing grins and let his hand fall limply to his side. "Since we find ourselves both on the floor, would you like to learn how to throw off an attacker who is trying to pin you to the ground? Or would that cause you more alarm? I do not wish to push you past your level of comfort again."

Georgina blinked rather owlishly. It was a moment before she spoke. "I—I don't think that would bother me like when you grabbed me about the waist. In fact…trying out this other technique would be…good. Very good."

Alexander struggled to keep his smile from becoming triumphant. It was indeed true that he wasn't the only one affected by their nearness. But he wouldn't take advantage of Georgina's flustered feelings.

"Straddle me," Alexander said, without thinking of the consequences of his automatic instruction.

Georgina tilted her head in confusion. "Straddle you?"

Every last bit of moisture left Alexander's throat as he realized just how dangerous this particular maneuver would be—and he wasn't talking about physical peril. He opened his exceedingly parched mouth to suggest another defense strategy. But before he could, Georgina jerked her head straight with military precision.

"Oh, I understand now. An attacker would assume a position like that."

Then without preamble, she swung one leg over his hip. Her skirts and petticoats should have hampered her, but she moved with surprising agility. Alexander supposed it came from years of managing to dig in her pit despite the voluminous layers that ladies had to don. He was suddenly exceedingly grateful for the number of petticoats separating their bodies. After all, his was having a very ungentlemanly reaction to the presence of hers.

"If our positions were reversed, what would I do?" Georgina leaned over his chest as she asked the question.

He nearly groaned. Firmly, he schooled his lower half not to buck.

"Grab my hands like you're restraining me, and I'll show you," Alexander said. As he demonstrated how a victim could leverage their body against their attacker's, he kept giving himself firm reminders of exactly why they were engaged in this particular activity.

This is a fight, not a seduction. This is a fight, not a seduction. This is a fight, not a seduction.

Chapter Ten

~~~

Georgina was focused on the mock battle. Unlike when Alexander had caught her around her middle, their current grappling didn't trigger bad memories.

"Let me know if I am frightening you," Alexander said as he firmly but gently pinned her hands to the floor. He'd asked a similar question before he'd placed his thighs on either side of her hips and when he leaned over her prone body. His constant inquiries reassured her that she had complete control over the situation.

"I'm fine."

Even with Alexander's heft pinning her down, she only felt determination to reverse their positions as easily as he had. Yes, she was untrained and more than several stone lighter, but she'd always been a wee bit competitive.

She catapulted her lower half into the air and swept her arms down toward her legs. The combination of the moves broke his grasp on her wrists and knocked him forward. As he flew toward the floor, she grabbed his stomach, burying her head into his abdomen, just as he'd instructed. Hugging his torso, she climbed up him as nimbly as a red squirrel. Quickly, she grabbed his shoulders and forced his body under hers. A moment later, he lay on his back with her kneeling on the ground between his legs.

"I flipped you! I actually flipped you!" Georgina tossed her hands upward and stared into the cloud-painted ceiling.

Alexander's warm chuckle brought her eyes back down to the floor, where he lay beneath her. Most of his auburn hair had escaped its queue during their tussling. It fanned out around his head, the red strands glowing in the light from the windows lining the ballroom's east and west sides. Just like when she'd first met him, the sun seemed to claim him as its own.

Alexander's laughter stopped abruptly, his gemlike eyes fixed on her face. She watched in fascination as the amber specks in his irises overtook the cooler blue and green hues. His gaze looked molten, like gold in a crucible. An odd ache started in Georgina's heart as she suddenly became acutely aware of just where she was situated. Her body was snuggled between his thighs. And her knees... her knees were pointing at a very intimate part of Alexander's anatomy.

Georgina didn't blush. She wasn't one for that.

Instead, needy heat coursed through her. If her cheeks reddened, it was from lust, not embarrassment.

Her mind and body simultaneously recalled how she'd scrambled up his torso. Despite the layers that they both wore, she'd felt the hard muscles of his chest against the softness of her inner thighs. And then when she'd squashed her face against him, the ridges of his stomach had pressed into her cheek. At the time, she'd been so focused on wriggling her way to the correct position to flip Alexander onto his back that she hadn't fully appreciated what a delectable climb it had been. Yet her antiquarian brain had very kindly registered, categorized, and neatly filed away each lovely sensation.

"We should rise." Alexander's voice had deepened into a warm tone that reminded Georgina of hot spiced cider. It made her want to launch herself forward and press her mouth against his for a taste. Before she could, Alexander slowly sat up, his body moving inexorably out from under hers. He rose to his feet. Leaning down, he reached his hand out, his other braced on his cane for support. His expression looked affable on the surface, but Georgina could see the strain around his eyes.

Although Georgina had little experience with love, she was extremely observant about things that interested her. And right now, Alexander Lovett, Marquess of Heathford, fascinated her. More intriguingly, she didn't seem inclined to fight against that attraction anymore.

She accepted his hand, allowing him to help her rise. As soon as she was upright, his fingers began to slip from her grasp. She held on.

Alexander cleared his throat. When he spoke, he sounded bright—overly bright. "It's about time to leave for Elysian Fields."

"Do we still have a few more minutes?" Georgina's heart kicked into a rhythm that it normally only did when she spotted a glint of metal or a shard of pottery in her pit.

"There's enough time for you to change into male clothing, if that is your concern. I assume you were able to pack some belongings before my sister and Calliope spirited you away from your brother's townhouse." Alexander lifted his thumb as if he meant to stroke the knuckles of her hand still clasped in his. But he seemed to stay himself.

"I did bring the disguise, but that wasn't what I was asking about. I was thinking about something more…pleasurable." A giddiness strummed through Georgina. She could not believe herself. She was flirting…and she was about to do even more.

Alexander's entire frame jerked as he grasped her meaning. When he spoke, the deep, deliciously rich tone had returned to his voice. "What do you desire, Georgina?"

She might be new to the art of seduction, but Georgina had

never lacked for boldness in pursuing what fascinated her. "A kiss. I've never had one before, and I suddenly desire my first with you. I want to know what it feels like. What it will do to this... this pressure I feel inside me."

Alexander swallowed. Hard. Georgina could see his Adam's apple convulse.

"That could be dangerous, Georgina. It could play into the plans of my father and your brother."

"How would they ever know? It is just a brief meeting of our mouths."

An odd choking sound emanated from Alexander. He was not grinning now. In fact, he appeared rather poleaxed. "I can promise you it will be much more than that, and it will *not* be brief."

"Interesting. How long are kisses normally? More than a minute? Perhaps two?"

Alexander's strangled coughing suddenly transformed into something that might have been a growl. Or maybe a purr. A growl-purr?

Before Georgina could fully define the sound, Alexander's mouth closed over hers, and she forgot all about terminology.

His lips—strong and deliciously warm—moved hungrily against hers, the friction utterly intoxicating. Shimmers of pleasure sparked inside Georgina until she felt alight.

She'd thought embracing him would relieve the tension coiling inside her. It didn't. It just made her greedier.

Georgina had read about coitus before. The Greek and Roman myths were full of lust. But she'd never truly understood the power and the utter madness of attraction. Was this heady elixir what had driven the ill-fated Helen and Paris of Troy?

Alexander's tongue traced her sealed lips, eliciting new but equally brilliant sensations. She hadn't expected him to lick her, but she rather liked it. Gently, he nudged, and she realized that he wanted her to open her mouth.

Curious, she complied. Alexander groaned, and the sound reverberated through Georgina. With one arm, Alexander pulled her closer. When she felt his glorious muscles, she freely plastered herself against him. He staggered, and she realized that it must pain him to support her weight and his. She tried moving back, but his forearm remained tightly banded against her.

Instead, she reached up to grasp his shoulders, guiding him gently down. He seemed to understand, and his cane clattered as he dropped it.

Their mouths still working madly against each other, they lowered themselves to the parquet floor. Once they were kneeling, Alexander changed the angle of their kiss, deepening it even more. If he hadn't been holding Georgina, she would have melted into an undignified but supremely happy heap.

With his right hand now free, Alexander caressed her body. First, she felt a delicate brush against her cheekbone. He traced down to her jaw, leaving a trail of sparks that joined the rest of the fire coursing through her. His fingers skimmed along her neck, resting hotly against her collarbone for several heartbeats.

He fiddled with the gauzy fabric above her bodice, and Georgina's muscles tightened. A need, strong and clear, blazed through her. Her breasts literally began to ache with the desire to be touched.

She moaned into Alexander's mouth. The sound should have embarrassed her.

It did not. She was too full of want to care.

Alexander understood the guttural request, and his warm hand closed over her bosom. His fingertips touched her bare skin while his palm rested against the satin of her stomacher. The fabric heated as he began to knead.

Georgina gasped at the onslaught of sheer sensation. Her head jerked back, and Alexander buried his lips under her ear. Sweet heat spiraled through her. Georgina didn't think. She simply reacted. She pressed her hands against his chest, pushing him backward. This time she was the one who captured his mouth.

His hands left her breasts as they both crashed to the floor. His fingers splayed across her back as she leaned over his prone body. Eagerly, she explored his mouth, her hands planted on either side of his face. He seemed to surrender—nay, open to her, allowing her to take not just the lead but her fill of him. Matching the rhythm that she set, Alexander kissed just as ardently.

A squeak—which was most definitely not from Georgina and too high-pitched for Alexander—broke into Georgina's pleasure. An echoing one definitely left her own throat when she realized that she and Alexander had been discovered. With a speed she did not know that she possessed, she half leapt, half spun and flipped off of Alexander. Georgina landed so hard on her rear that she bounced. Out of the corner of her eye, she saw Alexander slowly rise like a sleepwalker. Gripping his cane, he blinked twice before his eyes widened.

Taking a deep breath first, Georgina carefully turned to look over her shoulder. In an open doorway stood Alexander's sister and Calliope. Charlotte's entire face had pinkened. Calliope, however, showed no signs of embarrassment. She merely appeared amused.

"You shouldn't have made a sound," Calliope scolded Charlotte. "They were clearly enjoying themselves. We could have quietly backed away, and they would have been none the wiser."

"I wasn't expecting…" Charlotte trailed off and then helplessly waved her hands vaguely toward the space Georgina and Alexander had been occupying only moments before. "Well…that."

"I can tell you are not a writer," Calliope said, a mischievous glint in her eyes. "There are so many more suitable descriptors beside 'that.' For example…"

Georgina felt partially mortified and partially amused. It was odd having a friend tease her. Alexander and Charlotte, however, clearly did not see any humor in the situation.

"Please don't continue, Calliope. I beg you," Alexander ground out, his voice choked as he interrupted her.

At the same time, Charlotte plugged her ears and admonished, "Calliope, he is my twin! Who wants to hear those words about their brother?"

"I concede your point," Calliope said, "but you have to admit the circumstances are a bit comical. Georgina, your reflexes nearly rival a cat's. You must work on your landings, though."

"I am not exactly planning on a repeat," Georgina said as primly as she could manage while spinning around to face the women. Her embarrassment, she found, was fading. The ladies were not gossips, and Calliope had the right approach to simply laugh off the entire episode.

Charlotte removed her fingers from her ears. "Something similar has already happened—this time, though, is the reverse of the first. Alexander previously interrupted Matthew and me, so I know how you feel, Georgina."

Charlotte turned to her brother. "As the two of you have both expended great efforts to avoid a forced marriage, I recommend that you lock each and every door in the future."

Alexander scowled, and he looked a bit like a pouting schoolboy, especially with his hair so thoroughly mussed. "At least a ballroom is better than a glasshouse."

"Neither is a good place for assignations," Calliope said airily. "They both lack creativity and, much more importantly, seclusion. There is a certain art to *affaires de coeur*."

Alexander rubbed the back of his neck with his free hand. "I wasn't planning—wait, why am I trying to explain myself? Georgina and I must leave. We have plans."

"Of course you do." Calliope smirked. Broadly. Then she winked.

"Not those kinds of plans." Alexander tapped the ferrule of his cane against the hardwood floor. "Ones of an investigative nature."

"Oh, an *investigative nature*. Is that your term for it?" Calliope spoke so impishly that Georgina could not help but be amused. It was rather fun watching Alexander squirm. He always seemed so confident; Georgina hadn't thought him capable of awkwardness.

"Calliope!" Alexander roared, and he then glanced at Georgina. "I apologize on Calliope's behalf. She means to tease me, not you."

"It's novel to be part of banter like this. I don't mind," Georgina admitted.

Calliope swung her arm around Georgina's middle and gave her a gentle squeeze. "I am glad someone appreciates my humor."

Georgina wondered if this is what it felt like to belong. It was something she hadn't experienced for a long time.

Chapter Eleven

W e should leave."

Georgina's panicked tone instantly caused Alexander to stiffen. He should have been focused on asking the other patrons at Elysian Fields about Pendergrast's last whereabouts. Instead, he'd been reliving the ballroom kiss, which seemed a paltry term for what had transpired between Georgina and him. He wasn't inexperienced, but he'd never encountered such sweet fire before. It had obliterated all his other senses until he felt nothing but the wildness Georgina evoked in him. He'd nearly lost his control—even though she'd been the one leading their passionate embrace. If Charlotte and Calliope hadn't interrupted them...

Swounds! He was daydreaming again. He needed to focus, despite the fact that he felt like a red-hot ingot in the forge.

Quickly, he glanced around Elysian Fields, looking for signs of danger. Everything appeared ordinary to him: neat rows of tables; reedy, scholarly-looking men; mugs of coffee, some steaming, some long-forgotten at the elbows of those in deep debate.

The atmosphere was different from even in the front room of the Black Sheep, which was similarly configured. The Black Sheep always seemed on the edge of happy chaos. So many conversations happened at once, each more boisterous than the next. Here, at Elysian Fields, the chatter was still constant but more restrained. Fellows leaned intently over the scarred tables, but they did not gesticulate madly.

Elysian Fields certainly did not have the comfortable uphol-stered furniture of the Black Sheep's secret back room. And Alexander could only smell the acrid scent of black coffee, not the delicious brews with the surprising flavors that Sophia Wick dreamed up. Certainly, no women customers graced Ely-sian Fields. The place was traditional.

And boring.

In short, it did not appear to be a venue housing hidden dan-gers. But Alexander had learned early in life never to place his trust in appearances.

"What concerns you?" Alexander took care to keep his voice low as he continued to scan the building, making sure that his thoughts did not stray back to their embrace in the Estbrook ballroom.

"Do you see the men at the end of the first table?"

Alexander followed her instructions and spotted two finely dressed gentlemen, whom he instantly recognized. The thin, elderly peer of middling height was the Duke of Foxglen. Across from him sat his grandson, a hulking bruiser in a perfectly tai-lored silk suit. Despite his refined attire, the young man looked like a prizefighter or a ruffian. But the Marquess of Malbarry was neither. He was a quiet fellow who refused to gamble and barely danced at balls. He only talked about politics with aging members of the House of Lords who were contemporaries of his grandfather.

If Malbarry was reserved, Foxglen was dour. The peer rarely attended the ton's functions, and when he did, he glowered through them as if in a constant state of disapproval. Alexander had always done his best to avoid the aging lion of Parliament, who would never countenance the types of reforms Alexander dreamed about. In fact, Alexander might not have even recognized the cantankerous man if he hadn't been accompanied by his grandson.

"Do you mean the Duke of Foxglen and Lord Malbarry?" Alexander asked.

"Yes."

It was a good thing Georgina was whispering, as she'd forgotten to lower the timbre of her voice. Alexander was about to warn her to adjust the pitch, but she must have remembered herself.

When she spoke again, her tone was huskier. "His Grace was my father's chief scholarly rival. He's forever attempting to rebut the pieces that I write under Percy's name, too."

Alexander leaned closer to Georgina but not near enough to draw attention. "Have you met Foxglen?"

"Yes, and his grandson. The duke has a holding in Essex, less than a half-day's travel from the land my father owned." Georgina's voice began to rise again, but she caught herself and deepened it. Clearly, she was nervous.

Alexander wished he could squeeze her hand or offer some modicum of comfort. However, any such gesture would draw unwanted attention, especially with Georgina dressed in male attire. And it might be dangerous in other ways. He was like dry powder in a pistol, and one small spark could set off a powerful reaction.

"Do you think they will recognize you? People often accept what they think they should be observing rather than identifying what they are actually witnessing." There. He sounded calm, logical. Certainly not like someone having the occasional—or constant—lustful thoughts.

"I am not sure. I have not seen either of them for over a

decade," Georgina explained. "The Duke of Foxglen hardly paid me, a girl child, any mind. The marquess is different, though. While my father and his grandfather debated, we were left together. He was a quiet sort, and we mostly sat in silence, reading separate books. But I do recall him being observant and very quick-witted. I would not be surprised if he did see beyond my disguise."

"Then we'd best leave." Alexander pressed down on his cane as he prepared to pivot toward the exit. However, before he could even begin to turn, a familiar taunting voice stopped him.

"Why, if it isn't Alexander the Galling. If I didn't know you better, I'd think you were hunting me. Don't forget, Galling, that I am the predator, and you are the mere prey."

"Rather the fox than the dog following its owner's orders," Alexander quipped, keeping his voice bright as he turned in Talbot's direction. When he caught a glimpse of his old tormentor, an involuntary chortle almost bubbled up inside Alexander.

In the fellow's arms was a rooster—a very puffed-up, extremely annoyed, and absolute behemoth of a fowl. The bird stretched its neck, nearly bopping Talbot in the chin. A hideous screech escaped its open beak. Despite the babble of low voices, the call echoed off the bare walls.

Everyone turned in their direction, including Foxglen and Malbarry. There was no escaping undetected now.

"What an impressive chicken." Alexander somehow managed to keep both his face straight and his voice from wobbling with suppressed laughter.

"If you are intending to mock me, I shall have you know that I have it on good authority that roosters are highly fashionable. The Duke of Blackglen started the trend himself." Talbot stuck out his chest, looking like a veritable cock himself. He just needed to start strutting to complete the charade.

"Ah." Alexander forced a neutral tone when he just wanted to throw his head back in triumphant hilarity. Georgina's brother and sister-in-law must have already gossiped about the Banbury tale he'd told. He sorely hoped that Lady Craie had purchased a chicken herself.

"As scintillating as new fashion trends are, Lord Heathford and I must beg our leave." Georgina spoke low and soft as she kept her eyes trained on the floor.

Alexander nearly winced. He realized she wanted to keep her identity hidden, but Lord Henry would interpret her stance as weakness. And the damned man liked nothing better than to toy with those that he perceived to be defenseless.

"You seem familiar, yet I do not recall seeing you here before." Talbot spoke slowly as he moved his muscular body between Georgina and the door.

Georgina tried to shuffle back, but Talbot moved forward. He bent over, shoving his face in hers.

Alexander angled his cane between the nobleman and Georgina. Talbot tried to kick it aside, but Alexander held it firmly. The bully turned on him, just as Alexander had intended. Changing his grip on Hercules and the Nemean lion, Alexander prepared to defend himself.

"Please stop bothering my guests, Lord Henry."

The voice was quiet and cultured but full of undeniable authority. Talbot whirled toward the new speaker, his hands clenched into fists. Alexander watched as, one by one, Talbot's fingers went limp.

As soon as Lord Henry's hands hung at his sides, Alexander carefully maneuvered his own body so that he could both watch the newcomer and monitor Talbot. Although Alexander was not a short man, he found his gaze looking up and then up some more.

Looming over them was Lord Malbarry. His face remained placid, his shoulders relaxed, and his frame clearly not poised for a fight.

The marquess didn't need to flex to intimidate. He could just stand up.

"Come and sit down." Malbarry gestured for Alexander and Georgina to follow.

Alexander noticed that the massive man's gaze lingered a beat or two on Georgina's downturned face. Had he recognized her? If the marquess did, his expression never changed. But could that be the reason that Malbarry had come to their aid, or was he simply a kind soul who didn't like bullies?

Trapped now, Alexander and Georgina had no choice but to trail after their unexpected champion while Talbot and his giant cock slunk away to the opposite corner of the room. As long as Georgina's identity wasn't exposed, this might even be a fortunate turn of events. After all, if Foxglen was a competitor, then perhaps he was behind the disappearance of Pendergrast and the helmet.

"Must you involve yourself in matters that do not concern you?" Foxglen snapped at his grandson as the three of them joined the elderly peer.

"Do unto others," Malberry replied, his words a soft explanation rather than a defiant rebuttal.

Foxglen's lips thinned, but he did not argue. Instead, he fixed his icy stare on Alexander first. "You are Falcondale's heir apparent—one of those sporting sorts."

"Yes. That would be me." Alexander gave the dour man one of his brightest grins.

"My words were not a compliment." Between his age and his power, Foxglen had long since abandoned politeness.

"But I shall take them as one." Alexander made his smile even broader. He had a lifetime of dealing with censure, and even the biggest curmudgeon couldn't intimidate him.

Foxglen grunted, the sound an annoyed dismissal. With a slowness that either came from age or pompousness, Foxglen rotated toward Georgina.

"But who are you? I do not recognize you at all."

"He's Mr. George Harrington," Alexander answered, trying to draw the duke's attention back to himself.

"A Harrington, you say? Any relation to that scoundrel Lord Percy, whose mother was a Harrington? He besmirches the good name of antiquarians. If one wishes to have the honor of writing about our illustrious forebearers, one should live an exemplary life." Foxglen's entire countenance seemed to seize and wrinkle in disgust.

"I have always found Lord Percy to be unassailable in whatever course he sets." Alexander spoke with blithe cheerfulness that he knew would irk the old duke.

Lord Malbarry sent him a curious look, as if he sensed that Alexander was deliberately provoking his grandfather. If he suspected Alexander's true intentions, though, he did nothing to intervene. Despite his huge stature, the man seemed to have an ability to fade almost instantly into the background.

Georgina, for her part, kept her eyes trained on the table.

Foxglen bristled. "Lord Percy is a mockery to anyone who diligently seeks to learn about our glorious past." The duke thumped his hand on the table, causing his and his grandson's mugs to rattle. Coffee sluiced everywhere. The elderly man ignored the mess, but Malbarry withdrew a handkerchief and began mopping up the spill.

Alexander leaned over the table, ready to push Foxglen over the edge of his thinly held self-control. "Yet from what I've heard, he discovered King Arthur's helmet."

"He does not deserve such a boon!" Foxglen roared. "It is wasted on a mind like his. *I* should have been the one to discover such a priceless treasure."

Georgina's head snapped up before she quickly averted her gaze once more. Alexander knew that she was having the same thought as him. Had Foxglen wanted the antiquity so badly that he'd had Pendergrast robbed and abducted... or worse? The duke seemed like the type who would be horrified by the mere idea of sharing the same air as a ruffian, let alone hiring one, but perhaps his jealousy had overridden his pompousness.

"Grandfather, you said yourself that the helmet was not Arthur's. He's a mere legend from Wales." Malbarry's voice was a calm, gentle contrast to the duke's.

Alexander wondered, though, if Malbarry was as unflappable as he seemed. Was he merely trying to soothe his grandfather's nerves, or was he trying to silence the man? Malbarry could have been the one to arrange an attack on Percy. Hell, with his physique, he could execute the ambush himself, especially if Percy had been deep in his cups.

"Yes. Yes." Foxglen punctuated each of his words with a downward slash of his pale, age-spotted hand. "But it is still a piece of English history that the young pup will never fully appreciate."

"Lord Percy's articles indicate otherwise. Based on his scholarly work, he was exactly the right person to make the discovery." Georgina practically coughed out each word, likely in an effort to disguise her voice.

Alexander had to stop a fond expression from drifting over his face. Despite her worries at being unmasked, Georgina clearly hadn't been able to sit silently and hear her alter ego being maligned. But as much as Alexander enjoyed watching her defend herself, he knew she shouldn't risk exposure.

"Balderdash!" Foxglen's entire being seemed to transform into a thunderous glower. "That young whippersnapper—"

"Oh, you did come to Elysian Fields." Lord Clifville's monotone broke into the conversation, his gaze focused on Alexander. "How convenient. After writing down my thoughts, I had some additional questions about modern female boxers."

"What are you blathering about, Clifville?" Foxglen demanded as he turned to the earl, who was hovering near the head of their table.

Clifville blinked at the duke as if spotting him for the first time despite standing near Foxglen. "I do apologize. I did not see you there, Your Grace."

Foxglen flattened his body against his straight-backed chair in a clear attempt to look down his nose at the other peer.

Once again, Malbarry seemed eager to forestall any conflict. "You must be consumed with research, Lord Clifville."

As the marquess spoke, he pulled out a chair for the earl. "You had mentioned something about Amazons?"

"Indeed, I did." Clifville sank into the seat without acknowledging the gesture. He turned toward Georgina and started as if he just remembered something. "Oh, dear me. Here I am being forgetful again. Did you find your cousin? Penderblast, was it?"

"Not yet," Georgina mumbled in her hoarse attempt at a male voice.

"He's probably off whoring." Foxglen gave another dismissive wave of his hand. "Reprobate."

Before anyone could respond to the duke, a sudden crowing filled the air. Another, deeper *cock-a-doodle-do* challenged the first, slightly higher-pitched one. The battle of squawks succeeded in quieting the coffeehouse.

"Is it that ill-begotten poultry again?" Foxglen asked. "This is why membership to Elysian Fields should be restricted to true antiquarians."

"I believe there are now two fowls, Your Grace," Malbarry observed in that sedate manner of his.

Alexander pushed back his chair for a better vantage point. Sure enough, another patron had entered, holding a rather scrawny rooster. The poor creature did not seem to have an understanding of its underwhelming presence. Instead, it appeared to regard itself as the undisputed king of the barnyard. Its neck fully extended, it hollered its dominance to all and sundry.

Talbot's cock took clear umbrage at the newcomer's entitlement. The nobleman was clearly trying to clutch the bird to his chest, but the meaty chicken had other plans. Flapping its wings while *bock*ing most vigorously, it managed to kick a talon into Talbot's face. The brute screamed, loosening his hold. Desperate to attack its feathered challenger, the fowl shot across the table. In its mad dash, it knocked over a small item. Silver glinted as the metallic article rolled over the scarred wood.

"Not my snuff!" Talbot shouted as he dove after the box. His fingers missed by inches as the decorative little piece tumbled off the table. It crashed onto the floor and popped open. Dried tobacco flew everywhere. Distracted by the pulverized leaves raining from above, Talbot's rooster—who had jumped to the floor—halted its mad dash toward its nemesis. Instead, it began happily pecking at the floorboards.

But Alexander had little interest in the poultry. What had drawn his attention was the now-empty snuffbox. Unless Alexander was mistaken, it looked like a twin to his own sire's. The inside of the case was hewn from the same colorfully banded gemstone.

Georgina gasped. Her intake of breath sounded distinctly

feminine, but luckily everyone was distracted by the spectacle. Under the table, her foot nudged Alexander's repeatedly. With her eyes, she glanced significantly toward the snuffbox. Alexander had no idea what had excited her, but clearly it was important.

He stood up and took several steps to retrieve it, but Talbot's ego must have had enough embarrassment. The bully grabbed his rooster in one arm and snatched the small silver container in the other hand. He stomped from Elysian Fields without a single parting word.

"Dash it all," Georgina said quietly as she came up beside Alexander. "I really needed to look more closely at that snuffbox."

"My father has one just like it, if that helps," Alexander said.

"With the same interior?" Georgina's voice dropped an octave, which was fortunate, as her voice had risen a tad too high.

"I believe so." Alexander's own heart began to thump with tremendous force. He did not understand the significance of the trinket, but he trusted that Georgina did—or at least that she had a valid reason for her intense interest.

"I must see it. Immediately."

Chapter Twelve

※

"It is a good thing that we decided to leave the chickens at the Black Sheep," Georgina said as she stared up at the imposing Doric columns of the Falcondale townhouse. Somehow the stately edifice made even Algernon's fashionable city home appear slovenly. The blood-red bricks contrasted sharply with the brilliant white trim. The edifice was painfully symmetrical and austere.

Nervously, Georgina reached up and patted her hair. The gown that she'd borrowed from Calliope's sister felt tight, even though it had fit just fine during the carriage ride. But she was thankful for it. The ones she'd brought with her to Estbrook House were hopelessly outdated.

Alexander shot her one of his ever-present smiles. Even with Calliope and Charlotte flanking her, Georgina's whole body tingled. Goodness, how did Alexander manage to have such an effect?

"You look perfect," Alexander promised. "But I must disagree about leaving the flock at the coffeehouse. When visiting my parents, one must seek any possible source of levity."

Georgina managed a half smile at what she assumed was his attempt at a joke. When he turned and lifted the knocker, she took a steadying breath. She was so shaky it was as if she were actually visiting her future groom's parents. Silly, really. Yes, she and Alexander had kissed—and quite vigorously at that—but neither of them intended to marry the other.

Yet his parents were the Duke and Duchess of Falcondale. His mother was a legendary hostess. Even for someone like Georgina, who cared little for Society, it was daunting to burst uninvited into Her Grace's home, despite having the peeress's two children in tow.

Almost as soon as Alexander let the brass ring fall against the backplate, the door swung open. In the frame stood a butler dressed in a stiff, exceedingly formal uniform. His long, aquiline face matched the grand home.

When his crystalline blue eyes fell on Alexander, they hardened with an even more profound haughtiness. The sight took Georgina aback. Although she did not exactly expect the dignified man's countenance to soften at the sight of the heir apparent, she had expected some degree of welcome, however stilted.

"The Duke and the Duchess are not hom—" the butler began to intone.

"I have my sister, Miss Harrington, and Lady Calliope with me," Alexander interjected with his typical jovialness. "I assume that their presence has caused my parents to miraculously return to their lovely abode."

The manservant's cool eyes flicked behind Alexander's right shoulder to where Georgina stood with the two other women. When his gaze alighted on Calliope, he finally showed the deference that Georgina would have thought he'd direct toward his employer's son.

"Pardon. I did not see you ladies. Please step inside for a reprieve from the summer heat. You can wait in the drawing room while I check if their Graces are back from their outing." The butler spoke in formal tones—not too soft, not too loud.

Stiffly, he retreated into the foyer and gestured for them to enter.

The four of them were ushered into a finely appointed room that would have made Anne writhe with envy. It wasn't just the silk wallpaper dyed in the most popular of blue hues or even the plaster ceiling with its reliefs of Athena emerging from Zeus's head and turning Medusa into a Gorgon. It was the couches with their gilt wooden trim. They were art pieces themselves—long and sinuous with carvings of grapes, apples, and pears interspersed with flowers. They also looked deuced uncomfortable to sit upon, but that wasn't the point. In fact, they might even be intended to make the sitter feel slightly discomforted as they paid homage to the master and mistress of the house.

When the butler shut the door, Alexander gave a low whistle of appreciation. He turned to Calliope and bent slightly at the waist. "I must bow to your social clout, Lady Calliope. Mother never has me escorted to the blue drawing room. I'm always shoved away into the green one."

"Is that the family one?" Georgina asked in confusion, sensing there was something important behind Alexander's cavalier words.

"Mother and Father do not believe in intimate rooms for familial gatherings. Everything is always a grand show." Alexander's words were bitter, but the tone was not. He sounded exactly like his normal, cheerful self. But something was different, forced even. His entire demeanor had changed in some indefinable way as soon as he'd entered the foyer.

"Oh," Georgina replied, not sure what else to say. She sorely wished that she had not pressed him on the matter, especially with their audience.

Alexander's smile only widened as if he was trying to put her at ease even though she'd inadvertently made things awkward. "Mother's desire for perfect aesthetics is why she rarely has me ushered into the blue salon. In her view, my cane clashes with the décor, although I disagree. Hercules fits perfectly with the Greek theme."

Georgina barely stopped herself from blinking. Why did Alexander seem so blithe when speaking about such cruel rejection? Was he serious?

Quickly, she thought back to when she'd met his parents. Had there been tension then? She had been so focused on her own plight that she'd barely paid attention to anything. It was odd, his father being so keen on marrying Alexander off to a near nobody. What had Algernon said that day in his office when he'd been arranging the betrothal? He'd mentioned her bloodlines and connections to William the Conqueror. How had the other speaker responded, the one who she now assumed was Falcondale? He'd been waxing on about Alexander's prowess in sports. But wasn't misfortune mentioned too?

My cane clashes with the décor. Misfortune. Did Alexander's own parents condemn him due to his clubfoot? The idea chilled Georgina even as it made sense—a horrible, cruel sense, yet one that was all too common in a society that valued appearance and perfection above all else.

This certainly was not the time nor the place for questions, though. Not only did they have the audience of his sister and Calliope, but his parents could enter the room at any moment. And Georgina had the distinct sense that this very building put Alexander at ill ease. For the first time, she wondered if his constant joviality could be a protective mask to retreat behind. The thought brought another bolt of pain to Georgina's heart.

Before any of them could respond to Alexander's statement, his mother glided into the room. She moved like a royal swan on a clear, glass-surfaced lake. Her expression was as elegantly tranquil as her movements. She exuded no warmth as she regarded her children, although there was a slight defrosting when she glanced at Georgina and especially at Calliope.

"What an unexpected visit." The duchess fixed her son with a penetrating look. Then as if dismissing him, she turned fully toward Calliope. "If I had known you were coming, I would have had the cook prepare your favorite seedcakes."

"How kind of you to remember that I love them as well, Mother," Alexander said cheerfully, even though it was obvious that the duchess had not been addressing him.

Although nary a muscle twitched in Her Grace's smooth countenance, a faint shimmer of displeasure radiated from her. She gestured for them all to sit with an elegant sweep of her hand. Georgina sat between Charlotte and Calliope on one of the large sofas while Alexander took up a chair adjacent to them and farthest from his mother. As he adjusted his cane, his mother glanced at the object as if he'd brought a rotting cylinder of dung into her house rather than an exquisitely made walking stick.

No sooner had they all sat than the duke strolled into the room. Unlike his wife, he did not school his expression. Annoyance seeped from him. He managed the barest of greetings, only sparing a modicum of warmth for her and a bit more for Calliope. His own issue barely received grunts. He plopped down with an undisguised sigh and immediately began to drum his fingers against the gilded arm of his chair.

"To what pleasure do we owe this visit?" the duchess queried Alexander as she somehow acted both polite and disdainful at the same time. Georgina resisted the urge to shiver at the woman's easy coolness toward her son. Although Georgina had never been close to her half brother, she'd enjoyed a warm relationship with her dear papa. She remembered how she used to curl up in his lap as a child while he read her Greek stories and even his own essays.

"Since you both are so keen to have Miss Harrington and me marry, we thought it best to spend time as one happy family." Alexander managed to make the words sound not just sincere but hearty. He was utterly brilliant at obfuscating his sarcasm, but was he hiding something more? Pain, perhaps?

"I came to chaperone them on the carriage ride," Charlotte added, her tone just as bright as her brother's. "It is a wonderful benefit of being married—the ability to lend propriety to a situation by my mere presence."

Charlotte's father scowled openly, and his fingers moved even more rapidly against the abused wood. That tattoo sounded rageful now, instead of merely annoyed. Not a muscle of the duchess's face moved, but she somehow conveyed the impression of wincing. Perhaps she had squinted her right eye ever so slightly. The air had a decided chill about it.

Alexander was right. Georgina should have brought Crinitus Legatus for levity.

"And I accompanied them because you, Your Grace, are always a consummate hostess." Calliope's guileless look almost rivaled the duchess's. Still, the older woman studied Calliope for a beat or two, clearly trying to determine if she was being mocked. Calliope's expression remained absolutely serene.

"Thank you," Alexander's mother finally said.

"But do you know what I would like even more than seed-cakes?" Calliope asked.

"Tea?" The duchess suggested.

"No. I feel so dreadfully listless today. I need something even more invigorating." Calliope followed her weary statement with a long, laborious sigh.

"Coffee?"

"Even that strong brew won't cure my low spirits. What I really desire is snuff. I have heard that you have managed to find one of the best blends in England." Calliope turned to address the still-glowering duke. "My father mentioned how much he enjoyed the bit that Your Grace shared with him the last time you were together."

Calliope was truly a marvel at social manipulation. Despite her overly sugary words, she managed to make the flatteries sound real. The barest hint of a smile even touched one of the corners of the Duchess of Falcondale's mouth.

"I do not indulge in the pastime myself, but I ensure that any goods that enter my household are of the utmost quality." The duchess gracefully waved her hand toward her husband. "Please, Your Grace, would you be so kind as to share some snuff with Lady Calliope?"

"I wouldn't mind some myself," the duke grumbled as he pulled a silver box from his pocket.

Georgina barely prevented herself from leaning forward. She mustn't show too much interest in the object, at least not straightaway. From a distance, it did look similar to Lord Henry's. She thought she spotted the colorful stone lining, but she couldn't be certain.

When the duke took a healthy helping of powdered tobacco, Georgina resisted the urge to glance away. Although Algernon and Anne both indulged in the practice, she had always found it slightly revolting. She could not fathom why anyone would want to snort something up their nose—no matter how finely ground it was.

The duke handed the box to Calliope. She held it out from

her body, most likely to give Georgina a good view. At the sight of the lid's colorful interior, a jittery, almost sickening excitement swelled inside Georgina. It certainly looked like the gemstone that she'd kept digging up in her pit. The swirls of pink were the same startling hue as the rosy streaks in the helmet's mustache. The aquamarine shone like the Mediterranean Sea on a bright, cloudless day, contrasting against the pitch-black bands. The purple was the shade of the sky at dusk when the sun had just vanished over the horizon.

Calliope took only a small bit of the snuff. When they had schemed together on the way from Estbrook House, Calliope had confessed that she didn't much care for any tobacco products, especially after learning about their ties to the slave trade. But she had taken snuff before learning about its origins.

Georgina, though, was about to try it for her very first time. For a brief moment, she took her eyes off the box's lining to stare at the dark powdery contents. It looked like a sinister potion from a fairytale.

Think of Percy. If this is in any way connected to his disappearance, you can survive a bit of tobacco up your nose. You'll simply blow it out into your handkerchief later on.

"I would love to try some." Georgina attempted to sound nonchalant, but her request came out a bit too loud and a bit too bright.

"Oh, of course! It gives you the most marvelous jolt of energy!" Calliope immediately handed the container to Georgina. As soon as Georgina's fingers closed around the cool metallic lid, the duke cleared his throat.

"I did not take you for a snuff user. Your brother described you as a retiring miss from the countryside." The man's hazel eyes, more brownish-green than golden, flicked over her. There was a bit of surprise in those swampy depths and maybe even a hint of consideration.

Georgina suppressed a shiver. She much preferred his bored, lackadaisical greeting over this inspection. If he was anything like Algernon, attracting this man's attention boded nothing good.

"Do you mean to imply that it is unseemly for a woman to consume tobacco?" Georgina asked. "Queen Anne herself enjoyed snuff."

The duke's mouth hardened. Clearly, he had not expected her to refute him.

"I am certain that he does not think that, Miss Harrington." The duchess reached over and gently pulled on her husband's sleeve. She appeared to tug in the general direction of Calliope as she obviously warned her husband not to insult their well-connected guest.

"I was only expecting you to be more provincial." The duke was studying her now. Perhaps Georgina should have been more judicious with her response.

"Scholarly is the descriptor for Miss Harrington." Alexander's jovial voice burst through the room and thankfully drew his father's attention away from her. As the man turned toward his son, Georgina ran her fingers over the stone. It certainly felt like the same material that she'd been digging up.

When she touched the inner lid, she detected a few spidery indentations. Curious, she glanced at it closer. To her surprise, she saw that a single word had been etched into the gemstone: Merlin.

A chill tore through her. Why did everything circle back to a man who never existed? It seemed much too whimsical of a description for the staid duke. Yet, even though the lettering was a bit hard to read in the colorful mineral, Georgina knew she hadn't made a mistake.

"What are you looking at?" the duke barked in an imperious tone.

Georgina was so flustered that she nearly dropped the container. It bobbled dangerously to the side, but thankfully Charlotte reached over and helped steady it.

"I asked you a question," the duke snapped as he rose from his chair.

Some instinct informed Georgina to stay silent about what she had just seen. "I—I was just smelling it. Your blend gives off a very…um…pleasant smell."

It did not. It smelled like decomposing leaves in the fall.

"Have you actually partaken of snuff before?" The duke started to stride toward her.

"Oh yes. Most definitely." To prove her lie, Georgina grabbed a pinch of the tobacco. Holding it to her nose, she inhaled. Deeply.

That was a mistake.

A tickling sensation seized her right nostril. Desperately, she tried to contain the sneeze. It only made it worse.

Her whole body jerked back and then forward. Her eyes squeezed shut. Tobacco and goodness-knew-what-else flew from her nose. She might have also spat a little. Or a lot. It was difficult to determine exactly what was being expelled from her, the explosion was so violent.

She heard the duchess gasp. Calliope snorted. Charlotte made a little squeak that sounded like a smothered giggle. Alexander laughed openly. And the duke…the duke gargled something unintelligible.

Georgina cautiously opened one eye and dimly saw the duke frozen before her. She almost squeezed it shut again but realized avoidance would not make the situation go away. Slowly, she forced herself to focus her full gaze on the Duke of Falcondale. His face…glistened—that is, where it wasn't covered in dark flecks of wet tobacco.

The duke's mouth twitched violently, as if he was about to growl again. Given the rather drippy state of his face, he must have decided it might be prudent to keep his lips firmly pressed together. His body vibrated with suppressed rage, but he otherwise did not move. Disgust, ire, and shock had apparently rooted him in place.

"I suppose this snuff is not to my liking after all. It tickles my nose," Georgina said. Taking inspiration from Alexander's own approach with his parents, she made her voice as bright as possible.

Alexander absolutely roared with glee. Another suspiciously amused sniff escaped Calliope. The duchess *tsk*ed. Charlotte averted her gaze.

The duke simply did not move.

"But the case is very exquisite and unique. May I ask where you procured it? I would like to purchase one for Lord Alexander."

Falcondale pulled out his handkerchief and unfurled it with a snap of his wrist. With efficient strokes, he wiped his face, his glowering stare never leaving Georgina. Then with excruciating dignity, he folded up the cloth and returned it to his pocket.

He plucked the snuffbox from Georgina's hand. She desperately wanted to tug it back, but she didn't dare attract more attention to her interest in the item.

The duke straightened with great dignity, finally unlocking his gaze from Georgina's countenance. His entire bearing even stiffer than before, he regarded the room.

"I have a meeting with the steward of my property in the Lake District." Falcondale's words were clipped. With the precision of a soldier on drill, he turned and fairly marched from the room—presumably to change his sodden shirt rather than to actually discuss accounts.

"I do apologize." Georgina turned toward the duchess, who exuded a faint aura of exasperation. "That was the first time I have ever reacted that way."

It wasn't precisely a lie. She had never sneezed snuff before.

The duchess's lips tightened ever so slightly, but otherwise she showed no emotion. "I do purchase a more potent blend than most."

"It was exceedingly strong," Calliope chimed in, her voice remarkably free of laughter despite the amusement dancing in her eyes.

"Mother, I bought the most exquisite pocket-book the other day," Charlotte said, referring to the black and white pamphlets showing the latest fashions. The mention of the publication instantly steered the conversation away from the properties of powdered tobacco into the world of ruffles and bows.

Relieved to no longer be scrutinized, Georgina sank against the couch. Its straight back did not easily permit slouching, but Georgina didn't care. She'd take a bit of shoulder pain if it meant letting her tight muscles relax for one blessed moment.

The new information buzzed in her head along with the old conversation between Alexander's father and her brother. She had some pieces, but there were still so many missing. Perhaps she should try to write down the known facts as she did when trying to understand the disparate objects that she was unearthing in the pit.

Just then, Charlotte surreptitiously reached over and squeezed Georgina's hand while Calliope bumped her shoulder.

Georgina lifted her chin and her gaze met Alexander's. He gave her an encouraging wink. His perennial cheer injected a hope deep inside her.

Georgina wasn't alone anymore. She had friends—people whom she'd sought out to help her find Percy. Perhaps it was time that she shared her whole story with them.

Chapter Thirteen

reasure!" Pan called out gleefully as he circled above their heads in the back room of the Black Sheep. The coffeehouse was currently closed to customers, and Alexander and Georgina had gathered there with the group who had helped bring down Viscount Hawley.

"You are certain that your brother and my father were talking about treasure?" Alexander asked, ignoring the parrot and focusing on Georgina's recounting of the conversation that she'd overheard. Knowing that the damn betrothal caused her to be locked up made it hard for Alexander to listen. He wanted to fold her into his arms and protect her from any harm.

Yet, at the same time, he could not avoid the cruel irony inherent in his desire. His instinct to embrace Georgina perfectly suited his father's and Craie's schemes.

"Algernon spoke of a 'veritable treasure,' so there is a chance he meant metaphorically," Georgina said. "I am more and more certain, though, that he meant an actual one."

"You mentioned there was an upheaval during the week preceding the marriage discussion. You even spotted my father's carriage then, too." Alexander's voice sounded intense, even to his own ears. "Do you think their meeting had something to do with a treasure?"

"I—I am not sure." Georgina lowered her head and rubbed

her temples. "At first, I thought it could be my helmet that they were referring to."

"I am not precisely fond of Father, but I don't see him kidnapping people, especially someone of noble birth," Charlotte said. "It is not so much I believe in his goodness, but he would view such violence as vulgar."

"Does that mean we need to discover a recent gentlemanly pilfering?" Hannah rolled her eyes. "Have the crown jewels gone missing?"

Mr. Powys leaned forward, somehow infusing the commonplace action with dramatic flourish. He regarded each of them with a pointed, pregnant look before he spoke in a hushed tone. "Actually, there is an interesting rumor that the coronation spoon has disappeared."

"This is no time for theatrics or Banbury tales, Mr. Powys." Calliope sent an uncharacteristic frown in the playwright's direction. Since he was always chastising her for blitheness, she was probably only too glad to volley back the same criticism.

"I truly did hear murmurings about it." The theater owner straightened, and his Welsh accent deepened.

"The spoon is one of the few objects that survived the Glorious Revolution. If it disappeared, it would be the juiciest news in the land—not some idle piece of gossip." Calliope arched one golden eyebrow as if daring Mr. Powys to contradict her.

He happily accepted the challenge. "You may be from a high-ranked family with an impeccable Norman pedigree, but that doesn't mean that you are privy to all royal secrets."

"And you are?" Calliope retorted.

"One of the actresses at my theater has a sister who works at a certain kind of establishment that caters to royal guards, including those who protect the Tower." Mr. Powys tipped back in his chair as if daring Calliope to gainsay him again. "Two of her clients were discussing the matter, and she overheard."

"The Jacobite Rebellion may have been more than a decade ago, but its specter still haunts the king." Sophia thoughtfully tapped her finger against her cup. "It does make a certain sense that he would keep the disappearance of the spoon a secret."

"If the king even knows. The guards might be hoping to find it before anyone realizes it is gone," Hannah added.

"I don't believe Father would steal from the king," Alexander broke in, afraid the conversation was getting further and further afield.

"The trinket is rather useless. You couldn't sell it, and if you melted it down, the gold wouldn't be worth much," Mr. Belle pointed out.

"Can we please stop talking about a *spoon*?" Georgina burst out impatiently.

The room immediately went silent—even Mr. Powys looked sheepish. Still, he tried to defend himself. "Well, it isn't just an instrument for eating but for anointing—"

"I know what a coronation spoon is, and normally I would like nothing more than to discuss the details of an obscure antique object. But I highly doubt my half brother is skulking about with the Duke of Falcondale to pocket items from the Treasury. Frankly, Algernon has neither the imagination nor the intelligence for such a scheme. More importantly, I think the treasure has something to do with me."

"Then it is the helmet after all?" Alexander asked as renewed concern whipped through him. Although he still could not imagine his father abducting the son of a duke over ancient armor, Percy had disappeared while in possession of the antique. Already, Algernon had imprisoned Georgina for objecting to a marriage that he and his father were masterminding. What danger was she in?

Georgina shook her head and then sucked in a deep breath. "While you were all discussing the coronation spoon, I was finally able to organize my thoughts. I own a bit of land, you see, where my pit is. Algernon has control of it as administrator of my father's trust for me, but it is ultimately mine."

"Does it have any value?" Sophia asked.

"Not much—at least I didn't think it did," Georgina said. "My father bought it for the interesting mounds. He always hoped something was buried in it—his own miniature Herculaneum. But other than that, the property is just a narrow strip with a modest country house. It does have a bit of sea frontage but only at the tip."

"Do you feel differently about its value now?" Alexander asked, reaching for the top of his cane. Feeling the Nemean lion's teeth bite into his thumb steadied him, giving him something to concentrate on other than his worry for Georgina.

"While searching the first barrow, my workers and I dug up many objects made from a strange gemstone with bands of pink, purple, aquamarine, and jet black. Even the helmet has pieces inlaid as ornamentation. I'd never seen anything like the colorful mineral until Lord Henry dropped his snuffbox and I saw the inside," Georgina explained. "Then you said that your father owned a similar one."

"That's why you needed to see the box!" Calliope cried out. "You wanted to make sure it was the same material."

"Yes," Georgina nodded. "The coloration is identical. It must be mined from the same vein."

Worry coursed through Alexander. "You're thinking that the source of this gemstone is on your land."

Georgina huffed out a breath that was half a laugh. "It does sound absurd now that I voice it—a hidden trove of pretty rocks on my minuscule strip of soil in Essex. But if such a deposit does exist, and Algernon knows about it, he would want it—but by the terms of the trust, the gems are mine."

"But if you were to marry me, I'd have ownership—unless as part of the marriage settlement, it was agreed that your brother would get some rights to the minerals," Alexander said as his father's scheme with Craie became clear. He could picture his father helping another lord steal from a female relation if it meant securing a bride with impeccable bloodlines for his son.

Georgina jerked as if she'd just been splashed in the face with cold water. "Your words, they're so close to what the men were discussing that I can hear them clearly."

"Unfortunately, such a scheme does seem like something Father would be part of," Charlotte said softly. "He is exceedingly medieval in his views of marriage. He would not regard it as stealing, but only as enhancing both families' fortunes to a mutual satisfaction."

"I agree," Alexander forced out as old memories bombarded him, along with the guilt that he could not entirely escape.

"What exactly is this rock?" Mr. Belle asked. "And how valuable is it?"

"I am not sure," Georgina admitted. "It reminds me of a stone that Pliny the Elder described in his *Naturalis Historia*, but this one is more colorful than the purple and white one that he mentioned. Whatever it is, it's rare and pretty enough, especially when polished, that it definitely possesses some worth. It's not a diamond, but it's not fool's gold, either."

"Do you think their scheme has anything to do with Percy's disappearance?" Sophia asked. "You mentioned that the helmet had the gem inlaid into it. Could they have been afraid that your antiquity would result in the discovery of their illegal mine?"

"Perhaps…" Georgina said slowly. "Though I am not sure how they would have learned about it. Algernon has no interest in antiquities, nor do his friends."

"Neither does Father," Alexander said.

"But Lord Percy did claim that it was Arthur's," Charlotte pointed out. "There could be rumors circulating about the helmet because of that. Mother especially could have heard due to the literary connection. Perhaps she mentioned it to Father at breakfast."

"It's possible," Alexander agreed. His parents were barely companions, but they did engage in light conversation each morning—well, Mother did. The duke mostly concentrated on his customary soft-boiled eggs and kippers.

"Or it could be that the marriage scheme and your cousin's disappearance are entirely separate matters. You went to Elysian Fields. Did you meet anyone there who you suspect stole the helmet?" Mr. Belle asked.

"A few. Lord Clifville mentioned that Lord Henry Talbot wanted to purchase it, but Percy refused. There's also my father's old rival, the Duke of Foxglen. He knew about the find, too," Georgina said. "I've never liked him, and he did plagiarize my father. But purloining research is vastly different from ambushing a man. Foxglen isn't physically able to attack my cousin, but he could have hired men."

"Or sent his grandson Lord Malbarry," Alexander added.

"Malbarry is known as Foxglen's quiet shadow," Calliope said.

"Foxglen and Malbarry did it." Hannah punctuated her declaration by thumping her fist against the table in front of her. Alexander was used to his cousin being animated about her opinions, but she seemed even more intense than normal.

Everyone turned at Hannah's outburst. Georgina even jumped.

"Goodness, Hannah." Sophia gave her cousin a nudge. "There's no need to startle us."

"How can you be so nonchalant?" Hannah slammed her palm down this time. "It's Foxglen who they're talking about."

"Just because our fathers suffered due to Foxglen doesn't mean that he's guilty." Sophia gently patted Hannah's arm. "And we know nothing about Malbarry. He wasn't even alive when our fathers were caught poaching."

"Foxglen illegally enclosed common grazing land, and our fathers' family was starving. They had no choice but to poach, but Foxglen still had them deported to become indentured servants. If your mother hadn't attacked their ship and let them join her pirate crew, they would have spent fourteen years laboring in the colonies for trying to feed their siblings." This time Hannah waved her arms furiously instead of smacking the table. "We've suspected for a long time that Foxglen's family's wealth comes from something criminal. We just cannot figure out what."

"My middle brother is just as vicious as my elder one." Matthew broke into the conversation, his quiet voice a sharp contrast to Hannah's boisterousness. "I could see him attacking Lord Percy if Miss Harrington's cousin possessed something that Henry wanted."

"As can I," Alexander added as old memories once again sprouted up like a disgusting black fungus. "But like Sophia said about Foxglen and Malbarry, we cannot let past misconduct sway us. Pendergrast is missing, and there's no time to chase old prejudices."

"The only solid clue that we have is the snuffbox and its potential connection to your land," Sophia pointed out.

"Perhaps I should try to find the source of the gemstone,"

Georgina said. "The property isn't that big. It won't be hard to search."

"If it is such a small parcel, wouldn't you have noticed someone mining precious minerals?" Tavish asked.

"I avoid the headlands," Georgina explained. "I live in Essex, after all, and it is not good for one's continued health to be too interested about what is happening on the coast. But it seems like circumstances are compelling me to finally explore the cliffs."

An image of Georgina marching into a cave filled with armed smugglers popped into Alexander's mind. He wanted to protest, to tell her to stay safe in London at Estbrook House while he explored her property. But he didn't.

In the spring, he'd ended up placing his sister in more danger when he didn't include her in his plans to unmask the viscount. Revealing Hawley's crimes had been Charlotte's fight, just like this one was Georgina's. But that didn't mean that he couldn't assist.

"If you'll have me, I'll accompany you," Alexander said.

"We'll all go," Charlotte added, laying her hand over his.

Alexander glanced at his sister, and he could see the worry shimmering in her gaze. He understood it well, having felt it for her only months earlier.

Georgina shook her head. "I don't think that would be wise. A large group would draw too much attention, especially in this part of Essex. My village is extremely clannish. Alexander has visited before with Percy. Although no one would confide in him, they won't view his presence with as much suspicion."

"Just the two of you alone would be dangerous," Matthew added, looking just as concerned as his wife.

"If my brother and the Duke of Falcondale are the ones who

ambushed my cousin, I cannot alert them to the fact that I have suspicions about the gemstones. They could hide evidence…or worse. I can only hope Percy is alive. If he is, I don't want to trigger a panic that could result in his death."

"She's right," Mr. Powys said.

Charlotte bit her lip and then reluctantly nodded. "I suppose it can't be helped. But if you two have not returned to London within the week, we are all traveling down. You must also write to us each day. If I do not hear from you, I will follow."

"We'll be safe, Lottie. I promise," Alexander said with more conviction than he felt. He couldn't escape a sense of apprehension that had taken up an uncomfortable residence in his gut. He hoped that the trip to Essex would not prove to be a calamity.

⚜

The reason for the carriage ride might be ominous, but the day was otherwise lovely. A soft breeze countered the summer heat. Fluffy clouds—the perfect kind for make-believe dragons and puffy castles—dotted the otherwise blue sky. The hedgerows bustled with country life. The nesting song thrushes peeped out their cheerful, lilting tunes while fat hares full of clover slowly loped off the road at the sound of approaching hooves. Even the red squirrels seemed a bit lumbering, as if they were enjoying lazy, halcyon days before the hustle and bustle of fall foraging.

"I never thought a curricle ride could be so pleasant." Georgina, who was dressed in her male attire, stretched her arms out wide. It was their second day of travel, and they'd just left the coaching inn, where they'd slept in separate rooms the night before.

In a basket secured to the back of the vehicle, Ruffian Caesar emitted a snort, as if he agreed with his mistress. Alexander couldn't stop his lips from stretching upward, especially when Georgina's hand brushed against his shoulder. He'd plastered on so many fake grins throughout the years that even he had trouble telling which ones were real and which were fake. But with Georgina, each smile was absolutely genuine.

"Oops." Georgina yanked back her hand as if he were red-hot iron. "I do apologize."

Alexander half expected her to put her fingers in her mouth and suck them…which was probably not the wisest direction for his thoughts to meander. His entire body already felt bombarded by a million pinpricks of light by her mere proximity.

"I'm not sorry." Alexander didn't try to stop the huskiness creeping into his voice. Whenever he had a moment alone in the past three days, he'd thought about their kiss. At first, they'd been so busy chasing clues that there hadn't been time to mention their embrace. Then yesterday, he hadn't wanted to bring it up in case it made her uncomfortable. But he did wonder if she daydreamed about it as much as he.

"Pardon?" Georgina asked, sounding confused at first. Very quickly, though, understanding flashed across her countenance. To his delight, she did not seem embarrassed. Instead, her mouth quirked into an expression that he could only describe as intrigued.

"About those last minutes in the ballroom. I don't regret what happened. In fact, I very much enjoyed it. But I will understand if you regard it differently. If you do, I promise that I won't mention it again." Alexander spoke with a lightness that he didn't feel, but he did mean his words. He wouldn't pressure Georgina.

"I am the one who initiated the kiss. Why would I be opposed to discussing it?"

Alexander's entire being froze and then suddenly roared gloriously back to life. "Just discussing?"

The tips of Georgina's lips turned upward in a decidedly wolfish tilt. "I am amenable to additional explorations."

A hearty laugh escaped Alexander, and he couldn't help but lean over and buss Georgina's cheek. When she whirled in his direction, he was already staring ahead and whistling.

"Incorrigible rogue."

He started to chuckle, but then he felt her lips against his temple. When he turned in her direction, he found her looking at the road, humming her own jaunty little tune.

"Minx."

"I am being one, aren't I? I never suspected I possessed such potential."

Georgina's palpable pride caused warmth and something hotter to flow through Alexander. He wanted to pull back on the leathers and stop the curricle. He imagined securing the horses and heading to one of the copses of trees, far enough from the road for privacy. Or perhaps they could find an inn.

Or maybe he was the one needing to be reined in and not his matched set of bays. Yes, Georgina seemed keen on exchanging a kiss or two. But she was an innocent—an innocent who didn't want to marry him and who lived at the mercy of her relatives. Alexander had to ensure he didn't cross boundaries that should never be breached.

But that didn't mean all amorous activities were entirely proscribed.

"You know, I did promise to teach you to drive a curricle." Alexander leaned in Georgina's direction and gave her shoulder a teasing nudge.

"Ohhh…" Georgina hung onto the sound, clearly realizing his ploy.

"That would require me to place my arms around you…like an embrace."

"Hmm…" Georgina's mouth pressed together in a perfectly kissable pout. "Is that so?"

"Very. We wouldn't want to risk the team bolting." Alexander lowered the timbre of his voice and nearly whispered the words in her ear. To his absolute delight, she shivered.

"Oh, yes. We must consider safety." She pressed against him, almost leaning her head against his shoulder. He glanced down, and his heart simply stuttered at the desire shimmering in her brown eyes. It was a good thing that he was talented at the leathers and that his team was so well trained. If not, he might have crashed the carriage.

Before Alexander's consciousness completely turned into nothing but mushy thoughts, Georgina straightened. Her impish expression fled, replaced by her more familiar thoughtful one.

"But would we not attract attention?" Georgina asked.

"This is a lonely stretch of the road," Alexander pointed out. "And you're small enough and your features soft enough that someone in a passing carriage might think I'm a father teaching his teenage son how to drive."

Georgina still hesitated, and Alexander added, "I will take care with your reputation, Georgina."

His promise seemed to satisfy her as once more she pressed her body flush against his. "Show me how to manage a team."

As Alexander slung his right arm around her slim back, it struck him how good it felt just to hold her. It was madness, really. This need to be close.

"So you hold the reins like so," Alexander said, adjusting her hands around the leathers. There was both an elegance and a strength in her fingers. "Keep a firm hand on the reins. Just enough pressure to let the horses know you're there, but not enough to hold them back. Prospero and Caliban know what they're supposed to do, but that doesn't mean they always listen. Keep a close eye to make sure they're keeping straight ahead and not slacking."

Georgina sucked in one corner of her lip as she followed his instructions. She'd done the same when they'd wrestled at Estbrook house. Alexander found her ability to absorb new information absolutely fascinating. He wondered what it would be like to witness her writing one of her treatises—something he never would have imagined wanting to watch. Would she worry her lip the entire time?

❧

Ten minutes later, Alexander was still fascinated by Georgina's ability to concentrate on a task. He was even more taken with holding on to her. Despite the summer heat, it felt good to be pressed together as they crept along a straight stretch. Even the trees and tall hedges around them formed a green tunnel to guide the bays forward. It was the perfect spot for Georgina to drive the team without him hovering over her…but he didn't want to let go. At all.

That, however, would be a disservice to Georgina. He'd promised to teach her, even if he'd been clear that the lessons were partially an excuse to embrace.

"Do you think you can control Prospero and Caliban yourself?" Alexander asked, before he could succumb to pure selfishness.

"Oh, most certainly," Georgina said with utter conviction as she shifted away from him. "Do you think I'm ready?"

"Yes." Alexander tried not to sound miffed that she didn't seem at all reluctant to leave his side.

While he inched back toward his spot on the bench, Georgina

practically shoved him away. His disgruntled feeling faded when he spied her joyful expression. It was patently clear that she was pleased with her ability to control the powerful team rather than be a mere passenger. Alexander knew exactly how she felt. After all, it was what compelled him to race curricles.

"This is a glorious day, is it not?" Georgina's voice rang with a brightness that seemed to light up the dark places within Alexander.

"Yes. Glorious indeed," Alexander said, but he wasn't looking at the countryside. His entire being was focused on Georgina... which was perhaps why he missed the signs of danger.

Chapter Fourteen

When Georgina first heard the sharp crack, her brain registered it as a thunderclap, despite the cloudless blue sky. In the next moment, she wondered if a tree branch had split in two and fallen. By the third beat, she no longer had the wherewithal to attempt to identify the sound. Her entire concentration was centered upon preventing hers, Alexander's, and Caesar Ruffian's untimely deaths.

The horses had bolted.

Taut reins ran painfully through Georgina's hands as pain radiated through the muscles of her arms. She wasn't even capable of hauling backward. It took all her strength just to hold on to the strips of leather. Her body whipped back and forth, slamming against Alexander as the team shied to the left. To her horror, she felt herself fly half out of her seat as the bays halted abruptly. She was then yanked by the reins as the team surged forward again. Just as she began to pitch over the curricle's tongue, a strong arm encircled her waist.

Georgina slammed against Alexander's chest, the air nearly whooshing out of her. As she scrambled to make sense of the situation, he'd already unraveled one of the reins from her hand. He half spun, half pushed her away, sending her down against the carriage bench. Dazedly, she watched while he wrapped his fingers around the second leather strap. As he yanked back on the team, the silk fabric of his coat slid over his tightened muscles. His sleeves bunched back, revealing his straining tendons.

Ruffian Caesar, who was thankfully secure in his half-lidded basket, emitted a stream of panicked barks. His little head peeked out from the small opening at the top, but the rest of him remained inside the wicker container.

Georgina started to rise, wanting to help in some way. Before she could, Alexander pushed her back down with an elbow. "Stay down. We're being fired upon."

"Someone's shooting at us?" Georgina shouted.

As if in answer to her question, another boom crackled through the air. Ruffian Caesar growled. Dirt flew up from the ground to the left of their carriage. Alexander swore and leaned over the horses, calling their names. Under control now, the beasts moved faster.

"Get my pistols!" Alexander ordered, his voice sounding as strained as his body. "They're in the box under the seat."

"Why are you sitting upright? Duck!" Georgina yelled, even as she complied with his command. She tried to kneel, but at the speed they were traveling, she fell into a rather undignified heap in the well of the conveyance. Her shoulder slammed violently against the wooden dash. Ignoring the pain shooting down her arm, she tried to scramble to all fours.

"Just... give me... a firearm!" Alexander huffed out.

Realizing neither questions nor instructions were beneficial, Georgina focused on her search for a small chest. Sure enough, she discovered a rectangular container beneath Alexander's feet. It had a lock on it, but fortunately it was open. Throwing back the hinged lid, Georgina grabbed one of the ornately made pieces.

"Here!" she shouted. Still bouncing around in the well, Georgina held out the weapon to Alexander. Collecting reins in one hand, he grabbed it. Until now he'd only been bracing himself with his good leg, but he slammed both feet against the floor of the conveyance. Still gripping the leathers, he swung his body halfway around. Despite the jostling, he managed to keep the weapon steady...at least to Georgina's untrained eye. Georgina followed the direction of the barrel and spotted a figure on horseback lurking in the trees behind them. Alexander aimed the firearm toward their attacker. Between the distance, the carriage speed, and the shifting, dappled shadows, Georgina could not make out the fellow's features. Even his form was difficult to ascertain.

Sparks flew from the lock of Alexander's pistol, followed by a jet of smoke and flame from the muzzle. An acrid scent drifted past Georgina's nostrils. A scream welled up inside her, but she jammed it back down her throat. She didn't want to distract him. Ruffian Caesar's yapping was enough additional noise.

"Hand me the other pistol!" Alexander roared, his voice much louder than necessary. Georgina realized that his words were meant for the villain as much as for her. Thankful that her hands remained steady, Georgina passed him the second firearm.

Alexander didn't shoot this time. Instead, he swiveled back and forth. Somehow, he managed to control the thundering team even as he kept the assailant in his sights. Georgina had never imagined finding a sportsman heroic, but witnessing Alexander right now...seeing his muscles strain to handle the team one-handed...realizing that he was risking a lead ball...it was impressive. More than impressive.

The figure in the leafy shadows grew smaller and smaller. He didn't seem inclined to follow, not with Alexander's pistol at the ready.

"Keep watch." Alexander's normally jovial drawl was clipped, even officious. "The road's becoming curvy. At this speed, I'll need to train my eyes forward. If you spy our stalker, shout."

Georgina began to nod and then realized that the last thing Alexander needed was another visual task. "Yes. I will."

"Hold on!" Alexander shouted. "We're at the first bend."

The carriage swung violently around the sharp curve. Even clinging desperately to the seat, Georgina felt her body skid. Her knees chafed against the floor of the curricle, and her hip nearly left the carriage. Her thumb scraped along the wooden underside of the bench while her fingers dug desperately into the soft upholstery. Somehow, she managed to stay inside.

"You best get back onto the seat," Alexander shouted.

As the horses pounded down a short stretch of straight road, Georgina flopped onto the cushion. Her breath came in short huffs, both from the exertion and the excitement. Fear mixed with a strange exhilaration. Could part of her actually be enjoying this wild, wild ride?

Surely not. Yet she couldn't deny that it wasn't just terror making her heart dance inside her chest. Because amid all the alarm lurked a sense of adventure.

"Mind your grip!" Alexander called out.

She clung to the seat as she faced backward, her eyes peeled for their enemy. This time she pressed her knees into the padding for additional anchorage. Ruffian Caesar eyed her curiously before he burst into another series of yaps.

"Making a hard left!" Alexander roared.

Georgina's body swung violently to the right, just as the left wheel lifted from the ground. Her heart seemed to fly upward in her chest, or perhaps it was her stomach catapulting from its usual position. A sound tore from her lips...but it wasn't a gasp of alarm. To her shock, it was a battle cry—one that would make a Scythian warrior proud.

The conveyance slammed back down on the rutted path. Alexander let out a whoop of his own—the sound joyous and triumphant. It thundered through Georgina, triggering a swell of exhilaration. Somehow, despite the breakneck speed and the different positions of their bodies, their eyes met for the briefest of moments.

But it was enough to send sharp, twinkling sensations shimmering through Georgina's body. Enough to ignite the excitement already churning in her gut. Enough to confirm that they were sharing this adventure, this thrill.

Alexander laughed—a full-bodied one that almost drowned out the air rushing past Georgina's ears. An echoing rumble built inside her until mirth tumbled from her lips. Her high peals mixed with his low chuckle. Ruffian Caesar pointed his black nose into the air and woofed.

"Turning right!" Alexander called out.

This time, Georgina was even more prepared for being tossed about. The right wheel popped up. If she'd been in this carriage with anyone else, she would have been terrified.

But not with Alexander.

Instead, their enthusiastic shouts mingled. She trusted him, she realized. It wasn't just his skill—even though he had that in abundance. Nor was it his confidence. Instead, it was a bone-deep feeling—nay, a certainty—that he wouldn't place her in unnecessary danger. Even steeped in peril, he made Georgina feel safe.

She hadn't felt this secure for a long time. Not since her father drew his last breath after his wasting illness.

Nor had Georgina experienced this level of joy. And she wanted to hold on to it, revel in it as long as she could.

The road stretched straight again, and Alexander gave the team their head. The bays galloped down the wide path, their heads extended, their manes rippling in the wind they created. Even though Georgina still kept watch behind them, she couldn't help but steal looks over her shoulder at the magnificent horses... and their owner.

Alexander was smiling now—like always. But there was something different about his grin. It seemed deeper, more genuine. He was loving this—this fast, perilous ride.

A sweet ache started in Georgina's heart and spread throughout her body. A deep urgent throb thudded through her, demanding her to take action. But what action?

Alexander. She needed Alexander. This laughing, joyous, adventurous man.

She'd felt similar to this when she'd kissed him in the Estbrook ballroom. But this was more intense... more desperate. Raw.

The road began to branch off. Alexander slowed the team's pace as they passed a few small lanes. Finally, he turned off onto a small, shaded path. They had traveled only a few yards when he pulled the team behind a large hedge.

"Prospero and Caliban need to rest," Alexander explained as he climbed down from the curricle. He leaned more heavily on his cane than usual as he tied the horses' reins to a nearby branch. He put enough slack in the line that they could comfortably lower their heads to graze. He returned to the curricle and lifted Ruffian Caesar down from his basket. After he secured the dog's lead to a nearby tree, he turned in Georgina's direction. "We're sheltered from the main road here, but we can still see it. We have a chance to determine if the villain is following us."

"That..." Georgina tried to swallow back the unruly need pulsating through her. "That makes sense."

Alexander whipped his head in her direction, his hazel eyes golden with concern. Despite his uneven stride, he made his way

swiftly back to the curricle. Barely employing his legs as leverage, he used his arms to swing himself onto the bench next to
her. He reached forward and gently rubbed his thumb against
her cheek, leaving a trail of sparks across her skin.

But Georgina didn't want tender ministrations right now.
Or, at least, that wasn't all she desired.

"I apologize. I should have been more considerate of your
feelings. The ride itself must have been frightening—" Alexander began.

Georgina couldn't fight the impulse pumping through her.
She leaned forward, capturing Alexander's mouth with her own.
Her lips moved against his with a greediness that she wasn't
embarrassed to show. Latching her arms around his body, she
pulled him close. She wanted to feel all of him in the most ele-
mental way.

A surprise sound whooshed from him, but a moment later,
his tongue plunged into her mouth. He kissed with the abandon that she'd craved. Still, it didn't seem enough. They were
pressed against each other—her softness against his hard
contours.

She slid her hands to his back, wishing that he didn't have
on a coat, waistcoat, and shirt. The intriguing bands of muscles both beguiled and taunted her. She yearned to explore the
ridges without layers between them. What would it be like to
touch his bare flesh, to fully feel the heat he generated?

At least her man's attire afforded her an unexpected, but welcome, kind of freedom. Without her skirts and petticoats, there
was no pesky voluminous material separating her from Alexander. But their seated position still kept their lower halves apart.
And Georgina didn't want that.

Her fingers pressed against Alexander's firm chest. She gave a little but insistent push. His lips curved against her mouth, and his grin tasted as wicked as she felt. He lowered them both to the bench with her on top.

Their lips never left each other's. The kiss only deepened, their mouths moving in a rhythm that was at once new yet startlingly familiar. It called to something inside Georgina—that wild part that had awakened during their flight from their attacker. Her whole body wanted to move to the tantalizing tempo. Something hard pressed into the juncture of her thighs. Pleasure shot through her first, then understanding. This, this is what she'd read about in *Lysistrata*. But, oh, she didn't think a man's hardened cock could feel so good.

Alexander undid the buttons on her coat, and the fabric slipped from her shoulders. She reached for his outer garment and made quick work of the fastenings. They undid each other's waistcoats. Alexander's hands slid under her shirt, and he tugged at the binding around her chest. The strip of material fell away. Nothing but thin linen and silk breeches separated their bodies now.

Alexander's lips moved from hers and skimmed along her throat. His fingers were still under her shirt as they traced slowly over her bare skin. The calluses he'd acquired from driving carriages brushed against her, triggering the most wonderful shivers. The quaking of her body seemed to encourage Alexander, and his tongue darted against her moistened skin. Delicious sensations rioted through her already sensitized nerves. Helpless against the onslaught, she wriggled against him. Yet that only made the pressure inside her grow.

Alexander groaned, his body beginning to buck under hers. Experimentally, she kissed his neck, and the taste of salt touched her lips. To her delight, he also trembled. Their pants and moans filled the hot summer air, and Georgina found herself lost in a world that only contained Alexander and the brilliant sensations that he wrought.

Until the clop of horse's hooves.

In one swift movement, Alexander switched their positions. His broad back covered her chest, his legs still entwined in hers. But he wasn't kissing her anymore. Instead, his head was up, his eyes scanning their surroundings.

Cold fear dissolved the sparks of pleasure coursing through Georgina. Alexander was using his own body to shield hers. If their attacker discovered them now, they were vulnerable—the horses tied up, Ruffian Caesar sniffing a bush, Alexander's pistols back in their box, and half their clothes in a heap on the floor of the curricle.

What had they been thinking?

Well, they hadn't been. That much was clear.

"It's just a farmer off to market. I don't think the villain is following us." The relief in Alexander's voice was palpable to Georgina. After all, she felt it with all her being, too.

"Even if we're not in danger, we can't do this—at least not here." Alexander pulled them both into a sitting position. "If we don't wish a marriage foisted upon us, we cannot take matters too far."

"No. No, we can't." Georgina drew in a steadying breath despite a sudden pang of something that felt suspiciously like hurt. She didn't want to be wedded to a sportsman...right? But Alexander was different from her brother and his cronies.

"Less than a few hours ago, I promised to take care of your reputation, and now I've come a hair's breadth of seducing you right by a thoroughfare leading to London! If your half brother learned of our near-coupling and used this moment to threaten you more, I'd never forgive myself." Alexander shoved his hand in his already mussed hair. Auburn clumps fell from his queue, framing his face in fiery splendor.

Georgina's heart squeezed for more reasons than she cared to explore. Was Alexander truly just worried about her future, or was he also concerned that discovery would force his hand as well? And why did she care about the answer?

"Well, we weren't seen," Georgina said, trying to recover her practicality. "There's no harm done."

Alexander scrubbed his hands over his face. "Maybe it is too dangerous for us to embrace. I lose all control when I'm with you."

The dying embers inside Georgina flashed back to full flame. "Do I affect you that much?"

"Yes." The admission came out as a groan. Alexander still had his face buried in his palms as he dropped his shoulders to his knees. He looked like a man utterly overpowered by emotions— emotions for *her*.

"Truly?" Georgina prodded as euphoric giddiness hummed through her, reawakening that reckless wildness. His confession did much to dispel the prick of hurt.

"Yes." Alexander's shoulders sank even further in defeat. "If that farmer hadn't come by when he did…"

Georgina waited anxiously for Alexander to finish, but he annoyingly stopped talking. Her heart thud-skipped in a painful, yet also strangely pleasurable, pattern.

"Then what?" she prompted. Even to her own ears, her voice sounded breathless and more than a little strained.

"I might have gotten you with child, and then you would have had no choice but to wed me."

Alexander, a modern Adonis, found her, a wallflower, that alluring? Georgina had never thought herself the kind of woman capable of tempting a man—let alone beyond his limits.

Her blood thundered through her body, along with a new sense of power. She'd spent much of her life feeling trapped, but now there was a rush of freedom. And she wanted to seize it.

"But aren't there other things we can do? Things that do not lead to conception?" The naughty words flew from Georgina's lips, and she didn't have any desire to stop them.

Alexander's palms slid from his face. He turned slowly in her direction. His countenance was a lovely mix of pure shock, startled wonder, and, most importantly, blatant hunger.

An uncharacteristic giggle escaped Georgina. She was flirting, actually flirting. And she liked it.

"I don't mean here," she said as she reached down and handed Alexander his discarded coat and waistcoat. "You are right about the danger. But, fortunately, we are traveling to my cottage. My entirely empty cottage."

Alexander visibly swallowed. "Is that so?"

Georgina was absurdly glad that Alexander wasn't trying to play the gallant and ask her if she comprehended her own intentions. She may be a spinster, but she knew exactly what she was proposing.

"Most definitely." Georgina's words were a promise, not just to Alexander but to herself.

A huge grin stretched across Alexander's face. He smiled so often, yet this one was different. This particular beam seemed like a special gift meant just for her.

Chapter Fifteen

The first thing that Alexander noticed about Georgina's house was the dust. Each step they took disturbed hundreds of gray specks that floated in the waning light. If it wasn't for the pink-hued sunset, the large cottage might have felt like the abode of specters. An almost suffocating mustiness hung in the air, the smell of disuse and neglect. The cloths flung over the furniture had accumulated a visible layer of fine powder. Cobwebs hung everywhere, the strands glinting in the rosy glow.

With Ruffian Caesar prancing at her feet, Georgina stood in the center of the study, a fond, bittersweet expression on her face. She had the hazy look of someone not seeing the actual vista but an old, cherished memory.

Alexander lingered in the doorframe, giving Georgina space for her recollections. He felt like an interloper or perhaps even a trespasser. He'd grown up treated as an intruder, but this time, he sensed no malice, no annoyance at his presence. It was simply that Georgina's connection to this thatched dwelling had drawn her back into the past, leaving him in the present.

"I spent so many cheerful days here." Even Georgina's voice sounded far away. It contained a timbre that he hadn't heard before. She waved her hand in the direction of a vaguely desk-shaped lump covered in heavy fabric. "Papa would sit there, working on his latest treatise. Sometimes he'd have Roman artifacts in front of him. He was very good at sketching. I'd sit and watch, drawing them myself. I'd try to write descriptions, too. I had terrible penmanship back then and even worse spelling, but Papa always praised me. Oh, he'd correct my grammar and offer suggestions, but always kindly and wrapped in so many compliments. Sometimes, whenever I have a particularly difficult day, I still hear him encouraging me."

"He sounds like he was a marvelous man and an even better father." Alexander tried desperately to keep his own voice from thickening. He wondered what it would have been like to receive just a sliver of that affection from his own sire. His trips into the duke's study had always left him trembling and wracked with the sensation of never being good enough.

But this wasn't the time for Alexander to search his soul. It was Georgina's.

She'd fallen asleep on his shoulder about a half an hour after their passionate interlude. She hadn't woken up until they'd drawn close to her village. When she'd stretched awake and given him directions, her demeanor had been markedly different from the bold coquette who'd dozed off.

Alexander wouldn't be entirely truthful if he claimed no disappointment. He'd spent the last few hours imagining just how he could pleasure Georgina without risking pregnancy. He'd been keen to employ his mouth in very, very creative ways.

But it was apparent that introspection, and not lovemaking, was on her mind. There was a kind of melancholy wrapped around her, and Alexander respected her need for quietude.

It was probably for the best, anyway. His foot and leg were still smarting from the pressure he'd placed on his weaker side when he handled the team and shot at the villain. And being cooped up in a carriage for hours and hours had never been easy on him.

Quit sniveling. You've been sitting all day. My heir can't act like a weakling.

The old words cut through Alexander like a dull, rusty sword, leaving flecks behind to fester. He hadn't felt them this sharply in years. But something about being with Georgina, listening to her old recollections, made him vulnerable—as if layers of protection had fallen away without him noticing, leaving him exposed.

"The room used to smell like the soap Papa used," Georgina said wistfully, drawing Alexander out of his thoughts and back into hers. "That's gone now. Has been for years. Now it's just the scent of old, moldering books."

Alexander stepped through the threshold and entered the room for the first time. Carefully, gently, he placed his hand on Georgina's shoulder. She didn't shake him off, so he kept it there, offering what comfort he could.

"You mentioned that he was an antiquarian, too. Is that where your love of the past comes from?" Alexander asked, sensing that Georgina needed to talk about her father. And Alexander found himself wanting to know. He suddenly felt a swell of gratitude to this man who'd raised such a fiercely inquisitive daughter.

"Yes," Georgina nodded. "When I was a child, he took me to Europe, even when his own relatives told him it was no place for a widower to cart around a young girl. We visited all the grand sights: the Coliseum, the Parthenon, and parts of the Villa of Lucullus in Naples. Papa had even spoken of us traveling to Egypt to see the famed pyramids—the last of the seven ancient wonders. But he fell sick before he could arrange another trip."

"You were close to your father?"

"Oh, yes." Georgina leaned against Alexander's chest, her

head resting below his collarbone. "It was his dream to dig up the mound where I discovered the helmet. He—well, we'd—been inspired by the work we saw at Herculaneum—he in an academic way and me with the unbridled excitement of a child."

Alexander felt a true smile spread across his face. "I can just imagine you running around the mound, covered head to toe in mud."

Georgina laughed. "Indeed. And I wore breeches under my skirts. It horrified all sides of my father's family. Although he was a fourth son, he came from impeccable bloodlines, all dating back to William the Conqueror. Appearances must be maintained."

"Yes." Alexander breathed out the word, hoping Georgina didn't detect how much it hurt. He knew all too well about preserving precious familial lineage. But he wouldn't focus on the latter part of Georgina's statement. Instead, he'd picture her, spade in hand as she gamboled after her father.

"We had barely removed much soil when Father got weak," Georgina explained. "When he died, Algernon moved me into his house—the large mansion that we passed on the way here. This cottage was closed up, and all the digging stopped. I used to sneak over to my property and shovel a few clods of dirt, but it wasn't until I started making money assessing antiquities that I had the funds to hire men."

"You are remarkable, Georgina." Alexander meant the words. As a poor relation to a nobleman, she'd managed through her own intellect and wile to achieve her dreams.

"I've never been called that before you came into my life." Georgina shifted the position of her head against his chest to gaze up at him. "You are very free with compliments."

"Hardly. It is only that you keep impressing me." Alexander leaned over a fraction and bussed her lips. It was a soft meeting of mouths, yet it still caused demanding heat to sweep through him. The awkward angle made it hard to deepen the kiss, but this wasn't the moment for a passionate embrace. This was about comforting Georgina.

Alexander pulled back and ran his thumb over her cheek. "Your find is impressive—even to someone like me with little interest in England's past."

"It's not just the helmet. It's the other pieces as well. I believe I've found parts of a boat."

"A boat?" Alexander asked, finding himself honestly intrigued.

"I conjecture that a person of great prestige was buried under the mound in a small ship," Georgina explained. With each word, her voice transformed from pensive to academic. "His bones have decomposed, but given the placement of the helmet, two shoulder clasps, a buckle, and a sword, he was positioned in the center of the barrow. It is all inference, of course, but my findings support my theory."

"You don't dig for the treasure," Alexander said. "It's the history that attracts you, isn't it?"

Georgina nodded, her chin bumping against his palm. "I'm thrilled to have found something as beautiful as the helmet, but everything about the site fascinates me. I—I've drawn images of how I think the grave looked when its occupant was first buried. Do—do you wish to see them?"

Georgina's hesitancy caused a dull thump in Alexander's chest. She was expecting to be rejected—something he'd endured all too often.

"Of course." And he wasn't lying to make Georgina feel better. After watching how her face lit up when discussing the tomb, he wanted to see her artwork.

"Truly?" Georgina asked. "I won't bore you? Percy is the only one who tolerates my babbling about the ancient world, and that's just so he comprehends enough not to expose our ruse."

Alexander gently turned Georgina in his arms so that they were facing each other. His hand still cupping her face, he gazed down into her warm brown eyes. "Last month when Percy dragged me to your dig site, I only saw scattered debris and shadows in that hole of yours. But you, Georgina, you perceived the past. Not just the history or the ancient objects, but the people, the reality that was. And I want a glimpse at what you envisage."

Georgina pressed a giddy kiss against his mouth. Just as he was about to sink into it, she whirled around, tugging his hand and dragging him forward. "Come, then! I use my old bedroom as a study whenever I manage to slip away from my brother's house—at least on the rainy days. On the sunny ones, I'm exploring the barrow."

Alexander let her pull him through the cottage, their feet leaving clouds of dust as they ran. Ruffian Caesar padded after them, the wiry fringe on his legs growing increasingly gray. The stairs had a thinner coating of the powder, probably since Georgina used them from time to time to access the upper floor.

Her bedroom was a sizable room with a large window overlooking the mounds on the property. The drop cloths were neatly folded in a corner, the bed and desk uncovered. There were crates stacked along the wall with straw poking out of them. Perhaps she stored her finds in them. The shelves, though, were curiously empty, save for a few books. It did not look like a utilized room, yet then again, it was no longer a living space but a secret hideout.

"Here!" Georgina released his hand and grabbed a leatherbound journal from the small, scarred desk. She quickly flipped to a particular page and handed it to him. Georgina hadn't just sketched the scene in black ink but had also captured it in paint. Alexander swore he could see the flickering light from the torches she'd drawn attached to the wooden beams holding up the burial structure. The glow illuminated objects piled in the tomb—a goblet made from the same stone as the snuffboxes, the bow of the boat, drinking horns, spears, and even a ceremonial ax. But she had put the most work into the deceased's finery. The warrior-king lay in repose, the fierce helmet on his head, a linen cloak secured at his shoulder with clasps inlaid with the same banded stone as the drinking vessel. Around his middle, he wore an impressive belt made from the colorful precious gem, and in his hand, he clasped a dagger with a gilded handle.

"I feel like I'm peering into the barrow right before they sealed it." Alexander leaned closer to her masterpiece.

Georgina's studious expression melted into a radiant beam. "Would you like to see more?"

"Yes," Alexander said, not sure if he meant her research or her grin.

With almost childlike enthusiasm, Georgina unceremoniously dropped to the floor. Alexander laughed and joined her, resting his back against the wall. They could have gone downstairs and uncovered some suitable pieces of furniture, but this simply felt right. This—this was the place where she'd fantasized about the past, and it only made sense to share those dreams here.

They stayed huddled together, their heads bent over her journal and Ruffian Caesar snoring at their feet, until the candle that Georgina had lit flickered out. Alexander couldn't believe the time had passed so quickly while talking about history of all things. But the manner in which Georgina described her discoveries—how she considered not just the kings and warriors but the metalworkers, potters, and miners—made the past burst to life. And Alexander loved listening to how she employed her endless logic to speculate on the significance of finds as small as a shard of pottery.

"Thank you," Georgina said as Alexander heard her close her journal. "No one has ever listened so long to me—not since Papa passed."

"You should be lecturing in front of the Antiquarians of England Society," Alexander said.

Georgina sighed. "When I wrote under my real name, no one would read my work. Hence Percy. I wouldn't even be able to cross the Society's threshold."

"It isn't fair," Alexander said, even though he knew she was fully aware of the fact. Sometimes it helped to have inequities finally acknowledged.

"I've made some sort of peace with it." Georgina rose stiffly to her feet and lit another candle as Ruffian Caesar nosed at her skirts. She cleared her throat, signaling a change in subject. "We best head to bed. It has been a long day. You can sleep in my father's old room, if you would like."

"If you permit, I would prefer to stay here—"

"Pardon?" Georgina's brown eyes had grown as large as a seal pup's. Yet beneath her shock, was there a shimmer of excitement?

"On the floor. For safety. In case the villain who shot at us returns." Dash it all, he was doing a deuced terrible job at explaining. But the thrill in her gaze made coherent thought impossible.

"Oh," Georgina said.

Alexander thought he detected a bit of disappointment, but he didn't want to explore it. Given the nature of a rope bed and a feather tick mattress, they'd end up entangled in each other's limbs the entire night. And that... that might just snap both of their fragile control. Tonight he didn't feel capable of exploring with just his mouth.

"I only need a pillow and a blanket," Alexander lied. Given how badly his entire leg was aching, he really required a softer surface. But he certainly would not have Georgina sleeping on the floor.

Despite their intimate embraces only that afternoon, an awkwardness descended over them. Georgina hastily left the room with Ruffian Caesar trailing after her. When they returned, she had an armful of bedding. Georgina and Alexander didn't talk much while he made a pallet on the floor. As soon as he finished, she blew out the candle, plunging them into darkness. Tension swirled through the air, and the unforgiving floorboards weren't the only hardness that Alexander had to contend with. When Georgina's breathing eventually turned gentle, steady with sleep, the sound nearly drove him mad as he imagined what he could do to quicken her exhalations.

He wanted to toss about in frustration, but he didn't want to risk waking Georgina. Instead, he lay there stiffly until sleep overtook him. Unfortunately, when slumber came, it was anything but restful.

⚜

"This will not do!" The duke's voice was like a bone cracking—a sound that Alexander knew too well. "You promised that the foot would be fixed."

"And it will. It will." Dr. Smythe's voice was so bloody calm. "This time I recommend breaking and resetting the leg to rebalance the whole."

"But—but my leg is fine, Father!" Alexander cried out, his terror outweighing his better judgment.

"Silence!" Falcondale roared. "This is not for you to decide."

But it's my body. *The thought screamed through Alexander.*

"Do it," the duke told Dr. Smythe.

"No!" Alexander grabbed his father's arm in desperation. "Please. Don't touch my leg!"

"What is this behavior?" His Grace tried to shake off Alexander's grasp. There was not a single hint of compassion in his handsome, patrician visage. "Have some fortitude!"

"Alexander! Alexander! Wake up! Please wake up."

Georgina's voice. Calling through the darkness. Making him feel something. Like hope.

"Alexander?"

He blinked his eyes and found Georgina's worried face hovering above him instead of his father's stoic one. Still half caught in the dream world, he cupped her cheek.

"You were having a nightmare—" Georgina began to say, but Alexander barely registered the words. He was still mostly in the throes of the old, ugly memory. He only knew that she'd rescued him. Someone had finally stepped in.

He sat up and pressed his mouth against hers, wanting to blot out the pain and the past. Her lips went slack only for a moment before they moved just as furiously against his. Her hands moved across his back in wide, soothing circles. An emotional dam burst somewhere deep inside Alexander. He felt tears smart the back of his eyes as he hungrily accepted the comfort that she offered.

She seemed to instinctually understand what he needed. She gathered him to her in a close, tight embrace. The pressure both soothed and excited. When she slid onto his lap, he couldn't stop the moan that erupted from deep inside him. Her lips left his, trailing across his cheek and lingering naughtily at his earlobe before burying in the hollow beneath his throat. His whole body shuddered with desire as her hands continued their gentle caresses.

He felt... wanted. Cherished even. And he thirsted for more.

They'd both worn just their white shirts and breeches to bed. He could feel her soft curves, the dip of her stomach between her rib cage and hips and the press of her bosom against him. But that still wasn't enough.

And clearly wasn't for her, either. Her mouth worked against his neck as she tugged insistently at his shirt. Thick and clumsy, his fingers worked furiously at the lacings. When the linen spread apart, she pulled the cloth over his head. Her lips left his body only long enough to discard the unwanted barrier. When her tongue teased his skin, he groaned, his entire being tight with need.

He pulled at the string of her shirt and then waited for her signal before continuing. She nodded as she kissed a path along his collarbone. She was ever inquisitive and thorough—his Miss Harrington of the Essex mud pit.

He loosened the ties, and his fingers skimmed against her breasts. She gasped and arched into his hands. The material slid to the side, and he lowered his mouth. Capturing her nipple between his lips, he accomplished one of the things he'd daydreamed about in the carriage ride. She cried out, and she pressed his head more firmly against her. She ground her hips into him, and he instinctually began to thrust.

That's when his leg and foot muscles seized. He'd lived with the pain for years, but he still had trouble masking the agony from a series of horrible, sudden cramps. The yelp escaped him before he could stop it. He jerked away from her, his hands instinctually heading toward the knotted tissue.

"Alexander! Alexander! What is it?" Georgina's voice was drenched with panic. Her hands no longer moved seductively but were engaged in a frenetic inventory of his body.

"*Leg,*" Alexander managed through clenched teeth, embarrassed by the tears of pain gathering in his eyes. Quickly, he buried his face in his own knees as he drew them against his bare chest. Georgina scuttled backward, giving him space to curl up. He rubbed along the tightened sinew and wished she wasn't witnessing this. He'd even tried his best to hide these types of attacks from his sister and his best friend.

"Let me." Georgina gently brushed his fingers aside. Before he could stop her, she'd pulled down his hose.

She made a startled sound from the back of her throat before she silenced it. Her reaction was rather muted compared to others'. After a stream of doctors had finished with cutting muscles and breaking bones, his right leg and foot were both scarred, lumpy, and mishappen. Ever since he was a lad, he wore padding to obscure the damage the alleged physicians and surgeons had wrought.

To Alexander's shock, Georgina's fingers pressed into his throbbing muscles. She…she was touching him! He glanced at her before remembering that he hadn't wanted to observe the revulsion or pity on her face.

But he found neither. He only spied a look of concentration.

"Is this pressure acceptable?" Georgina asked matter-of-factly as if she was asking him if he preferred to eat carrots or peas for dinner. "I can deepen the massage if you desire."

"A…a little harder, if you don't mind," Alexander admitted. The cool pads of her fingers felt good against his burning muscles, but the knot hadn't begun to untwist.

As he watched her diligently knead his leg, a soft warmth washed over him. He wasn't accustomed to anyone fussing over him. Charlotte hadn't been allowed to "coddle" him, as his parents deemed it. There was an adorable fierceness to how

Georgina rubbed his leg. She was so focused on helping him that she was gnawing her own bottom lip in concentration.

"Is it starting to feel better?" Georgina asked.

"Yes," he spoke truthfully. "The tension is starting to leave."

She moved onto another knot, and the searing pain dimmed into a dull throb. Some of the air that he'd been holding whooshed out of Alexander. "I can continue from here, Georgina. I don't want you overworking your fingers. Then you'll be the one dealing with a cramp."

"I am fine," Georgina said. As she settled into a rhythmic motion, an unusual sense of peace began to flow through Alexander. Her next words, however, drove the nascent harmony straight from him.

"Who…" Georgina stopped, her voice shaking with an emotion Alexander couldn't identify. After an audible swallow, she continued in a steady, almost unyielding tone. "Who did this to you?"

"Numerous physicians—quacks, all of them. But the old duke believed their lies that they'd repair my clubfoot and make me into his perfect, undamaged heir." Alexander tried to sound wry, but he couldn't stop the bitterness. It seemed like this was a night for truths, whether he wanted it to be or not.

Georgina glanced at him, and the ferocity in his gaze caused him to freeze. He finally realized what had made her voice tremble. Rage. She was livid. Not at him, but for him.

"Your father is an addlepated fopdoodle."

Despite all the old and new pain swirling inside him, Alexander snorted. "I rather like that insult."

"I have more if you want: nincompoop, gowpenful-o'anything, lubberwort, smelfungus, saddle goose."

A surprised laugh bubbled out from Alexander. He didn't

know a chuckle—even a slightly bitter one—was possible after awakening from one of those old nightmares. But Georgina had a way of making him feel better.

"Smelfungus. That might be my favorite."

"It is a rather new one," Georgina said with satisfied pride as she worked the muscles in his foot.

Alexander couldn't help the fond smile drifting across his face any more than he could stop the sense of intimacy sweeping through him. It wasn't just her touch—as personal as it was—but the words flowing from both of them.

"The duke considers himself enlightened albeit staunchly conservative," Alexander said. "But he is not a man of reason, especially in regard to my foot. He considers it as retribution for a sin."

"But you were born with a clubfoot!" Georgina protested indignantly. "Furthermore, you are one of the most upstanding persons whom I have ever met."

Her compliment, along with her protective outrage, spurred him to share even more. Because, for once, he felt safe—safe with who he was. "It is not my transgression but that of my aunt's."

"Your aunt? That makes no sense." Georgina's fingers dug a little harder into his arch.

"In my father's mind, it does. She is my mother's identical twin, her very image. Right before Lottie's and my birth, she ran away with a pirate. Father was horrified to be connected with such a scandal, and my paternal grandfather even more so. The late duke had not even wanted my parents to marry, since my maternal grandmother and great-aunt ran a salon. Father convinced his sire, and himself, that my mother otherwise came from good stock. I suppose Father felt guilty, which turned into anger and resentment. In his mind, he had besmirched the family's name by his poor choice in a bride, and he made it clear to my mother as well.

"Then...then a few weeks later, in the thick of the hateful gossip, I arrived. Against the current scientific thought, he saw my clubfoot as a manifestation of God's wrath for my aunt's sins. He once again blamed my mother. It—it became an obsession for both of them. They tried everything to fix it, fix me. But it never worked, and they could never accept my body."

Alexander's throat tightened, and he couldn't force out another word. But then Georgina glanced up at him, her fingers warm against his skin. He saw no condemnation and no pity either. Just compassion and a dawning understanding.

"They could never accept me." The hideous truth that had haunted Alexander since his earliest memories finally escaped. It hurt, speaking it aloud, but not as much as keeping the pain dammed up.

Georgina held his gaze for several long beats, and in her eyes, he saw the acceptance that he'd always craved. Then, with a gentle smile, she bent over and kissed his leg—scars, uneven lumps, and all.

"How—how can you do that?" Alexander asked as an intense fluttering erupted in his chest. "It...it is not a pretty sight."

"How can I not? It is part of you, after all."

And with those words, Alexander fell hopelessly and utterly in love with Miss Georgina Harrington.

Chapter Sixteen

Georgina had never experienced so many conflicting emotions. Even as her heart seemed nigh near to bursting with tenderness for Alexander, she simultaneously wanted to rip his mother and father into the teeniest, tiniest scraps.

"Do they…" Georgina trailed off, unsure of how to ask the question but needing to know if he was in any current danger. "Have they…."

"Are you asking if I've suffered through surgeries as an adult?" Alexander asked, his voice so, so terribly kind, as if he was upset about worrying her.

Georgina swallowed at the burn of tears. She could not allow him to see any fall. He needed her strength and comfort, not the other way around.

"Yes," she admitted, steeling herself for the answer. Afraid that he would notice the sheen in her eyes, she focused her gaze on his leg once more as she continued to knead it. She had never seen a clubfoot, but she had known instantly from the silvery, puckered scars studding his flesh that he'd suffered through numerous attempts to "repair" his limb. The cruelty was written on his body.

"Not since I left for university in Scotland," Alexander said. "When I refused to see another surgeon or physician, Father cut my income. I must rely on him and Mother to select most of my belongings. That's why I only have a curricle—it is a sporting, virile young man's equipage."

Georgina's heart seemed to shift in her chest as she realized how thoroughly she had misjudged Alexander. She had thought him a frivolous rogue interested only in adventure. But she'd been wrong.

"Is—is that why you race? To prove something to your parents?" Georgina asked, finally able to glance back in Alexander's direction. However, his eyes were focused upon some indeterminate spot on the floor.

"Initially." Alexander's normally jovial voice was starkly hollow. "That and shooting. I even approached Championess Quick in some vain hope that my parents might approve of me if I could manage to defend myself."

A terrible ache spread through Georgina, and she wanted so badly to ease Alexander's emptiness. She reached for his hand, lacing her fingers through his. He lifted his head in her direction and even managed a weak smile. His constant cheerfulness was indeed his mask, and it hid even more pain than Georgina had suspected.

"But I truly do enjoy thundering down the road or hitting a target from a great distance. I made a vow years ago that I would never again try to win their affection or follow their whims. I listen to my own impulses now." With each word, Alexander seemed to return more and more into his sunny, confident self. But how much was real, and how much was playacting?

"I absolutely refuse to participate in any of their schemes to protect the family lineage." Alexander's voice suddenly hardened, his now palpable anger bubbling to the surface. "They want me wedded and producing able-bodied male children of the right bloodlines."

A new hurt stabbed through Charlotte with such force that she almost clutched at her chest. Snippets of old conversations flowed through her mind as their meaning suddenly became painfully clear.

What had the Duke of Falcondale said to her half brother the day that she'd overheard them talking in Algernon's study? *"...reputation is of the utmost..."* He'd been talking about her marriageability. Of this, Charlotte was now certain.

And how had Algernon responded?

"Unbesmirched...Both her father and our mother's lines... William the Conqueror..."

Back then she had wondered why a noble would be interested in wedding his son to an old maid. But Falcondale was focused only on blood, and she came from ancient stock.

Later, there'd been Alexander's own reaction to their potential union.

I knew nothing of our planned betrothal until yesterday. My parents wished to finagle me into meeting you. I have rejected all their other attempts at matchmaking.

"That's the reason you're so determined not to wed. You no longer want to play a role in your parents' schemes." It made sense, Alexander's desire to avoid the parson's noose. His reasons were just as personal and deep-set as hers. But why did the realization shred her insides? She should feel relief, not this awful turmoil.

"I'm not opposed to all matrimony—just one that would please my parents. Sometimes I'm of half a mind to run away with a piratess myself. I'd love to witness the expression on my mother's and father's faces then." Alexander's jovial mask had snapped back into place, and his smile cut more than any scowl ever could.

It wasn't all marriage that he wished to escape but one with her. Oh, Georgina intellectually comprehended that he meant every woman of similar lineage and class, but the rejection felt damnably personal.

Alexander didn't seem to realize what he'd just admitted. But he was wrestling with old, crushing memories. And why would he even suspect that his statement could hurt?

She and Alexander had been clear from the beginning that neither wanted marriage to the other. But lately... today even... Georgina's heart felt differently. No, it wasn't just that fickle, emotional center that had changed. Her mind was being swayed, too. Alexander wasn't a careless gadabout or a self-absorbed rascal. He was kind and thoughtful, and absolutely nothing like her half brother. Alexander had showed a true interest in her research in a way no other man had except her father. History might not be Alexander's passion, but he'd never discourage her love for it.

But just when some part of Georgina had begun to consider Alexander as a real partner, she had to face the truth that she wasn't the ideal person for him. After all he'd suffered for his father's pursuit of the perfect heir, she understood his refusal to enter into a marriage that could possibly produce just that. She could not, would not, pressure him.

"Thank you," Alexander said softly. "Not just for the massage but for listening. I've never felt this much peace after a nightmare. Normally, I'm in turmoil for the rest of the night."

Oh, why did Alexander have to say those words? To make it sound as if something special had arisen between the two of them?

Georgina had to barricade her heart, but she couldn't start tonight. She didn't want to push Alexander away when they were both hurting. They had a connection, even if it might not be forever. He needed comfort, and she needed to soothe.

Georgina reached for Alexander. She could feel the heat and strength of his body—an athlete's physique. But the power in his frame didn't make him impervious to hurt.

"I'm glad I can be here for you right now," Georgina whispered in his ear.

He gathered her close, burying his face against the crook of her shoulder. She ran her hands down the muscles of his back, letting her touch console them both. His parents may have hurt him, but they hadn't destroyed him.

"Can I kiss you again, Georgina?" Alexander's voice was low and heartbreakingly earnest.

She should say no. To protect herself, that was the right choice. But she couldn't deny either of them this moment.

"Yes."

His lips touched hers, soft and light as eiderdown. It was nothing like the hungry kisses they'd exchanged earlier. Yet somehow it affected her the most.

She allowed the embrace to overtake her worries, and she felt like she was sinking into a freshly heated, rose-scented bath. Beneath her palms, Alexander's muscles uncoiled. His hand gently cupped her cheek, and in that moment, she experienced the forgotten sense of what it was like to be cherished. She wanted to stay here, in this moment, with Alexander.

But that wasn't to be. They had different goals and different wants.

Yet tonight, they needed the same thing. Comfort. Acceptance. Each other.

When they broke apart, Georgina stood and tugged Alexander's hand. "Sleep next to me. Staying on the floor cannot be good for your leg."

Alexander glanced at her bed dubiously. "With my heft, you'll definitely roll toward me, and we'll be stuck in the middle together."

A dangerous place indeed. But Georgina had never been a coward.

"Come on." She gently gave another pull. "It's just for resting. It's too late for anything else."

Alexander made a sound that indicated that he didn't fully ascribe to her reasoning, but he didn't try to prove her wrong. Instead, he allowed her to help him to his feet. He limped woodenly to the feather tick, but he didn't lean on her.

When he flopped onto the mattress, he heaved out a sigh that filled her room. Smiling, she tried to focus on the humor of the situation and not on the lust prancing merrily through her body. As soon as she climbed onto the rope bed, the soft bedding immediately collapsed under her. She slid, with more speed than she'd even anticipated, straight into Alexander's exceedingly warm and exceedingly hard chest.

He wrapped his arms around her in a tight hold. "I feel better now. At peace even."

Georgina was experiencing the exact opposite. Sharp, needy want shot through her, and she had to fight the urge to kiss him.

"I'm glad you're comforted," Georgina said truthfully, even as she tried to steady her own wild heartbeat.

A few minutes later, a soft, gentle snore emanated from Alexander. Then another.

His ability to tumble into sleep didn't surprise her. He'd been in a lot of pain, and he must have felt exhausted when his body had finally relaxed. Georgina was glad one of them was getting rest tonight.

Because she certainly was not.

But maybe it was for the best that slumber escaped her. She

could savor this moment of lying abed in Alexander's arms—a chance she would likely never have again. For once they found Percy, they would permanently part ways.

⚜

"These scraps of metal were part of a boat, then?" Alexander asked as Georgina shone her lantern directly on one of the pieces she'd just unearthed.

They didn't have much time for digging, but she hadn't been able to resist showing him the site again. Luckily, she knew a spot where most of the rivets lay, and it hadn't taken long to excavate one. The rest were safely stored in an old cruck barn by the main house, along with her other finds that weren't tucked away in her former bedroom in the cottage.

"I believe they once held together the planks of a ship," Georgina confirmed.

"It is astonishing to think of an entire vessel being buried under the ground." Alexander started to reach for the piece and then stopped. "Is it acceptable for me to touch it?"

"Very gently," Georgina instructed. "It is more fragile than you would think. It is amazing it has survived so long."

Georgina watched closely as Alexander very, very gingerly stroked one finger against the brittle iron. His face shone with the reverence that the antiquity deserved. And in that single moment, Georgina sank even further into a wellspring of affection for Alexander.

"It is much different seeing history like this than reading it in some musty tome. I can't help but think of the long-forgotten hands that forged this metalwork." Alexander gave the fragment one last stroke before he slowly rose.

"That is precisely what draws me to ancient objects. It is not so much the gold and the jewels, but the history of those who made and used such pieces," Georgina said. "And thank you for being so careful. Percy never asks before touching. He's unexpectedly clumsy, too."

Georgina uttered the last sentence unthinkingly, but once the words left her mouth, a deluge of sorrow slammed into her. Perhaps Percy would never again plague her with his rambunctious presence. Right now, if his laughing face appeared above her, she'd let him touch whatever piece he wanted.

"We'll find him." Alexander laid his hand upon Georgina's shoulder, immediately understanding the weighty silence that had filled the opened tomb.

Georgina drew in her breath and gave an officious nod. Wallowing in grief and worry wouldn't save Percy...or bring his attackers to justice.

"We should search for the source of the many-hued gemstone," Georgina said, her voice almost martial.

"You ascend the ladder first." Alexander stepped back to allow her to pass. "I'm afraid it will take me a bit of time."

Still wearing her men's attire, Georgina scrambled up the wooden frame with even more alacrity than usual. She and Alexander had debated if it was riskier for her to wear skirts or the disguise, especially since someone was more likely to recognize her in Essex. In the end, they'd decided that a local would more readily notice that she was unchaperoned compared to realizing that a "man" was actually her. People generally accepted what they saw, and she wasn't particularly close to any of the nearby gentry. Her workers might identify her, but they'd be tightlipped.

Alexander's head had just appeared over the top of the pit when Georgina heard an unusual sound for her little plot of land: the clop of horses' hooves. By the sound, there was more than one steed. Tossing his cane up first, Alexander heaved himself from the barrow. As soon as he rose to his feet, he pulled his pistol from his bandolier and angled his body between her and the approaching riders.

"There's no need to shield me," Georgina protested.

"I want to," Alexander replied, matter-of-factly.

Georgina was about to ask what if she wanted to protect him, too. But before she could, three mounted figures appeared from a dip in the landscape. The horses were all well-formed, expensive equines, and the men wore gentlemen's garb. These were not ordinary cutthroats, but that did not make them any less dangerous. After all, Percy probably wasn't taken by ordinary footpads. The trio was still too far away for Georgina to distinguish faces, but they each possessed a distinctive build. One rider was massive with broad shoulders akin to a knight of old. Beside him was a shorter slight fellow, while the final interloper was tall and reedy.

As they drew closer, Alexander surreptitiously eased his pistol into his coat pocket, but Georgina noticed that he did not change his grip. It took her a few moments longer to recognize the men. Surprise crashed into her, and she was exceedingly glad to be wearing her male disguise.

Her father's old rival, the Duke of Foxglen, was in the middle with the scholarly Lord Clifville on one side and his grandson, Lord Malbarry, on the other. They were an odd group to find outside London, although she supposed that they all had connections to Essex. Yet, the duke's estate was not particularly close, nor was Clifville's. Perhaps they were staying at the local inn, as she could not imagine His Grace traveling far on horseback. In fact, she did not recall him riding much during his visits with her father even over a decade ago.

There was one reason, and one reason only, why Foxglen would choose to trot over the countryside rather than sit comfortably in his well-appointed coach. The duke wanted to explore her land in a way he couldn't by carriage.

Georgina marched forward, determined to make it over the small hillock still between her and the invaders to her domain. The gentle swell in the landscape would obscure her pit, something she did not want the three to witness. She would not allow anyone to steal her find. If she had to fire Alexander's gun to frighten them away, then so be it.

"Mr. Harrington!" Alexander called out, clearly upset by her charge.

She did not heed him. She had her and her father's legacy to protect.

Freed from the confines of swirling skirts, she found that she could sprint exceedingly fast. She safely made it over and down the small rise. She almost stood with her arms akimbo but recalled at the last minute that the pose was often associated with women. Instead, she spread out her feet, trying to make her frame appear as large and intimidating as possible. She really should have grabbed one of Alexander's pistols.

"Mr. Harrington! What are you doing here?" Lord Clifville called out first, his voice cheerful and neighborly.

She was not charmed. "I should be the one originating the inquiries. Why are the three of you on my—" Georgina paused, almost realizing too late her assumed identity. She quickly added, "cousin's land."

"Miss Harrington invited us," the duke said confidently as he drew his ridiculously large mount to a stop in front of Georgina. His grandson sent him a quelling look, probably because he recognized the lie.

Georgina made a disgusted sound at the back of her throat. "I am fully aware of who my cousin invites onto her land. You are not among them."

The older man straightened his back as if commanding every dukely fiber in his being to stand at attention. Some would say he appeared regal, but Georgina had little use for such airs.

Lord Clifville glanced at Foxglen in befuddled concern. "You said you were invited. That is why I agreed to come see if this is where Lord Percy unearthed the helmet."

Lord Clifville turned back to Georgina to further explain. "You see, I have been very intrigued by Lord Percy's find, which I assumed would be on his ancestral land. But His Grace mentioned that Lord Percy's maternal uncle had purchased property with intriguing mounds on it sometime before his death. I just had to see for myself if one could be the barrow that contained such a marvelous treasure."

"*Pffft*. Of course we are welcome here." Foxglen waved his hand dismissively as he otherwise ignored Lord Clifville's impassioned speech. "I am an old friend of Miss Harrington's father."

"You were rivals, and barely civil ones at that by the end of my uncle's life." Georgina's voice started to go high at the end, but she quickly lowered the register. The duke and the earl didn't appear to notice, but Malbarry's gaze bored into her.

"I will not stand here and be maligned!" the duke protested. "Who are you to judge the relationship of your elders? You're just a young upstart with more sense of importance than actual substance. You don't even possess a title."

"I don't need one to defend my cousin's own land." Georgina had to work hard to keep her voice sounding masculine despite the anger sweeping through her.

"Mr. Harrington makes a salient point," Lord Malbarry

said, a calm and conciliatory contrast to his grandfather. Not a single emotion flitted across his countenance as he spoke with a dispassion that was at odds with everyone else's heightened emotions.

Foxglen whirled on his stoic heir. "I have reared you better than to question authority."

"I may be a cheeky fellow myself, but it appears to me that Mr. Harrington is the one with the law on his side." Alexander was slightly out of breath as he joined them, but his voice remained relentlessly cheerful.

"But I am—"

"The Duke of Foxglen," Alexander finished for him. "A very laudable title that harkens back nearly to the days of William the Conqueror. Yet I do not believe that even your impressively ancient letter of patent includes the right to freely trespass wherever you wish."

The duke's lips twitched with palpable displeasure while he pointedly directed his gaze toward Alexander's cane. Protective anger flared through Georgina. How many times had Alexander endured similar speaking glances, including from his own parents, the people who were supposed to defend him the most?

"I would be surprised that your father had not curbed your glib tongue and instilled better respect in you, but then I've heard you're a perennial disappointment." Foxglen's voice had obtained a brittle quality as rage seemed ready to break through his control at any moment.

"That is an unfair assessment of—" Georgina began to protest.

"Your Grace, perhaps it would be best if—" Lord Malbarry said in that quiet tone of his. It was telling how he used his grandfather's public title instead of a familial name.

Even Lord Clifville attempted to relieve the tension with a

clumsy apology that would have been more suitable earlier. "I am exceedingly sorry. I truly thought we had permiss—"

But it turned out that none of them needed to come to Alexander's defense. He already had his arsenal of wit.

"A disappointment is precisely what I endeavor to be. It is so much more fun than trying to live up to expectations, don't you think?"

The duke appeared downright apoplectic. Malbarry stepped closer to his grandfather, his expression dutiful. "Your Grace, you mustn't give over to anger like this. Remember what the physician said after your last—"

"I told you not to speak of it," Foxglen snarled. "Who are you to offer me advice? Have you still not learned your place?"

Was the duke in poor health? He had always been a presumptuous man who thought he should be more respected as an antiquarian than Georgina's father simply because he bore a prestigious title. It did not seem out of character for him to boldly strut onto her land to claim her discovery as his own, but he seemed even more bellicose than she'd recalled. He'd always possessed an almost lethal disdain, but before, he'd wrapped it under more layers of dignity. Had ill health and perhaps impending death made him thirsty to leave a legacy? Finding Arthur's helmet would certainly ensure fame even after death.

"I am only saying that we should be careful, Your Grace," Malbarry said, remaining utterly calm and gracious despite his grandfather's cutting words. "I am thinking of the reputation of the dukedom. It would do no good if anyone learned that we were chased away under the threat of gunfire from the land of a daughter of a mere fourth son."

"Gunfire?" Lord Clifville blinked, looking a bit like a slumberous owl disturbed in its roost. "Why would you mention that?"

Malbarry nodded to Alexander's coat pocket, where the decorative handle of Alexander's pistol was visible. "Lord Heathford is armed and is a very keen shot."

Georgina glanced over at Alexander for his reaction. She didn't think he was particularly friendly with the reserved marquess, so how would Malbarry know about his prowess with a pistol? Had he been their assailant yesterday? Or was Alexander's talent simply well known?

"Will you shoot at us?" Lord Clifville asked, sounding oddly eager.

"Pardon?" Alexander asked, clearly as confused as Georgina was by Lord Clifville's reaction.

"A warning volley, I mean. I wouldn't actually like a gun trained at my person. But over my head, at a safe distance, would be exceedingly thrilling. I could better understand the chaos of battle—for research purposes, of course." Lord Clifville spoke with a cheerful earnestness that did not contain even a hint of sarcasm.

"You wish for me to discharge a weapon in your general direction for research purposes?" Alexander asked, disbelief drenching his voice.

"Have you entirely lost your senses?" Foxglen snapped. Lord Clifville's ridiculous statement had evidently chased away the duke's anger and replaced it with patent incredulity.

Even the dispassionate Malbarry looked disgusted. "How privileged is your existence that you would consider coming under fire a lark? Do you realize how many people of all races and backgrounds are dying around the globe because of our war with France, Russia, and Austria? If you wish to experience battle, join that conflict."

Georgina's estimation of Lord Clifville dropped precipitously. The man was more fool than scholar.

Lord Clifville seemed unperturbed by Malbarry's criticism. "It is not necessary for me to actually participate in a fight. I just wish to understand the feel of it. Besides, it was not me who decided to face danger today. His Grace is the one who hoodwinked me into engaging in the crime of trespass."

"I thought you were an intelligent man even if too given to woolgathering. I see, now, that I have assessed you wrongly. I no longer wish to collaborate with you." Foxglen managed to look down his nose at Clifville despite being much shorter, even on his huge mount.

"Are you here together to steal my—Lord Percy's discovery?" Georgina stepped forward as renewed anger coursed through her. "How much of your scholarship is purloined from others?"

Lord Clifville smacked his hand against his chest so hard that his body swayed a bit in the saddle. "I never poach from others! My findings are all my own."

"How dare you malign me!" Foxglen snapped. "My body of work shall be my legacy along with the dukedom."

"Then prove you are not here for some nefarious purpose. Turn around and leave!" Georgina barely managed to keep her voice deep. The outrage pumping through her naturally raised her tone, but she battled against it.

"Your Grace, there is nothing more to do here," Malbarry said. "It is best we depart. We still have to travel northeast for some distance to reach your holding."

"I, for one, plan to leave. I will not have my honor further besmirched." Lord Clifville's narrow chest had puffed out to an absurd degree.

"Very well," Foxglen said. "I came for a friendly visit, but I will not remain with such ungracious hosts. Let's return to the inn for luncheon. I'd rather sup with the odious Lord Henry Talbot than consort with these ingrates."

Even the mention of the belligerent Lord Henry did not dim Georgina's immense relief as the three men turned their steeds around and headed back toward the main road. Still, she could not move from her position. Alexander did not urge her, either. Instead, he stood by her side as a salty breeze from the sea buffeted them. Only as the minutes passed did he reach out, his warm fingers curling around hers.

She should withdraw. She had to start their separation sometime.

But she couldn't. Not now. Not when she needed his quiet but steady support. Her heart knew this would only make it harder on her when they parted ways, yet she'd face future pain to have this moment now.

Chapter Seventeen

Alexander stood on the headlands, his hands gripping the handle of his pistol. He saw no trouble—either from the blue-gray sea below or from the grassy hillocks behind him. Gulls cried as they dove into the water, some emerging victorious with flashes of silver in their beaks. Sandpipers scurried on the golden stretch of beach between the bumpy red cliff face and the white-capped waves. Tufts of sea thrift bobbed in the wind, their spring pink flowers long gone, but their greenery remaining.

It was a bucolic summer day, perfect for picnicking at the shore. Yet despite the beauty, danger permeated the air. Foxglen, Malbarry, and Clifville's unwelcome visit had shaken Alexander more than he'd realized. He wasn't sure if the trio posed any danger, and their trespassing had verged more on the absurd. But their presence had reminded Alexander of the very real perils that he and Georgina faced.

Even setting aside their ambusher from yesterday, Georgina was literally treading close to a potential den of thieves—or, at least, of smugglers. Transporting illicit goods from France was the lifeblood of the people of Essex, and they would kill to protect their source of income. In these cliffs, there was a better chance of stumbling upon a smuggler's cache than locating a cave of gems.

But if Alexander joined Georgina in scrambling over the rocks below, he could bring her more danger. Although he could pick his way down the path, he'd be unsteady. If he tumbled, he could bring her down with him. It was better to stand at the edge and stand guard. She was close enough that he could still protect her with his pistol. And he had a good vantage point. It wasn't as if the smugglers would be curled up in a cave on a bright day like some storybook dragons protecting their horde.

"I found an opening!" Georgina appeared on the strand below as she waved her arms enthusiastically. "It's not too far from the bottom. You can take the normal path down."

Alexander nodded and picked his way along the narrow passage. The edge was crumbly, and twice his cane sent red chunks of gravel bouncing down the hillside. His movements became even more hampered when he finally made it down to the beach. Loose sand was one of the hardest surfaces to traverse, and he knew he'd pay for it with more muscle spasms tonight. But it was a pain he was willing to endure to assist Georgina and search for Percy.

"Here!" She pointed to what at first appeared to be a shadow between the main cliff and a crumbly outcropping of sandstone. "It is narrow, but I do believe it is a deep crevice."

"It is your cave, so you choose who goes first. Since I am the one who can shoot, it might be safer for me to lead." Alexander wanted to insist on the more dangerous position, but this was Georgina's search.

Georgina worried her lower lip and glanced at the lantern in her hand. "But you wouldn't have any light. You'll need your cane for support, and your other hand will be holding a weapon."

"You could follow close behind. It would give me some illumination," Alexander offered.

Georgina shook her head. "That is unnecessarily perilous.

What if I crouched low and we entered at the same time with you above me?"

"That may be the best plan," Alexander agreed. If smugglers were indeed hidden in the recess, they'd aim their weapons high. And it would help to have the glow from Georgina's lantern if he needed to fire his own pistol.

Together, they moved slowly toward the gap. The crevasse was too small for them to simultaneously squeeze through. Using hand gestures, they agreed for Georgina to smoosh herself in first. She kept her body as low as possible, giving Alexander space to reach over her head. He followed close after her, trying to ward off an uneasy sensation as the red rock seemed to grip him in a rough embrace.

Georgina moved more easily than he did. His broader shoulders kept scraping painfully against the walls and loosening flakes of sandstone. The powdery bits danced in the dim light of Georgina's bobbling lantern. Alexander tried not to sneeze as his lungs constricted almost as if the cave was actually compressing him.

Then suddenly there was a release. The two of them popped into a broad tunnel. The flickering flame revealed a carved passageway. Uneven marks from chisels dotted the soft stone walls along with curious deep grooves. Even through Alexander's untrained eyes, it was apparent that something had been extracted.

"Footprints," Georgina whispered as she held her light a little higher. Sure enough, the soft sandy floor was littered with the outlines of human shoes. They were far enough inside the entrance that wind and rain wouldn't wipe away the impressions, so it didn't mean anyone was inside. But that didn't stop Alexander from checking his grip on his pistol and straining his ears for the slightest sound.

"It looks like they've dragged crates through here." Alexander nodded toward a flat trail where other marks had been compressed.

"It would have been difficult to get through the entrance, but not impossible," Georgina agreed. "Do you think this is a smuggler's hole? Rather than a secret mine?"

"The tight entrance certainly would deter the excisemen," Alexander pointed out. "Although I do wonder why they went to the effort of making a deeper tunnel. It seems like this was far enough in the hillside just to carve out a decent storage area."

"I believe something was dug from the walls." Georgina aimed her lantern at the missing chunks that Alexander had noticed earlier. Even though Georgina spoke softly, an almost palpable excitement hummed in her voice.

Alexander knew her well enough to surmise that it wasn't the prospect of gems that thrilled her, but the peoples who might have removed them. "Do you think this is the ancient quarry, and the smugglers repurposed it?" he asked.

She nodded. "Can't you imagine ancient Britons or Anglo Saxons spotting a sparkle in the rock and following it farther and farther? Would their tools be cruder than ours? What would their light source be?"

Personally, Alexander's entire being was entirely focused on alive smugglers, but he didn't want to spoil Georgina's vivid image of their forebears. So while her mind created scenes of the past, he tuned all of his senses to the present.

They moved as they had originally planned. Georgina shuffled awkwardly below Alexander as he led with his weapon extended. The passage twisted, parallelling the missing portion of rock. Then, just as suddenly as the switch from natural crevice to man-made tunnel, the rocky chute opened into a small cavern.

Wooden boxes and crates were shoved into every nook, barely leaving much space to move. Glinting in the lantern's light, the necks of glass bottles peeked up from nests of straw. Barrels were stacked neatly, their copper bands shining like thin, emaciated moons. Despite the cramped quarters, the entire inventory seemed meticulously organized.

A cool dampness clung to the air along with an eerie stillness. This was not some abandoned operation but an active one. Despite the sandy conditions of the smugglers' lair, no layer of dust lay over the goods—not even a fine one. No one seemed present at the moment, though, and there was no sign of Percy.

"Since we did see evidence of mining, we should look quickly to make sure no current excavations are occurring. But I don't wish to tarry," Alexander said.

"Neither do I," Georgina admitted. "I felt at ease in the passageway but not here."

As they stepped fully into the storage area, Georgina raised the lantern above her head. The sandstone appeared brown instead of red in the dull light, making the space even more oppressive. Alexander's heart thudded against his chest, and he tried to focus the energy building inside into heightening his instincts, just as he did when racing his curricle.

When Georgina suddenly gasped, he tightened his muscles and lifted his pistol at the unknown threat. Then he saw it too: the glistening band, sandwiched between two plain layers of sandstone. Georgina followed the sheen with her lantern until it suddenly stopped. It had been gouged out of the wall, leaving behind a gaping hole that was more sinister than those in the entranceway. Perhaps it was seeing such beauty torn away, or maybe it was because this gash was less neat.

"Where did the seam start?" Alexander asked.

Georgina once again illuminated the line of gemstone. It curved around a corner and disappeared.

"Another passage!" they both exclaimed before they hurried toward the overlooked opening. It, too, was hand-dug and followed the precious mineral. This seam was positioned lower to the ground, making it easier to examine. Although the gemstone was not as brilliant as the polished lining of the snuffbox, it was clear that it was the same material.

They glanced at each other, both not ready to voice what this meant. They moved deeper into the tight chamber with Georgina leading the way. More of the gem had been ripped from the sandstone, and the channel suddenly stopped after a few yards. Mining tools were left neatly by the dead end, clearly to be used again in the near future. It was looking more and more obvious that not only was Georgina's brother involved in smuggling, but he was stealing from her as well.

And so, most likely, was Alexander's father.

A thousand different emotions clawed at Alexander—too many to make sense of right now. But he had no trouble detecting the guilt. Georgina—brilliant, intelligent, no-nonsense Georgina—had been locked up because of this unexpected wealth and a scheme between their relatives. Their greed appalled him, and so did the hypocrisy. Falcondale had blamed Alexander his entire life for allegedly bearing the consequences of his aunt's sins. Yet she'd simply married a pirate. Even if that had been a truly dastardly act, Alexander had never been a party to it. But the duke—his father—was actually participating in smuggling.

Oh, Alexander was under no illusion that his father was haunting beaches at night and flashing signals with a dark lantern. Falcondale had nothing to do with the actual work—of that Alexander was certain. But the man had invested in this illegal enterprise and filled the precious coffers of the dukedom with the dirty gains. Yet Alexander was supposed to be the one besmirching their illustrious family history?

Pain—old mixed with new—serrated him. Wounds that Georgina had soothed only hours before burst open anew, ugly and festering.

But this wasn't just his agony. He was more of a bystander.

Georgina's legacy was being robbed. Her brother had treated her worse than a pawn. She was a burden to be shuffled about for the sake of the earl's profit. Alexander could not fathom all her emotions, but he could empathize with so many of them.

"I am sorry." Alexander's voice sounded rumbly even to his own ears. There was a deepness he'd never heard before, but it made sense. His feelings for Georgina had depths that sank far into his soul. Alexander reached for her, his fingers lightly brushing over hers. He wanted to offer comfort yet also give her a chance to pull away.

He wouldn't blame her if she did.

"It isn't your fault," Georgina said softly. But even though she rejected his apology, she accepted his comfort. Her palm pressed tightly against his as if he were the only bulwark while the very land shifted under her feet.

"My father is involved." Alexander clutched the Nemean lion with his other hand, feeling the beast's claws against his thumb.

"He probably is," Georgina said, her voice carefully controlled as her eyes flicked from the vein of the colorful mineral to the neatly arranged tools. "But we have no direct evidence, just supposition."

"I admire your calm, Georgina." Alexander squeezed her fingers. "If I were in your position, I would be raging."

She turned to fix him with a surprisingly fond smile. "No. You would be making pointed quips with a grin on your face."

And just like that, she managed to alleviate the hurt roaring inside him. "You know me so well."

"We've both endured wretched relatives," Georgina sighed. "I am only so tranquil because I'm not surprised. My half brother has always been scurrilous. I did not suspect him to be involved in smuggling, but in retrospect, I probably should have guessed."

"How do you wish to proceed?" Alexander asked.

"I—I am not sure." Georgina shook her head. "I cannot allow him to steal my land for these gems, but how do I fight against smugglers? After we find Percy, then I'll consider what my choices are. But not now. Not until my cousin is safe."

"Do you think Percy could have discovered something about the illicit trade?" Alexander asked. He could not imagine his father kidnapping a lord, but he also hadn't suspected him of smuggling, either.

"Doubtful. Percy was in London when he vanished." Georgina tapped her foot against the mine's floor, sending puffs of silt into the air. "And his silence could be easily bought with a supply of good French brandy. Algernon knows that. There'd be no reason to resort to abduction."

"Percy might not have said a word about the smuggling, but he wouldn't have kept quiet about the gems on your land," Alexander pointed out. "He's a rogue, but he does have a sense of honor. Moreover, he cares for you, Georgina, and he wouldn't let Algernon steal your inheritance so blatantly."

"I'd like to think that, too." Georgina drew a circle in the dust with her shoe. When she lifted her head to face him, both fierceness and pain lurked in her eyes. "If he'd discovered this cave, he would have told me before he left. How would he have learned about the gems in the city?"

"Perhaps he drew the connection between the antiquities in your barrow and the snuffboxes like we did."

"That's a bit too observant for Percy, don't you think? He's not lacking in intelligence, but he's too self-absorbed." This time Georgina swung the lantern in clear frustration, rather than her foot. "I almost wish that he had realized Algernon's scheme. Then we'd have a better lead on where to look next."

There was a small glint of bright red, like a scarlet star, winking among the powder on the floor. It didn't look like the banded gemstone, but something that would come from a faceted jewel.

"Wait!" Alexander shouted.

"What?" Georgina asked.

"Shine your lantern there!" Alexander pointed in the direction where he'd seen the unexpected twinkle.

When the beam fell on the floor, he spied it again. Keeping her lantern steady, Georgina slowly moved forward. Alexander followed, his eyes trained on what he prayed was an actual clue.

"I...I'd know those garish garnet hearts anywhere!" Georgina's voice vacillated between fear, hope, and triumph, echoing the emotions clashing inside Alexander. She released his hand as she ran toward the semiprecious stone.

He watched as she reached down and pulled a familiar shoe buckle from the dirt. She blew off the extra dust, but Alexander didn't need more confirmation. It was one of Percy's favorite ornamentations. Alexander had even accompanied him the day he'd picked up the hideous things from the jewelers. Percy had boasted about designing them himself. There wasn't another pair like them.

"Percy...Percy must have been here!" Georgina clutched the buckle tightly as she raised her fist to her chest.

Alexander didn't voice the questions racing through him—not when they could puncture Georgina's temporary feeling of success. Had Percy lost the buckle while exploring the cave...or had he been brought here against his will?

No matter the answer, it seemed that Algernon was indeed connected to Percy's kidnapping...which meant that Alexander's father was likely involved as well.

Ignoring the sick sloshing in his stomach, Alexander focused on what he and Georgina could control. It was clear that Percy wasn't still tucked away in the main room or in either tunnel. The closest known place that they could investigate was Lord Craie's property. Perhaps Percy had been moved there, or maybe they could find information on other nearby smuggler holes where he could now be held. "We should head to your brother's estate."

Breaking into the earl's country home could bring dangers as unexpected as the visit to this mine. But to save Percy, they needed to face them.

Chapter Eighteen

W hen Georgina emerged from the smugglers' lair into the summer sunshine, it wasn't just her eyes that were having trouble adjusting. She'd always known that Algernon was an underhanded scoundrel, but had he become a true monster? What had he done with Percy? Was her cousin still alive?

She hoped the shoe buckle meant Percy had been taken captive and brought to Essex from London. But what if the perennially careless Percy had simply lost it while exploring the secret cache? When Percy had last stopped by her pit, they had discussed that the unique gems could have been originally excavated nearby. Perhaps Percy had become curious and hadn't wanted to endanger her when he'd spotted evidence of smuggling. Had he confronted her brother in London?

Oh, how she missed that cheeky, cavalier rascal!

"We will find Pendergrast, Georgina." Alexander's voice was strong, confident—exactly what she needed. His fingers once again slipped between hers, and she clung tightly. She should be seeking her own strength, especially when she knew that they had no future together. But right now, she couldn't let go.

Before Georgina could speak, a loud crack rent the air. At first, she thought perhaps a large chunk of the cliff had broken free and crashed to the shore. But when Alexander pushed her to the ground, his body splayed over hers, she realized the truth. It was the same sharp noise that she'd heard only yesterday on their wild carriage ride.

Someone was shooting at them.

Moments later, sand flew from the beach about a yard away. Alexander wrapped his hands around her head, pressing her into his chest. Then he rolled them into the shelter of a nearby rock ledge. Pushing her back against the wall, he withdrew his pistol and crouched in front of her, once again using his body as her shield.

Already shaken by what they'd discovered in the cave, Georgina tried to steady her breathing. She needed to have her wits about her. She wouldn't help either herself or Alexander if she succumbed to a case of the vapors.

Another spray of silt exploded into the air. Alexander craned his head, but he didn't seem to locate the shooter. Georgina tried looking, too, but she just spotted startled gulls, frantically flapping their wings and screaming with indignation.

"Those may only be warning shots," Alexander told her, "but I cannot be certain."

"The ambusher on the road was aiming at us, right?" Georgina asked, trying to marshal her thoughts into some semblance of order. But fear had seized her mind. Unlike yesterday, they were trapped on this beach. If their attacker was standing on the edge of the headlands, he could easily pick them off once they left their meager shelter.

"Judging by how close the lead balls came yesterday, yes, that attacker meant to hit us." Alexander spoke a bit distractedly as his eyes scanned their surroundings.

"Do you think they are the same person?" Georgina asked.

"I don't know," Alexander admitted grimly. "If it is the first assailant, there's no telling when he'll switch from warning shots to real ones."

Just then a series of sharp barks filled the air. Georgina stiffened at the familiar yips. It certainly sounded like Ruffian Caesar. Had he escaped from the cottage and followed them?

A growl and more yapping, then the fiercest rumble that Georgina had ever heard from her little dog. Terrified for his safety, she started to bolt from their rock shelter. Alexander gently but firmly gripped her arm.

"You don't have a weapon, Georgina. If anyone should be hurrying into the fray, it should be me."

Fear and panic collided. She yearned to save Ruffian Caesar, but she didn't want to place Alexander in the path of a firearm.

Before either of them could move, the sound of ripping fabric floated down the cliffside. There was a man's muffled curse, miraculously tinged more with annoyance than rage. More canine snarls punctuated the air. Running footsteps followed. The thud of boots grew fainter and fainter, but Ruffian Caesar's low, threatening growl still echoed over the beach.

"Your dog chased off the miscreant," Alexander said. "He's certainly earned the title of emperor today."

"Ruffian Caesar is, and always will be, a prince," Georgina responded with more pluck than she actually had. Right now, she wanted to grab her dog and then sink back against the sun-warmed rocks. But she had no time to collapse, even as she felt the intense energy that had filled her body start to drain away.

"He deserves a piece of steak fitting a king tonight." Alexander sounded half distracted, and she realized that he was listening to hear if their attacker was returning.

"That or a turnip," Georgina said, mostly under her breath. Her pup did have the most peculiar tastes.

"A turnip?" Alexander asked, swiveling his head and giving her his full attention.

"It's one of his favorite treats," Georgina answered, feeling a bit defensive over Ruffian Caesar's curious eating habits. "He truly does love them. He occasionally finds them and drags them back to my room. I have yet to discover his source."

"You have an affinity for unique creatures," Alexander said fondly as he returned his pistol to a holder on his bandolier. He grabbed onto a shallow shelf of rock and hoisted himself to his feet. Still steadying himself with one hand, he offered Georgina his other. "But we unfortunately don't have time to discuss either the mutt or the fluffball. We should move quickly. Our attacker is definitely gone, but he may return."

Georgina accepted his offer of assistance. Neither of them had worn gloves for their adventure, and the warmth from his bare palm seeped into her. Alexander possessed a singular talent for making her feel secure—not just in a physical sense but in a deeper, more complete way. With him, she could simply be.

As they stepped from the rock shelter, he yanked sharply on her hand, and she realized he was having trouble maintaining balance on the sandy beach. His cane was a few yards away, abandoned when he'd rolled them to safety. Georgina looped her elbow through his, offering him more support. He immediately allowed her to take some of his weight.

Even after they'd retrieved his walking stick, Georgina didn't remove her arm. It just felt right to be walking side by side. And she didn't feel so bewildered as she had when she'd left the cave. Together, they could fight whatever peril came their way.

❧

"Do you think we should use the servants' entrance?" Georgina asked as she and Alexander peered at Algernon's manor from the copse of trees planted at the edges of the well-manicured lawn. "It will be open."

"But it's still broad daylight," Alexander pointed out. "It will likely be bustling with people. With your brother and sister away, the main part of the mansion is actually safer."

"But we can't just stroll up to the front door." Georgina tried to tamp down on her frustration. It was exceedingly annoying trying to break into her own residence. But she couldn't just boldly strut around dressed in men's attire with Alexander in tow. The servants would quickly recognize her, and they owed her no loyalty. Gossip that delectable would quickly spread.

"Perhaps a window has been left open to air the place out." Alexander craned his neck as he scanned the brick façade. "The indoors must be stifling in this heat."

Two furry feet suddenly pawed Georgina's leg, followed by a cold wet nose against her palm. Glancing down, she found Ruffian Caesar staring expectantly up at her. Ever since they'd been reunited on the headlands, the terrier had been clingier than usual. She and Alexander hadn't wanted to take the time to bring the dog back to her cottage, and they also worried about another ambush there.

Georgina bent, brushing her fingers against Ruffian Caesar's springy fur. "What about you, boy? Do you know a way into Algernon's home?"

Ruffian Caesar ignored her question as he focused on licking her wrist. When she rubbed his left ear, his eyes drifted half closed in pure doggy bliss.

"He did prove himself excellent at escaping." Alexander slowly crouched down to join her in patting Ruffian Caesar.

Basking under the dual attention, the dog began to wag his entire hindquarters.

"Did he ever disappear and reappear at your brother's?" Alexander asked.

"He generally stayed by my side," Georgina said slowly as she flipped through her memories. "Anne didn't like him, so I tried to make sure he was never underfoot. There were times, though, that he'd slip away and come back with muddy pads and his treasured turnips."

"Let's quickly cross the lawn and follow Ruffian Caesar around the perimeter of the house. Perhaps we'll see an open window or maybe he'll show us a trick for getting in and out," Alexander suggested.

Despite the direness of the situation, Georgina couldn't help but laugh at the idea of them skulking through the bushes after a trotting terrier. "I suppose he is named after Rome's greatest general, so it only makes sense to appoint him as our leader."

"And, as we've mentioned, he is living up to his name today." Alexander donned his cheerful grin like a knight of old would his armor. Given the renewed confidence she was feeling, Georgina couldn't deny his strategy.

"Plus, we need dogged determination." Alexander gave an exaggerated wink as he spoke the awful pun.

Georgina groaned theatrically. "Upon that, I believe we should move before the jokes devolve even further."

"What?" Alexander pretended to be miffed as they moved as quickly as possible over the open grass surrounding the mansion. "I thought it was one of my better quips and not ruff at all."

Ruffian Caesar, who was padding after them, chose that perfect moment to snort. Georgina shot Alexander a look as they slipped around the fountain, trying to use it as a temporary screen.

"Even the dog realizes how bad your jokes are." Georgina pretended to gripe as they moved behind a statue of a plump cherub hugging an equally rotund fish. In reality, she was glad for the levity that kept her stomach from churning with anxiety.

"My humor is paaawsitively brilliant!" Alexander added as they ducked between another winged-child—this one clutching a pudgy, indignant goose.

His exclamation was so intentionally terrible that Georgina couldn't suppress a giggle as they slunk behind a putto riding a fat aquatic mammal that was neither dolphin nor whale but some puffy hybrid. For the first time, Georgina had an appreciation for her sister-in-law's love for cherubim statuary. But not as much as she was grateful for Alexander's irreverent presence.

"Don't you want to give me some apaaawse?" Alexander asked as they finally reached the shrubbery surrounding the brick edifice.

"How many words are you going to insert 'paws' into?" Georgina asked as they began to trail Ruffian Caesar as he sniffed his way around the boxwood.

"I am not pawsitive," Alexander replied quickly.

"That is a repeat. Try being a little more creative." Georgina feigned a scolding tone as she watched her terrier mark the branch that he had been so thoroughly inspecting only moments before. "Are you sure this is a sound plan? I feel all that we're learning is how to properly be a Ruffian Caesar."

"I would say that I was 'pawsitive,' but then you would accuse me of banality." Alexander sounded airy, but Georgina hadn't failed to notice that he had his hand in the pocket where he kept his pistol. Although her reputation was likely in more danger than her person, there was no telling when their attacker might return.

Georgina shivered despite herself, and she saw the flicker of concern in Alexander's eyes. She tried to think of her own pun, but the fear had started to swirl inside her again.

"Ruffian Caesar is moving." Alexander tugged on Georgina's hand, pulling her forward. Branches caught at their clothes as they bent nearly in half. If Georgina had been wearing skirts, she was sure the loose fabric would have been snagged in the rosebushes.

"How absurd do you think we look?" Georgina asked as they attempted to shrink behind a neatly pruned rhododendron while their doggy guide thoroughly investigated a clump of brown pellets that Georgina did not want to study too closely.

"Very," Alexander said jovially without a hint of self-consciousness.

"Do you think we are wasting time?" Georgina asked nervously.

"We haven't found a better way into the house," Alexander pointed out. "If all we manage to do is stay hidden until night-fall, it will be easier to slip inside the servants' entrance. We don't precisely have a better option."

Just then Ruffian Caesar ambled between the house and a large boxwood shrub. He did not emerge from the other side. Georgina sidled after him. A gasp of excitement escaped her as she spied a low rectangular window designed to allow light into the cellar. The shrub must have been planted to obscure the opening, which clashed with the impressive array of symmetrical sash windows.

Giving up any pretense of dignity, Georgina lowered herself

to her belly and slithered like a snake. The glass had been broken, leaving a gap big enough for a small terrier. But if she removed the remaining shards, she and even Alexander could squeeze through. Peering inside, she found herself looking into the kitchen larder. The astringent smell of turnips hit her first as she scanned the barrels and sacks that had been piled under the window, half obscuring it. The stacks of foodstuffs were arranged in such a manner to make perfect steps to the floor below for a dog… or two intrepid humans.

⚓

"I'm sorry we didn't find any trace of Percy in the cellar," Alexander whispered to Georgina as she led him up the main staircase with Ruffian Caesar loping behind them, one of his precious turnips firmly clenched in his maw.

As they'd suspected, the servants weren't in the family rooms, and it was relatively safe to move about. Still, Georgina couldn't escape the sense of dread that had settled over her like a thick, oppressive blanket. They'd managed to avoid the cook and the kitchen staff when they'd slipped through the lowest level, quietly checking the storerooms. But that didn't mean that they wouldn't blunder upon a maid tasked with dusting the empty parlors.

"Maybe we'll find a clue in Algernon's office," Georgina replied softly as they headed down the hall to her brother's study. Her last words were drowned out by a terrible creaking sound. In horror, she stared down at her left foot. She'd squarely stepped on the same board that she had last time when she'd tried to be stealthy. A bubble of nervous laughter pushed its way up her throat. She slammed her hand against her mouth in an attempt to stifle her sudden attack of the giggles.

"I don't think anyone heard." Alexander patted her back as she swallowed her snickers.

"I. Am. The. Worst. Spy." Even as she quietly huffed out the words, she clomped down on another loose piece of flooring right outside Algernon's study.

"Your espionage skills are on paw with my puns." Alexander winked as she pushed open the door.

"Oh, please don't start those again." Georgina pretended to plead even as his awful quip helped settle her anxious energy. "Although I must agree with your assessment."

Together they entered Algernon's domain. Alexander silently shut the door while Georgina moved to the drawn drapes. She tugged them open just enough to provide adequate light. Alexander moved to stand next to her, somehow making less noise despite his cane.

"Matthew told me that, when he searched Viscount Hawley's office for incriminating information, he was able to open a secret drawer by pointing a bust of his brother in the direction of a certain painting. Perhaps your brother has something similar." Alexander glanced around the room as he spoke. Although he seemed at ease, Georgina couldn't help but notice that he was gripping his cane tighter than normal.

"That sounds too clever by half for Algernon." Georgina strode over to her half brother's desk. "He's not nearly that imaginative. I wouldn't be surprised if he has evidence of the smuggling ring locked in a drawer."

Systematically, she began to pull each handle. All moved but the lower left.

"Surely it can't be that easy," Alexander said while he fiddled with the paintings as if one of them would open a secret door if nudged the right way.

"Why not? He's arrogant and doesn't expect anyone to root

around in his personal belongings in his own home on his sizable country estate. He is lord here." Georgina began turning over the objects on the desk. "Now just where would he hide the key?"

"Perhaps he has it on him?" Alexander asked as he walked over to join her after his unsuccessful picture-shaking venture.

"No." Georgina lifted up a clock and placed it on the floor. "He's forever losing things like that. Even if he carries one, he would have a second."

After finding nothing under the inkwell or the blotter, she returned to the drawers—this time rifling through them. In the third one, she felt a small, rectangular object shoved deep into the back. As her fingers closed around the cool metal, her heart started thudding faster and faster. Even before she pulled it out, she knew what she would see.

A snuffbox—which looked exactly like the Duke of Falcondale's and Lord Henry Talbot's—lay in her hand. She flipped it open, and the colorful banded gemstone glistened in the sunshine.

"Is that—?" Alexander asked.

"Yes," she affirmed as she leaned forward to read what was engraved on the inner lid. The light wasn't bright enough, but she could spy faint markings. Shutting the case so as not to spill the powdered tobacco, she raced to the window. As she did, she thought she heard something clink inside it.

"What does it say?" Alexander asked as she held the box in the bright beam.

"Lancelot," Georgina read. "Of course he chose that appellation. He's always fancied himself a chivalrous, dashing Lothario, when in truth he's simply a scoundrel. But an appellation like that would appeal to him."

"The investors in the smuggling ring must use Arthurian

names as a kind of cowardly nom de guerre." Alexander leaned over her shoulder to get a better look at the evidence. "It always seemed odd that my father had Merlin carved into his snuffbox. He's not the least bit fanciful."

"I don't think Algernon's alias is the only secret in this box." Georgina upended the container on the windowsill. Sure enough, a key thudded onto the wood.

"Do not tell me that he hid an object connected to his illegal activities in an item literally emblazoned with his clandestine name?"

Georgina shrugged as she began to replace the snuff to hide the evidence of their visit. "I told you that he was an uncreative sort."

"I cannot believe that my father chose him as a partner in an illegal undertaking." Bitterness laced Alexander's voice.

Georgina paused in opening the window to sweep the remaining powder outside. She had been so focused on her brother's misdeeds that she hadn't truly considered those of Alexander's father. Like she'd told Alexander, she did not hold him responsible for the duke's machinations. But even if Falcondale's involvement was unimportant to her, his perfidy must slice at Alexander in ways she should have realized before now. After all, Alexander's father had, in his warped logic, placed the sins of piracy upon the innocent Alexander while he himself was financing a smuggling operation.

"Our families are both truly terrible." Georgina reached out and squeezed Alexander's arm.

A faint smile drifted over his face. It was not a strong one, but neither was it the fake, cheery grin that he used to mask his pain. "Yet I like to think that neither of us turned out badly."

"Very true." Georgina wanted to lift her hand to cup his dear face, but she couldn't afford such intimacies anymore. Her heart was already too entangled. Removing her palm from his sleeve, she turned sharply in the direction of Algernon's desk. "And it is time to learn exactly what my brother and your father have been up to."

Sitting in Algernon's seat, Georgina used the key to unlock the bottom drawer. Inside lay a pile of ledgers along with a handful of documents. Alexander lowered himself into a chair across from her. She pushed one of the records in his direction and scanned through another.

"He doesn't even try to obfuscate the fact that this is a record of smuggled goods." Alexander shook his head in disbelief.

"I told you before, it's conceit. Your father and my brother have been treated with deference their entire lives. They simply believe they are above everyone and everything. They probably regard this as their rights as lords—to earn as much money as possible to fill their coffers." Georgina didn't even look up as she flipped a page. Nothing about the lists of transactions surprised her. She was simply trying to discover something that might explain Percy's whereabouts.

"They did use their aliases for the distribution." Alexander frowned as he nudged the ledger he was reviewing in her direction. He jabbed his thumb at the list of names. "It appears there are three of them: Merlin, Lancelot, and Arthur."

"Merlin is your father, and Lancelot is my brother. Does that make Henry Talbot Arthur?" Georgina wondered aloud. "He has the third snuffbox."

A darkness settled over Alexander, and his entire body stiffened. "Henry would definitely involve himself in something illegal. He'd also have no qualms about kidnapping."

"My brother is friends with him." Georgina glanced down at the desk as old memories haunted her. "During my debut,

Algernon tried to arrange a marriage between Lord Henry and me. It...did not go well, to say the least."

Suddenly, Alexander was on his feet with his cane gripped in one hand and his other balled into a fist. His normally sunny expression had turned downright glacial. "Did Talbot hurt you? Attack you? What happened?"

Georgina blinked, taken aback by Alexander's desperate fierceness. His expression almost immediately softened, but his warrior stance did not change. "I am on your side, Georgina. No matter what he did to you, I will not judge you."

"He only called me a wallflower to his cronies," Georgina said. "There were one or two other unkind observations, but only my pride was pricked. I was never fond of him, so I didn't even nurse a broken heart. He never touched me."

Alexander sank back down, but he still looked grim. "I'm sorry that you had to endure his unkind comments. He is a mean-spirited fool. I am sure you were as lovely then as you are now."

Normally Alexander's compliments caused a rush of warmth, but Georgina was too shaken by his reaction. She was used to a jovial Alexander. The only time she had seen him like this was when he'd revealed the surgeries that he'd endured.

"Alexander..." Georgina paused as she tried to determine how to broach the subject. She could sense his old wounds and perhaps even fear. "You went to boarding school with Lord Henry, didn't you?"

"I did." Alexander's voice was unusually sharp. "The man is also Matthew's middle brother."

A chill stalked through Georgina. "Did he hurt you?"

"Yes." Alexander's response was swift and short.

"Do you wish to talk about it?" Georgina asked, trying to

meet Alexander's gaze. Although he had not bowed his head, he managed to look everywhere but at her.

"It … it is embarrassing, even after all these years."

"You said you wouldn't judge me. I can promise you the same, Alexander." Georgina reached for him again, unable to suppress her urge to connect with him in the most fundamental way.

His fingers suddenly gripped hers, and his story came in a low rumble. Anger, sharp and hot, pierced Georgina as Alexander haltingly told her all the ways that Viscount Hawley and his middle brother had tormented him. Now she understood Alexander's ferocity when she had mentioned her past connection with Lord Henry. A surge of protectiveness roared through her. She wanted to rush back in time and use all the fighting skills that Alexander had taught her to protect the boy he'd been.

"When I wrote to my father about the abuse, he never responded. When I saw him that summer, he only said that I should learn to defend myself." Alexander shook his head sharply and then plastered on one of his cavalier grins. "But that is the past, and we must focus on the future if we're to save Pendergrast."

"I don't want to gloss over your pain," Georgina told him softly, wishing she could take him into her arms but afraid of what it could do to her heart. "You didn't deserve your father's treatment or what the Talbot brothers did. Your pain is real, but you needn't feel embarrassed. It is their shame, not yours. You are the strong one to not just endure but to stay a good person."

Alexander's fake smile dropped, and his gaze held hers. "How is it that you always know the right thing to tell me?"

Because we unexpectedly fit each other. Every fiber of Georgina wanted to say those words, but she wouldn't burden him.

Instead she spoke another truth, one she knew would comfort. "Because I know how wonderful you are, so it is easy being your champion."

Alexander groaned. "I wish I could kiss you, but I am afraid the fervor of my affections would delay us greatly."

Oh, how Georgina desired that, too. But their mission to rescue her cousin wasn't the only reason she should avoid Alexander's embrace.

Ignoring the passion simmering between them, Georgina swallowed. It was time to return their attention to the mystery at hand. "We have a few more documents to skim, but if we learn nothing from them, perhaps we should visit the local tavern. The Duke of Foxglen mentioned that Lord Henry is there."

"Lord Henry may simply be staying there on his way farther north to his father's estate in Essex, but he could also have been following us." Alexander reached for his cane, which had been resting on the side of the desk. He rubbed his fingers idly over Hercules and the lion. "I've never gone shooting with him, but I've heard he's an average marksman. That fits with our pursuer's skill level."

"Lord Henry seemed glad to be in London. I don't see him returning to Essex voluntarily." Georgina suppressed a shiver. She had never liked the man, and the thought of him stalking Alexander and her left her unsettled. Only Algernon would pick such a dangerous snake as an illicit business partner.

"I did wonder if Lord Malbarry could have been the shooter, given that he was on your land immediately before the second attack," Alexander added. "I don't think the duke has the stamina to ride a horse the way our ambusher did, although he certainly could have sent Malbarry or hired a ruffian. Lord Clifville doesn't seem familiar with firearms, so I don't think he would be the attacker. But now it appears that Talbot is the villain."

Georgina handed Alexander half of the stack of folded papers. "Perhaps we will discover proof in these."

Georgina quickly glanced over the letters, but they contained no information pertinent to Percy or clues to the identity of Arthur. She spotted the pact in which the three men outlined the smuggling operation, but they'd all signed their fake names. Neither Georgina nor Alexander recognized Arthur's handwriting, but they also weren't familiar with their suspects' penmanship.

"You'll want to look at this," Alexander said suddenly, his voice grave.

"Does it mention Percy?" Georgina asked as both hope and dread shot through her.

"No." Alexander slid the long document in her direction. "It's our proposed marriage contract."

"Oh," Georgina said as a dullness washed over her. Although she did not want the match plotted by Algernon and the Duke of Falcondale, she had begun to yearn for a true union with Alexander. The loss of that unconsummated relationship hurt more than her half brother's betrayal.

Alexander pointed to a particularly lengthy paragraph. His gaze was soft with compassion. "It is here where they lay out how I will grant your brother the right to your lands and all contained within it."

"Well, it is what we expected." Georgina folded her hands and tried her best to stop the tears that suddenly wanted to flow from her eyes. Why did looking at this scrap of paper hurt so much? It was the proposed record of a fake marriage. The union was never meant to be a true one. The document was just a tool of manipulation. So what was this keen sense of loss pulsating through her?

"I am sorry." Alexander's voice was rough.

Faint hope whispered through Georgina. Did he also feel a pang of longing for the wedding that would never be?

"As I said before, it is not your fault," Georgina assured him. She nervously wet her lips as she wondered how she could gauge his feelings about marrying her.

"I want you to know that I never would have signed such a travesty of an agreement. Even if I had been inclined to wed a woman of my father's choosing, I would have rejected this. There is nothing in here that protects you." Alexander gripped the vellum so hard that half of it crumpled. "No wonder you did not wish to enter into a union with any man after living under the guardianship of a tyrant like your half brother."

Even if I had been inclined to wed a woman of my father's choosing.

Alexander certainly hadn't intended those words to be a dagger, but they sliced at Georgina nonetheless. He wasn't feeling wistful about nuptials that would never occur or vows never to be spoken. What was roaring through him was guilt. It should be a balm that he felt so protective of her, but it only served to hurt Georgina more. He did care for her, but not in the way she longed for the most. And she feared that he might have even begun to pity her.

"I am not opposed to all marriage. I simply do not want to wed a man like my brother or Henry Talbot—or even Percy." The words came from the wellspring of hurt deep inside Georgina. She didn't know if she'd even initially meant to speak them aloud, but once she'd begun, she found that she could not stop. "If I could find a quiet, scholarly fellow like my father who is somber and deliberate in every undertaking, I could be persuaded to plight my troth to him."

"By someone like your brother or Percy…" Alexander hesitated a beat. "Do you mean a sportsman?"

His long pause almost caused her to relent. But it was like she was a wild, wounded animal, lashing out at the hand trying to comfort her. Because Georgina didn't want to be soothed. Not by him. At least not in that way. And definitely not like this. So instead she spoke a truth, even though she knew it would sting both of them.

"Yes. That manner of man has only ever broken my heart."

Chapter Nineteen

Alexander stabbed rather too ferociously at the innocent slab of beef on his plate. Yes, the meat at the local inn was a bit tough, but it didn't warrant such force. Yet when Alexander lifted his knife to cut it, he pressed so hard that the metal scraped against the glazed clay plate.

I do not want to wed a man like my brother or Henry Talbot. Was she clumping him into the same category as them? And what had she said about sportsmen? *That manner of man has only ever broken my heart.*

Did she really consider him a callow brute who toyed with women? Before, Alexander had just assumed that she did not wish to marry at all. But it stung—nay, it burned—to know that she was particularly rejecting him.

A scholarly man. That's what she wanted. Did she actually prefer a dunderhead like Lord Clifville, who wanted to be shot at for research purposes? Was that truly Georgina's idea of a good match? She was clearly too spirited for such a man. She should marry someone like...

Like him.

The words burst inside Alexander like a firework—the sparks both iridescent and painful. He'd known since last night in her bedchamber that he loved her. And somewhere, deep in his heart, he'd already started planning their life together. They'd go for long rides in his curricle, and she'd chatter away about her latest treatise. While she dug for antiquities, he'd amuse himself with target shooting and riding over the countryside. And when he came into the title, he'd run the estates while she explored them for any ancient structures. They could sit together on candlelit evenings and write. She would scribble about history, and he could pen one of his satires.

It had stopped mattering to Alexander that marrying Georgina would please his father. Because Alexander wasn't willing to sacrifice his own happiness. He'd thought he could bring the same joy to Georgina's life.

That manner of man has only ever broken my heart.

Once again, her words speared him. He could not even blame her considering what she'd endured living with her half brother. After Alexander had read through that awful marriage contract, he'd discovered a letter in the pile where Algernon admitted to Alexander's father that Georgina had no dowry because he'd embezzled it. Georgina had only shrugged at the news and admitted she'd assumed he'd gambled it away long ago.

Percy, too, had misused Georgina's trust. As much as Alexander enjoyed his friend's company, he knew Pendergrast wasn't the steady, reliable sort. Hell, Pendergrast would admit to that failing himself.

Alexander could see why his shooting and racing would worry Georgina. And he certainly wasn't somber and deliberate in every undertaking. He was a writer, but not of dry, academic pieces.

He supposed that he could try to give everything up for Georgina and mold his personality into what she desired. But he wouldn't. Even for her.

He'd spent his entire childhood trying to remake himself into someone who his parents would accept. He couldn't waste his adulthood in the same fruitless endeavor. He was who he was, and he wasn't about to change himself.

If Georgina didn't want a sportsman, then she didn't want him. And he simply needed to accept that fact. Even if it felt like his heart was being torn apart by a million tiny, red-hot pokers.

"That's it!" Georgina suddenly cried out, breaking into his misery. Under the table, her hand gripped his, and he almost shook her off. But Georgina didn't deserve his foul temper for simply making her needs and desires clear.

"That's why there was such a commotion in the weeks before Algernon and Anne brought me to London!" Georgina was enthusiastically pumping his arm now, whacking his knuckles against the wooden board. He doubted that she even realized what she was doing.

"I am afraid I missed something important," Alexander said as he gently tried to disentangle himself from her grasp.

"Didn't you hear what the men behind us were discussing?" Georgina asked. "I thought we were eavesdropping while we wait for Lord Henry's appearance?"

Well, that's what they were supposed to be doing, but Alexander was wallowing. Something that was entirely inappropriate given the circumstances. At the very least, Georgina needed him alert for danger. If Talbot was involved in the smuggling ring, he would be very dangerous indeed. Even if their suspicions were wrong, he still wasn't a fellow to trifle with.

"What did you hear?" Alexander asked, forcing his senses to sharpen.

"Week before last, the body of an exciseman washed up on shore a few miles from my parcel of land. He had been shot and killed." Georgina leaned forward as she whispered so softly that Alexander had trouble understanding her.

When he did piece together her words, his innards froze. If

the person they were chasing had murdered once, then he was capable of doing so a second time. Worse, anyone who attacked a government official wouldn't hesitate to harm a mere miss like Georgina.

"You think Arthur was the perpetrator?" Alexander asked.

"Or one of the underlings in the smuggling ring. Even my brother would be capable of it, especially if he was deep in his cups," Georgina admitted.

"I don't see my father shooting another person, nor can I imagine him skulking around on a dark beach participating in smuggling." Alexander reached for his cane to fiddle with. The facts were starting to arrange themselves into a pattern now, and he didn't like their deadly portent. "Talbot has always been bloodthirsty. As a youth, he and his older brother enjoyed forcing the other lads to engage in dangerous games."

"You think that just like Hawley played at being a highwayman, his middle brother tried his hand at smuggling?" Georgina asked. "It does make sense—in a terrible way. If Lord Henry found it a lark, Algernon would, too. And I do think the smuggling ring precipitated the murder. That is why the carriages converged upon Algernon's manor. It would have been at the right time. Your father came from the west, and Arthur arrived from the northeast. They probably convened to address the death. It likely put their entire operation at risk and added substantially to the crimes they were committing."

"My father wouldn't have liked being embroiled in such a travesty, but he was already too deeply enmeshed. The fact he was negotiating a marriage between you and me indicates that Algernon wasn't directly involved in the murder. Or, if he was, my father is unaware."

How were they to untangle this mess, and how had Percy gotten caught up in it?

"I wonder if the duke and my brother are trying to form a tighter alliance to push Arthur out?" Georgina tapped her fingers against the tabletop.

"That sounds like His Grace. He wouldn't want the taint of murder affecting him." Alexander tried to ignore the churning in his stomach. "But it could make Arthur even more dangerous."

"Arthur is the one who caused Percy's disappearance, isn't he?" Although Georgina had been talking in extremely hushed tones this whole time, her voice became even smaller.

"Most likely." Even though he knew he was risking more heartache, Alexander reached under the table to covertly give Georgina's hand a reassuring squeeze. This was about her need for comfort, not his.

Without warning, her fingers dug into his palm. Her brown eyes had grown enormous, yet she seemed more determined than frightened. "He's here."

Alexander didn't need to ask who. Immediately, he stiffened. He didn't want to confront his old tormentor, but it couldn't be helped. If Pendergrast was still alive, they had to follow every clue to save him.

"You said that you'll pretend to accidentally knock into Lord Henry, but it's my cousin who's missing." Georgina planted her hands on either side of her plate as she rose. Their goal was to try to grab Henry's snuffbox and confirm that "Arthur" was inscribed in the lid.

"No." Alexander used his cane to push himself quickly to his feet. "It's too dangerous for you. He could see through your disguise. He almost has in the past."

"But I don't want to place you in—" Georgina said as she shifted out from the table.

"You will bear more risk—" Alexander protested at the same time while he shuffled sideways to stop her.

Unfortunately, Georgina tripped over his outstretched cane. She pitched forward into his chest before he could brace himself. His bad leg buckled under the unexpected weight, and he toppled backward...right into something hard and unyielding.

"Oooof!" The grunt near Alexander's ear was accompanied by the exceedingly strong smell of ale.

Alexander righted himself, only for a hand to painfully grip his shoulder. Its owner immediately pushed Alexander, forcing him to awkwardly spin around. If Alexander's reflexes hadn't been honed under Championess Quick's tutelage, he probably would have collapsed into a heap. Instead, after using his cane to steady his body, he found himself face-to-face with Henry Talbot.

"Well...well...well." Talbot drunkenly slurred the words. "If it isn't Alexander the Galling—the reason for my banishment."

Banishment? Was Talbot not in Essex of his own volition? Or was he blaming Alexander for leaving London and forcing Talbot to stalk him all the way to Georgina's home village?

Alexander did not have much time to parse the meaning of Talbot's words as the man's fist came flying in his direction. Alexander easily ducked, but if he had any hope of triumphing over Talbot, he'd need to knock him to the ground. Henry swung again, and this time, Alexander had a harder time avoiding the blow. Pain shot up his bad leg as he awkwardly put pressure on it.

"Do. Not. Touch. Him." Georgina growled out the words, her feminine voice thankfully deep with rage.

All around the tavern, the other patrons watched. None seemed inclined to join the fight, but they were definitely interested in watching it unfold.

Henry straightened. He blinked sluggishly at Georgina, his senses clearly dulled from alcohol. Shock washed over his countenance, making him look even more inebriated. But why was he stunned to find Georgina at the inn? Hadn't he been trailing them? And given how deep Talbot was in his cups, could he have actually been today's shooter? Taking into account how much liquor the reprobate could hold, it seemed like he'd been drinking for a least a few hours to be in such a state.

"You!" Henry jabbed an unsteady finger in Georgina's direction. "You're also the reason for my exile! If you two hadn't plagued me at Elysian Fields, Father wouldn't have ordered me back to the bloody countryside."

So Talbot was here on the Duke of Lansberry's orders. Perhaps he wasn't Arthur after all. But if he wasn't, why did he have the snuffbox?

One thing was certain, though. Alexander needed to draw Talbot's attention away from Georgina. Even this drunk, he was a dangerously powerful brute, perhaps even more so. Some of Alexander's worst beatings at the other man's hands had come when Talbot had drunk brandy that he and Hawley had smuggled onto school grounds.

"You're the progenitor of your own ill luck," Alexander taunted. Unfortunately, Talbot didn't seem to register the insult. He only staggered toward Georgina, somehow managing to be both clumsy and purposeful.

"Who are you to order me to unhand Alexander the Galling? You're nothing but a short, annoying mite." As Henry lurched forward, he kept stabbing his finger in Georgina's direction. Alexander began to lift his cane—ready to intervene before Henry poked Georgina in the chest. If he discovered her bound breasts, her reputation would never recover.

Georgina backed away, which made Talbot's mouth stretch into an unkind grin. He threw back his head, his cruel chuckle a haunting echo of his schoolboy chortle.

"Afraid, Little Mite?" Talbot balled back his hand, preparing to strike.

Alexander started to sweep Talbot's leg with his cane, but Georgina was faster. With no hesitation, she kicked up her leg and rammed her shin between Henry's thighs. Hard. Exceedingly hard.

Just like Alexander had taught her.

Henry stiffened and then seemed to collapse on himself, his arms sweeping downward. As his body sagged forward, Georgina slammed the heel of her palm into his chin. Not expecting the blow, Henry toppled backward. With his hands gripping his groin, he didn't have time to brace himself. His head conked against the floor followed by his back. A roar of rage and pain erupted from him.

Around the room, the other patrons began murmuring in astonishment. Although they didn't know that Georgina was a woman, it was still a spectacle to witness a large, muscular nobleman felled by a small fellow.

"Now run!" Alexander shouted to Georgina as Henry began to thrash in her direction.

"Not yet!" Georgina yelled back, fortunately remembering to deepen her voice. Alexander realized that she wouldn't escape until they'd secured the snuffbox.

Talbot's hand snaked toward Georgina's ankle as he began to surge to his knees. Alexander didn't wait as protective rage thundered through him. Tossing his cane to the side, Alexander tackled Henry. His wrath was so intense that he barely registered the hollers ringing from the onlookers. "Plant a facer!" "Ribroast that jackanapes!" "Give him what you've got!"

Talbot flung his fist at Alexander's head, but Alexander easily blocked the hit with his forearm. Talbot next tried to land a blow with his other hand, but Alexander was faster. Although he was still less muscular than Talbot, he wasn't a weakling, and he'd been taught by a prizefighter who knew how to defeat her bigger opponents. Using his body as leverage, Alexander pinned Talbot down. It took all his willpower not to slam the brute against the ground. He just needed to subdue the bully, not beat him into a bloody mess.

Alexander didn't even need to shout to Georgina to grab the snuffbox. She was already kneeling beside them, searching Talbot's waistcoat. Talbot writhed, but he wasn't using his bulk strategically. It wasn't hard to keep him pinned, especially with the anger pumping through Alexander. This man hadn't just attacked him over and over in the past, but he'd lunged at Georgina.

Trying to keep his fury at bay, Alexander watched as Georgina fished out the silver-covered piece. Quickly, she bent over the object, shielding it from both Talbot's and the spectators' view.

"What does it say?" Alexander asked as Talbot attempted to headbutt him.

"It simply says 'To Viscount Hawley.'" Georgina turned to him in shock, no longer trying to obscure the snuffbox. Instead, she shook it in Talbot's face. "Where did you get this?"

"Why do you care about that useless trinket of my brother's?" Talbot spat out as he ineffectively twisted his body in an attempt to wriggle from Alexander's grasp. "I thought it might be of some value, but no one knows what the bloody gem is."

"My father must have gifted it to Lord Hawley when he was going to marry Charlotte," Alexander told Georgina, ignoring the thrashing Talbot. "I don't think it's the one we're interested in."

"Why the hell are you addlepates searching for a damn snuffbox?" Talbot bellowed as he increased his struggles to break free. "Bloody arses."

Alexander wanted nothing more than to repeatedly smash his fist into Talbot's face. But they'd studied the trinket, and he wasn't the villain they sought.

"I'm going to release you," Alexander warned. "But if you attack either Mr. Harrington or me, I won't hold back."

Slowly, Alexander relaxed his grip on Henry's upper body but still immobilized his legs. Talbot bolted into a seated position, his balled fingers nearly walloping Alexander in the temple. Alexander pivoted but took a painful hit to his shoulder. Before the blackguard could sock him again, Alexander whacked the fleshy part of his elbow against Talbot's cheek. A single groan escaped the bigger man's lips before he slumped bonelessly to the floorboards.

Fueled by untrammeled vigor and pent-up ire, Alexander raised his fist. But he stopped mid-strike. Because he wasn't Talbot. He didn't clobber those who were already down.

"Alexander! Alexander!" It was Georgina yelling. He heard her shouts now, and he wondered how many he'd missed. Her hand touched his arm, and he let her guide him to his feet. She pressed his cane into his hand, and he accepted it. Together, they turned from Talbot's prone body and strode out the inn's doors. Dimly, Alexander heard the congratulations from the other patrons, but he didn't care.

His limbs began to shake, but he'd expected that. He had an unharmed Georgina by his side to keep him steady. Somehow, he'd defeated his childhood tormentor. And better yet, he hadn't become him, either. Triumph filled him even as the wild energy inside him ebbed away.

The cooler evening air washed over Alexander as they emerged into the twilight. The horizon burned a glorious red, almost as if in celebration of Alexander's victory.

"That was an exceedingly impressive blow." Georgina's tone

was bright. She, and the sound of her voice, buoyed him even more.

Using his cane as a pivot point, he slowly spun in her direction. But when Alexander faced her, the joy suddenly whooshed from him. How could he kiss her? Especially now? Would his victory over Talbot only make her think of him as a violent man? Yet she hadn't seemed to mind when he'd successfully outrun their ambusher yesterday. In fact, he knew the escapade had thrilled her.

But Georgina had still declared that she didn't desire a sportsman. At least not for a husband. And Alexander didn't want only a fleeting romance with Georgina anymore. Not with the way his heart felt around her.

Perhaps he should be honest. If he suddenly withdrew his affections, could that not hurt her?

"Georgina, I…" Alexander stumbled over his words as he tried to explain his feelings, even while fully expecting rejection.

"Miss Harrington!"

Alexander stiffened at the use of Georgina's real name. Instinctually, he stepped between her and the speaker, who was somewhere behind them. As Alexander turned toward the newcomer, he reached for the gun hidden under his coat. The man had spoken with a local Essex accent rather than a London one, but that didn't make him any less of a threat.

Perhaps he was even a greater one.

"Jack!" Georgina called out. "Were you having a drink at the inn? I didn't see you inside."

"Who's Jack?" Alexander asked Georgina quietly. Perhaps this fellow wasn't dangerous if she was greeting him with such warmth. She certainly wasn't attempting to hide her identity, although it was apparent that this chap had already recognized her.

"He's one of the young men who helps at my pit," Georgina answered in a low voice, before she added brightly, "Is Tom with you?"

"No." The answer was short and tinged with an ominous darkness.

Alexander pulled out his pistol just as the figure stepped away from the bright glow of the tavern. As the interloper drew closer, his features became more apparent in the faint lingering rays of the sun. His boyish features were drawn, making him look like a wizened elder instead of a lad on the cusp of adulthood. A wildness haunted his eyes that could have been desperation or something more sinister.

"Don't step any closer." Alexander leveled his weapon at the local's chest.

"I'm not here to hurt Miss Harrington or you. I'm trying to warn you." Jack lifted his hands, showing that they were empty.

"Jack," Georgina said, her normally crisp voice marred with worry. "What's wrong?"

"Telling you will only put you in more danger." Jack's expression turned pleading, and Alexander finally saw the fear in the youth's face. "Please return to London. Stop looking for snuffboxes, and never return to where they are mined."

"How did you know we went to the cliffs?" Alexander demanded as he cocked his weapon. Jack's palpable terror had almost caused Alexander to lower his guard, but he was thankful he hadn't. "You were the one who shot at us, weren't you?"

The lad didn't even try to refute the accusation as he visibly began to shake. "I never intended to hit you. I was trying to scare you away."

"Jack, I have always known you were a smuggler." Once again, Georgina sounded like her pragmatic self as she stepped around Alexander to face her worker. "I have no intention of reporting you or any of the locals."

"You don't understand, miss. I'm not worried about the government. It's the nob you need to fear. The one your brother calls Arthur. He's unhinged, that one. He murdered the exciseman. Shot him in the back, Tom said. He was yelling about how he was the descendant of King Arthur and the real law of England when he pulled the trigger."

"You know who Arthur is?" Alexander said.

Jack shook his head. "Just that he's a gent. It's Tom who met him and saw the murder. I got a glimpse of him once, and that was all. Tom told me to keep away, and so should you, Miss Harrington. From what I hear, Arthur would likely kill a dove, too. Those gems aren't worth your life."

"I'm not worried about a bunch of rocks—no matter how colorful they are. I'm searching for my cousin, Lord Percy Pendergrast." Georgina stepped even closer to Jack.

Alexander reached out and gently snagged her arm. He didn't fully trust the lad, and he didn't want Georgina blundering into a trap.

"Lord Percy is as good as dead, and so is Tom. There's no saving them, if they're even still alive." Jack's eyes glistened in the fading light, and his face crumpled. He attempted to look stoic, but his anguish and concern were palpable.

"Tom is missing, too?" Georgina asked.

This time when she shifted toward Jack, Alexander let her. It was clear, even to him, that the broken youth wasn't a danger. He was simply scared and doing his best to save Georgina.

"Since right before you went to London, miss. Tom knew that this Arthur fellow was keeping your cousin among the loot, and Tom left one evening to rescue him. He never came back. When I finally mustered enough courage to check the cave, there was no trace of any of them." With each word, Jack sagged a little more, his gaze fixed on the ground.

Georgina seemed to wilt, too, and Alexander grabbed her arm once more. He felt flattened as well, but he wouldn't accept this lad's word as defeat.

"Did you spy any blood or signs of a struggle?" Alexander demanded, steeling himself for the worst.

"No. Just an empty corridor where they'd been keeping Lord Percy." Jack swallowed hard. "I should've gone with Tom that day or stopped him altogether."

"You can help now," Alexander said firmly.

"How?" Jack asked. "The best I can do is keep Miss Harrington away from Arthur."

Alexander ignored the sickening churn in his stomach as he concentrated on the facts. "You saw the villain's form. Could he have been Lord Henry?"

"Who?" Jack asked in confusion.

"The man whom Alexander and I fought in the inn just now." Georgina's voice was back to being logical without a single quaver. Hearing the return of her pragmatism brought a wave of relief through Alexander, bolstering his own confidence.

They had a witness. All was not forsaken.

"No. It wasn't him," Jack said. "His frame is all wrong."

"Is Arthur even more hulking?" Alexander asked, thinking of Lord Malbarry.

"He's tall but skinny as a reed. He looks like a puff of breeze would bend him straight in half."

"That sounds like the Earl of Clifville," Georgina gasped out.

"He does own a crumbling old castle to the northeast," Alexander said slowly, "but I cannot imagine that bookworm killing an ant, let alone a human being."

"Do you think he'd strut around London proclaiming that

he's a murderer?" Georgina asked. "Besides, scholars can be exceedingly underhanded and vicious."

"Yet you want to marry one!" The accusation flew from Alexander's mouth before he could stop it.

"I beg your pardon!" Georgina shouted, sounding confused and more than a trifle annoyed. "My marriage preferences have nothing to do with this conversation."

Jack cleared his throat awkwardly as he studiously looked anywhere but at Georgina and Alexander. "I...I did hear Lord Craie mention an earl once, along with a duke. He didn't use their full titles, though. I never met the other nobs, like I said. I wasn't supposed to know even that much."

"The duke would be my father," Alexander said, still trying to accept the fact that the man who wanted to experience gunfire for research purposes had actually shot a government official in the back. "It does sound as if Lord Clifville is the one who kidnapped Percy for discovering the smugglers' lair."

"That isn't why he was taken—not according to Tom," Jack interjected. "It's because of that helmet you found, Miss Harrington. Arthur wanted more treasure. He kept Percy in that cave and demanded that he reveal where he'd found the grave goods. From what Tom said, the earl thought the barrow was on Percy's family's estate and not your parcel."

"That bastard!" Georgina clenched both fists and looked ready to knee a man in the groin for the second time that evening. Then her fingers went limp as she realized the darker meaning behind Jack's words. "Did—did he hurt my cousin?"

"I-I do not know." Jack stared at a spot over Georgina's shoulder.

"Why didn't Percy just reveal that the barrow was located on my land?" Georgina asked. "My dig isn't worth his life."

"Most likely for the same reason Tom didn't see fit to reveal it, either. Once Arthur knows, he'd have no need to keep your cousin alive," Jack explained.

"But Clifville now has a good idea where the burial mound is located after the Duke of Foxglen practically led him straight toward it." Georgina's face showed the same horror that was piercing Alexander.

"Shite!" Jack said and then glanced at Georgina. "Sorry, Miss Harrington, for my language."

It was unlikely, however, that Georgina had even heard him. She was pacing now, clearly trying to make sense of all the new facts.

"Why is Lord Clifville so obsessed with the barrow?" Jack asked.

The reason suddenly became clear to Alexander, but he felt no thrill. Not when the answer showed just how deluded the earl was. "He believed Pendergrast when he bragged that the helmet was King Arthur's."

Georgina stopped her nervous marching and whirled in Alexander's direction. "But Lord Clifville dismissed Arthur as a legend."

Alexander gripped Georgina's arm as his concern for the well-being of her cousin and now Tom grew exponentially. "The earl hid the fact that he was a deranged murderer and kidnapper, too. It would have been much easier to lie about his belief in the Round Table. Think about it. He chose Arthur as a nom de guerre. I wager that he dreamed up the other appellations, too. And Jack, didn't you say that Tom heard Clifville call himself a descendant of King Arthur?"

"He did," Jack confirmed.

"But...but none of that is logical," Georgina protested.

"No, it isn't. Clifville is clearly troubled," Alexander said.

"That is precisely why we need to rescue Pendergrast and Tom as soon as possible."

Jack shifted nervously. "It isn't safe, but…"

"But?" Georgina prodded.

Jack shoved his hand into his hair, loosening his already sloppy queue. "When I was at the tavern making sure you didn't get in more trouble, I overheard two other nobs talking—an old man and a big mountain of a fellow. They mentioned that a Lord Clifville had returned to London on some urgent business."

Alexander tried to ignore the sense of doom that had settled over his soul. He didn't want to drag Georgina further into danger, but he knew she'd never stay behind. He braced himself and made the declaration they were all thinking.

"Then tonight is the perfect time to invade Camelot."

Chapter Twenty

‗‗‗

"Clifville's abode is indeed a proper castle," Alexander said with an exaggerated sigh. "It's even crumbling in a picturesque way. I suppose it is the dream of every boy to storm one. I didn't think it would be the legendary Arthur's, though."

Georgina tried to muster a smile, knowing that Alexander was attempting to dull the fear sweeping through her, Jack, and even Alexander himself. The ancient fortress was designed to impose, with its keep rising out of the cliff. Half of the once-massive edifice had fallen to ruin. Judging by the east wing, part had even tumbled into the sea.

"I'm a smuggler, not a burglar," Jack said, his normally hearty voice faint. "How are we to even begin breaking into such a place?"

"We follow the dog." Alexander gestured to Ruffian Caesar, who was gnawing his own back leg with great gusto in the small circle of light that they were allowing to escape from their dark lantern.

"The…the dog?" Jack asked, glancing helplessly in Georgina's direction. The poor lad probably thought he'd exchanged one deluded noble for another.

Georgina shrugged. "Ruffian Caesar is actually very adept at sneaking in and out of buildings."

"Your mutt…" Jack trailed off and shook his head. "This… this isn't how this sort of thing is done."

"Do you propose that we just walk up to the front gate and demand entrance?" Alexander asked.

"Well, no," Jack admitted, "but surely we could climb into an open window or…"

"But then we'd be on the main floor of a huge structure with a layout completely unknown to us," Georgina pointed out. "We all agreed on the journey here that Lord Clifville would likely imprison Percy and Tom in the dungeons."

"As befitting a man who thinks he's a direct descendant of King Arthur," Alexander added. "I would wager my curricle that there is a round table somewhere in that castle."

"With my helmet sitting in the middle of it," Georgina concluded bitterly and then felt ashamed for fretting over her treasure when Percy and Tom were suffering. "But more importantly, castles of this age often had escape tunnels in the event of a siege. If there is a secret passage, Ruffian Caesar will hopefully find it."

"For how long are we to stalk after a mutt?" Jack asked wearily.

"Just until there's enough daylight to look ourselves. It's already close to dawn."

"But the terrier is still chewing its leg," Jack pointed out.

Georgina knelt down by Ruffian Caesar. She had little hope in their plan working, but it wasn't as if they could see much in the dark. And the little dog did love his treats. A cool dungeon dug into an ancient hillside would be the perfect place to store his favorite crunchy vegetable. Georgina mustered all the enthusiasm that she could and shouted, "Turnip!"

Ruffian Caesar's head immediately shot up. In the faint moonlight, his left eye glistened against his white patch of fur while the rest of his small face was lost in the darkness.

"Find the turnip! Can you find the treat?" Georgina cajoled.

Ruffian Caesar sprang to his feet. Georgina braced herself to follow, glad she was not encumbered by skirts. Beside her, Alexander adjusted his cane. Even Jack shifted his body into a running stance.

Ruffian Caesar gave a joyful bark...and then turned in a circle. Six times.

"Perhaps we should dig for an entrance here?" Alexander joked.

Georgina sent him a baleful look. Jack snorted and then lifted his hand to his mouth in an attempt to hide his mirth.

"Turnip. Go get the turnip." Georgina bent low as she tried again.

It worked. At least a whit.

Ruffian Caesar executed a happy bounce and started sniffing. Everywhere.

"It is a good thing the sky is starting to lighten," Jack muttered.

Georgina ignored him. She didn't think their plan would succeed, but admitting the truth would mean acknowledging the seriousness of their circumstances. Perhaps Alexander had begun to influence her more than she'd thought. Laughter really could be the best shield.

Ruffian Caesar snuffled along the bumpy cliff, scrambling here and there. Georgina trailed him closely, with Jack reluctantly accompanying her. Alexander stayed on the beach, and Georgina knew that he was scanning their surroundings, his hand resting on the butt of his pistol.

Just as the sky began to turn a pearly gray and a thin band of light appeared on the horizon, Ruffian Caesar gave a happy woof. He performed a little doggy dance, his entire body writhing in utter joy. As Georgina climbed over the mounds of grass and lumps of exposed London Clay, she heard an unexpected, but entirely familiar, sound: doggy toenails scrabbling against wood.

Georgina fell to her knees and pulled away a thin layer of vegetation beneath Ruffian Caesar's paws. Sure enough, a trapdoor emerged. The planks were weathered and dried by the sea air. Ignoring the orange flakes that rubbed off onto her hands, Georgina yanked on the rusted metal loop in the center. The ancient wood had become light with age, and she easily lifted the cover. Below was a tunnel that sloped into the hillside.

"I don't believe it." Jack crouched down next to Georgina. "It beggars belief."

Georgina didn't wait to respond to Jack. She simply sprang to her feet and flew down the hillside toward Alexander. "Ruffian Caesar found it! He actually discovered a tunnel!"

"I never doubted our little conqueror," Alexander said and held out his arm. "Care to assist me up the slope?"

Georgina linked her elbow with his and together they climbed. Jack half slid down the grade to join them. He took ahold of Alexander's other side. Despite no path existing, the three of them managed to get Alexander swiftly to the secret entrance.

Pausing to whine mournfully every few moments, Ruffian Caesar paced impatiently. He didn't even wait until the humans reached him before he darted into the opening in a clear pursuit of turnips.

"Do you wager that it's safe?" Alexander asked as he tapped at the hard-packed ground with his walking stick while Georgina shone their dark lantern into the circular gap.

"London Clay is good for making passageways," Jack explained as he stuck his head and shoulders inside. "Much easier than mining in Wales. I'll go first, since I'm armed and familiar with narrow spaces."

"Here. Take the lantern," Georgina said as she held it out to him.

The passage was smaller, tighter, and definitely longer than that of the cave on her land. As they drew deeper and deeper into the hillside, an astringent, rotting odor permeated the narrow space. Her eyes watered from the stench, but she could hear Ruffian Caesar noisily licking the air. The scent did have a turnipy twinge, as if it was coming from a giant decomposing pile of the vegetable.

Suddenly, Ruffian Caesar emitted an excited sound halfway between a huff and a woof. All she could see in front of her was Jack's feet and legs, but she could clearly hear the dog's paws thudding against the London Clay. The tunnel didn't only funnel sounds but amplified them.

A few beats later, Georgina detected a noise that made her limbs shake. Not from fear. But from utter relief.

"Swounds, is that a dog?"

Percy.

That was Percy's voice!

"What is a mutt doing in this bloody dungeon?" Percy asked, sounding remarkably like...well...himself. "Is...is it eating one of those disgusting turnips?"

"Apparently so, my lord." Tom was speaking now, his tone respectful on the surface, but wry underneath.

They were both alive! Perhaps not unscathed but in good enough health and spirits to have retained their sense of humor.

"The only dog that I've ever witnessed enjoying that noxious root so much is..." Percy trailed off. "Wait, that scruff does look exactly like Ruffian Caesar!"

"He does indeed!" Tom no longer sounded covertly sardonic but excited.

Georgina wondered if she should call out. A guard could be

stationed with the men, but the two were talking so freely. Still, she did not wish to expose their presence too cavalierly.

"Here, boy!" Percy called. "Come here…Oh, would you release the bloody turnip for one moment and come over here!"

"I don't believe shouting will make the dog wander more closely to us," Tom observed drily.

"I am going to have to reach over and grab one of those disgusting, slimy roots, aren't I? Why am I the one locked in with the turnips?"

"Most likely because you started shuddering and gagging when the earl brought us down here," Tom pointed out. "Be glad we have access to a food cache."

"But they stink!" Percy complained. "And are, ugh, slick to the touch. Ewww. If only they'd shriveled instead of half rotted. Here, Ruffian Caesar! Here's a lovely, half-putrefied treat. Mmm! Mmm! Mmm! Moldy, lumpy, rooty goodness. Mmmmmm!"

Just then Georgina noticed a glow that wasn't coming from the lantern. She was almost certain now that Percy and Tom were alone, but there was no point in stopping precautions. Not when they were so close.

The tunnel opened enough for the three of them to crouch now, although Alexander continued to crawl—probably since he could move faster that way with his leg. She had a good view of Jack, who had his gun at the ready. The flickering light grew brighter.

"Jack!" Tom sounded overjoyed, but then his tone changed to worry. "What are you doing here? You'll be caught!"

"Georgina! What the hell! And what are you wearing? Alexander, is that you, too?" Percy shouted when Georgina finally stepped into the exceedingly malodorous dungeon with Alexander close behind.

Although the torches burning on the wall were not exceedingly bright, it took a moment for Georgina's eyes to adjust. When Percy wasn't nattering away, she could hear the steady drip of water. A mildewy scent mixed with the more powerful stench of the turnips. When she could see, the undercroft matched what her other senses were telling her. There were cracks in the masonry, and the stone walls glistened with moisture—at least in the places where mold wasn't growing. It was hard to tell how deep each cell was, but Percy and Tom stood pressed against the iron grates in front of theirs. The other chambers contained crates and barrels, presumably of foodstuffs.

Percy had fading bruises on his face, and he'd lost weight. His normally impeccable clothes were stained and even torn. Still, instead of leaning heavily against the strips of metal, he stood straight. His eyes were alert, and he didn't seem to be in obvious pain. Tom, who'd been taken captive later, looked in better shape. He only had a scrape on his cheek, and he wasn't much thinner than before.

"Alexander, did you bring my cousin here? I never took you for a fool!" Percy attempted to rattle his door, but the sturdy bars didn't even jiggle. "Do you have any idea how dangerous this is?"

"Alexander is accompanying me, not the other way around," Georgina told her cousin crisply. Despite the fear pulsating through her, she had no intention of being viewed as a helpless damsel. "And yes, we are well aware of the current peril, which is why we have no time to dawdle. This discussion can occur after a successful rescue. Now, do either of you know where a set of keys are?"

"Over there." Tom pointed his thumb in the direction of an iron rod sticking out of the wall with a large ring hanging from it.

"Well, that was unexpectedly easy," Alexander said. "It's definitely quieter than shooting the locks with our pistols. Saves lead, too. I suppose it's so convenient since this is chiefly a warehouse now."

"Good lord, when did you become so logical?" Percy asked. "You sound like Georgina. I thought only she could transform a dungeon escape into a series of practical steps."

"Our chief strategy has been relying on a dog's love for turnips, so I think you might be a tad premature in calling us rational." Alexander sent Percy a grin before he unhooked the key ring and began unlocking the doors.

"Can you both walk unassisted?" Georgina asked, ignoring the banter entirely. She wanted to be free of this frightening place. She didn't trust that a guard wouldn't appear, even if Lord Clifville was allegedly on his way to London.

"I might waver like a drunken sailor from eating nothing but turnips for over a week, but I'll make do," Percy said as he exited his cell. He was favoring his right foot, and he did sway a bit, but he stayed upright.

"I will be fine." Tom's gait was stiffer than normal, but he seemed steadier than Percy.

"We found—or rather, the dog found an old hidden tunnel," Jack said as he gestured to the entrance.

"Jack should lead, as he's armed," Alexander instructed. "I'll guard the rear."

"We can't leave yet!" Percy protested, shocking Georgina.

"Whyever not?" she demanded. She was accustomed to her cousin acting cavalierly, but certainly he understood the gravity of their circumstances.

"We need the helmet, the spoon, and the painting!" Percy insisted. "I saw them when Clifville dragged Tom and me through his castle before tossing us into the dungeon. We even had to stand in front of that damn artwork while he explained his plans."

"I cannot believe I am saying this, but the helmet isn't important right now." Georgina gripped her cousin's hand. "I have no idea what the other objects are or what precisely you're talking about but—"

"Clifville is on his way to London to poison the entire court and kill the king!" Percy exclaimed.

Chapter Twenty~One

━━━◦◦◦━━━

"I never thought I'd see a painting more unsettling than medieval depictions of the Last Judgment." Alexander stared dumbfounded at the wooden triptych in the castle's former Great Hall. The picture on the left showed a young Clifville being visited by what Alexander assumed was the ghost of Arthur and the Lady of the Lake. Instead of handing him Excalibur, though, they were offering him the state crown of King George I and the Stone of Scone, the ancient rock used in the coronation of Scottish kings. Evidently, phantom Arthur possessed superhuman strength, as he had seemingly no trouble hefting the huge slab of sandstone. The entire illustration had a biblical feel, almost like an image of the Annunciation, when the angel appeared to Mary and announced her pregnancy with the Christ child. It was also the most prosaic of the three panels.

The tableau on the right was exceedingly gruesome. It depicted recognizable members of King George's court and parliament succumbing to poison. There was a tangle of limbs, blood seeping from mouths and eyes, lolling and discolored tongues, and mottled flesh. Clifville strode triumphantly through the chaos, swinging an ornate sword and randomly maiming the dead and dying.

The center was not completed but was fully sketched out. Clifville stood triumphantly in the middle, wearing a full suit of armor, his head bare. In one hand, he held Georgina's helmet. Parts of it had been painted in, including the colorful eyebrows, while other aspects remained simple charcoal lines. The effect was rather chillingly dreamlike—a half-realized, nightmarish fantasy.

Clifville clutched the coronation spoon in his other gauntlet with his metal-covered foot grinding into the severed head of King George II. The likeness of the monarch was disturbingly accurate, made more unsettling by the graphic effects of a deadly toxin. The sovereign's eyes were bloodshot and more protruding than normal. Spidery veins, the color of mauve, covered his face. His tongue was a marbled purple and black.

"Whenever I closed my eyes in the dungeon, that picture haunted me. To think that Clifville spent years creating such gruesome images." Pendergrast shuddered theatrically, and Alexander was glad that his friend seemed like his normal self. But Alexander also knew all too well that humor could mask pain. Pendergrast might be making the same quips as before his kidnapping, but that did not mean his captivity hadn't affected him deeply. Alexander would make sure to spend time with his friend after this, checking up on him, even if Pendergrast outwardly seemed fine.

"This painting makes no sense," Georgina tapped her finger against her chin as she contemplated the first panel. "Even if Arthur existed, he's Welsh or maybe English. He wasn't Pictish, so why did the earl include the Stone of Scone?"

"That is the aspect of this monstrosity that you choose to quibble with?" Pendergrast turned slowly toward his cousin.

Georgina visibly bristled. "Well, Lord Clifville is a historian."

"A deluded one," Alexander pointed out. "After all, he does believe that he is the heir to the Round Table—which we have oddly not yet seen."

"Yes, but even with Lord Clifville accepting that fallacy as the truth, if he adhered to the rest of the legend, it would not make sense to use a Scottish rite in something meant to be exceedingly English. I do realize that Edward I stole the Stone of Destiny in 1296 and installed it in Westminster under the Coronation Chair, but it still seems poor symbolism when Lord Clifville could have drawn Excalibur or the Holy Grail or—"

Jack cleared his throat. "Pardon me, my lady and my lords, but this mightn't be the best place for debate."

"He is right, Georgie." Pendergrast limped to his cousin's side and slowly raised his arm to sling it around her shoulders. "When Clifville last visited me, the bastard said, and I quote, 'You must decide now if you will join my side, as I will claim my kingdom in five days hence.' And that was three turnips ago."

"Three *what* ago?" Alexander asked.

"Turnips," Pendergrast said as if it was common to mark the passage of time with root vegetables. "Since I had no writing implement, I created a pile of them instead of tally marks. Hopefully, I was correct in estimating the length of a day—since he kept those bloody torches burning day and night when darkness didn't cause me to spill my secrets. So by my turnip count, that only leaves us less than forty-eight hours to reach London. And we're three normal travel days away from the capital."

"I could go by horseback," Alexander said, "but that means I couldn't take the triptych with me."

"It would be exceedingly difficult to be granted an immediate audience with the king without it. Both of us have a reputation for frivolity," Pendergrast said, showing an unusual glimmer of seriousness and an even more rare kernel of introspection. "I doubt anyone would believe that boring old Clifville is plotting a mass poisoning. How he became a favorite of the king,

I shall never know. George II is notorious for not liking book learning."

"Clifville has helped the king acquire rare antiquities and also lent His Majesty a sheen of Englishness," Alexander said. The German-born ruler's entire reign had been beset with claims that he and his father should not be on the throne, but rather the Stuarts living in exile in France. The Stuarts were technically next in line, but their Catholic beliefs had made them untenable candidates for Protestant England. But the Jacobite Uprising of '45 proved that not all agreed. "King George doesn't have to bother himself with learning the history of our shores. He can just have Clifville drone on. But his reliance on the earl will make him more reluctant to believe our claims."

Alexander rubbed the handle of his cane as he stared up at the wooden triptych and tried to determine how best to transport it. The middle section was three feet wide by six feet tall. The other panels were the same height but half the length. The pieces wouldn't fit in saddlebags, although Alexander could fasten them to the back of his carriage.

"I'll have to drive my curricle back to London," Alexander said with more confidence than he felt. "It'll be the ride of my life, but I'll make it." Alexander's political interests lay in stopping the slave trade, improving prison conditions, and ending cruelty to animals. He cared little whether a Stuart or Hanoverian king sat on the throne, but he certainly did not want Clifville commencing a bloodbath.

"Jack and I can carry the painting from the castle," Tom said.

"Are you certain?" Georgina asked. "Percy said that neither of you have eaten well in days."

"I'm accustomed to hefting objects much heavier, my lady. And there is an exit to the outdoors on the other side of the great hall. Lord Percy and I were dragged through it when we were first brought here." Tom nodded his head to the far end of the long, cavernous room, still half shrouded in shadows. Dawn had begun to seep through the narrow windows, but it hadn't yet penetrated the gloomy space.

Jack and Tom folded the triptych and then grabbed opposite ends. Alexander took the lead, keeping his pistol at the ready. The massive castle seemed all but abandoned, especially in the wee hours of the morning with the servants tucked away in their wing. But the threat of violence still swirled around them. Pendergrast—who had Jack's gun in his hand—trailed behind with Georgina lending him support.

As they drifted as noiselessly as possible through the crumbling stronghold, more and more pearly pink light illuminated the ancient space. One beam suddenly bisected the room, lighting the one thing that had been missing.

A very, very gaudy replica of the Round Table.

It was painted in the same style as the triptych but with more fantastical images of Lord Clifville slaying wyrms and villainous storybook knights. In the center, he proudly held a golden goblet, most likely intended to be the Holy Grail.

But Alexander knew the decorated piece of furniture wasn't what elicited the sharp gasp from Georgina. It was her helmet, boldly displayed next to the purloined coronation spoon. Alexander watched as Pendergrast released his grip on his cousin's arm and made a shooing motion with his hand.

"Go. Go save your helmet."

Georgina dashed to it, then stopped. Bathed in the rosy glow, she should have looked ethereal. But the serious expression on her face as she inspected her precious find marked her as what she was. A preeminent scholar. Very carefully she reached for it, cradling it against her body.

From a distance, Alexander watched. He wanted to share

her joy, but he didn't feel invited. She didn't want a sportsman by her side, but a fellow antiquarian—one who would understand this treasure without explanation. This was Georgina's moment, and Alexander had no wish to intrude.

Pendergrast, however, had no sensitivity to Georgina's quiet, personal triumph. He limped forward and snatched the coronation spoon. "We best take this, too. Coupled with the painting, it's undeniable proof of Clifville's villainy."

"The sun is climbing higher," Tom warned. "There didn't seem to be too many servants here, but they will start stirring soon."

Alexander hustled the group forward, listening for any footsteps other than theirs. They moved without incident through the rest of the Great Hall and its hodgepodge of rusting armor, which Clifville must have purchased from impoverished aristocrats. Everything had a hint of desperation to it, even the moth-eaten ermine cloak and a collection of ancient-looking goblets.

As they pushed through the heavy wooden door and spilled out of the castle, Alexander thought they'd reached safety. But a hulking figure stood against the bright wash of the morning sky, the barrel of his gun glinting in the emerging sunlight.

It looked like Lord Clifville had another, menacing accomplice: Lord Malbarry.

◦◦◦

"Two large coaches are barreling down the road!" Lord Malbarry shouted over the thundering hooves of his own mount and Alexander's latest team.

It was a good thing that Malbarry had turned out to be investigating the theft of the coronation spoon rather than being part of Clifville's maniacal schemes. Despite his bulk, the man had proven to be a swift rider as he checked the road ahead for dangers.

The marquess's vanguard skills weren't the only way he was helping Alexander and Georgina race to London at an impossible pace. If he hadn't financed the hiring of new horses at multiple coaching stops, Alexander would have been forced to wait to rest his own bays. But his warmbloods were happily munching hay at the same inn where Pendergrast was holed up with Tom and Jack. Alexander was furiously driving day and night to the capital with Georgina sleeping intermittently at his side and Malbarry riding as a scout.

Alexander slacked their pace to one at which he could easily stop the curricle. As they turned the bend, two rumbling carriages thundered into view. At the sight of the lead one, relief swept through Alexander. He knew that livery. It belonged to Tavish Stewart—Matthew's benefactor.

The coachmen drew back on their reins while Alexander did the same. His sister popped out of the conveyance, closely followed by her husband and Calliope. From the other coach spilled the Wick cousins, Mr. Stewart, and Mr. Powys. All the women wore men's clothing, although Hannah hadn't bothered to hide her red mane of hair. Cradled in Charlotte's arms was a familiar white fluff, while Pan perched self-importantly on Hannah's shoulder. It was a wonder that they hadn't brought the monkey, but Alexander didn't see the impertinent little face among the group.

"I assume that they're friends of yours, given that your sister and your best friend are among them," Lord Malbarry said to Alexander in a low voice that wouldn't carry to the others.

Alexander nodded as he shot the marquess a look. "I didn't realize that you knew so much about my family and friends."

A grin that was more grim than pleasant stretched Lord Malbarry's normally expressionless lips. "My grandfather ensured that I know everything about the nobility—anything to make me useful to the king."

"Yet His Majesty doesn't trust you."

Malbarry snorted in disdain. "My father was a notorious Jacobite and died a traitor's death, according to the Crown. His Grace is forever hoping to change the king's opinion of our family, which is why he ordered me to discover what happened to the coronation spoon."

"Alexander! Georgina!" Charlotte called as she ran toward them. Although a pouf of feathers obscured Fluffus Legatus's face, the rooster radiated grumpy disdain as he bounced up and down in Charlotte's arms, his head perfectly straight. "What happened! You look like you haven't slept in days, and we never heard from you. We were all so worried."

Alexander and Georgina launched into an abbreviated version of Percy's rescue and the Earl of Clifville's treasonous perfidy. While their friends from the Black Sheep gathered around, Malbarry stood off to the side, towering over them like a distant mountain.

"Blackguard! Villain!" Pan screeched as he paced on Hannah's shoulder, his feathers puffed up.

"Why are there birds here?" Lord Malbarry finally interjected after staying silent for the entire exchange of questions and answers.

Everyone from the Black Sheep turned in his direction. By their expressions, Alexander assumed that they'd somehow overlooked the giant noble. Alexander wondered if the Wick cousins recognized him as the grandson of the man who'd sent their fathers to prison. Judging by their faces, they didn't.

Sophia's expression was open and pleasant, while Hannah looked…intrigued. Very intrigued.

Swounds.

Hannah most definitely did not realize Malbarry's identity. Although the marquess had just spoken with a refined accent, he wore rough linsey-woolsey clothes rather than his normal tailored wools and silks. He didn't look like a lord but rather a hardworking laborer. Alexander debated whether he should enlighten his cousin, but he didn't know if the reveal would be wise. She had a fiery temper, and a fight would delay their journey.

Hannah stepped up to Malbarry, a broad, welcoming smile on her face that was tinged with more than a little friendly flirtation. "Pan is our constant companion and an excellent partner in mischief of all kinds. Besides, we were taking the chicken, and Pan would not be left at home. He is an exceedingly jealous type."

"Oh, I see," Malbarry said, sounding a bit awkward and more than a tad confused. To Alexander's surprise, red stained Malbarry's cheeks, but perhaps it was just sunburn from their long, seemingly endless journey. Alexander immediately forgot about the fellow's potential blush, however, when the viscount did something even more unexpected. He bowed. To the parrot. "Well, uh, pleased to make your acquaintance, Pan."

The bird was not impressed. "Blackguard." And then, because Pan was Pan, he started squawking out vulgarities. "Beast with two backs! Beast with two backs!"

There was no doubt. The stiff, normally self-composed man was blushing. Lord Malbarry's face was as bright as an ornamental tomato from the New World.

"How did you come to help Alexander and Georgina?" Sophia asked.

"He was about to storm Clifville's castle in search of the coronation spoon," Alexander said quickly. He had decided it was best to wait to disclose Lord Malbarry's identity.

Not even trying to hide her appreciation, Hannah glanced at the marquess. "You look very storm-worthy or storm-ready. Either way."

Lord Malbarry choked, and then his lips twitched into the faintest of real grins. Before the poor fellow could respond, a gasp arose from Charlotte and Calliope. The two had wandered over to the back of the curricle and had spotted the hideous third panel.

"Is this what Lord Clifville is planning?" Charlotte asked, horrified.

"That…that is my maternal aunt and her husband." Calliope pointed to two of the prone bodies. For the first time that Alexander could recall, she sounded subdued. "I had tea with her earlier this week, and she mentioned attending a banquet hosted by the king. It is tonight. You'll never be able to make it to St. James's before the meal is served. By the time you arrive at the outskirts of London, the roads will be too congested."

"You're such a fast rider, Calliope." Charlotte grabbed her friend's hands. "You should go and warn your aunt."

Calliope shook her head. "Even on horseback, I doubt I could get through. If by some miracle, I did, it still wouldn't work. I may be able to convince my aunt, but not my uncle. He finds me vulgar and prone to excessive whimsy. My aunt will never gainsay him."

"If only we could stop London traffic," Alexander said as frustration burned through him.

"Maybe we could send a rider ahead and ask George Belle for help," Sophia said. "His main stables are on this side of London, and he is there today taking care of business. Belle could map out the best route."

"Doesn't he control a large number of London's hackney carriages?" Georgina asked.

"Yes," Sophia said.

"Is it a well-organized network with communication between the drivers?" Georgina asked.

Alexander turned to watch her closely. Georgina definitely had a plan.

"Yes. Belle likes his drivers to pass on information to others about traffic situations and places needing carriages. The coachmen have a series of hand signals that Belle developed with my help," Sophia said.

"Perhaps if all of his coachmen coordinated their efforts, they could halt traffic and provide us passage through the streets," Georgina said. "It would be a bit like controlling the flow of water."

"It sounds difficult to coordinate," Sophia said slowly, "but if anyone could manage such a miracle, it would be Belle."

"Who shall deliver the message to him?" Mr. Powys asked. "I'd volunteer, but I didn't grow up around horses, and I can't ride."

"I'm lightweight, and I travel fast," Calliope offered.

"Here, use my steed." The marquess dismounted and handed the reins to the duke's daughter. "The stallion is rather fresh and has a few miles left before you'll need to exchange him for another at a coaching inn. There's one in Pudingham. Give them my name."

Calliope nodded and then sprang onto the horse. Lying low over the beast's neck, she took off at a gallop. She practically melded with the animal, making a single unit.

"Bye-bye! Bye-bye." Pan cackled the words gleefully until he turned on Hannah's shoulder to glare with his one eye at Fluffus Legatus, who was still nestled in Charlotte's arms. "Birdie bye-bye. Birdie bye-bye."

"Pan has a low tolerance for other feathered beings," Hannah said wearily. "It is why we put them in separate carriages. Things have not been calm at the Black Sheep with the rooster in residence."

"If Alexander and Georgina are to invade a dinner at St. James, then they should take Crinitus Legatus." Charlotte walked back to the curricle. "Chickens have become a necessary accessory for the fashionable set. You might look amiss without one."

"Are you bamming me?" Alexander asked as amusement trickled through him despite the dire circumstances. "Did my joke actually take root, especially so quickly?"

"Impressively so," Charlotte said. "Shall I place him in the basket with Ruffian Caesar?"

"Yes. I wouldn't want him flying out on the curves," Alexander said.

"I'll ride with you and Miss Harrington in the curricle until I can hire another mount," Malbarry said as Charlotte carefully nestled the rooster beside Ruffian Caesar.

When Georgina pressed tightly against Alexander to make room for the marquess, he tried to calm his natural reaction. It would be a crush until they reached Pudingham, and Alexander couldn't spend the entire time with an overheated body. He needed to be primed for another sort of action entirely. And he couldn't risk thinking about his attraction for Georgina, not with their relationship doomed before it even began.

He could hurt later when he wasn't responsible for carrying off the impossible. It would take all of his skill at the leathers—and even more luck—to reach the outskirts of London in time, let alone to accomplish the mad dash through the city streets.

But he'd always enjoyed a challenge.

⚜

Alexander should have been steeped in exhaustion. After all, he'd driven hard for two days and two nights. His jaw hurt from clenching it so tightly as he barreled toward curves, judging how fast he could take them. Even with his thick gloves, his hands were rubbed raw, but he'd stopped registering the pain long ago. The muscle aches in his arms had become familiar companions. He was only glad that he still had the strength to yank on the reins. His throat had grown scratchy from yelling commands, but even if rough, his voice was clear enough. His bad leg—well—it was a cramping mess, but he'd suffered worse agony from the surgeries.

Yet despite the soreness and downright pain, exhilaration rushed through Alexander as he dodged yet another farm wagon. The driver yelled, shaking his fist. Fluffus Legatus began his nervous *bock*ing, inspiring Ruffian Caesar to let loose a string of barks. Georgina shouted an apology above the hullabaloo before the four of them swung around another bend. Out of the corner of his eye, Alexander watched as she now expertly shifted her body to avoid being tossed about. The basket kept chicken and mutt safe, despite the animals' protestations to the contrary.

His dear Miss Georgina Harrington of the Essex mud pit was a remarkable woman. She'd kept him company the whole time, only dozing in small snippets here and there. He'd loved her stories, even those about antiquity. History through her keen observations fascinated him.

Yes. He could play the scholar for her, but he couldn't forsake his wildness. But watching her whoop joyfully as they snaked down a windy hillside, Alexander knew Georgina possessed just as much daring as he—perhaps more. Why couldn't they be both scholar and adventurer? He needed to at least present the idea to her. If she still rejected it, rejected him, then he would listen. But he owed it to himself to be honest about his feelings.

However, racing pell-mell down the road was not conducive to love confessions—no matter how heartfelt.

Three riders suddenly appeared on the crest of a hill: Malbarry, Calliope, and Mr. Belle. When they drew up beside them, Mr. Belle tossed a rolled-up map to Georgina.

"Can you read it?" he asked as she flattened it out.

"Yes—although I'm more accustomed to ancient ones with less road details and more monsters."

"London itself is the belly of the beast." Mr. Belle tempered his ominous words with a cocky grin. "But I've already slayed it for you. It's a madcap plan, but it just might work. Lord Malbarry, Calliope, and I will ride ahead to guide you and ensure the roads are properly blocked."

"Thank you," Georgina said.

"Are you ready for fun?" Mr. Belle asked Alexander.

"It'll be a treat racing through London's streets unhindered." When Alexander said the words, he realized that they weren't just false cheer. He wanted to whip through the capital at a breakneck speed with the woman he loved by his side. "Let's go."

As Alexander drew deeper into the city, he wasn't precisely sure what to expect. Then he heard the shouts and the yells. As they burst into an intersection, Mr. Belle's carriages were blocking two of the thoroughfares. Wagons, other hackneys, and elegant coaches were piled up behind. Men of all social classes milled about the jammed streets, but Mr. Belle's men held them back. Horses whinnied, and ladies with powdered hair poked their heads from curtained conveyances. Some of them were hurling invectives even worse than the fellows.

In contrast to the chaos on the dammed thoroughfares, the path in front of Alexander was clear. It was odd and thrilling to barrel past the half-timbered buildings with their exposed wooden supports and white plaster walls. At a dizzying speed, they thundered by shops with dangling signs. People poured from the coffeehouses and taverns, eager to watch the spectacle.

Sometimes they were greeted with cheers, other times with jeers, and normally a mixture of both. The whole city had come alive, brimming with curiosity, confusion, and outrage.

Even with Mr. Belle's men eking out a path for them, Alexander still had to remain alert. Children darted into the streets—sometimes followed by their panicked mothers. A big dog ran alongside them, barking at Ruffian Caesar and Fluffus Legatus. A burly fellow burst through Mr. Belle's line of men at one intersection and stood wide-legged in the middle of a thankfully large thoroughfare. On a windy back alley, they encountered a bleating goat that almost rammed the curricle. The surly animal even chased after them for several blocks as Ruffian Caesar growled and Fluffus Legatus cowered.

There were dirt-packed lanes and bone-rattling cobblestone ones. They whipped through twisty alleys with sudden sharp turns obscured by the hodgepodge of buildings and charged down fancy thoroughfares with huge townhouses. Alexander led the horses around crescents and over bridges. The curricle crunched through piles of refuse and groaned as it swung past grand statues. Waifs in dirty threadbare clothes waved, and well-dressed ladies in fine gowns gasped. He, Georgina, and their animal companions traversed rich neighborhoods and poor ones, but at every intersection, there was the same jumble of humanity trying to break through.

Triumph roared through Alexander as he and Georgina pulled up to St. James's Palace just as members of the nobility were departing from their carriages. He'd done it. They still needed to breach the royal residence and convince the king, but Alexander had accomplished a truly Herculean task. He'd finally wrestled and beat his own Nemean lion.

Chapter Twenty~Two

G eorgina never thought she'd glimpse the inside of the famed St. James's Palace. She certainly would never have pictured herself strolling through the state apartments wearing men's clothing that hadn't been changed in days while clutching a fluffy and extremely frightened rooster. She was fairly certain she smelled fouler than the bird. Alexander likely did, too, but he managed not to appear rumpled as they strolled behind the triptych carried by Mr. Belle and Lord Malbarry. Calliope had stayed outside of the palace to avoid recognition whilst in male clothing, but her relatives were at the front of their strange procession. Calliope's uncle hadn't wanted to help them enter the royal residence until he'd seen the panel depicting his gruesome death.

Their motley assembly bustled through richly appointed chambers so quickly that Georgina only caught glimpses of gilded woodwork, imposing tapestries, and expensive carpets. When they halted in front of the King's Presence Chamber, Georgina started to turn her head to study her surroundings. But before she could, Alexander leaned close.

"If the king asks who discovered the helmet, you should name yourself," Alexander whispered.

Georgina's heart, which had already been beating abnormally fast, catapulted into her breastbone and then settled into a mad gallop. She inadvertently squeezed Crinitus Legatus a little too hard, and he clucked in dismay.

"Are you saying that I should claim that I, as George Harrington, made the find? I suppose I could continue using this male identity, but it would be a great scandal if anyone found ou—"

"No." Alexander's voice was still low, but he managed to inject it with urgency. "You should use your real identity—Miss Georgina Harrington."

"Do you mean that I should reveal who I am? To the king?" Georgina wondered if it was even legal for a woman to appear before His Majesty in such attire. It certainly would result in her social demise.

"No. Just state that your female cousin—meaning you—unearthed the helmet," Alexander said. "If the king champions your discovery, then no one at the Antiquarian Society of London can gainsay you."

"Do…do you think he would?" Georgina asked, trying not to squish Crinitus Legatus again.

"We're about to save His Majesty not just from death, but from his entire reign ending disastrously," Alexander said. "He will support what we say."

Before Georgina could question Alexander further, their entire group marched forward. Nervousness flooded her, and she could barely pay attention to her environs. Peering around Mr. Belle and Lord Malbarry, she caught a glimpse of George II. He was sitting on his throne holding a rather regal-looking rooster with green tail plumage.

Then she spied him. Lord Clifville. He was standing relaxed among the other courtiers already gathered around the monarch. When his gaze fell upon the folded triptych, the color leached from the scholar's already pale face. His body swayed, and he had to stagger to stay upright. The king glanced at him curiously but then turned his attention back to the parade of people entering his chamber.

Georgina, though, kept her gaze on Clifville. His face was no longer devoid of color. It was aflame. His fists were clenched, and his body primed for violence.

"What!" King George bellowed as Calliope's uncle explained the conspiracy. Mr. Belle and Lord Malbarry unfolded the wood panels. A collective gasp arose from the gathered courtiers. There was one strangled scream. Those who were depicted as maimed in the painting reached for their body parts as if to ensure they were still attached.

Everyone appeared frozen in horrified shock. But not Clifville. His lanky body sprang forward like a coiled spring. Before the guards could react, he grabbed a sword from a slack-jawed admiral.

"This will serve as my Excalibur!" Clifville shouted out the words as if leading a grand charge.

He rushed toward the sovereign, hefting the piece over his head like a battle axe. Even Georgina, who knew nothing about the handling of modern weaponry, was fairly certain that was not the way to attack. It was, however, still dangerous to anyone in Clifville's path.

As the self-acclaimed heir to the Round Table rushed past Georgina, she simply stuck out her foot. Clifville tripped. He didn't even have time to stop himself before he ingloriously toppled onto his nose. At impact, the purloined sword flew from his grasp. It clattered along the floor until it rested near the king's feet.

For a beat, no one moved. Then the guards launched themselves at Clifville. They hauled the stunned academic to his feet and began dragging him from the room. About halfway to the exit, Clifville's fight returned, and he struggled against his captors.

"I am the true heir to the English throne!" Clifville screamed. "My father's ancestors can be traced back to before the Norman Invasion! His forebears hail from Colchester—built on the Roman Fort Camulodunum, which was named for Camelot! I am the divine ruler!"

"The fort was named after Camulus—the Celtic god of war! It had nothing to do with King Arthur, who was a *mythical* Welshman. *My-thi-cal!*" Georgina shouted, thankfully remembering after the first word to deepen her voice. She really should have stayed quiet, but she could not allow such flagrant misinformation to stand. Her cries must have startled Crinitus Legatus, for he threw back his fluffy head and crowed. Emphatically.

"Mr. Harrington is right," Alexander said, his tone a calm contrast to Crinitus Legatus's avian battle cry.

Clifville, however, just kept yelling. "If only I'd successfully shot you in the Essex countryside! You two are the most annoying of my rightful subjects! I am the proper sovereign! I am…"

As Clifville's protestations grew ever fainter, silence once again descended over the throne room. The king fixed Georgina with a penetrating look.

"Who are you?" George II asked, his voice carrying an accent tinged with both French and German and more than a little command.

Georgina felt the scrutiny of the entire room of high-ranking nobles, military men, and clergy. She was accustomed to living in obscurity. But the attention did not feel as heavy as she'd expected. After all, she and Alexander were the heroes of this adventure, and she'd more than earned her right to speak.

"I am Mr. George Harrington, the cousin of Miss Georgina

Harrington." Georgina could feel Alexander's gaze on her, warm and supportive.

The king blinked. "And who is she?"

Georgina glanced over at Alexander, who was smiling brightly, the grin on his face entirely real. Not even needing to draw in her breath for fortitude, she turned back to George II.

"Miss Georgina Harrington discovered the ancient helmet that Lord Clifville is holding in the middle frame. It is not of Arthurian origin, but it is a remarkable part of English history. When the priceless antiquity and Miss Harrington's other cousin, Lord Percy Pendergrast, went missing, Miss Harrington—along with Lord Heathford and myself—tracked them both down at Lord Clifville's castle. That is how this whole conspiracy was uncovered." Georgina felt like a trumpeter heralding not royalty but her own hard work. For the first time, she was not hiding behind a male relative. Even if she was speaking as Mr. George Harrington, she was still claiming her success under her real name. She would not be denied any longer. She was staking claim to everything. Not just her life's work but her very existence.

She was Miss Georgina Harrington, the discoverer of the greatest find of antiquity on English soil.

◈

"You put a cocked hat on Crinitus Legatus?" Georgina asked in mostly mock dismay as she climbed into Alexander's curricle. The mud and dust from their wild dash to London had been cleaned off, and the sleek equipage shone in the summer sun. Georgina felt a bit like the vehicle herself—sparkling and ready for another adventure. Particularly one with Alexander.

"Of course." Alexander wore one of the cheekiest smiles that she had witnessed on his face. "*Fluffus* Legatus is off to see the king. He must be properly attired."

"But *Crinitus* Legatus already has a pouf on his head!" Georgina complained.

"It wasn't nearly dignified enough for His Majesty." Alexander flicked the reins as he shot her a rather naughty wink.

"But our rooster has already been to court, and we're just meeting King George in the gardens," Georgina pointed out, refusing to concede this point. Really, clothing on chickens. It was getting absurd. She had no idea why Alexander had even brought the bird—although she supposed she should be grateful for the feathered companion.

After two nights of good sleep, she no longer had the frenzied, chaotic energy that had buoyed her during her first encounter with the sovereign. Nor was she meeting him in her male garb. He'd commanded a private audience with Miss Georgina Harrington and Lord Heathford—even going so far as to request that she not bring a chaperone. The king was doing his best to quell any rumors about the near-poisoning of his court, fearing it could bring undue unrest, especially with the current war against France and Spain.

"Our rooster," Alexander repeated. "I like the sound of that."

The joy that had been bubbling through Georgina collapsed into a puddle. Why—why had she uttered such a silly sentiment? Of course, she and Alexander did not have a chicken together. They would be parting soon and might already have said their goodbyes if not for His Majesty's summons.

"We…we do need to talk about who will take custody of Crinitus Legatus when I leave for Essex. I know we said we would share, but that was when Anne and Algernon would not allow a pet. Hopefully, with my brother's crimes being known,

I can finally live on my own." Georgina glanced down at her hands and rubbed the callus on her right thumb.

"I…" Alexander paused, and he sounded as nervous as Georgina felt. Shocked, she glanced up at him. Sure enough, he was visibly swallowing as he stared resolutely ahead. Although the London street was crowded as usual, it did not warrant that much strong attention.

"I have been giving that a great deal of thought." Alexander finally completed his statement, his voice as rough and dry as a long-weathered wooden plank.

"Over whom shall retain ownership of the rooster?" Georgina asked, thoroughly befuddled.

"No, not that—or maybe, yes, indirectly. I suppose it would resolve that matter as well. I mean if you are amenable. Which you don't need to be. Amenable, I mean."

She really did not know what he meant. "I am hopelessly confused."

"You're not just a scholar, Georgina. You're an adventurer, too."

"Pardon? What does that have to do with Crinitus Legatus? I suppose I did rescue him, but—"

"Ignore that." Alexander squeezed his eyes shut.

"Should you be doing that? We are proceeding down one of the busiest thoroughfares in the city." Georgina wondered if she should grab the reins—either the physical or metaphorical ones. Unfortunately, she didn't know the direction they were headed in either sphere.

Alexander's eyes popped back open. "It was unfair of me to make it about you. This is about me—or rather you accepting me. So it does involve you, but not that you need to change. Well, I mean I don't need to, either. Or rather I can't. But I don't think it's necessary for either of us to alter our innate characteristics. I believe we fit—as is."

"Alexander, I really have no earthly idea of what you're getting on at." Georgina felt hopelessly adrift. Yet at the same time, an undercurrent of excitement began to hum through her. It was as if part of her comprehended his garbled explanations.

"I am a sportsman," Alexander announced, as if this signified something.

"Yes. I am aware."

"And I shall probably be a sportsman even when I am old and tottering and the reins shake in my hands. I shall still want to race and feel the wind against my balding head, because that is part of who I am."

"Yes?" Georgina asked, trying not to laugh at the image that he so emphatically painted even as she tried to decipher his deeper meaning.

"You will still climb down into mud pits even after your hair has turned a beautiful shade of silvery white."

"Why are we both aging so dramatically in this discussion?"

"Because I want us to do it together," Alexander blurted out.

Georgina was beginning to understand exactly what he meant, and a wonderful, wonderful joy spread through her. But still, she could not help but tease Alexander a bit more. After all, he was always the one making quips. It was only fair she managed her share, too. And now that she realized his intent, he seemed adorably flustered.

"Accomplish what, precisely? Losing our hair together?" She lightly bumped his arm.

He glanced at her and must have detected her impishness. He chuckled. "No. Mine is falling out. Yours will remain in a glorious mane."

"Then what are you saying?" Georgina asked as her every fiber strained to hear his answer.

Alexander inhaled so deeply that his chest visibly inflated. For a moment, Georgina thought he might pop a button on his waistcoat. She knew that she felt ready to burst.

When Alexander did speak, all of his words came out in one heart-stopping jumble. "I know you imagined yourself wed to a scholar and that you associate curricle-racing men with your brother. But I promise that, if you agree to marry me, I will always support your work as an antiquarian. You can dig up every single barrow on your land. When I inherit, you can scour my estates for more. And I will listen. Every night, we will sit by the fire as you describe in impressive detail how ancient peoples likely used the objects that you've dug up. I'll read all your treatises, and I won't think them dry because you wrote them. I may not be a perfect academic, but I swear I can become the ideal helpmate of a very capable scholar."

And Georgina had thought herself ready to explode with bliss before. A wonderful headiness filled her, and she wanted to allow the sheer ecstasy to send her floating. But her ever-present logic weighed her down.

"But—but wouldn't that destroy the vow that you made to yourself—that you would no longer try to please your parents? Your father doesn't just find me a suitable bride. He selected me himself."

"To hell with living to spite the duke and duchess. I want to be happy, Georgina, and I am discovering that you are a very essential component to my joy. Nay, not merely joy, but something imminently more lasting. You make me feel comfortable, Georgina. With who I am. Even though you make me smile, I don't feel obligated to grin in your presence. I can frown with you, Georgina."

How could Georgina argue against those wonderful words? Emotion swamped her, and tears sprang to her eyes. "I never thought I could be so moved by someone saying that I make them frown."

"I didn't say that you make me frown!" Alexander said, clearly aghast. "I mean that I am able to show my real feelings around you, even those that I've kept hidden for years. Maybe especially those."

Georgina took pity and squeezed his biceps again. What she really wanted to do was throw her arms about Alexander and kiss him passionately. However, lustful embraces were probably more at odds with driving a carriage than simply closing one's eyes.

"I understand. And yes." She couldn't resist bussing him on the cheek. That, at least, should not cause an accident.

Alexander started to pull on the reins. Then he shook his head and relaxed his grip. Maybe even a press of the lips against his temple was too much.

"A yes to what?" His voice was even more hoarse than before.

"If I clarify, you're not going to yank on the reins and cause the team to rear, right?" Georgina queried.

"I won't," Alexander promised.

"I would be extremely happy to marry you, Alexander." Georgina could barely form the words because her mouth was stretched in such a wide grin.

Alexander whooped loudly. People on the street and those passing in wagons turned to stare at them. But Georgina didn't care. They were getting married and could stir up all the scandals they wanted. So she joined him, which of course caused even more looks. Crinitus Legatus—who had fallen asleep in her arms—arose with a surprising strident *bock*.

"We'd better stop," Alexander said. "We're nearing the

gardens, and we don't want to cause a scene before our clandestine meeting."

Georgina smiled. "I thought I was supposed to be the logical one and you the carefree one."

"Perhaps we're influencing each other for the better."

"You have brought brightness into my life, Alexander." Georgina leaned briefly against his shoulder, but not long enough to attract notice.

"Can I refer to you as my affianced?" Alexander asked as they turned into St. James's Park.

"It is hardly something to keep a secret if we are to be married," Georgina laughed.

"Maybe we should elope like my sister did. This new requirement of banns is a nuisance," Alexander said.

"I have heard that Scotland is lovely this time of year," Georgina said just as the curricle pulled up to a rather secluded dock.

A man dressed in plain, unremarkable clothes was waiting in a punt to ferry them over to Duck Island. The trip across the canal was quick—although Georgina did spy two of the park's famed pelicans bobbing along in the still water. As the three of them—well, four, counting Crinitus Legatus—approached the other bank, a raft of mallards took flight, quacking their anger at being disturbed.

Instead of going to the cottage built by William III, Georgina and Alexander were led to the back of the building, where a silk pavilion had been set up. The king lounged on a chair in the shade, a veritable feast of sweet delicacies set out before him. His green-tailed rooster was happily pecking through the grass for insects.

Although Georgina had been nervous about the formalities of meeting the king again, Calliope and Charlotte's emergency training that morning had prepared her. The introductions went smoothly…at least until Alexander identified Georgina as his fiancée. The relaxed stance of George II immediately stiffened into a more regal one.

"That is a happy development. It shall make my request and other plans much easier," the king said rather cryptically.

What request? The question burned through Georgina, but she didn't dare voice it. The anxiety that she'd been keeping at bay seeped out.

"Sit." King George waved toward the seats across from him. As Georgina and Alexander started to obey his instruction, the sovereign fixed Georgina with a penetrating gaze. "You look very much like your cousin, Mr. Harrington."

Georgina froze, her rump hovering midair. It was not the most dignified position and most likely against all sorts of protocol. But she was too startled to move.

His Majesty knew her secret. She was certain. If her masquerade as a man became public, the gossip would destroy not just her reputation but now Alexander's, too. Although she would suffer more, she didn't want Alexander to face any more ostracization than he already did.

Then King George winked. Actually winked.

Georgina plopped into the chair with a resounding thud. She was not cajoled into thinking that the sovereign was a soft, kind-hearted soul. After all, he had not only banished his late heir from the palace but had a horribly contentious relationship with him until the previous Prince of Wales's untimely death. King George was also bellicose, eager to enter into fights in the European theater and to expand the empire, no matter the cost to the peoples living on the lands England conquered.

But it appeared that His Majesty would not reveal her identity as Mr. Harrington. Momentary relief flooded Georgina.

"I do hope you marry quickly," the king said. "I was concerned about your status as an unmarried miss for propriety's sake, but I was still going to make my request."

Alexander was already sitting straight, but he seemed to grow a few extra inches at the rather alarming words. "What is your meaning, Your Majesty?"

"As you are aware, I have lost my informal advisor who assisted me in the acquisition of antiquities. I would like Miss Harrington to take his place." King George paused to turn to Georgina. "I generally find history and book learning dull, but I am convinced you will have a rather intriguing way of conveying it—much like how Mr. Harrington lambasted Lord Clifville for his poor understanding of the origin of Fort Camulodunum."

"You want me... to advise you... on the provenance of antiquities?" Georgina asked, almost forgetting to keep her voice loud as Calliope had instructed. Evidently, the elderly man was hard of hearing. In her arms, Crinitus Legatus emitted low *bock*-ing noises.

The monarch pulled a face—almost like a young child's. "The king of Naples has been exceedingly smug about the treasures his men are finding in Herculaneum, and I want to increase my own collection. The Prince of Wales has expressed his interest as well."

"Would my assistance be publicly acknowledged, or are you asking me to do this discreetly, Your Majesty?" Georgina asked as her heart stuttered in her chest. Like her, it didn't seem to know precisely how to react.

Alexander shifted. His expression mirrored the eager hopefulness burgeoning inside Georgina.

"The point of such objects is to boast about them. In order to increase your standing as a scholar—and thus to secure the reputation of my collection—I shall lend my support toward

your publication of a series of treatises. I would also like to purchase that helmet of yours."

Georgina's dreams were shimmering within reach. She just
needed to reach out and grab them. But could she sacrifice her
greatest find?

"Would you put my helmet on public display?" Georgina
asked. If the piece would be hidden away, she didn't think she
could part with it—not even to secure royal patronage.

"I shall add it to the Royal Armouries Museum in the Tower.
It will make a spectacular centerpiece, don't you think? And I
shall be the king who acquired something so ancient."

"It wasn't Arthur's, your majesty," Georgina said, once more
hoping that her scholarly integrity would not jeopardize this
opportunity.

The king chuckled. "Mr. Harrington made that exceedingly
obvious when he burst into the Presence Chamber. However, the
helmet was the property of some heroic English leader, correct?"

Georgina tamped down on the excitement thundering
through her. Although she had not been schooled on how to
properly respond to a request like this, she was fairly certain
that loud squealing would be frowned upon.

"I cannot identify the man, but given the grave goods that
accompanied his body, he was of high status and a warrior."
Georgina couldn't prevent her voice from rising at the end, but
the king didn't appear to mind.

Alexander stayed silent, but he was not hiding his reaction.
His face beamed with pride, and Georgina basked in his silent
support. Alexander had been right. He was perfect for her, and
much better than any partner she could have imagined.

The king waved his fingers nonchalantly, obviously already
bored with the topic of conversation and ready to move onto
another. "Yes. Yes. Write a book about the warrior-king's

burial, a piece that scholars will love and I won't read. You can summarize it for me and the Prince of Wales so we can sound knowledgeable. It is settled then—you will help me improve my antiquities collection?"

"I would be honored, Your Majesty." Georgina dipped her head. She was very proud of the fact that she didn't start visibly vibrating with joy. The bubbly feeling was certainly fizzing merrily inside her.

"Are you tolerant of your future wife performing such duties?" King George asked Alexander.

The fact that Georgina did not fear Alexander's answer was telling of her trust.

"Nothing would make me more pleased. My fiancée's brilliance has long been overlooked, and I am honored that Your Majesty has recognized her intelligence." Alexander employed his full charm, and a wry smile crossed the king's countenance.

"I have heard you are in possession of both flattery and wit." King George now turned his attention to Alexander. "It seems that your father made a grievous mistake in aligning his fortunes with a scoundrel like Lord Clifville rather than with his own son."

Alexander's expression faltered a fraction, and Georgina had to squeeze her hands together to prevent herself from reaching out to comfort him. But it turned out that the king was surprisingly the one to demonstrate empathy.

"I, myself, am no stranger to the strain between a father and son," King George said. "In your case, the estrangement proves fortunate. After all, had you been part of the smuggling conspiracy, you would be headed to exile, too."

"Exile?" Alexander echoed the question ringing in Georgina's head.

The monarch smiled. This one was not kind. "Yes. The duke and Lord Craie both."

Lord Craie? Algernon was being forced to leave England! What would happen to his lands, his title? A storm of emotions swelled inside Georgina. She wanted to see her brother punished, but she had not imagined something so extreme. A trickle of guilt slid through her, along with a sense of satisfaction that he could no longer easily steal from her.

"My advisers inform me that we should seek the execution of the Earl of Clifville under charges for both his murder of the exciseman and his involvement in the smuggling ring," King George continued. He did not mention the obvious cover-up. "It would make little sense not to punish the other two co-conspirators of the smuggling ring, so we are planning to strip them of their titles and confiscate their properties. I am assured that we have the appropriate support from both the Whigs and the Tories in Parliament."

Georgina spun toward Alexander. If his father was no longer duke, that meant that Alexander would become a mere mister. She did not care a fig. She had enough income from her father's estate to provide a simple but comfortable living for the two of them. There was also the financial support that she would receive from the king for her publications and work as an antiquarian. Yet would Alexander be content, especially after all that he'd suffered for the alleged sake of the dukedom? Or would he feel freed?

No matter Alexander's reaction, Georgina knew her own decision. She would remain by his side and help him grapple with the consequences of his father's misdeeds.

Chapter Twenty~Three

The dukedom was going to go extinct—or perhaps not extinct, but dead nonetheless. At first, Alexander could feel nothing but shock. What the king was proposing was not an easy accomplishment, even for a sovereign. But high-ranking nobles from both political factions had been painted into Clifville's gruesome tableaux. They were shaken and angry. Given the Jacobite Rebellion of '45, the king had no tolerance for individuals involved in conspiracies to seize the throne— even those who were guilty by association. Alexander doubted that either his father or Georgina's brother had known about Clifville's wild dream of usurpation, but it didn't matter.

So, in the end, there had been no legacy to suffer for. Alexander's clubfoot hadn't destroyed the house of Falcondale, nor had his aunt's elopement. His father had accomplished the destruction on his own.

And Alexander? Alexander was finally free.

"If Falcondale and Craie wish to escape the noose, they shall not fight my decision," King George said. "But enough about them. Let us talk about you."

Alexander warily studied His Majesty as his stomach sloshed nervously. He had, of course, attended the same functions as the monarch, but he had never before had a true conversation with the sovereign. Although Alexander had become good at deciphering people, the king's intent remained a mystery.

"You need an award for stopping a political disaster and saving my life. Such heroics normally result in the granting of a peerage, and there will soon be several empty ones along with choice estates. I am prepared to ask Parliament to issue a letter of patent for you to receive the title of the Duke of Falcondale—and all its accompanying courtesy ones—and the lesser title of the Earl of Craie." The king smirked as he finished speaking, and part of Alexander wondered if the man was vicariously getting revenge against his own sire, who had mistreated him to the point of separating him from not just his mother but his own child. But most of Alexander's mind was too stunned to consider anything at all.

"You're making me the duke? In my father's stead?" Alexander could barely speak the words. He felt curiously numb—or perhaps the opposite. He was experiencing too many feelings to register any of them.

"Not in his stead. The chain of inheritance will be broken. It will be your own peerage, to make what you wish of it." The king reached over and popped an expensive pastry into his mouth.

His own peerage. Unfettered by the past. Not something to live up to, but something to create, to mold. Alexander wouldn't have to concern himself with a legacy that he'd never wanted. His focus could be on bettering the lives of those who relied on the estates and creating a place for his own children to thrive, no matter their abilities or their appearance. He could join the House of Lords and begin publicly advocating for social reforms.

"I did have concerns if you were being treated equitably." The king turned toward Georgina. "After all, you helped expose

Clifville, but you were losing your residence. But your upcoming nuptials will fix all that."

The king waved his hand over the delicacies set out before him. "Now eat. You are both likely famished after the news I've imparted."

Alexander gingerly picked up a marzipan shaped like a swan. His stomach was churning too much to consume sweets, but he wasn't about to refuse the monarch's orders. He bit off a wing, chewing slowly. He was to be the duke. The. Duke. Not in some unknown, indefinite future. But soon.

"What will happen to the local people who were involved with the smuggling?" Georgina inquired cautiously as she picked at a seed cake. "They are very impoverished with no other good income. They weren't a party to Lord Clifville's deluded fantasies."

Alexander instantly felt a stab of remorse that he hadn't thought to ask about the inhabitants of Georgina's village. If he was to receive Algernon's estate, he had responsibility to the community as the chief landowner. Although he might be able to plead for leniency for Tom and Jack, it would be harder to protect the others.

"Enough efforts have been expended to discover the noble ringleaders. There is no reason to expend resources to root out petty underlings," the king said dismissively. Alexander sensed that the king wasn't being generous. A prolonged investigation might mean that more of the real truth would be revealed.

"When will my parents and Lord and Lady Craie be informed?" Alexander asked.

"Oh, they have already been." The king plucked a fruit tart from the table and jammed it into his mouth. When he swallowed, he turned back to Georgina. "When things are settled with your marriage, you must visit to view the antiquities that

I've acquired. I wish to know exactly what my collection is missing."

⚜

After the king bid them adieu, Alexander remained quiet while the servant poled them and Fluffus Legatus across the canal. Even when he and Georgina had secured the rooster in its basket and climbed into the curricle, Alexander still found himself unable to speak.

As the horses plodded down the tree-lined lane, Georgina laid her hand gently on his arm. "Perhaps we should pull off into a less well-used path. We could rest a bit before fighting through London traffic."

Alexander nodded, picking a dirt road that looked overgrown. They hadn't gone far when it abruptly ended.

"Let's just tie up the horses and sit here. That log over there would make a good bench." Georgina pointed in the direction of a large fallen branch that was perfectly curved to accommodate two people.

As they made their way to the makeshift seat, Georgina took his elbow and rested her head against his upper arm. "That was a whirlwind of rapid changes."

"Yes." Alexander nodded as they sat. Georgina stayed tucked next to him, and he relished the close contact. It was anchoring.

"How do you feel about it?" Georgina asked hesitantly.

Alexander sucked in his breath and then let it out in a huffing sort of laugh. "Pleased. Guilty. Excited. Nervous."

"Same with me," Georgina admitted.

"I need to start thinking like a duke," Alexander said as he stared at the dappled pattern made by the sun shining through the gently swaying leaves. "I should have thought to ask the king about the locals in Essex."

"You would have in due course. You were a bit stunned." Georgina leaned more heavily against him, clearly lending her support. "The more pressure I am under, the more logical I become. You are apt to sort through your feelings first. It is why we shall make a wonderful team as the Duke and Duchess of Falcondale."

"You aren't worried that managing multiple households will distract from your antiquarian work?" Alexander asked. "We can hire good butlers and housekeepers to take the burden off you."

Georgina lifted her head and pressed a quick kiss against his cheek. "Your consideration is why I'm happy to be your duchess. But you needn't worry. I am accustomed to juggling multiple endeavors."

Alexander threaded his fingers through hers and squeezed tightly. The swell of happiness that he'd experienced when she'd agreed to his proposal returned. "I feel like I'm in a rough sea today—sometimes at the top of a wave feeling absolutely glorious and then battling through the swells that I never saw coming."

Georgina laughed. "That is very apt. But I don't think we need to fight through the choppiness. Perhaps it is best to simply bob along for the moment and accept that our emotions are a shifting mess. We can feel joy and freedom while also mourning the familial relationships that never became proper ones."

"How did I get so lucky to have a fiancée as wise as you?" Alexander rested his forehead against Georgina's, finding comfort in their closeness.

"By being exceedingly sage yourself," Georgina responded.

"My finely honed intellect is telling me that we should kiss now," Alexander whispered.

"That is indeed the most sensible course."

Their lips met, and the rollicking emotions settled inside Alexander. Georgina was his lodestone, guiding him when the world set him adrift. Their lives would have chaotic moments and quiet interludes, but they would face them together with logic and humor—and definitely a lot of passion and love.

Epilogue

I am truly happy for you, cousin. You shall make a wonderful royal antiquarian, and you have chosen an excellent husband." Percy reached forward and clasped both of Georgina's hands.

They, along with Alexander, were traveling to the Black Sheep in the Falcondale coach for a wedding reception. Yesterday, Georgina and Alexander had hosted a traditional wedding breakfast after their nuptials, but their friends wanted to hold a more intimate event today.

The sincerity with which Percy held Georgina's hands shocked her. Her cousin had always been an affectionate sort, but in a more rambunctious, puppyish way. Now there was a quiet deliberateness to how he squeezed her fingers.

Worried, Georgina studied him closely. His face was still gaunt and definitely paler than before his captivity. The bruising had mostly faded, but she noticed purplish shadows under his eyes. Was the previously cavalier Percy beset by nightmares?

"Have you been sleeping properly?" Alexander asked the question before Georgina could.

Percy released Georgina's palms and sank against the squabs. He rested his right ankle atop his left knee, striking a relaxed pose that also showed off his new buckles festooned with peridot half moons. Yet he seemed to be trying too hard to appear carefree.

"Being back in my own featherbed has done marvels." Percy rolled his shoulders and slouched into an even more exaggerated lounge. Since he was ensconced against plush upholstery, he succeeded—or rather he appeared to succeed on the surface. A stiffness clung to him, as if his muscles would not entirely unbend no matter how hard he tried.

"If you ever wish to talk about what you endured, I will always be ready to listen. I know what it's like to hide behind smiles." Alexander kept his tone low as he leaned slightly toward Percy.

"I am here for you, too," Georgina said. "Once Alexander and I finish setting up our household, you can come and visit us anytime." Alexander's parents and her brother and sister-in-law had fled to the Colonies shortly before Parliament had agreed on the new letter of patent for the dukedom. Alexander and Georgina were currently in the process of reviewing their massive new holdings and settling into Falcondale House in London.

Percy seemed to truly brighten at the mention of their marriage. "I don't know what surprises me more. That you married under special license that His Majesty himself helped procure from the archbishop of Canterbury, or that you wed Alexander. Probably the latter. I always figured you'd choose a scholarly fellow, and that Alexander would remain a confirmed bachelor."

Alexander slung his arm around Georgina and pulled her close. He had been regularly eschewing the rules of propriety, and Georgina was not inclined to enforce them, either. "Georgina and I are the perfect match—wit and logic."

"That we are." Georgina pressed against Alexander. "A mere academic would have bored me in the end. I've decided I prefer life with a bit of adventure."

Percy spluttered out a sound between a laugh and a surprised choke. "My, you have blossomed into a fierce one, Georgie. I was worried that you might feel awkward with the attention you'll receive as a royal antiquarian, but you'll be brilliant."

"You are not upset that I will no longer be using your name for my scholarly endeavors?" Georgina asked.

"Not in the least. It was always your work, not mine. I was a rascal to have accepted the honors. I should have thought of clever ways to give you as much credit as possible."

Georgina blinked. "Did—did you just express regret?"

Percy's laugh was tinged with self-recrimination. "I've always been a cavalier scoundrel, haven't I? When I was tied up at the mine and then locked in the dungeon, I had time to engage in long overdue reflection. It is time that I cultivate my own talents."

"Are you planning to join the military or clergy?" Georgina asked.

Percy gave a theatrical shudder. "I have not altered that much. I'm not one to follow orders, and could you imagine me leading a congregation? It would definitely become a sordid metaphor about a wolf shepherding sheep. But I am resolved to do something other than be a mere gadabout. I just don't know precisely what."

"You'll figure it out in due course. I have faith in you," Alexander said—good friend that he was. Georgina could not help but adore her husband even more for his innate kindness.

"As do I," Georgina agreed.

"Well, that makes two people." Percy gave a lopsided grin. "But enough about my ambitions or at least my attempt to cultivate some. Have you heard any news about Tom? Has he fully recovered from our ordeal?"

"Yes." Georgina nodded. "He and Jack arrived in London two days ago, and they'll be at the Black Sheep today with my former maid and Tom's sister, Mary. Yesterday, the two men had a secret audience with King George and were awarded rather generous gifts. The three would like to learn a trade at Mr. Stewart's school and start a reputable enterprise in Essex."

"I am planning to invest in their business and others," Alexander added. "I want to help provide the locals with options for income that doesn't come from smuggling."

"Look at you. Already talking like a duke. I can't believe that you're the same fellow who wrote ribald essays as Willoughby Wright."

Alexander groaned and cast Georgina an obviously mock look of annoyance. "Why did you share those articles with him? I managed to keep that secret for years!"

"How was I to know that Percy would recognize your writing style so readily? And I knew he'd laugh at the piece where all the nobles strut around with erections and compare their girth."

Alexander groaned. "Do we have to mention my first work? It is the epitome of sophomoric banality."

"Even in that absurd, ribald piece, I could see how much you care, Alexander." Georgina nestled against her husband. "You fight for those who society has forgotten—human or beast. You will make the most wonderful peer, and I will be proud to be by your side."

"Ugh. This is getting too mawkishly sentimental," Percy groaned. "Whyever did I get in a coach with a newly wedded couple?"

"Because you mixed up the location of our second reception and arrived on our doorstep," Alexander pointed out.

"Oh, well, there is that," Percy conceded sheepishly.

Georgina couldn't stop beaming. Her cousin might have accidentally ended up in the wrong place, but she was exactly where she wanted to be.

·❦·

"I cannot believe that you made a separate 'cake' for each of the animals," Georgina said, her gaze fixated on Fluffus Legatus.

Alexander turned to also look at the rooster, who was happily pecking at apple skins that had previously been artfully arranged into a rose by Sophia.

"You did not witness the disaster at Dr. Talbot and Lady Charlotte's wedding feast." Mr. Powys shuddered as he gingerly touched the flesh around his right eye. "The color of my cheekbone only recently returned to normal. It was a hideous yellow-brown for days. At least the stage makeup did a good job covering it."

"The battle was truly epic, Georgina." Alexander slung his arm around his wife.

"At least the rice wasn't moldy this time." Sophia nodded her head toward a large sack hanging on a nail near the entrance, all ready to be tossed.

Alexander's throat constricted at the memory of celebrating Charlotte and Matthew's nuptials. He'd been so anxious that day, wanting everything to be perfect for his family. And now his sister and his friends were doing the same for him. He'd grown up feeling like an outcast, but here, at the Black Sheep, he'd always belonged.

"Who just threw a currant?" Percy demanded, pulling Alexander out of his rush of sentimentality.

A triumphant chitter filled the air. Pan flapped his wings, shouting "Lovey! Lovey!"

"That would have been the capuchin," Matthew said wearily.

"Why is the monkey here again?" Sophia rubbed her forehead. "Especially after the last disaster?"

"It was at the groom's request." Tavish shot Alexander a look as pointed as his clipped words. He had the fortune—or perhaps misfortune—of being the one who carted the little devil around, since Banshee lived on his estate.

"Isn't the rascal more attached to your sister than to you?" Mr. Belle asked.

"She is, but her presence is tradition," Alexander said, feeling a tad defensive.

"I thought you said that Banshee's sweetheart was Pan," Tom said, glancing up at the bird that was strutting merrily on the rafters above.

Beside him, his sister nodded. "Not that it makes much sense—a monkey and a parrot."

"I believe it after watching that dog over there sniff out a secret tunnel simply because he loves turnips." Jack tilted his head toward Ruffian Caesar, who was gnawing on a chunk of the root vegetable that had been carved into the shape of a lily.

"I feel as if we're starting a menagerie." This time Sophia dropped her head onto her folded arms.

"Birds of a feather! Birds of a feather!" Pan bopped along his beam.

"At least Pan is tolerating Fluffus Legatus's presence," Alexander pointed out.

"Crinitus Legatus's presence," Georgina corrected.

"I really do think we should put his name to a vote again." Alexander reached down to stroke the creature, who was enjoying apple slices next to Alexander's chair.

"I am not subjecting my rooster to such nonsense a second time. His name is Crinitus Legatus," Georgina said crisply.

"It is more linguistically pure," Calliope pointed out.

Mr. Powys rolled his eyes. "It is a rooster of fluffy ridiculousness. It does not need a pretentious Latin name. Fluffus suits such a silly bird."

"Plebian," Calliope sniffed.

"Nob," Mr. Powys rebutted.

"Are those two in a relationship?" Percy asked no one in particular.

"What?" Mr. Powys roared.

"Never!" Calliope dramatically clutched at her bosom with so much theatrical flourish that one would think she was the actor, not Mr. Powys.

"You two bicker with more passion than most couples flirt," Percy observed before taking a sip of his coffee. "Mmm. This is a delicious brew, Sophia. I have no idea how you accomplish such a miracle."

Alexander tried his best not to guffaw at the aghast expressions of Mr. Powys and Calliope. They might disagree about almost everything else, but it was clear that they had the same reaction to Percy's cavalier observation. Percy, of course, had already moved on to a different conversation, while the rest of the group vainly tried to hide their mirth.

"It's a shame the newly minted Duke of Foxglen isn't here, although I suppose he is still in mourning for his grandfather," Percy said, completely oblivious to Hannah's immediate scowl.

The elderly man's passing had at first shocked Alexander, but when he'd learned that the peer had been hiding his illness for months, the late duke's recent actions made sense. He'd probably hoped that if he claimed the discovery of the helmet with Lord Clifville, then the other scholar would give His Grace posthumous credit.

"We do not mention either the name Malbarry or Foxglen in this establishment." Hannah pierced everyone gathered around the table with a dark look. "I shall never forgive you all for not telling me his identity immediately. You let me lust after a bloody duke!"

"Well, technically, he was a marquess when you met him," Pendergrast pointed out with a cheeky grin.

Hannah whirled on the rogue and delivered her best death glare. "That is not the point!"

"Blackguard!" Pan cried from his perch in the rafters.

Hannah glanced up at him, her chin set at a fierce angle. "That's right, Pan! I should have listened to you from the very beginning. To think I had *those* types of thoughts about the grandson of the man who destroyed my paternal family."

"I don't think Lord Malb—I mean the Duke of Foxglen—is a bad sort," Georgina said, thinking of the shy, quiet boy who'd read beside her. "He was invaluable in helping us arrive in London in time."

"So he saved his own kind." Hannah thunked down a mug she was holding with such gusto that Georgina was afraid the pottery would crack. "That doesn't make him any less of a—"

"Blackguard!!!" Pan sang gleefully as he swooped happily through the air. Then without warning, he landed on Ruffian Caesar's back. "Gee-up!"

Ruffian Caesar scurried forward in an obvious attempt to dislodge the parrot. However, the cheeky critter merely whistled and hung tightly to the wiry fur. The two thundered past Fluffus Legatus, startling the benighted bird. In a desperate attempt to avoid the fray, the rooster ran, flapping its wings. It hurriedly jumped onto one of the low, swinging perches that Hannah had installed for the chickens of the coffeehouse's patrons.

Everyone stood at once in an attempt to rescue the beleaguered Ruffian Caesar. Hollering joyfully, Banshee bounced up and down. The dog barked, and Fluffus Legatus began panic-crowing.

"Gee-up! Gee-up!" Pan croaked out louder than any teamster.

Hannah lunged for the dog and parrot. Unfortunately, Ruffian Caesar swerved sharply at just the wrong time. He shot across Hannah's path, tripping her. She grabbed wildly, her hands grasping at the rice. At just that precise moment, the door to the Black Sheep opened. The bag slipped off the hook. Hannah stumbled forward, upending the entire sack into the midsection of the newcomer.

Lord Malbarry—or rather, the Duke of Foxglen—seemed unperturbed by either the deluge of grain or the dog-riding parrot careening in his direction. He calmly reached down and grabbed Ruffian Caesar around his belly. He hoisted both pup and bird into the air.

Foxglen carefully disentangled the bird's claws from Ruffian Caesar's fur while rice poured from his silk breeches and ran down his stockings. Disgusted, Pan flew from the dog and landed on the newly minted peer's head.

Cradling the dog in one arm and with the parrot clinging to his hair, Foxglen bent at the waist in a perfectly executed bow. More rice rained from the folds of his waistcoat. He straightened with a dignified solemnity that miraculously contained no hint of irony.

"I do beg your forgiveness for interrupting this celebration, but I wished to speak to all of you privately. I deduced you would be gathered here today," Foxglen said in that calm, steady tone of his. "I come to humbly ask for your assistance in locating my mother and older sister. They've been in hiding from the late duke since my father's death when I was six years of age. Now that he's dead, I want to reunite with my family."

Acknowledgments

Thanks to my editor, Alex Logan, who once again helped me streamline my writing to allow my characters and plot to really shine. Without her, Dear Readers, you would need to suffer through four separate endings and numerous unnecessary repetitions. Thanks also to my copyeditor and proofreader, who ensure that my writing is polished.

Once again, Forever's art director, Daniela Medina, has designed the perfect cover. My heart just squeezed when I saw how perfectly the illustration captures Ruffian Caesar and Fluffus/Crinitus Legatus along with the frenetic energy of the carriage race through London.

Thanks also to my publicist, Dana Cuadrado, and the rest of the Forever team, who work tirelessly to make sure my books get into the hands of you, my Dear Readers.

As always thanks to my agent, Jessica Watterson. Her belief in and championing of my work are the reason that my books are ultimately published.

My fellow author Sarah Morgenthaler has once again lent her invaluable critique and expertise. I wouldn't have been able to write the vibrant fight scenes without peppering her with questions about her background in Krav Maga and Muay Thai. Any mistakes in these passages are my own.

Thanks again to the Rebelles for keeping me sane during

the writing process. You guys are always there, whether it's an inquiry about punctuation or the tougher life questions.

My husband—who grew up on a farm—was a great resource for all things poultry- and equine-related. He has even designed and constructed coops, although not chicken swings. And yes, Sean, the brief reappearance of the goat from *Lady Charlotte Always Gets Her Man* is for you. Any errors regarding livestock were made by me and me alone.

My mother, as always, was my first beta reader. Thank you for again exercising your English major muscles and helping me wrestle with comma placement.

And to my daughter, I appreciate your understanding of the times when Mommy needs to write and your unbridled enthusiasm for spotting my books in the wild. No one can spy them as quickly as you, not even me.

Dearest Readers, thank you for picking up my books, posting on social media, recommending my works to friends, and generally helping my characters come to life by reading and enjoying their stories.

About the Author

Violet Marsh is a lawyer who decided it was more fun to write witty banter than contractual terms. A romance enthusiast, she relishes the transformative power of love, especially when a seeming mismatch becomes the perfect pairing.

Marsh also enjoys visiting the past—whether strolling through a castle's ruins, wandering around a stately manor, or researching her family genealogy online (where she discovered at least one alleged pirate, a female tavern owner, and several blacksmiths). She indulges in her love of history by writing period pieces filled with independent-minded women and men smart enough to fall for them.

Marsh lives at home with Prince Handy (a guy who can fix things is definitely sexier than a mere charmer), a whirlwind (her toddler), and a suburban nesting dog (whose cuteness Marsh shamelessly uses to promote her books).

Marsh loves to interact with her readers on social media:
www.facebook.com/violetmarshauthor
www.instagram.com/violetmarshauthor